Andrew Blades was born in South Africa and educated there and in Australia. He holds three degrees, two at master's level. He has worked variously as a social worker, reforming corrupt police officers and in various departments of government at a senior level. He has also written for a newspaper in Africa. Among his published works is the successful fantasy series for children, now sold as readers for school aged children, and a supernatural thriller called *The Flame of Heaven*.

Andrew is currently working on a sequel to *False Flag*. He lives in Sydney, Australia, with his wife and two sons.

To Kathryn, Lewis and Declan.

To the most excellent of editors, Faith Moore, and as always to K, who makes all seem possible and my children, Lewis and Declan.

# Andrew Blades

## FALSE FLAG

AUSTIN MACAULEY PUBLISHERS™

LONDON ∗ CAMBRIDGE ∗ NEW YORK ∗ SHARJAH

A CIP catalogue record for this title is available from the British Library.

ISBN 9781398471504 (Paperback)
ISBN 9781398471511 (ePub e-book)

www.austinmacauley.com

First Published 2022
Austin Macauley Publishers Ltd®
1 Canada Square
Canary Wharf
London
E14 5AA

# Prologue

**Portugal Azores, Sao Jorge Island, Velas**
**Present Day, at Dawn**

The hull of the trawler boomed like a drum as it ploughed its way through the breakwater out into the deep Atlantic, leaving behind a widening wake. The roofs of the port city of Velas were still visible from the deck, their terracotta tiles reflecting the rosy dawn light. Konstantin Bogatov smiled to himself, remembering the events of the night before.

He turned his attention from the receding town back toward the deck. His flat Slavic face and deep-set sky-blue eyes remained impassive as he watched the crew at work.

They were struggling to fit the second manipulator arm on the research submarine strapped to the deck as the trawler bucked on the restless sea. Perhaps they should have done this in port, but he'd wanted as few curious observers as possible and absolutely no difficult questions from port authorities.

His eyes flicked over the men appraisingly; they seemed relaxed and in good spirits despite the difficulties. The open bar and brothel were always a good idea with soldiers. Small price really, considering the goal. This mission was potentially far more dangerous than the run-of-the-mill murder and mayhem they usually dished out. They'd all had a well-deserved, good, last bit of fun if it all turned to shit.

He sighed and then walked over to the men; his thinning blond hair disturbed by the blustering sea breeze.

"Vasyli!" he called out to the lanky technician kneeling at the keel of the submarine. "We're nearly there. We're going to be lifting atomic weapons, not treasure. Have you checked the lights, scaling laser, temperature probe, Geiger counter? Those're more important than the manipulators at this stage. That is what will keep you alive!"

Konstantin noted the surreptitious exchange of glances between the men working with Vasyli. Their surprise was clear—the object of this salvage operation had top secret status and they'd had no need to know the objective too early.

"Up next, Commander," Vasyli said to Konstantin with a grin.

Old habits, thought Konstantin. After all these years together, Vasyli still called Konstantin by his old moniker. The wars in Chechnya and Syria had been brutal and saving his life more than once along the way probably explained Vasyli's respectful use of his old military rank. That and gratitude for rescuing the quiet engineer from a life of drunken boredom as a Russian soldier too, no doubt.

Konstantin's lips curled in a half smile. A mercenary's life had been far more rewarding for both of them. Broken men often make the best soldiers, he thought.

He rotated sharply on his feet, walked swiftly to the companionway, climbed the narrow stairs to the bridge, and entered the wheelhouse accompanied by a gust of cold air.

"Ok Alexey, here are the coordinates," he said to the burley captain manning the helm.

Konstantin watched as Alexey punched the coordinates into the ship's navigation computer and felt the ship veer in its course toward the northeast; their destination was less than a half an hour away in this weather.

Alexey was an old soldier too, but he'd gone his own way. Still, Konstantin trusted him because of their shared past—that was an invaluable commodity in this dangerous trade.

Konstantin observed his old comrade. Alexey was a squat, powerfully built man, with a crop of dark hair now graying slightly at the sides. He had the weathered good looks of a man of the sea. Still single, no children he knew of, no encumbrances, one could almost say a man wedded to the ocean. He was useful for all those reasons and, most importantly, he was a man who could keep his mouth shut.

In only a matter of minutes, the powerful sonar had picked up their target; the USS Scorpion nuclear submarine lying in two pieces on the ocean floor like a broken, unloved toy.

"Concentrate on the front section, there," Konstantin said. "Get the ship right over it. We'll go straight down with the sub."

"Udivitelinye!" Alexey exclaimed in amazement. "How were you able to find it when the Americans could not?"

"It's an old wreck. They were looking for it in 1964. The equipment we have now is much more sophisticated. Still, it was a good find for us; a hunch that paid off."

There was silence between the men for a few moments. Konstantin could sense Alexey's unease. He was an ex-military man and knew it was a nuclear sub.

"It hasn't posed a problem for the Americans in more than fifty years. From their point of view, why waste time on trying to find it now? It's best just to let it lie quietly down there and hope no one notices," Konstantin added in answer to the unasked question.

The captain pulled the corners of his mouth down, nodding once, acknowledging the logic.

"When you put it like that it makes sense."

Another moment of silence.

"And why the front section, Konstantin?"

"Full of fucking questions today, Alexey, aren't you?" Konstantin said and then patted him on the shoulder.

Alexey did not reply.

"These missions are kept secret for a reason, you know that." Konstantin chided.

Alexey snorted softly, but said nothing.

"I suppose you will know soon enough anyway, but I don't want anyone to become anxious. The front section houses nuclear torpedoes. Those are what we're after today. If they're in good shape we bring them up. If not, we leave them."

Alexey glanced at Konstantin, a fleeting look of disbelief passing over his features.

"If you're going to shit in your pants, Alexey, then don't ask questions, okay? Yes, it's dangerous, but my men will do the risky work in the sub. You've worked with me many, many times. My work is always dangerous, but you and your crew are always paid well and on time, no?"

Konstantin grasped Alexey by his shoulders and shook them gently. His smile was friendly, if patronizing.

"Alexey, you're so tense. Please—for fuck's sake. Be calm. I know what I'm doing! Show some faith."

Alexey shook his head. "Yes, I know you know what you're doing, but I just wish you would have told me it was an old atomic weapon we were bringing up. I could have made preparations…"

Konstantin bowed his head slightly. "Sure, sure, also maybe next time Kraznodar Inc. goes with another salvaging company who doesn't ask stupid questions? Ha?"

Alexey chose not to answer.

Konstantin looked out at the choppy sea as Alexey spun the helm and then engaged the bow thrusters expertly, maneuvering the trawler directly over the shattered submarine below. When he was satisfied at their position, he dropped the anchor with a push of a button.

"Be careful! We don't want the anchor to strike the hull. It's fragile!" Konstantin snarled.

"Good of you to explain, Konstantin," Alexey said, somewhat morosely. "I will remember for next time…if we survive, that is."

Konstantin swallowed his anger. Alexey had a point. He was right to fear this mission. This was definitely the most dangerous—and for that reason the most lucrative—mission the Kremlin had ever authorized for Kraznodar Inc.

To enter the sealed torpedo room of a drowned sub and retrieve lost nuclear weapons—broken arrows as the Americans called them—was going to prove a very difficult task. He wondered what the Kremlin needed them for, where they would be used. They were old technology…but that was not his problem.

If God existed, as his old Babushka insisted he did, then prayer would be worth the effort about now, he thought.

Instead, he filled his mind with the crazy young girl from last night and the thought of what he'd do with the money.

# Chapter 1
# Brooklyn, New York

When Gideon Dunbar answered the advertisement for MMA instructor, the owner of the gym had shrewdly guessed that his class would become popular with women. His muscular 6.1 frame was helpful, but it was his steady, friendly gray eyes and his habit of really looking at you when you were speaking that did the trick. And of course, where young women frequented, so did young men.

For Gideon, the class was fun and easy money. Now, walking home, he mostly felt the after-effects in his calves. His gait brisk, despite his slight fatigue; his mind relaxed—for the moment. His dark, curly hair was still a little damp from the shower.

Gideon's empty apartment in Williamsburg made him feel restless. No point in being alone with his thoughts, so no need to rush to get back there. Besides, the leafy peaceful streets of Brooklyn Heights were pleasant in the evening and very different from the back streets of the West Bank and Beirut, which was what he was really escaping.

He caught his mind drifting back to the last operation—again. Everything had gone wrong from the get-go. Faulty radio equipment, bad intel. The bloody, lolling head of Ariel floated up into his mind. He squeezed his eyes shut for a moment and cursed.

PTSD? Hell, he hoped not? Maybe psychological leave had been a good idea after all.

He took a left off Atlantic Avenue, now buzzing with evening traffic, and onto Hicks Street: much quieter and lined with trees and Italianate-style brownstones. The trees were what he missed most in Israel and what he loved best in Brooklyn. They were the same trees that had been on these same streets when he'd been a boy. It seemed a million years ago now. All that was the past.

His father dead, his mother now living in England with his aunt. He smiled wanly at the memory.

It was at his school, not two blocks away, that he and Ariel had decided to join the Israeli Defense Force and render a service to Israel. His father had been proud when he told him, his mother less enthusiastic, though touched, because she was Jewish herself and, of course, Gideon had been born in Israel, so there was that. As an American soldier his father had wondered why Gideon did not want to join the American Army. Then 9/11 happened. He'd finished his studies not long after and there were no more questions about which army to join, just a burning certainty that these monsters had to be stopped.

Sun slanted off the windows of the brownstones, making them look like golden mirrors. The lilting croon of a Leonard Cohen song wafted from a café further up the street.

Gideon's subconscious registered a change in the pattern of behavior on the street before his conscious mind had even comprehended it. He felt his adrenalin spike and the fatigue left his calves as if by magic.

His eyes flicked across the scene trying to make sense of it. The first kink in the calm was the two bull-necked men: buzz cuts, large hands, dark clothing, wearing sunglasses on a relatively shaded street. Next was the point man on the opposite side of the street. Then the white van moving slowly toward him—about 200 yards away. This was trouble, no doubt.

Who was the target?

*An image of Ariel's bloody head shocked through his mind again.*

He shook his head to clear it.

For a moment he thought he might be the target. But no. There was a young woman walking toward him. Slim, dark hair, beautiful, maybe late 20s, hands stuffed into the pockets of a dark gray parka, her eyes covered behind large sunglasses. Her stride was brisk, her boots clacking on the pavement above the buzz of filtered traffic noise.

*The hornet buzz of a sniper bullet missing him by inches, striking Ariel in the back of the head. Blood, blood everywhere.*

Gideon flinched involuntarily and felt a tremor start in his hands—Get a fucking grip!

The heavies should've come from opposite directions to do the job properly, he thought. They looked like cardboard cut-outs of bad guys; the two of them together just too obvious—regardless, shit was about to get real, he knew it with the certainty of death.

Gideon slowed his pace slightly to take in the unfolding picture. There were two men in the van, their faces obscured behind sunglasses and hoodies. One driving, one riding shotgun.

*The slowing car, the sudden buzz of silenced rounds. Ariel knocked off his feet.*

Gideon pushed his knuckles hard into the side of his head. Focus—control your breathing. Another ten yards gained on the girl by the heavies.

The bizarre battle joy that made him so right for soldiering flowed from his stomach and rose like a tide into his chest, sparking clarity in his mind. He took in the scene with perfect precision.

The woman was the target for sure. Gideon turned as if he was going to cross the street. Point Man was closing in on the target too, slightly ahead of him, cutting off any angle of escape for her. Clack-clack went the woman's heels. Gideon kept the thug twins and the girl in the periphery of his vision to his right. Further up the street several people exited the café, momentarily slowing the twins' predatory glide. Decision time.

Point Man's eyes flicked back over his shoulder for a second, appraising him, assessing the threat level. He seemed half aware that Gideon suspected something. Both hands in his coat pockets, jacket pulled to the right, right hand bunched like a grapefruit inside the jacket. He was holding something heavy in that pocket. The thug twins quickened their stride. The girl was still unaware. Point Man was halfway across the street—something had to give.

Suddenly the white van sped up.

The girl was maybe 12 yards from Gideon now. Her features relaxed, sweet, her long hair drifting in the cool evening air.

*No. I can't...Ariel lying like a rag doll on the ground. His right arm caught under his body; his left grotesquely propped against the wall, a parody of an attempt to save himself from a fall...I can't let this happen, his mind stuttered.*

Now or never!

A massive surge of adrenalin slammed him into action. Point Man's eyes widened in surprise as Gideon lunged for him. His right hand came up out of his pocket. Gideon saw the blunt slide of the Glock. That was all he needed. He struck Point Man on his Adam's apple with a quick chopping punch. Hard enough to spasm his larynx, but not crush the windpipe. Point Man went down, gagging. He would be breathless for about 40 seconds. Not much time.

A quick glance up and Gideon saw surprised looks all round. The girl had stopped, her hands rising to her mouth as if stifling a cry of alarm, the heavies' expression halfway between shock and disbelief, still 50 yards from their target, the driver's expression obscured in flickering shadows on the windscreen; the van now only twenty yards from the target.

Point Man was writhing in the middle of the street, but he wasn't giving up. He was still trying to extricate his right hand from the pocket of his coat. Gideon grabbed Point Man's hand and pulled, flicking his wrist down and out. The gun dislodged and fell to the ground with a clatter. He sent it skittering across the street with a deft kick, then he wrenched Point Man's arm up and back, dislocating the shoulder and, in the same movement, put Point Man between himself and the oncoming van. If Point Man could have screamed, he would have, but his larynx was locked shut in a spasm. Instead, he writhed in agony on the ground like a speared animal.

The van slowed, now Gideon could see indecision in the driver's face. Good, the driver was a newbie. The hesitation cost the team maybe another five seconds. The driver screeched to a halt, slightly overshooting his mark. He switched gears and reversed the van, putting it between the bewildered girl and Gideon. She stood frozen in place, registering a threat for the first time, but still not aware she was the target.

"Run!" Gideon bellowed at her.

He could see her through the side window of the van; a look of shock spreading across her face as she turned to run. Gideon heard the sliding door slam back. Someone—a woman—was screaming instructions from the innards of the van.

Gideon let go of Point Man's arm and sprinted diagonally to his left to get around the van. The twins kept to the game plan. They were definitely pros. They loped like pumas, closing the distance between themselves and their prey. They came up next to the girl, one on each side as she began to run, and grabbed her, jerking her completely off her feet. The force knocked her sunglasses off her face and sent them spinning to the pavement. Their churning feet smashed them to pieces.

"Help!" she screamed. "Help me, please!"

She struggled wildly and screamed again—an inarticulate, savage battle cry for survival.

Several people on the street and in the café froze in fear, rictuses of disbelief and horror on their faces.

Gideon knew he would get no help from the watching crowd. He raced toward the van. The girl had managed to wedge the heels of her boots against the edge of the van's floor and was pushing back with all her might as the twins tried to shove her in.

Twin One registered Gideon charging toward him and let go of the girl. At the same time, someone inside the van reached out and pulled her into the van by her long hair. Twin Two shoved her, finishing the job.

She screamed again and thrashed her legs as Gideon and Twin One smacked into each other. Gideon, though the lighter of the two men, had momentum on his side and sent Twin One sprawling backward. Gideon followed him and lashed out with his booted foot, giving Twin One a sharp dragon kick to the sternum. The thug fell hard on his ass, completely winded.

Gideon turned toward Twin Two just as a large fist slammed into the side of his head. Stars. He staggered backward and tripped over Twin One, hitting the sidewalk hard himself. Thudding blows from a boot: once, twice to the head, then to his back as he rolled into a ball, protecting his head.

The rain of blows stopped. Gideon was only dimly aware of movement around him now. He lifted his head as he lay prone. Twin One seemed to float by him toward the van. Point Man followed still gasping for breath. His mind hazily registered the muffled struggle of the girl. Then, near his head, the click-clack of a cocked weapon. A low female voice speaking urgently in Farsi.

"Leave him, Arash!"

Every fiber in Gideon's being screamed at him to move! With all the strength that remained to him, he rolled to his left.

"Boom!"

Gideon heard the percussive explosion. Almost simultaneously, a spray of hot lead and concrete penetrated his neck and back as the shot rang out.

A chorus of screams from the cafe. Then the Farsi again, this time raised in anger.

"Arash, you idiot! Go! Go!"

Gideon raised his head, ears ringing, and looked directly into the eyes of the terrified prisoner.

"Help me!" He saw her mouth move, but he could barely hear her voice above the revving engine and the ringing in his ears.

The sliding door slammed shut. The gears engaged. Tires screeched on the tarmac. The acrid stench of burning rubber filled the air. Gideon shook his head and tried to rise, staggered and fell hard. He felt hands on his shoulders, hands gently turning his head, murmurs of concern. And then he was gone—drifting in velvety darkness.

*** 

Gideon blinked and looked to his left. A fiery pain lanced through his neck. The blurred outline of a paramedic hovered near his head, dabbing gingerly at his temple, neck and back with a swab. He heard the tinkle of something small and hard striking a kidney dish. He could feel a bruise rising, making the rest of the skin pull tightly on his face. He tried to rise, but the paramedic gently pushed his shoulder back down.

"Not yet, buddy," he said.

A wave of nausea washed over him and he groaned. There was another presence in the ambulance. He opened his eyes again, turning his blurred vision to the back of the vehicle. A tall gray-haired man, his head slightly stooped under the ceiling of the ambulance, stood silently, holding onto the safety rail set into the roof. He swayed gently as the driver negotiated Brooklyn traffic. His steely blue gaze never once left Gideon's face.

That would be the law, Gideon thought.

***

Mahram struggled against the strong pair of hands pressing her into the floor of the van's cargo area. She kicked and thrashed wildly. Her boots struck flesh. She screamed again, her heart hammering. The inside of the van was phantasmagorical—indistinct shapes lunged at her out of the dark, grabbing at her legs and arms.

Someone was shouting commands in a language she did not understand, then a fist sledge-hammered into the side of her face. There was strangely no pain, just a distinct diming of consciousness, an almost out of body experience as she felt herself flipped over like a rag doll. A huge knee planted itself against the small of her back, forcing out her breath. Someone twisted her arms forcefully until her wrists met behind her back. She felt the sharp plastic edges of zip ties slip over her wrists and cinch tight.

Her mind stammered in amazement—Bloody hell! How many times had they done this to be so proficient at it?

A white canvas sack was forced over her head. She lay still—that might be best.

The knee was removed, she could breathe again. Now her ankles were zip tied together.

The very odd but definite odor of flour pervaded the bag over her head. Her mind slowly cleared.

"Mahram?"

Mahram did not answer.

"Obey everything I say. Don't struggle and you will not be hurt," the woman said in Arabic. She had an accent that Mahram could not quite place.

"Yes," Mahram answered in the same language.

Her voice sounded small, somehow weak in the dark. Salty tears suddenly stung her eyes. She swallowed hard.

"What do you want?" Mahram said more forcefully, her voice breaking on the last syllable. There was no answer.

One of the men groaned in pain.

A loud, angry exchange burst out between the woman and one of the big men who'd grabbed her, in a language she did not understand.

"Arash…"

That was an Arabic or Persian name and the only word she understood in the exchange.

The van had slowed considerably, no longer a mad dash but an efficient speed registering in its revs. She felt the van turn every few minutes, her body swaying to its motion, causing her to roll involuntarily against its side. She heard other bodies shifting around her to the sway of gravity but remembered seeing oddly shaped plastic handles protruding from the van's surfaces when she was thrown inside. No doubt hand holds that the others were hanging onto to stop themselves rolling about the floor like she was. She turned and lay on her side in a foetal position; as she did, she felt the toes of her boots lightly strike the wall of the van. Her heartbeat became less frantic. She tried to picture where they were. The sounds of the city filtered to her through the van's metal side. She decided, in an indefinable way, that they must be heading in a westerly direction.

East: water, south: Manhattan…the traffic wasn't heavy enough to be Manhattan. Maybe scream again. They hadn't gagged her.

Her face, now throbbing with pain from the impact of the punch, warned her against any heroics. There was another moan, another sharp exchange between the woman and one of the men.

Farsi? Why would Persians want anything to do with me?

The van moved slowly now in traffic, then stopped. She heard the muted engines of other vehicles sidling through the van's walls—traffic light? Silence in the van.

"I think you might have the wrong Mahram," she said, her voice wavering, sounding desperate to her own ears. "My name is Mahram Ammar. I'm not Persian. I'm a primary school teacher."

No answer.

Mahram shifted position, trying to put a little distance between herself and the wall of the vehicle. A thought flitted like a bright blue bird through her mind—kick the side of the van, attract attention in the traffic.

The woman in the van gave a sharp order, almost like she was reading her thoughts.

Large rough hands picked her up as if she weighed nothing, one by the shoulders the other by her ankles and moved her into the center of the van. They placed her face down.

"Don't move. Don't even try. You will only get hurt," the woman said.

The van started moving again and then picked up speed. The revs mellowed as they merged onto the expressway. Her focus narrowed now, moving inward toward herself, no longer in denial, assessing the damage. Aside from her face she felt no pain. Her senses became acutely aware of her own breathing and the smell of flour and the darkness in front of her eyes. Her mind flitted like a small, frightened bird in a cage, rerunning the experience.

Why me? Why now? She wracked her memory trying to think of anyone she may have offended.

Who was the young man who'd tried to save her? She hadn't recognized him.

# Chapter 2

Gideon spooned another helping of red Jell-O into his mouth from a white plastic bowl. It must have been fifteen years since he last tasted Jell-O. A kind of watered-down sweetness. Not terrible. He took another mouthful and then washed it down with some water from a white and blue paper cup.

His memory of what had happened was vague. He remembered gaining consciousness as they arrived at the hospital. The paramedic pushing him from the ambulance on a gurney. It had been getting dark then and he remembered the cold breeze stroking his face and bare chest as they entered the hospital. Gideon had noticed the tall gray-haired man standing near the entrance of the ER in the glare of the fluorescent light, speaking softly into a cell phone, his gaze never leaving Gideon's face as he passed by on the bed. And there had been pain and the sound of a groan he'd realized was coming from his own mouth.

Later, there had been a nurse—Tara her name badge said—pretty, blonde, with a warm smile. He'd smiled back and decided he wouldn't make a fuss. Besides, his back and head ached. Tara had brought him the Jell-O, some water, and a few pain killers.

The door to his room swung open again. Gideon looked up.

"Tara?" Gideon said. She smiled slightly.

She hesitated for a second, looking at him, then picked up the empty cup.

"You seem a little better. Would you like me to remove the Jell-O? Would you like more water, Mr Dunbar?"

"No, I'm enjoying the Jell-O, thanks," he said.

She smiled and moved slightly closer, fluffing up the pillows behind his head.

"Actually, some coffee would be good, if possible."

"Sure. Are you comfortable, Mr Dunbar?" she said. Gideon smiled.

"Tara, my wallet and watch—where are they?"

"The detective has those," she said. Her voice had a lovely, smoky timbre to it.

"I see." He grinned and rolled his eyes dramatically.

He could see she was trying to suppress a smile. His eyes followed Tara's neat figure as she exited. Just across the hallway from the door to the room sat a large African American police officer on a ridiculously small chair. He was reading a newspaper. The police officer looked up as the door opened and his dark eyes met Gideon's. A wash of human sound came from the hallway into the room. Nurses moving about busily, their shoes squeaking slightly on the linoleum floor. Somewhere close by someone moaning in pain. The smell of disinfectant. That he could smell was a good sign, he thought.

Gideon spooned another mouthful of Jell-O into his mouth. Then the hydraulic piston began to close the door.

"I see you there, officer. Nice to meet you," Gideon said.

The door flicked closed with a loud clack, but not before Gideon saw a sardonic smile spread across the policeman's face.

Gideon eased himself back gingerly onto the pillows. The bed had him propped up at a 45% angle. He probed at the bruise on his left temple with his index finger. Not too bad.

Suddenly he felt tired. That didn't surprise him. His military and martial arts training had conditioned him to expect the post adrenaline come down. His thoughts turned to the girl in the van. He admired the way she'd fought back against her assailants. He wished he'd been able to help her. Who was she? Why did they want her? And who were 'they' exactly? Gideon thought through the incident again carefully; the relative sophistication of the kidnapping would seem to suggest that she was a high value target, otherwise why waste the money? Why not hire local hoods? He sighed heavily and moved his head right to left, testing the tenderness in his neck. He thought about his unit in Israel and why he had been sent home in the first place, 'For rest and recuperation after Ariel's death,' he remembered his commander saying. Gideon snorted out loud at the memory.

"So much for that," he caught himself saying under his breath.

The shrinks wouldn't let him back into the unit until his blood pressure started to normalize. He glanced over at the blood pressure monitor—not much chance of that now.

The door swung open again. The doctor and the tall detective who he'd seen in the ambulance walked through the door, together with a woman, probably mid-fifties, dyed dark brown hair, olive skin. A world-weary face that had been beautiful once—it was her eyes that struck Gideon—bright, light green and alive with intelligence. She held a large, but slim leather case in her right hand.

The doctor gave Gideon a quick, tired smile.

"Mr Dunbar?"

"Please, quit with the 'Mr' business. Call me Gideon," he said.

"Ok Gideon, my name is Doctor Lehmann, this is Agent Hunter of the FBI and this is Ms Alda Dibra."

The doctor checked his chart, then spoke to no one in particular.

"No concussion. His skull bones are intact, although there are several superficial lesions in the scalp, neck and upper back tissue. Fortunately, the blows didn't quite catch him on the temple or the spine. A bullet struck the pavement about a foot from Gideon's body and sprayed small shrapnel into the back of his head and back. All vitals are fine."

Turning to the man and woman, the doctor said, "Agent Hunter, Ms Dibra, Gideon needs rest so I would like this interview to be as quick as possible."

"Thank you, Doctor. We'll be mindful of Gideon's health," said the detective in a dry baritone voice.

The doctor looked skeptical but left the room. A silence descended as Agent Hunter and Ms Dibra contemplated Gideon and Gideon looked back at them.

Hunter held a sheaf of paper in his hand. He rasped his fingers over the stubble on the side of his neck with the other, sticking out his jaw as he did so, then sighed heavily. He lifted the paper to eye level, flicked his eyes over the writing and then resumed staring at Gideon. This was a man who did not seem to blink much at all.

"It says here you serve in the Israeli Defense Force. An 'Aish Machal'." He made a quote mark with his free hand. "So, not a conscript, but a foreign national who has voluntarily joined the Israeli army?"

"Yes, Sir," said Gideon.

"Your unit?"

Gideon remained silent.

"Duvdevan," said the woman. "Unit 217, to be precise. An elite special-forces operation unit that specializes in undercover operations in urban areas. Trained in human and mechanical counter-surveillance. High-risk, complicated operations, included targeted killings and, significantly, kidnappings…and a range of other undercover work, mostly in Arab areas."

Gideon did not answer immediately. He looked from one to the other. "What does my service have to do with any of this?" he said flatly.

"That's what we'd like to know, Gideon."

Her voice was low, more of a purr. The two of them were a powerful combination. Gideon gave them a wan smile.

"We've seen CCTV footage from the café and the apartment directly across the street from the incident. Regrettably, the footage is grainy. Cheap security. Installed mostly to get insurance coverage, not really there to help criminal investigations, so we're going to have to rely on eyewitness testimony," she said.

Gideon again remained silent.

"We feel sure that you can fill in some of the blanks for us, Gideon."

"I'd be happy to help if I can, Alda, but first I'd like to see some ID. Someone did just try to kill me, after all," he said facetiously.

Alda did not smile, neither did Hunter.

Hunter stepped forward and flipped out a slim black wallet with an FBI badge inside. Gideon flicked his eyes over it. It seemed authentic enough. The gold-colored Lady Justice and photo looked genuine.

"I didn't catch who you worked for, Alda?"

"CIA, Gideon. I think you know how this works."

"How what works?" he said.

Gideon looked from one to the other. There was no response from either of them.

"Is your ID in that big briefcase of yours?" Gideon said sardonically, indicating the leather case Alda held.

They both continued to stare at him.

"Oh, I get it. I either cooperate or I get arrested for trying to help someone who got kidnapped."

"Yes, your cooperation would be nice," Hunter said.

Their tone seemed accusatory to Gideon.

"You have it…for now," Gideon said. He did not appreciate the insinuation in Hunter's words.

"You're right about the crime. We are treating this as a kidnapping," Hunter said.

Gideon stared at Hunter for a moment, letting the tension build.

"It's self-evident. Someone got snatched off the street. It's a kidnapping."

"You reacted very well in the face of some fairly formidable odds," Hunter responded.

"Is that a question or a statement?" Gideon said.

Hunter didn't answer.

"I'm a trained soldier. And you're correct, trained in counterterrorism," Gideon added.

"Do you know of, or have you had any association with Mahram Ammar, the young woman who was kidnapped?"

"No, never saw her before in my life."

"Have you ever had any operational involvement with the Northern Oil Company in Libya?"

"No, sir. But I've heard of that company."

"Do you know her father is Basar Ammar, the head of the Northern Oil Company in Libya–in Libya that position passes for the Minister of Oil or Energy?"

"I've heard his name, but I've never met the man or had any operational involvement with him."

Hunter raised one eyebrow questioningly.

"You get to know a thing or two when you work for Unit 217. Sometimes our work entails hot pursuit of our targets abroad. Many of these Middle Eastern companies funnel money for political activities in Israel, the Gaza strip, West Bank and Beirut. All of them have financed factions within the civil wars in Libya and Syria. Weapons have to be bought with something. That something is usually oil. But I'm sure you know that."

Hunter's steely gaze raked over him from top to toe, then back again. He said nothing.

"Okay let me give you my theory. You say this girl is the daughter of the oil minister or minster of energy? My guess is she's going to be exchanged for either oil or money to buy armaments for one of the factions in the Libyan civil war," Gideon said.

"Why do you think that, Gideon?" Alda said.

"Because it's the Middle East and there's a civil war raging right now in Libya. Fairly obvious."

"What were you doing on Hicks Street this afternoon?" Hunter said.

"Walking home from work. I take the subway to Williamsburg."

"Okay, tell us from the beginning, in broad terms, what happened," Hunter said.

Gideon skimmed through the story.

"Where's work, where's home?"

"I'm sure you know that too."

"We do, but indulge me."

"Work is the Gym, near Pier 6. I'm an MMA instructor for the moment. Williamsburg, Juliana Place is home."

"Which subway station were you walking toward?"

"Clark Street."

"Why not Court Street; it's closer?"

Gideon smiled. "I like walking down the quiet leafy streets of Brooklyn Heights in the evening and there's a nice little Thai restaurant on Hicks that sells good take out. I usually get some for dinner. Check my credit card if you don't believe me."

Hunter and Alda glanced at each other. It seemed they already had. Gideon could not help feeling impressed at the speed with which they had gleaned information about him and the incident.

"So, an Israeli counterterrorist expert with just the right kind of military training to recognize a kidnapping in progress, just happens to be walking down the right street when the daughter of the very influential Libyan Oil Minister just happens to be kidnapped; is that what you're telling me?" Hunter said.

"I'm describing what happened."

"You're an American citizen. Why do you serve in the IDF?"

"Because I figured it would be better to kill the bad guys there before they got here. Do you remember what happened the last time they got here in numbers?"

Gideon let the last statement hang in the air.

"Also, I happen to be Jewish and hold Israeli citizenship because I was born there. And in case you haven't noticed, Israel needs all the friends she can get. She's surrounded by enemies."

"Dunbar is a Scottish, not Jewish name."

"My mother's Jewish, my father is an American of Scottish heritage. They met in Israel."

"Do you work for Israeli intelligence?"

"No."

"Do you work for Mossad?"

"I told you, no!"

"Was this an Israeli operation?"

"No, it was not!"

"Let me tell you my theory, Gideon. You're a Mossad agent and you're giving cover to a False Flag Mossad operation," Hunter said.

Gideon snorted in derision.

"Ten out of ten for a vivid imagination," he said to Hunter.

"Are you willing to take a polygraph test?"

Gideon eyed them both coldly for a moment.

"Sure, why not. But you're wasting time focusing on me. I actually do have some useful information I can share with you about the bad guys," he said.

"What's that?"

"There was a woman in the back of the van. She was calling the shots."

"Did you get a good look at her?"

"Partial—but that's not the important point. The important point is that I heard her speak Farsi."

"How'd you know it was Farsi?"

"My mother's Persian."

"I thought you said your mother was Jewish?"

"She is. She and her family moved from Iran after the Shah fell and the Muslims started to persecute Jews and other religious minorities. So, I know a bit of Farsi. It's literally my mother tongue."

The two exchanged another glance.

"Anything else of use that springs to mind?" Hunter said, in a slightly less hostile tone.

"Yes, the woman called one of the men—the one who tried to shoot me— 'Arash'."

"*Arash* you say? And what does that mean in, er, Farsi?"

The sarcasm was so New York, Gideon thought. He could not help smiling at Hunter.

"It's a man's name in Farsi. It means something like 'Archer.' So, the people you are after, are Iranian…probably."

"Is that so?" said Hunter.

"Also, the van was a Nissan VR 1500."

"We know that. We're not idiots," Hunter said.

26

Alda took a step forward and laid the portfolio-size carry case on the bed, then opened it. There was a series of photos in it.

"You're an interesting man, Gideon, with an interesting skill set. Tell me, why did you leave the IDF?"

Gideon sighed again.

"I haven't left," he said. "I'm on leave. A good friend and fellow soldier was killed in action in a recent operation that went sideways."

"The Middle East is a dangerous neighborhood. Hard to control outcomes," Alda said.

"Not if you're good enough."

"You don't feel good enough, or the IDF don't think you're good enough?" Alda smiled. This time there seemed to be some warmth in it.

"There's always a mandatory rest when one of your unit dies. Especially if you're having murderous thoughts about it."

"You like to kill people?" asked Hunter through a slanted smile.

"Let's just say there is a certain satisfaction in ridding the world of people who blow up innocent children on school buses," Gideon said, his eyes cold.

"You must be getting a little tired, Gideon. Just a bit more, then we'll leave you be," Alda said.

Gideon looked at them without responding. The good cop, bad cop routine did work, he knew that. He'd be doing exactly the same thing if he was in their shoes, but he could not help feeling slightly affronted at the tone of the questioning.

Alda took out a handful of 8.5x11 sized photos.

"I'm going to run through this series of photos relatively quickly. I'd like you to tell me if you can identify these as any of the people involved in the kidnapping this afternoon."

Alda held up a photo of a middle-aged Arab man with a small neat moustache. She passed it to Gideon. Gideon shook his head.

Then another of a man, then a woman, then several young men.

The pack of photos started to thin, but suddenly there he was: 'Point Man.' Gideon flicked the photo. "That's 'Point Man.'"

"Point Man?" Alda said.

"The guy who acts like a lookout," said Hunter. "Is this the guy whose arm you dislocated?"

"Yep, that's him."

"How certain are you?" Hunter said. Gideon saw a look of excitement cross his features.

"About one hundred and ten percent. I got up real close," Gideon said.

"Do you know this man?" Alda said.

"Do we really have to go through all that again?" Gideon said, arching his brows.

Alda laughed softly.

"Who is he?" Gideon said.

"Delir Hashemi. He's a facilitator. Part of the Quds Force and, yes, Iranian. A very bad man. He usually operates in the Americas and has ties to Hezbollah. I'm surprised you don't know him, Gideon. I thought you guys in the IDF knew a thing or two about your enemy?" Alda said.

"There are a thousand Hashemi's out there. I won't know them all, just what is operationally necessary," Gideon said.

"Did you get a good look at the woman in the van?" Hunter asked again. "No, like I said, I didn't, but I heard her voice."

"Would you recognize her voice again if you heard it?" Alda asked.

"It's likely. It was distinctive. A low harsh voice for a woman."

There was silence again for a few seconds while Hunter and Alda scrutinized him.

"You've been very helpful, Gideon. Get some rest," Alda said.

"If I could only avoid the kidnappers and attempted murderers of the world, I ought to be able to manage that," Gideon said, then smiled.

"We'd like to meet again. Say 9 am tomorrow?" said Alda.

"Sure," Gideon responded.

"We'll have someone pick you up. Oh, and don't try to leave. The officer outside has strict instructions to keep you safe."

"Am I under arrest?" Gideon asked.

"No, but it would be helpful to us if you stayed put. There are dangerous people out there who just tried to kill you. We'd prefer not to have any more gunfire in the neighborhood. I'm sure you understand. And you're injured."

"See you tomorrow," Gideon said without enthusiasm.

Alda zipped away the photos. She and Hunter turned to leave.

"Oh, and one more thing, Gideon." Alda spoke over her shoulder. "Keep this to yourself for the moment, okay?"

"Could I have my wallet, cell and watch back?" Gideon said.

Hunter dug into his jacket pocket removing the cell phone, watch and wallet and put them on the bedside table next to Gideon.

They walked out. He saw Hunter speaking to the officer outside his room before the door flicked closed.

Gideon leaned back too quickly and groaned as his bruised and pockmarked back made contact with the pillow.

***

The nurse came in again at about 8 pm with another paper cup and a small jug of fresh coffee.

"It's decaf. We want you to sleep," she said.

He smiled at her. "Thanks."

"Lift up your shirt. I must give your wounds fresh dressings."

He lifted his shirt obediently and she cleaned his wounds gently. It was painful but somehow, he didn't mind that.

***

Ronaldo Lopez put down his mop and bucket, using both hands to smooth back the fringe of glossy black hair that had fallen across his forehead. He looked up and down the hospital corridor. No one in sight. He glanced at his watch: 10 pm. He knew this stretch of corridor was the best spot to take a quick smoke break because it didn't have any cameras on it. He opened the exit door and pushed his wheelie bucket and mop outside and onto a strip of concrete under an awning, dimly lit by a grime-covered fluorescent light. He took out his bag of smoke, as he liked to call it—a mixture of marijuana and tobacco—and some paper and started to roll a joint.

"I wonder if you could help me?"

"Fuck!" Ronaldo exclaimed as he jolted with surprise.

The beautiful, dark-eyed woman in front of him laughed softly.

"Sorry, did I startle you?" she said, her voice like cream. "My name's Vanessa Habib. I'm a reporter for the New York Times. You've heard of me?"

"No, sorry lady. I haven't," Ronaldo said with churlish satisfaction. In any life he knew she would be out of his league.

29

The woman flicked open a security pass with New York Times written on it next to her photo.

"What do you want?" Ronaldo said.

She smiled again; she was quite stunning Ronaldo decided.

"I need your help."

Ronaldo lit his joint and blew smoke up toward the awning then smiled back, his teeth stained by years of smoke.

"There's a young man who was shot this afternoon and is in the ER. He's being guarded by a policeman. I'll give you 500 dollars if you can find out the man's prognosis. Is he expected to live, what his wounds are etc….any other information, like his home address…his name, anything you can find out."

"500 dollars! Okay," Ronaldo hawked, but caught himself before he spit the gob of mucus and swallowed it instead.

"I'll meet you back in an hour or so. Okay?"

Ronaldo took another deep puff of his joint then dropped it and ground it out dramatically with his booted foot.

She smiled again, but this time the smile did not seem to reach her eyes.

"Okay, I'll be here waiting for you," she said softly.

*** 

Gideon woke from a shallow sleep with a start, trying to cling onto a shred of memory—something the women had shouted to the thug who had tried to shoot him; but it dissipated on a rising tide of consciousness.

There were raised voices outside his door. Two men arguing, then Tara's voice. The door to his room opened and a cleaner pushed his wheeled mop and bucket through the doorway. The cleaner glanced at Gideon for a second and then down at the clipboard at the end of his bed. He glanced back up at Gideon and then used both hands to slick back his head of thick glossy black hair before turning and pushing his bucket and mop into the restroom area. The large policeman stood in the doorway of the room scowling at the cleaner who was muttering under his breath now as he cleaned the toilet and then mopped the bathroom floor. The cleaner walked backward toward the bed, mopping the floor as he went.

A slight frown passed over Gideon's features as the cleaner took an exaggerated step backward and knocked the bucket with the heel of his boot.

Water sloshed over the side of the bucket and traced a streak of dirty liquid right to the foot of Gideon's bed.

"What the f…" the police officer began.

"Sorry sir, sorry."

The cleaner turned.

"Sorry, you're making me nervous, man. I was rushing! I'm jus' tryna do my job, okay?" the cleaner said. Tara came into the room again to find out what all the fuss was about.

"Are you sure you know this man?" the policeman said to Tara.

"Yes, Ronaldo, he's one of our cleaning staff," she answered.

Gideon noticed the cleaner's eyes flick down to the chart at the side of his bed—the chart held his details on it and the spillage had conveniently made its way across the room to the chart. The cleaner's upper lip glistened with sweat.

The policeman kept a vigilant eye on the cleaner until he left the room.

Tara smiled at Gideon.

"Get some rest now," she said and switched off the light.

The policeman closed the door behind him and Tara with a thud.

***

Gideon's sleep was restless. In his dream he rolled on the ground and a gunshot went off close to his head and then a woman screamed something out of the darkness, but when he looked up to try to see who it was, a van door was slammed shut in front of him.

# Chapter 3

Jack Hunter and Alda Dibra exited the Brooklyn Methodist Hospital on 7th Avenue in Park Slope.

The traffic was slowing, but it made little difference to the ambient glow of light in the night sky. Their shadows gyrated like boxers under the lights.

"What do you think? Alda said.

"I think we'd better keep an eye on him. The last thing we need is the Israelis involved in this mess on our soil," Hunter said.

"This has become an international incident now. I'll need to let the Director know we're dealing with a possible terror cell…or a possible Mossad operation. Whoever it is, they're almost certain to try to move the victim offshore. We'll need to contact the Libyan ambassador to let them know one of their citizen's children has been abducted on US soil and, assuming Gideon is telling the truth about this being an Iranian operation, we'll also need to keep the Iranian consulate under surveillance," Alda said.

"This is still a criminal matter, not an intelligence matter and Mahram Ammar is likely still on US soil, so this is an FBI investigation regardless of the international connection."

"Jack, if the Quds force is involved, it's almost certainly a terrorist matter. You know and I know that this will move offshore and then we'll have an international incident. Once that happens it'll be a CIA matter."

"They're still on US soil. There's no way they could be anywhere else."

Alda said nothing. The truth was the girl could be anywhere by now.

"We work well together, Alda. Let's keep it that way. I'll speak to Carl tonight and have Gideon picked up tomorrow. Let's meet at FBI HQ in the morning."

\*\*\*

Executive Assistant Director Carl Sullivan, National Security Branch, counterterrorism unit of the FBI, sat in the conference room on the 26th floor of the FBI Headquarters, Federal Plaza, New York. It was a large room with pearly light spilling through the window from the Plaza. Dimmed downlights cast a contrasting yellow glow over an impressive 18 seat oval shaped, cherry wood table. The table faced a large screen. Carl Sullivan sat on one side with Hunter to his right, Alda to his left, and a team of five Joint Terrorism Task Force agents, led by Tyler Gutierrez, seated across the table from him. Carl Sullivan rewound the apartment complex CCTV footage for the third time.

Gideon came into frame walking briskly, the slightest hesitation in his gait as he clocked the bad guys, and then slowing as he made to cross the road before exploding into action.

"He's good," Sullivan said.

"Yes, they train their boys well in the IDF," Hunter replied.

"Did he pass the polygraph test?" Sullivan asked.

"Yup, flying colors. But it means virtually nothing. The IDF special forces get training in evading polygraph," Hunter said.

"Alda, your thoughts?"

"I think he's clean."

"So do I, but that doesn't mean we should forget about him," Sullivan said.

"We've pegged a tail on him," Tyler said, "and a little something in his cell phone while he was on the polygraph," he added after a pause.

"I assume you've got a warrant for that. He's a US citizen too, you know," Alda said sharply.

"FISA warrant came through this afternoon," Hunter replied.

"How did you manage that so quickly?" Alda said.

"The judge in question likes my work. I don't give him bad information, he knows that, plus I've helped him with difficult cases before in another life," Hunter said, a sparkle in his eye.

"Good interagency co-operation," Sullivan said, then gave a short barking laugh. He turned to Alda with a faint smile. "Can't be too careful these days, Alda. I'm sure you'd agree, particularly if it turns out to be a terror cell."

Sullivan turned to Tyler, "Any news on the vehicle?"

"A vehicle matching the description was stolen outside a bakery in Queens early yesterday morning. A Sunrise Bakery van. The company logo is burgundy lettering on white, so all they had to do was roughly spray over the logo with white paint and presto, a white van, like a million others. Using plate recognition, we've managed to track the stolen vehicle's movement going south on the Expressway and then over the Verrazano Narrows across Staten Island via the Goethals Bridge into Jersey. Possible sighting on the New Jersey Turnpike near Newark, but then nothing. We have the tristate and local police on the lookout for the vehicle."

"What about the Pakistani embassy in D.C.?"

"A small pick-up in electronic traffic last night in the Iranian section of the embassy, but no useful intercepts."

"Have we got a tail on the Iranian ambassador?"

"Yes."

"Any known Iranian assets we can squeeze? Especially medical staff. We have one terribly injured Iranian."

"Yes, and yes we're doing that as we speak."

"Watching the ports and airports?"

"The main ones, like a hawk sir. But as you know there are thousands of possible unofficial routes out of the country."

"Well, we have at least one positive ID, so get this, er… 'Delir Hashemi's' photo out there will you, and let the Canadians and Mexicans know too."

"Will do, sir."

"What about the Israelis? Have they said anything, done anything to indicate they know about this?"

"Not a peep, sir. We've been monitoring their embassy too," Tyler said.

"What you're telling me is we basically have nothing. Is that what you're saying?" Sullivan said dryly.

"Yes, sir." Tyler said, looking around the room.

"Let me know immediately if we come into some useful intel. Make sure Gideon Dunbar doesn't disappear anywhere. We may need him soon to identify suspects. Okay, let's go."

The group broke up and Tyler and his agents left the room.

Hunter and Alda got up to go.

"I now have the very unpleasant task of flying to D.C. to inform the Deputy Secretary of State, the Libyan Ambassador and a worried father, that one of their nationals and an only daughter, has been kidnapped on American soil and is now in the hands of suspected terrorists." Sullivan said.

"You have my sympathy, sir. Would you like some company?" Hunter said.

34

"No, but thanks, Hunter. You look like crap, by the way. Go get some sleep, will you. I need you functioning on all cylinders. You've got the lead on this one."

Hunter smiled, then said, "Okay, Carl."

Sullivan turned to Alda. "I assume you've let Langley know what's going on?"

"I have, sir," Alda said.

***

The same young male officer with bright blue eyes and sandy hair who had picked Gideon up at the hospital that morning approached him as he sat in the lobby.

"You're free to go now Mr Dunbar," he said in a public relations tone. "Would you like me to give you a lift home?"

The officer reached into his jacket pocket and took out Gideon's cell phone and handed it to him. "You almost forgot this."

Gideon stood and smiled, accepting his phone and said, "No thanks. I'll catch a cab."

The officer indicated the direction they should take with his hand.

"Are you planning on leaving town anytime soon?"

"Nope," Gideon answered.

"Okay, if you do, let us know immediately."

The officer handed Gideon Jack Hunter's card with a cell number on it as they walked from the Federal Plaza building onto Duane Street. Gideon accepted it and placed it in his wallet. He hailed a cab and Gideon got in. The officer gave the cab driver Gideon's address; a not too subtle reminder that he was being watched.

He bent low, holding Gideon's eyes. "Let us know if you think of or remember anything else, okay?" he said with a tight smile, then closed the door firmly.

Gideon's back and neck still ached. He took a capsule from a small box of painkillers the doctor had given him that morning at the hospital and popped one on the ride home.

His apartment was a rental, two bed walk-up on the third floor in a surprisingly quiet and leafy street. The reason Gideon had chosen it was because the walls were painted a creamy white and got good morning sun inside. The floorboards were newly sanded and lightly stained. The kitchen was new too, and painted white with a white marble benchtop. The cheerfulness he knew was a direct counter to his state of mind. He closed the solid door behind him and dumped his wallet and keys down on a small table that held his computer. He moved to the kitchen where he made himself a Nespresso coffee, opened the pantry cupboard and grabbed an energy bar, then returned to the table that held his laptop, sat down and turned it on. His eyes narrowed as he thought through the day, sipping the hot brew. The series of questions they'd asked him were telling, concentrating on the Northern Oil Company in Libya and any association with Mahram's father.

Gideon switched on his TOR search engine—much more secure than Google. The internet was a treasure trove if you knew how to interrogate it. Soon he had enough information to give himself choices. He shut down the laptop with a snap and popped it into a gray and black nondescript backpack, then gathered a few crucial belongings. An idea was taking shape in his mind, an idea that quickened his pulse. Several items of clothing and his army go-bag with a dozen or so items made it into his backpack; unremarkable items to the untrained eye but crucial for what he did for a living.

Yes, he thought, time to resign and move quickly. He rehearsed the words he'd need to say to David, the owner of the gym where he worked.

Gideon walked slowly up Division Avenue in Williamsburg toward the Marcy Avenue station. He could not shake the half-remembered words spoken in Farsi; something about those words was important, but somehow eluded him. Then his mind turned to the girl. An image of her reaching out to him, crying out for help seemed indelibly inked onto his memory. The FBI would do their best to locate her, given the profile of the kidnap victim and the kidnapper, he was sure of that at least. He tried some breathing techniques to calm his racing heart. He had to clear his thoughts and make sure his decisions were being driven by rational thinking and not adrenalin; he knew what he wanted to do but were they wise thoughts? At the very least he'd have to contact his unit commander soon and let him know what happened.

The tingling feeling of hair rising on the nape on his neck, Gideon knew from experience, meant something was wrong. He slowed his pace and withdrew his wallet from an inner jacket pocket, pretending to be looking for something, while surreptitiously glancing up into a glass shopfront several feet away. He immediately spotted what had made him sense something amiss. He had a tail. Possibly more than one, he thought. That surprised him, so soon after his 'interrogation'. Well, they'd be disappointed, and he was going to have some fun at their expense he decided. He led them down into the Marcy Avenue station and made at least three possibles while walking along the platform. The train rattled and hissed to a stop. A blonde woman, her hair pulled into a tight ponytail, stepped into the car, one up from his, and sat so that she could observe him through the window of the gangway connection. Too pretty to be a good surveillance officer, he thought. She was dressed in jeans, a black jacket, and sunglasses, which she did not remove on the train. She may as well have had FBI stenciled across her back in bright yellow letters. Then there was a guy with a carefully trimmed beard further down the carriage and another small dark older man with a New York Yankees baseball cap on, furtively glancing around the carriage behind his black rimmed glasses.

Gideon got out at Court Street, Brooklyn Heights. The woman from Marcy Avenue got off too and followed him, digging in her shoulder bag, as she exited the train. The Beard Guy in the dark green sweater got off moments later. He was a little more subtle: he exited the train at the last possible instant and turned in the opposite direction to them. The other guy did not get off. Gideon took a circuitous route to Hicks Street and walked slowly down the street toward the Gym.

It was quiet on Hicks Street, but the tail was still there. He noticed her reflected in the back window of a bus, as it pulled up to disgorge its passengers. A cool breeze moved the leaves on the tree-lined street. The brownstones stood like silent sentinels as he wandered past; windows like dead eyes.

The sidewalk and part of the street where the action had gone down the afternoon before was marked off with crime scene tape. A police officer stood nearby looking bored.

The images spilled through his mind as he walked slowly by—his attack on Hashemi, the kick, the punch, the bullet striking the sidewalk and the girl's cry for help. Gideon felt the bruising where the shrapnel had penetrated his good leather jacket. He stopped and stared at the spot pockmarked by the bullet on the pavement. The woman's angry words came back to him now:

"Arash you idiot. Go! Go!"

His breath left him in a rush. He was surprised by the violence of his emotional response. He felt the old anger mounting in him. These pricks never learned. This was the cold fury that animated him in action. He'd been wondering when it would show up; his old dark friend, the uneasy companion who had stalked his life ever since he'd broken the nose of a bully at school when he was 10. Now it struck with force. A feeling that had been mounting all day resolved itself into a cold determination. He was involved for better or worse. In reality he knew he could not make himself walk away from this now. Not after discovering someone like Hashemi was involved, plus the idiot called Arash had tried to kill him. He also knew realistically that the terrified young woman was likely to die; this was not his first rodeo with kidnappers, and he owed it to her to try his best to help.

He looked up to see Green Sweater Beard Guy getting a table at the Hicks Street café. Gideon decided his hair was too short and his facial hair too carefully groomed for him to be a good surveillance officer after all. They should be Johnny average, not noticeable in any way. He thought he might have a word with Hunter about the FBI's tactics. For the second time in one morning, he felt surprise. They were pretty bad at this. He felt a strong urge to walk over and tell the Beard Guy that his careful grooming was a dead giveaway, but he pushed the temptation down and walked on to the gym.

***

"Aw, you're kidding. We're gonna miss you, man," David said when Gideon gave him the news. David, was a tall, good-natured man and his disappointment was genuine. The hangdog look accompanying his dismay made Gideon want to chuckle it looked so theatrical.

"But I understand…crazy shit, man. I heard about it. They tried to shoot you? I'm glad you're in one piece, is all," David said, his eyes bulging slightly.

"Yeah, me too," Gideon said, then took off his jacket and showed David the wounds on his neck.

"Sheeeit. I'm not gonna lie to you. That's just gnarly, man."

Gideon chuckled. "David, I'm no longer an employee but I need to use the bathroom, would you excuse me?"

"Yes, sure and good luck and all that. I gotta go and take a class now," David said. They shook hands.

"Your paycheck's on the way," he said over his shoulder.

Gideon smiled again.

He glanced through a window near reception that looked out onto the car park below. He noted a black sedan pull up. No one got out. Gideon thought quickly. He had to phone his Unit commander and bring him up to speed and he had to get out of the States before the authorities restricted his movements. He used the ATM in the gym to draw several thousand dollars in cash, then walked to the men's change room and closed the door.

Time to lose the tail.

The gym itself was relatively quiet, but the 'Movement Floor' as it was called, was filled with mostly women doing Pilates and yoga at this time of day. In the bathroom there were three stalls, a urinal and four showers—all empty. He took the far stall and closed the door. From his pocket he removed his cell and wallet and undid the watch around his wrist. Agent Hunter had only had the wallet in his possession for a short space of time and it was unlikely he'd have had the time to do anything illegal, thought Gideon, but his phone and watch had been taken from him when they did the polygraph that morning. The phone's battery was unusually hot. The power was half of what it should be— compromised for sure, thought Gideon. He quietly lifted the toilet's tank lid and slipped his phone inside. He took a coin from his wallet and levered the back of his watch open. Nothing unusual there. He carefully closed the watch up again and replaced it on his wrist. Then he closely inspected every card holder and pouch and all the stitching of his wallet looking for filamented homing devices— they seemed fine.

Gideon turned his attention to the windows in the stalls. He inspected the louvered window in each one, then entered the last stall again and closed the door. The window in this stall had the least amount of grime and years of careless paint slopped over the grooves in which the louvered panes rested. He knew he had only minutes before one of the tails would come up to find him. The first three panes were removed easily enough. He placed them carefully on the window ledge. The last three proved trickier than the first. The panes of glass were the kind reinforced with wire mesh through their centers, so were quite tough, and this was fortunate because he had to wrench backward and jiggle quite forcefully. Each came from its grimy metal prison with a reluctant squeak. After about a minute of this there was finally an opening big enough to crawl through. He listened carefully for any movement outside the stall. All quiet. He mopped the beaded sweat on his brow with the back of his hand, then standing on the toilet, he shuffled head first through the opening, wedging his head and one of his arms through first and then with an ungainly worm-like wriggle brought his other shoulder and arm through. There was a fall of about four foot to the asphalt roof below. Gideon allowed gravity to take him, cushioning the fall with his arms extended before him and allowing the rest of his body to follow, like a slow-motion dive which he converted into a roll as his hands hit the asphalt. He sat for a moment catching his breath, then stood and carefully replaced the louvered windowpanes.

From a birds-eye view, the roof of the building resembled a large H. Gideon found himself standing on the crossbar of the H. Moving quickly, he jogged across the asphalt roof to the far left-hand wing of the building that looked out over the Hudson River, and the furthest point from the parking lot. He knew he had to move fast. Getting through that window had taken longer than he'd imagined it would. The surveillance team would be losing patience and one of them was bound to come looking.

The building was seven stories high. He had hoped to find an external fire stairwell, but there was none and the drop to the ground was way too severe to attempt a jump down to the street below. He turned toward the hut that housed the opening to the internal fire stairs, but as expected, access was secured behind a padlocked door. He jiggled the door. The padlock was sturdy, nevertheless the bolt that secured the door was part of a flimsy screw-in system. Gideon shook it again; there was some give. The door itself was old plywood veneer and half-rotted through. Nothing for it. Gideon took a step back and gave the door a violent sidekick just below the padlock. He kicked again and was rewarded with the sound of splintering wood. On the third kick, the whole bolt mechanism splintered out of the door, screws and all. He descended the stairs quickly and, on reaching the ground floor door, opened it cautiously and peered out onto a bricked-in footpath. Next to the footpath was a street which led to a main road. On the other side of the street was a densely foliaged garden, part of the Pier 6 park which extended via the pier into the Hudson River. He took another quick look around and then walked briskly across the street into the inviting shadows and squatted behind the trunk of a large tree. Diagonally opposite the park was a bus shelter where several people sat waiting for the next bus. None of them seemed to have noticed him and if they had, they did not show it.

About a minute into his vigil, he was rewarded. He saw Beard Guy make his way around the building, a frown on his face. He looked into the doorway vestibule Gideon had just left and tried the door. It was a one-way locker and did not allow people in from the outside. Beard Guy turned and peered into the shadows of the park where Gideon hid, shading his eyes from the sun with his hand. Gideon was positive he could not be seen, but watched Beard Guy walk all the way toward the Hudson River and then turn right and disappear behind the building before he moved.

Another minute passed and then the B36 bus to Manhattan rumbled toward the bus stop; the advertising on its side heavily covered with inane, but colorful graffiti. He broke from the bushes and hurried across the road, keeping a sharp lookout. Once aboard, he glanced around the bus. A sullen young woman with purple hair and oversized white earphones gave him a dead-eyed look and then dismissed him. Several overweight older ladies who had been waiting at the bus stop scattered themselves like confetti down the length of the bus, talking to one another loudly about grandchildren. Halfway down, an old black guy with a grizzled beard stared with rheumy eyes out of the window at memories. No threat here, he thought.

Gideon sat down and pulled the hood of his jacket up over his head as the bus turned left and rolled past the parking lot of the gym and toward the Brooklyn Bridge. He risked a quick glance into the lot and saw the blonde woman who'd followed him on the train speaking urgently into her cell phone. A man, the guy with the baseball cap Gideon had seen earlier that day, came running from the front of the building toward the waiting sedan holding up what appeared to be Gideon's cell phone.

***

Gideon felt sure that he'd given his tail the slip before he approached the Israeli consulate in Manhattan on West 2nd Avenue, a building that sat almost, but not quite, adjacent to the United Nations Headquarters. The Israeli consular staff were surprised when Gideon flashed them his special forces card—a black card with his identity on it that could be instantly verified and which allowed him onto any scene involving causalities or potential terrorist threats. They quickly ushered him up to the 15th floor and into a quiet office where a video phone stood like a sphinx in the middle of the table. Gideon dialed a number from memory—the Duvdevan Unit had a dedicated number for urgent and private matters and was well disguised as the reception of a hotel.

After a bit of clicking and whirring a feminine voice answered:

"Hotel Golan, Reception." This was said in Hebrew; the video screen blank. Gideon spoke his ID number distinctly into the phone receiver.

"Gideon Dunbar. How may I help you?" the voice said.

"I'm phoning in from a secure line in the Israeli consulate in New York. I need to speak with my Unit Commander Dani Gilad. An urgent matter," he answered in Hebrew.

"Putting you through now."

Gideon glanced at his watch. It was 4 pm in New York, about 11 pm in Jerusalem. After a short pause Dani Gilad, the unit commander, answered.

"Yes?" the commander sounded grumpy.

"Hope I didn't wake you. Gideon here." Gideon looked down at Dani in the monitor. He looked like he'd been woken from his sleep; his hair in disarray.

"It's late. Where are you?" Dani said, rubbing his eyes.

"In New York. Something's happened, I thought you should know," Gideon said.

"It couldn't wait to the morning?" Dani said, looking at his watch.

"It's afternoon here, Dani and it's important. I would have called earlier but I had to lose my tail. It took time."

"Wait…what? You had a tail? What, is this a joke? I send you home on a vacation and you give me this? It better be good," Dani said sardonically.

"You know I wouldn't have called otherwise, Dani!" Gideon said, with some force, surprising himself with the level of emotion in his outburst.

"Woah! Okay. I didn't mean anything by it. Let's start again. What's concerning you?" Dani said more reasonably.

Gideon told Dani everything from the beginning. Dani interrupted only once to clarify a point.

"You're absolutely 100 percent sure it was Delir Hashemi?" Dani said.

"Yes, absolutely."

"Shit," Dani said. Gideon saw Dani look down for a moment in thought, then his eyes narrowed and after a pause he added, "How are you?"

"I'm fine. I have some antibiotics for my back and I'm starting to work out the stiffness. Otherwise, feeling strong." Gideon said.

"I mean emotionally, psychologically…after Ariel…"

"Really, I'm fine Dani," Gideon said. He could feel the untruth in his statement.

"You want to come back here?" Dani asked.

"No, I want to kill these snakes and find the girl before something bad happens."

Dani remained quiet.

"Jack Hunter thinks I was running cover for a Mossad operation on US soil," Gideon added into the silence.

"That's ridiculous!" Dani responded in an irritated tone.

"It's obvious what they're doing, Dani. Her father runs the Northern Oil company in Libya. They mean to extort oil from the Libyans in exchange for the girl and use the oil to barter for weapons or money to buy weapons and manpower. But they weren't banking on me being able to identify anyone."

"Maybe. This is essentially an American problem. She's an American citizen. The extorted money could be for the civil war in Libya after all. It may have nothing to do with Israel. Anyway, we'd need a green light to take action."

"Not likely with Quds force and Hezbollah involvement. Israel is the target. Dani, they won't catch them on American soil. It was a slick team and if this Hashemi is Quds, they are unlikely to track him down. These guys will have a well-financed network Stateside. The girl is probably already halfway to Africa somewhere."

Dani did not answer.

"This is an Israeli problem. The only reason Hashemi and his crew were in the States is because the girl was here. If oil or money changes hands in Libya and the Hezbollah are involved, that immediately becomes an Israeli problem. The money they make from the kidnapping turns into guns, or missiles aimed at Israel, or worse. Any which way, Israelis die."

Dani sighed and rubbed his face again. "Yes, probably true," he said. "But we still need a green light. Also, the girl could be anywhere."

"Hashemi will need to contact the father somehow, if he hasn't already. The father should be our target. The handover will need to be in Africa," Gideon said.

"Africa's a big place, Gideon."

"The father is in Tripoli. I can go there, do some surveillance and, if possible, find the girl," Gideon said.

"The father is a very powerful and wealthy man. This could just be about personal greed or political leverage," Dani said.

"Unlikely, given the Iranian involvement," Gideon shot back.

"Maybe," Dani said, then paused.

Gideon filled in the silence. "This is about a revenue stream for terrorism. Hezbollah is involved. Why, Dani?"

Gideon heard a faint hiss over the line as Dani remained silent, staring down at the table in front of him. The silence lengthened.

"You okay?" Gideon said.

"Yes, I'm thinking!"

"How positive are you that it is Delir Hashemi?" Dani said finally.

"Very."

"That really is not good. He's not small fry."

"Let's make this easy. Tell the Chief I'm already in transit to Libya following the leads."

"You will do as I say, Gideon! I'm your commanding officer."

Gideon ignored the emotion. He realized he'd had time to think about it while Dani had not.

"The Americans will try to get the girl back; it's a reputational thing. The easiest way to do that is for the father to pay up. It's not a security threat to the Americans, but it is to Israel. Why would the Americans pursue it? They won't try to stop the exchange of money or oil," Gideon said.

Dani remained silent.

"Dani?" Gideon knew he was pushing his luck. The Israeli army encouraged their soldiers to think and challenge their Commanders, but there was a limit.

"I'm thinking!"

"Have the Americans contacted our embassy? Or our prime minister? I bet they haven't. It's not in their interest to get into a shit fight about this and it's why they had me under surveillance. Think about it? It's likely the Iranians know who I am."

"Believe me, I am thinking!" Dani said forcefully.

"She asked for my help, Dani. I can't ignore that," Gideon said.

"Okay, go if you must! But do you think you should be doing this after the last operation?"

"I'm fine, Dani. I'm getting bored, anyway. I need a weapon and a phone. Where?"

"Go to Tunis, we have an agent we work with there. When you're there, give me a call. I should have the politics sorted out by then. And Gideon, if they say no, it means no. Then you come home, you understand?"

"Have you ever known the PM to say no when it comes to Israel's security?

"I have actually. But not often, that's true," Dani replied.

Dani waved his hand vaguely and nodded his head, then hung up. Gideon heard the click on the other side of the world, then silence. For some reason he caught himself smiling. He took the back way out.

# Chapter 4

A fragile calm descended over her—a sort of acute awareness of her immediate environment. Something like a small animal might feel when it knows a hawk is nearby: alert to shadows, apprehensive, but not terrified into immobility. Mahram heard the woman make a call. She could not understand what she was saying, but the tone she used was universal in any language: threatening, cajoling.

The injured man continued to groan. She could feel the Gorilla Twins ogling her despite the sack over her head. Their breath swept over her while she lay on the van's floor. She curled more tightly into a foetal position and forced herself to calm her breathing, her mind still flitting through scenes of what had just happened. She could feel shock turning into anger in the back of her mind and forcing its way forward. Her body trembled involuntarily all over—the after effects of an adrenalin storm.

The van slowed, then turned onto a gravel road. It came almost to a stop, then turned again and traveled in low gear down a potholed track. Mahram turned over onto her secured arms, placing them underneath her body to try to minimize the discomfort to her hips as the van bumped along the rutted path. Her arms were already numb, so why not let them take the battering. After about a minute, which seemed an eternity, the van stopped.

Dead silence for a moment—inside and out. Must be dark by now, she thought. The door of the van slammed open, then several voices began talking all at once.

The woman's rose above them giving a sharp instruction as the gasping, injured man was lowered from the van.

Mahram struggled to sit up, the hood still blinding her. A large hand clamped down on her shoulder, pushing her roughly to the floor.

Mahram stifled a scream.

"Don't move until you are told to," an accented male voice said in Arabic.

Mahram tried to control her sobbing breath, but could not. From behind her she heard a low mirthless laugh.

Then she heard the rasping command of the woman and the two men in the van dragged Mahram into a sitting position.

"Get up, woman!" the one called Arash barked.

Rough hands wielding a knife sliced through the zip ties around her wrists and ankles like they were made of butter. The hood was yanked from her head, pulling strands of her hair with it.

She stepped from the van on shaky legs, rubbing the pins and needles out of her numb arms. It was dark outside and a billion stars sparkled up above them. The moon stood like a sentinel, high and small in the sky. She sent a prayer skyward. Her night vision was startlingly clear—probably thanks to the hood, she thought.

The van's headlights bathed the outside of a large log cabin in white light. The bull-necked twins were on either side and slightly behind her. The cabin stood in the middle of a square clearing of tall maple and birch trees. Somewhere, pines grew—she could smell rather than see them. Closer to the cabin and on the right, leading down and back toward the road, was a thicker copse of birch trees, silver ghosts in the night. There were no other dwellings or lights in sight.

The man on her right pushed her shoulder. She stumbled forward awkwardly, gravel underfoot making her slip, but she did not fall. They climbed the porch steps and entered a large open room flooded with florescent light—almost too bright after the darkness and the hood. A couch, two overstuffed old chairs with a floral design that might have been popular in the 50s and a TV to her left, a solid dark stained wooden dining table, surrounded by dining chairs dominated the middle of the room. To the right was a kitchen. Further back and to the left was a passageway that led, she presumed, to the bedrooms.

The two men who'd acted as driver and shotgun stood in the kitchen under the glare of the light, one of them stirring a large silver pot, the other slicing and buttering white bread. The aroma of instant tomato soup filled the room.

Arash pulled aside one of the dining chairs and made her sit down on it, then he turned and locked the front door. The old chair made a rickety wooden shriek as she lowered her weight onto it. Arash was definitely the worse of the two brothers, she decided.

The men in the kitchen were younger than the Gorilla Twins—longer hair, darker, with straggly beards and high cheekbones. The woman who gave the orders wore her hair in a tight ponytail. She also had high cheekbones with widely spaced, dark angry eyes—her face was beautiful, but cruel.

On a chair in front of her sat a good-looking, dark haired, lightly skinned man with hazel eyes. This was the injured one. Looking at him over his glasses was an elderly man with balding gray hair and dark skin. A large black bag rested on the table next to them. The elderly man felt around the shoulder of the seated man with great care, then helped him to remove his shirt, all the while speaking softly to him and the woman in that same foreign language. They looked Persian.

The elderly man, presumably a medic or doctor, opened the black bag with a click and removed a syringe. His face seemed a controlled mask of repressed fear. As he drew some clear fluid from a small glass bottle into the syringe, Mahram noticed his hands shaking. Despite this, he gently inserted the needle into the man's shoulder. The man groaned loudly; beaded sweat on his brow shining in the bright light spilling from the kitchen florescent. A feeling of schadenfreude washed over Mahram as she watched the doctor instruct the woman to help the man onto the table. His pain-filled face told the story of his well-deserved agony.

The injured one lay down with care. The doctor lifted his arm. Mahram noticed a sheen of sweat on the doctor's forehead. Despite this and with calm authority he extended the injured man's arm 90 degrees from his body and then slowly, but with some force, pulled the man's arm outward.

The man gasped in short percussive breaths.

"Inshallah," one of the twins said under his breath.

There was a meaty 'clunk' as the ball of the shoulder re-entered the socket. A relieved expression flitted over the woman's face.

Mahram looked away from them to the two young men preparing supper. They were ladling the soup into bowls and placing the bread onto a large platter.

One of the young men, the more confident of the two, wore a large gold signet ring on his left pinkie finger. He turned to look at her, feeling her scrutiny, and gave her a quick smile. He noticed the Gorilla Twins scowling at him and held their eyes for a good five seconds or so, then turned back to the range. No love lost there, she thought. Pinkie Ring hoisted a large copper kettle off the stove and brought it, and a tray of small tea glasses, over to the table. Although it was modest fare, Mahram's stomach growled with hunger. Never had the aroma of tomato soup smelled so good. Judging from the meal and the furnishings, Mahram decided they were in transit. This did not look like a final destination.

The doctor quietly but efficiently placed the man's arm in a sling, knotting it around his neck. He shut the bag with a final angry snap and handed the woman a sheet of tablets without a word.

Mahram's eyes narrowed. The doctor appeared to not want to be here either. Mahram stared at him hard, hoping he would look her way, but he never did.

The woman escorted him to the door, all the while speaking to him in a low tone. She shut and locked the door behind him.

Pinkie Ring put the bowls in front of each person at the table, then nodded to Mahram, beckoning for her to come and join them. Mahram looked at the woman, but she said nothing, just stared back at Mahram and took a mouthful of soup and dipped some bread into her bowl. Mahram got up and moved her chair to the table. A bowl of soup scraped across the table into her view. She looked up; Pinkie Ring tried to hand her a plastic tablespoon.

She refused to take it—how could you accept kindness from monsters. A well of tears rose in her chest threatening to spill from her eyes, but she clamped down hard on it. She would not give them the satisfaction.

He set the spoon down gently into her bowl.

"Eat. You will need your strength," he said in fine Arabic.

She glanced up at him. He smiled thinly and nodded again, encouragingly.

Mahram decided that self-preservation was the best course of action. She spooned some soup into her mouth tentatively, noting in a dissociated, unbodied way that her hand was shaking as she did so. Then she spooned with more gusto. She was ravenous. This was not the sort of food she usually ate, but she was wise enough to know they did not have to feed her.

She glanced around the table. The Gorillas, as she dubbed them, spoke to each other in low tones, ignoring Mahram, but the injured man glared at her intermittently throughout the meal. The two younger men said nothing, though Pinkie Ring glanced at her occasionally while they ate their meal. The woman said no more to her, in fact made a point of ignoring her completely and spoke to the injured man, who answered her monosyllabically in their foreign tongue. Through their conversation she learned two more facts. The woman's name was Fairuza, his was Delir. They seemed fond of each other.

After the meal the woman clicked her fingers.

"Come with me," she said to Mahram in English.

Mahram's blood pressure spiked as she saw the Gorilla Twins also rise from their seats and follow them to the bathroom.

"You have two minutes," she said and pushed Mahram gently but firmly into a toilet cubicle and shut the door.

Mahram glanced around the small room frantically. The room was about a meter wide and held a toilet with cistern and a small hand basin. A frosted window directly over the toilet looked out into a black void her eyes could not penetrate. The frame of the window had bars screwed into it. No escape there. A solid ceiling above. She found her hands quivering and her eyes burning with unwept tears of frustration and rage as she did her ablutions. She finished and washed her hands then her face, then flushed the cistern. The door opened immediately and she was all but marched into a bedroom.

The Gorillas made her lie down on a thin mattress placed on the floor of her room. Her wrists and ankles were once again zip tied by them as the woman looked on with a faint sneer on her face. The room she was in had been beautiful once. The logs had been covered in render and painted a daisy field yellow. Five rough planks of wood were nailed across the window, so that no light could penetrate the room. Small plaster chips of wall lay on the floor where the nails had smashed through the render. Cobwebbed dust hung in strands in one corner of the ceiling. There was no closet. The only other object was a naked light bulb screwed into the ceiling, nine feet above her head.

No chance of suicide then—a fleeting thought.

The two thugs laughed and joked in their language as they secured her, then left the room. The woman snapped off the light and locked the door as she followed them.

The dam finally burst as she lay alone in the dark. Bitter, silent tears welled in her eyes and flowed down her cheeks. She moved her head to wipe them off on the mattress. Images flashed through her mind, especially the last, of the young man who tried to rescue her; raising his dazed and bloodied head from the pavement, looking directly into her eyes.

Why me, she thought? Who was it that tried to save her? He'd been so brave. Was he just a passer-by that saw her distress, or was there something more complicated going on? She wondered about her father. This probably had something to do with him; about his involvement in oil in Libya. In fact, the more she thought about it the more certain she became. Maybe she was a bargaining chip of some sort? Then she prayed fervently for a long time, tears streaming down her face, imploring God for help.

She woke with a start as the light came on with a loud click. She was astonished that she'd fallen asleep.

"Get up," the woman ordered in a monotone voice.

"Who are you and why are you doing this to me?" Mahram said in English.

The woman gave a short laugh. "Don't speak to me in the language of Satan," she said in Arabic.

"Who are you?" Mahram said in Arabic.

"Who we are is none of your business."

"Is it my father's business, then? I have no money," Mahram said.

The woman regarded her in expressionless silence for several seconds.

"I see your spirit has revived, Mahram. I shall let those two friendly men know. They seem to have taken a great interest in you. Shall I do that, Mahram? They liked your tight jeans."

Mahram swallowed hard, biting back her terror. The woman looked down at her smugly.

"A woman without a veil? You are nothing but cat meat."

"Strange, you are not wearing a veil!" Mahram said with force.

"It is Taqiya, because I am among the infidel. I have not chosen to live here like you, without modesty. I wear the veil when I'm at home."

"And where is home? Iran?" Mahram said smoothly.

The woman sneered at her.

"I said get up!"

"I cannot get up. My ankles are tied together!"

Just then Pinkie Ring appeared. He had a kitchen knife with him. He gestured to the woman. She nodded.

Mahram flinched as the young man bent down and gently sawed through the zip ties around her ankles. She rose awkwardly to a sitting position, her wrists still secured by the ties behind her back. The young man bent down and gently helped her onto her feet. Once up, he abruptly turned and left the room.

Outside, the sky was still dark. The van was gone. In its place was a large, gray SUV. She heard the Gorilla brothers behind her, then felt rough hands on her backside. They picked her up like a sack of potatoes and forced her into the trunk. Laughter from the two Gorillas and the woman, but Mahram noticed that Pinkie Ring guy and his friend did not laugh.

Her heart thumped, but she tried not to show fear as the thug twins ziptied her ankles again.

Thoughts of hate, hot as embers, burned their way through the veil of fear that enveloped her mind.

She braced herself for the back door of the SUV to be slammed shut. Instead, she heard the familiar musical note of a cell phone chime. The woman answered. There was a quick exchange of information. She could hear that the woman was somehow happy with what she'd heard. Then the woman spoke to the injured man. He replied with authority to the woman. The woman relayed the message to the person on the other end of the call. The only words she could make out in the stream of conversation were two very distinct English words, repeated several times. A name: Gideon Dunbar. Then, with a suddenness that made her start, the cargo security shade was drawn over her and boom! the back door of the SUV slammed shut.

The engine under her thumped to life. A noose of claustrophobia tightened around her neck; she hoped the drive would be a short one. Her body rocked as they crossed the bumpy track, her breath quick and shallow. As they turned onto the tarred road, her whole body rolled and her cheek grazed across the carpet in the trunk.

"Get a grip," she whispered to herself.

Mahram rolled onto her side and moved into a foetal position again and lay diagonally across the trunk space so that her feet and shoulders wedged her firmly between the back seats of the SUV and wall of the trunk. This at least stopped her from being tossed about every time the SUV changed direction. She concentrated on slowing her breath. There was one positive she thought, at least they had not placed a hood over her head. She could make out thin filaments of light lancing around the edges of the seats in front of her and the cargo security shade cover above her head.

Finally, the twisting and turning was over and the steady hum of the wheels suggested a motorway. This lulled her into a shallow sleep.

She woke with a start, surprised once again that she had slept. The drive had seemed interminable, about three or four hours to Mahram's reckoning, judging from the discomfort in her bladder. She could hear light Arabic pop music playing over the car radio interspersed with sporadic conversation between the people in the car. A wave of nausea threatened to overwhelm her as her mouth suddenly filled with saliva. She swallowed hard several times to stop the rising gall. Sweat broke out on her brow, despite a chill in the air. Now there was the low growl of stop-start traffic and the slightly metallic odor of carbon monoxide filtering into the back of the SUV; they were back in a city. Which one, she wondered dully?

Then the unmistakable fragrance of the ocean broke in on her senses. The SUV came to a smooth halt. The faint shrill cry of gulls and the hollow slap of water against the hull of a boat sent a thrill of panic through her heart as she lay in the dark. Were they going to leave the States? Maybe she was just the victim of a people smuggling ring. Her throat threatened to clamp up on her once more. Just to see sunlight again would be such a joy.

Car doors opened and slammed shut and she felt the SUV rock as people got out. Then the back of the SUV opened and the luggage cover zipped back with a loud clack. Mahram blinked as the wan silver light of an overcast early morning spilt over her. She sat up. Pinkie Ring looked down at her with a slight frown on his face that somehow to Mahram looked like concern. He took a small pen knife from his pocket. She could not help flinching slightly as he cut through the zip ties around her wrists and ankles.

"Help her out," the woman said to Pinkie Ring.

He did so, taking her weight as she climbed from the back of the SUV on rubbery legs. He was so much gentler and more respectful of her than the twins, that Mahram felt an almost overwhelming rush of gratitude toward him. She stood blinking in the early morning light, taking her bearings.

Above the woman's head, about a hundred yards away, Mahram could make out a sign: 'Boston Yacht Club: Inn and Marina.' She rubbed her arms mechanically trying to get the circulation going again.

"If you make a sound, or try to do anything to attract attention, you will die alone and painfully," the woman said in a low voice. "We do not necessarily need you alive, your corpse will do just fine."

Mahram shuddered slightly and looked into the woman's unblinking but tired looking eyes. Mahram believed her.

The Gorillas and the rest of the crew formed a loose cordon around her.

"This way," the woman said in her low voice.

They were alone on the quay and walked a short distance diagonally to their left, onto a boardwalk. Somewhere to their right Mahram heard the guttural sound of a powerful boat engine roar to life, as the sweet, chemical odor of diesel fumes wafted across the water.

A small delivery truck made its noisy way onto the wharf and came to a halt in front of a restaurant called 'Harry's Grill and Bar.' The driver got out of the truck, whistling to himself. He did not even glance in their direction. He opened the back of his truck and started to unload cartons of beer with a sort of gusto and good humor that made Mahram want to scream. She felt her legs itching to run toward him. He was only about 50 yards away. One of the thugs reached out and grabbed her left wrist, squeezing it hard; so hard that she thought it might break. She flinched and tried to draw away. The movement caught the eye of the delivery truck driver. He gave the group a long hard look as he picked up a pack of beer.

The woman spoke sharply to the man called Arash. He let go of Mahram.

"If you want to save that young man's life do not make a fuss. If he tries to be a hero, we will kill him, and that will be your fault," she said to Mahram in Arabic.

Mahram turned sharply and walked toward the gangway of the motor yacht.

They boarded the navy blue, 45-footer named *Liberty*. Mahram snorted under her breath at the irony of being a prisoner on a boat sporting such a name. She was led down into a state room where she was made to sit on a bed with a bare mattress while one of the Gorillas secured another zip tie around her wrists. Mercifully, this time her wrists were secured in front of her body.

"The yacht *Liberty* is beautiful. Who does it belong to?" Mahram asked with subtle sarcasm.

The woman and the Gorilla Twins ignored her question.

"Good behavior will get you water, food and toilet breaks. If you become an annoyance, you will get none of those," said the woman. She pointed to a CCTV camera bolted to the ceiling.

"Wave to the camera when you want food, a drink, or relief." The woman closed the door gently behind them. Mahram heard the slight but definite click of a well-oiled key mechanism being locked.

There were no more tears now, instead she felt a smoldering rage and the poison plant of hatred putting down firm roots in her heart. She flopped down onto the mattress, vowing to herself that someone would pay for this.

\*\*\*

After many hours of sailing, some food and a toilet break the yacht slowed in the late afternoon and Mahram was freed from her zip ties once more. All except two people aboard *Liberty* were moved onto a small cargo ship in a makeshift lift, using an onboard crane, nylon rope and pallets. It seemed pretty precarious to Mahram and she clung to one of the ropes threaded through the pallets they stood on. The ropes in turn were looped around the crane's massive metal hook so that it looked like they were standing in an open-sided pyramid with the pallets as the floor and the ropes as the walls. The contraption was surprisingly sturdy and was drawn upward and then swung with dexterity over the ship's railing before being deposited carefully onto the deck. They performed the maneuver twice and Mahram was relieved to see that Pinkie Ring guy was one of the last to leave *Liberty*. The only people to stay on board the yacht were Pinkie Ring's companion and the captain of *Liberty*. The injured man gave the captain on board the yacht an order to take it back to Boston.

Somehow being aboard this vessel without any other girls reassured Mahram that at least she had not fallen victim to a sex trafficker.

# Chapter 5

The van used for the kidnapping was found in a gully off Route 52 near South Wind Lake, Woodbourne in New York State. Some school children on the way to class noticed a plume of dark smoke coming from the forest and pointed it out to their teacher, who contacted the fire department, who contacted the police. Patrolman Nash responded.

Nash knew right away what he was looking at. The sergeant's brief that very morning was about a stolen white van.

"Car Patrol one, nine, zero Patrolman Nash here. I think I've found the van. It's been burnt-out though. Over," he said. He felt like a real cop for a change, calling it in.

About an hour later, the FBI showed up in a helicopter. Secretly, Patrolman Nash was enjoying the drama. He'd become a cop hoping for excitement, but he mostly helped local farmers with their stuck pick-up trucks, or busted hippies for growing weed, and that was likely to be legal soon anyhow. Plus, there were fewer and fewer hippies every year…but more and more meth-heads lying in gutters, who were a different animal altogether, come to think of it.

FBI Agent Tyler Gutierrez was in no doubt either as to what he was looking at and set into motion an amazingly effective chain of events. All ships and light air traffic heading east out of the tri-state area were analyzed. Then he asked his team to cross-reference a hundred square miles from the vehicle site with all medical personnel from a middle-eastern background. They found Dr Kamran Farshid from Scotchtown in the late afternoon. As soon as the doctor saw the police car outside his medical practice, he hurried outside.

"It is I. It is I. You are looking for me. I'm sure, sir," he confessed with his rolling 'r' rich accent. Tears pricked in the back of his eyes.

He invited Agent Gutierrez into his office and tearfully told him that the Iranian authorities kept tabs on all Iranians that had left Iran and would routinely ask them for favors, no questions asked. If they did not comply, they could always make life hell for family members who remained in Iran.

"Officer, you must believe me, please, sir. I'm a doctor and someone called for help. I did not ask them how the injury occurred, sir. You must believe me."

"I do believe you, Doctor. But now you have to help me," Tyler said.

"Anything, but please do not send me back to Iran, or let anyone know what I have said. They will kill me and my sister and her family. She still lives in Tehran. Please sir, please!"

"Don't you worry, Doctor. Just cooperate and all will be well. Tell me, what was the injury that you treated?"

"A man with a dislocated right shoulder."

"Do you know the man?"

"No, sir. I have never, never seen him before in my life, sir."

Quite an attractive accent in a way, thought Tyler. "Did you recognize anyone else in the house?"

"No, sir."

"How many people were in the house with you?"

The doctor thought for a second, "Five men and two women."

Tyler took a photo of Mahram out of his jacket pocket. It was a security photograph from the school that she worked at, in Brooklyn.

"Do you recognize this woman as one of the women you saw?"

The doctor peered down at the photograph through his glasses. He did not have to say a word; his expression said it all. It registered shock.

"Yes?"

"Yes, sir. This young woman was present. They made her sit on a chair, away from the others."

"Can you show me where the house is?"

"Yes, certainly sir," the old doctor said.

An hour later, the FBI raided the log cabin. They found only a very slightly warm copper kettle, a neat stack of clean soup bowls and a mattress in one of the rooms from which they took hair samples. In the driveway, they found several tire tracks of a motor vehicle that did not belong to the burnt-out van. The forensics team determined them to be from a heavily laden sedan, or SUV, with Goodyear tires.

Tyler put out a call for all reported stolen vehicles in the immediate vicinity. He did not have to wait long. At 5 pm, they were able to track down a gray SUV that had been reported missing that morning in Orange Lake just off the New York State throughway. Grainy footage from interstate traffic management cameras showed the same SUV entering Boston in the early hours of the morning, with approximately six adults on board. Later, Boston police apprehended two young men from Southie, driving the SUV. When Tyler interviewed them that night, they told him they had found the car abandoned and with its doors wide open and the key still in the ignition, so naturally they had taken it for a joy ride.

At 8 pm they had the manifests of all the ships that were heading toward Africa from the east coast of the United States that day. There were 12 of them, all registered under foreign flags. By 9 pm they knew they were too late. All of the ships in question were in international waters. The option of boarding vessels under a foreign flag in international waters was discussed at the highest level and rejected as a realistic option by 10 pm. To board 12 ships, all foreign registered and all going in different directions in international waters would be a political disaster, and boarding them with troops would potentially constitute an act of war.

At about the same time Carl Sullivan, Jack Hunter and Alda Dibra were receiving the bad news, Hunter took a call.

"We tracked Gideon Dunbar down, sir. He was on a flight to Tunis that left this morning."

Hunter swore under his breath.

"Sir, it gets worse. We have footage of him entering the Israeli consulate…from this morning, right after we lost track of him."

Hunter thanked the officer and ended the call.

"A problem?" Alda asked.

"Yes," said Hunter tersely and told her and Carl Sullivan the news.

"So, the Israelis know. Alda, this is a CIA problem now. What do you want to do?" Sullivan said.

Alda's green eyes flicked from one man to the other.

"No change of plan," she said. "Keep Hunter in charge of the operation and get him to Tripoli as soon as possible and in touch with Mahram's father. It's likely there'll be a ransom demand. Hunter, you have hostage negotiation experience. We want to control that process from the beginning and before the Israelis can throw a wrench in the works. The Israelis will be assessing the actual and political risks differently from us, obviously. Mahram Ammar is an

58

American citizen. We want her back alive and in one piece and, above all, under the radar. No interviews, no media, and, if necessary, we bargain for her life."

***

The flight to Tunis left at 10 am from JFK and cost just under a thousand dollars.

Becoming a 'gray man' was what Unit 217 specialized in. Their mission was to infiltrate behind enemy lines and look and act like locals in order to dismantle terror cells. They collected intelligence, and targeted kidnappings and assassinations. Gideon always found becoming 'mister average' was much more difficult than one initially thought. You had to know the culture which you were immersing yourself into well. His commander had noticed his propensity to choose bright colors before his training and that tendency had had to be knocked out of him. Now Gideon chose his clothing with great care and an eye to his new identity or 'legend'. In this case, a lower-middle class young American if anyone asked. Gideon bought a cheap G shock digital watch, a nondescript black baseball cap from which he removed the glued-on logo, cheap sunglasses, a fairly large unremarkable gray daypack, a make-up kit, some indeterminate brown chinos and a good black jacket with a hood. Nights could be cold in the desert in early May. He also bought two GSM burner cell phones and sim cards at the airport. At a currency kiosk he exchanged five hundred dollars into Tunisian dinar and a two thousand dollars into Libyan dinar. He changed into his new clothes in the airport restroom and dispatched his old clothes into the restroom garbage can. He thought about throwing away his beloved leather jacket, now covered in shrapnel holes, but decided against it and stuffed it into his daypack.

He used his American passport. Israeli passports were not welcome in many Arabic countries, especially Tunisia and Libya. He took the make-up kit to the restroom and in a toilet stall, applied some base to the large darkening bruise on the side of his face. Walking around with a bruise on his face would very definitely attract attention he could ill afford.

The flight to Tunisia was full. After take-off, Gideon walked the cabin slowly, wearing his sunglasses. No-one seemed to be paying him any undue attention. His mind was alert to surveillance, but he did not feel the tingling at the back of his neck that usually meant he was being observed—there were minor cues that his training alerted him to, almost at a subconscious level now, and his personal radar was picking up nothing. He had 11 hours to kill. Air travel was not a problem for him and he was blessed with the ability to sleep just about anywhere.

***

Dani Gilad woke with a start. His cell phone buzzed like an angry insect on his bedside table. He got up quickly, cursing under his breath.

He glanced over at his wife—she snored intermittently next to him; her orange earplugs still lodged in her ears. She could be grumpy if woken early.

He grabbed his phone and left the room, closing the door quietly behind him.

"Yes," he said curtly.

"Sorry for waking you, sir. Gideon Dunbar on the line. He's on a burner."

"Put him through."

Dani looked at his watch—4.30 am.

"Hello," he said.

"Hello Father," Gideon said in Arabic. "You asked me to let you know when I arrived. I've just landed in Tunis and been through customs. Is Uncle Ahmet okay to pick me up?"

Dani smiled. This was their agreed cover story.

"Yes, he is. Uncle Ahmet says he is curious to see what you think of the city. He will show you around. It's a bit early for Uncle Ahmet to pick you up now, son, but he will. Go to Belvedere Park in the city and wait for him at the Oasis Café. Off Allee Jeanin street. You know the one? He'll be there between 8 am and 8.30 am."

"Sure, thanks Abba. Sorry to have woken you up."

Dani's eyes narrowed. He sensed rather than heard the playfulness in Gideon's tone, but he could not fault Gideon's cover. Dani thought he would get in on the act.

"Not to worry now, my boy. Just remember to behave yourself while I am not around."

Gideon chuckled. "I wouldn't do anything you would not do, Abba. By the way, the daypack and baseball cap you bought me have worked well on my travels so far."

"Which ones? I can't remember. I'm getting old."

"The gray daypack and the black baseball cap. Surely you remember, Abba? We shopped together."

"Ah, yes, yes, now I remember," Dani said. That was the description of the person their agent in Tunis would have to look for.

"Ma'a as-salamah," Dani said, saying goodbye, then pressed the screen to end the call.

\*\*\*

There was a sudden rush for taxis as 400 people made their way out of customs. Gideon was not in any hurry, so turned back and strolled to the nearest restaurant where he ordered breakfast—Lablabi, a spicy chickpea dish served in pasty cumin and garlic-flavored soup, topped with a poached egg. He also ordered a pot of coffee which came in a small copper pot accompanied by a diminutive glass, a spoon and a heap of sugar cubes. Tunisians like their coffee sweet, black and strong. The waiter was in a surly mood; probably too early for him, thought Gideon.

Gideon liked spicy food and strong coffee. He sat with his back to the wall at the rear of the cafe and watched the crowds pass by as he slowly ate his food and drank a second cup of coffee. Afterward he picked up a local Tunisian newspaper and watched the crowds just over its rim. Nothing seemed out of the ordinary. More flights arrived and the terminal became busy. He paid cash and left a tip, not too mean and not too generous. He would be forgotten within a few minutes by the busy staff. He went to the men's restroom and, after making sure no one else was there, took the SIM card from the burner phone he'd used to phone Dani and disposed of it in the trash can. He then snapped the SIM in two and deposited it, wrapped in some tissue paper, into a garbage can on the way out of the airport terminal. As he took the last few steps toward the terminal doorway, the hairs on the back of his neck prickled up. He changed his trajectory smoothly and went to a news stand, pretending to search the shelves. Something had caught his attention in the periphery of his vision. He scanned the crowds again from the sanctity of the bookshelves.

"Sir. May I help you?" The magazine vendor asked in Arabic.

Gideon shook his head and smiled, continuing to scan the crowd with a magazine in his hand. About 70 yards away a tall male figure moved away from him toward the door. He had his back to Gideon, but Gideon was certain he'd seen that dark green jumper and close-cropped hair before. The man turned his head slightly as he exited the building. That well-groomed beard—he'd definitely seen that before.

"Shit! Shit! Shit!"

The FBI was onto him again. That was quick.

A taxi driver looking for work accosted him as soon as he walked out of the airport building. Best not to argue and be remembered.

Gideon scanned the crowd before he ducked into the taxi. No sign of Beard Guy.

The ride to Belvedere Park took about 25 minutes in the light morning traffic. Gideon arrived at 7.30 am and asked to be dropped off on the side opposite the small lake, or oasis, as they called it in Tunisia. Gideon paid the taxi driver in cash and once again left a tip verging on generous. Gideon could pass for an Arab. He'd spoken no more than six words to the driver and those he did speak were in Arabic, so hopefully he'd be forgotten almost immediately. It struck Gideon how against the grain it was for human beings to want to pass through life anonymously, but not so for him. He disliked being the center of attention.

The park was set on a gently sloping hill and the oasis was located at the bottom, near its border with the street. Gideon decided to approach the rendezvous point obliquely. He'd never been to Belvedere Park before, though his work had taken him to Tunis once. That mission had ended satisfactorily, with a Hamas operative bobbing face down in the ocean, just off the coast.

It was a beautiful park, full of swaying trees and several fountains out in the oasis jetting their plumes high in the air, creating a cooling mist which wafted gently ashore. It irritated Gideon that the park was full of litter. It reminded him of the parks on the outskirts of London near his aunt's home. He remembered fleetingly the disappointment he'd felt at how dirty they were. Order was important to his mind.

He ambled into the early morning shadows among the trees, employing some counter-surveillance tradecraft: searching for any tail by doubling back, then sitting on a bench, then walking quickly and changing his direction as if he'd forgotten something and then slowing down. Nothing he could detect.

Finally, he made his way to the Oasis Café. The meet/drop point was almost certainly the most hazardous part of any operation; that had been drummed into him in his training. It was the one place where agents could be caught red-handed. Despite all his own precautions, the agent meeting him could have been followed and there was nothing Gideon could do about that.

The Oasis Café had just opened for the morning. It was essentially a glass box with a back wall constructed out of the ubiquitous but beautiful light sandy-colored Tunisian limestone. Two doors pierced the back wall; one to the kitchen, the other to a restroom. He sat down inside the café, back to the wall. He had a 270-degree view of his surroundings. A very cheery young waiter, dressed in black pants and white shirt with a wine-red waistcoat took his order; his second pot of coffee for the day. Gideon was pleased that the waiter assumed he was Tunisian and addressed him in the local Arabic dialect. Gideon used the more formal classical Arabic.

"You are not from here, sir?" the waiter asked good-naturedly.

"No, I'm from America, but my father is from Tunisia originally and I'm visiting my father's family. I have not seen them in many years."

"Your Arabic is good. Do they teach such language in America?"

"You can learn anything in America if you want to," said Gideon, smiling.

The boy laughed. "Everything is bigger and better in Ameeeerica!"

Gideon chuckled at the bigoted humor.

"Maybe bigger. I'm not so sure about better," Gideon said.

The boy's smile widened. "Very wise, my friend."

"Do you serve white coffee, you know, with milk?" Gideon said.

"Not a problem. Yes, we can give you some milk, sir, with your coffee. Not a problem," the boy said in English.

"Your English is very good!" said Gideon in English, then smiled.

The boy whisked away, obviously pleased with his efforts, and came back, chuckling to himself, holding a pot of coffee, a small ceramic cup, and a less than generously sized jug of what Gideon discovered was goat's milk. A large glass of sugar cubes was already on the table. Gideon paid the boy right away in case he had to move fast.

"Not a problem," the boy said in English, as he accepted the money, then laughed when he saw the generous tip.

"Hyee, that is nice, sir," again the careful English.

Gideon had to smile. He placed his gray bag on the table and pulled his baseball cap more securely down onto his head so that it obscured his features. The gray bag and black cap were what 'Uncle Ahmet' would be looking for. The lake, diagonally to his right, was very pleasant, with three fountains, spraying their white plumes into the air. The refracted early morning light sparkling in the fine mist was mesmerizing.

The city was waking up. Another perfect day beckoned with not a cloud in the sky and the peculiar fragrance of the desert in the thin air. Gideon felt a subtle temptation to relax, but he knew he shouldn't. Pedestrians made their way to work slowly, and traffic hissed around the park in an unobtrusive rhythm. On the brick pathway in front of him leading to a copse of dense trees 150 yards away, Gideon noticed an elderly lady walking her dog. The dog strained on its leash, wagging its tail, as if to get to something or someone in the shadows of the trees. Gideon remembered he'd sat on a bench underneath those trees only minutes ago when doing his recce of the meet point, but couldn't quite see if anyone was sitting on it from his vantage point. The sun was rising rapidly and he was looking into its slanting rays, making the shadows among the trees darker still. Probably not the best drop point after all at this time of day. He must remember to tell Dani.

The old woman had to coax her dog to keep it from straining at the leash. At this distance, he saw rather than heard the old woman mutter an apology. It must be a person then, not an animal.

Gideon moved uncomfortably in his chair, keeping an eye on the shadows. The hairs at the back of his neck began to tingle again. No one had come down that pathway, except the old woman and her dog, and no one had been on the bench when he'd passed it earlier. Someone must have made their way through those trees with care.

Moments later, a man walked purposefully into view from the opposite direction. 'Uncle Ahmet' was a middle-aged man of about 50, wearing the traditional black chechia—the Tunisian beret, over gray flecked curly dark hair and a close shaven beard. He wore a light blue cotton shirt and baggy dark trousers. Strapped over one shoulder was a mid-sized green canvass messenger bag. He entered the coffee shop and moved purposefully toward Gideon. Gideon stood, keeping an eye on the sidewalk behind Uncle Ahmet.

"So good to see you. I have not seen you since you were a little boy. It's me, Uncle Ahmet. Surely you recognize me?" he said in Arabic.

"Uncle, of course. It's been a while."

Gideon gave him the traditional three cheek kisses. Left, right, then left again.

"You must come to the house later today. Your auntie and cousins want to see you. We can have some dinner together."

"Yes, of course. Sit, sit uncle."

The boy came back smiling. "More coffee, my friend?" he asked in Arabic. "Yes please, for my uncle."

Ahmet took his coffee black and strong.

The waiter again left with a grin, after receiving another generous tip.

"Something's not right," Gideon said.

"You sure? Followed?" Ahmet said.

Gideon described what he'd just witnessed and the man at the airport.

They both took a sip of their coffees.

"I was careful, but I had to come in on my own passport."

"If you were followed, who could it be?"

"Well, presumably the FBI." Gideon said.

"Tunisia has an extradition treaty with the U.S. If the FBI did not want you here, they would have had you stopped at the airport and sent back to the States."

Gideon's frown deepened. His eyes flicked up to the shadowy recesses among the trees again. Ahmet took another sip of his coffee. "This is good," he said loudly in Arabic.

A couple of young businessmen came in wearing western suits. Gideon watched them warily. They seemed interested only in their take-out coffees and office gossip.

"That's not good. The only other players it could be are the people who kidnapped Mahram," Gideon said.

His mind flicked through recent events and settled on the cleaner at the hospital. He'd not thought much of that incident, but it had struck him as odd behavior at the time.

"Shit. We've gotta leave. I'll explain as we walk," Gideon said.

"Okay, let's walk and talk. The bag is near your feet," Ahmet said.

Gideon bent down and scooped the messenger bag into his backpack. It was quite heavy. There was nothing for it; he hoped that no one would notice that Ahmet was no longer carrying it when they left.

"It's got everything you asked for. Weapon, suppressor, papers, camera."

They left the café, crossed the busy street, and strode toward the old quarter of the city. Gideon caught Ahmet up on the situation. Ahmet listened carefully.

"Okay. Yes, I think we have a problem. Do you know the city?"

"Yes, I've been here before and studied a map on the way in," Gideon said.

"Take the metro to Nelson Mandela station, head west until you cross Avenue de La Liberte, then head south on the Avenue until you pass the Grand Synagogue; the safe house is apartment 215 on the next block, above Ben's Café. If you have a tail, shake it off before you get there."

Ahmet took off in the direction of the old city, walking fast. Gideon walked at a moderate pace for three blocks, bought a ticket to a station three stops further down the line than Nelson Mandela station, and took the escalator to the metro platform. Three young men came down after him, making a great deal of noise and laughing loudly, closely followed by a couple, pushing a stroller with a baby in it, and then, about thirty seconds later, a young woman in a hijab and sunglasses. The woman in the hijab passed behind Gideon and emerged from among the roof support columns, about 20 yards further up the station. Gideon's neck tingled as he watched her, watching him. The laughter of the young men echoed around the platform. Gideon moved back slightly. So did the young woman. She was clearly keeping him in the periphery of her vision.

The tracks began to buzz. A train came around the bend in the tunnel twenty seconds later. The doors of the train hissed open. Gideon entered. So did the Hijab woman.

Just as the doors began to close, Gideon stepped off the train again. As the train glided past Gideon, he saw the woman clock him on the platform, a fleeting look of shock on her face. She immediately lifted a mobile phone to her ear.

Alarm bells sounded in his mind. He raced up the escalator stairs, through the barrier and out into the busy street, walking due west, until he reached the Avenue de La Liberte. There were large numbers of pedestrians now—good and bad from his point of view. Good if they did not know where he was, bad if they already had a tail on him. The buildings rose and fell in an eclectic fusion of old and new. The Avenue was a bustling, tree-lined thoroughfare, filled with small businesses and vendors hawking their wares, and a constant stream of motorized traffic. Gideon stopped at a vendor selling headscarves and bought one. A black and white shemog popularized by the late Yasser Arafat. He stepped into a shop selling spices, stuffed his baseball cap into his backpack and wound the shemog around his head like a turban as he walked the aisles of the shop and left the same way; the shopkeeper did not even glance up from his newspaper.

The safe house was due south. Gideon walked several blocks until he reached a large supermarket situated on the side of the Avenue. Supermarkets usually had handy back doors that were open to accept goods. He took a chance and walked directly to the rear of the supermarket with cool authority and through the swing doors, into a large storage area. This was dimly lit and about ten degrees cooler than the supermarket floor. Several employees in the room wrangled with the store produce—the ambient noises of trollies and boxes being moved or ripped open all around. No one noticed his sudden appearance. Unless he met someone with some rank, it was unlikely he would be questioned. He walked briskly to the very back of the storage room and into a passageway. Two employees chatting and smoking moved aside as he sauntered past. At the end of the passageway was a loading dock and cargo bay. A truck was backing into it, screeching its high-pitched warning. Two young men stood on the dock waiting to unload the contents. Gideon jumped down from the dock and moved quickly toward the opening that led onto a street running parallel to the Avenue.

"Hey, careful you fool!" one of the young men shouted, as Gideon pushed himself deftly between the reversing truck and the metal frame of the entrance to the building.

Once outside, he looked up and down the street. He saw no one. He turned left and jogged a few hundred yards down a street called Rue de Cologne and then stopped abruptly, edging himself into the large darkened vestibule area of an apartment complex. This was a tree-lined street and gave him a great vantage point from which to do some counter-surveillance. He did not have to wait long. Gideon saw the two young men emerge from the dock entrance with a third man, pointing in the direction he'd gone. Even from this distance Gideon realized there was something familiar about the man the other two were speaking with. They were gesticulating, nodding at what the man said and again pointing him in the direction that Gideon had taken. Gideon watched from the edge of his vantage point as the man walked rapidly down the street toward him, searching the shadows as he went. Surprise registered in Gideon's mind as the searching man's features came into focus. This was the guy who'd been sitting at the Café in Brooklyn Heights, the same guy he'd seen at the airport. Beard Guy.

Gideon melted back into the shadows of the deep vestibule and squatted behind a row of large black plastic bins about ten yards from the entrance.

Firm, quick footsteps—then a hesitation. He could picture the man in his mind, scanning the vestibule. Gideon held his breath.

He sighed as the footsteps resumed, rapidly moving away. Gideon got up warily from his hiding place and took a quick and careful look up the street from the shadows of the vestibule. The man was up ahead, still searching. There could be no mistake. They knew he was here. Gideon appraised his quarry. The man moved fluidly, like an athlete, about the same height as Gideon, but more heavily set and muscular—probably late twenties.

Gideon moved forward, squatting behind the trunk of a large Jacaranda tree, his eyes on the man moving down the street. He dug into his backpack for his cell phone, found the second burner, then flipped open his wallet and quickly dialed the number Jack Hunter had left him. He watched Beard Guy continue his search as he waited for Hunter to answer on the other side of the world.

"Hunter, here."

"Gideon Dunbar here. Do me a favor, Hunter and get your goons off my back."

"You in Tunis?"

"I'm watching one of your goons as we speak," said Gideon, keeping is eyes on his quarry.

"Listen up, Gideon. Are we on a secure line?"

"No, a burner."

"We don't have anyone in Tunis. So, whoever it is, he's not one of ours. What we do know for certain is that the 'product' is on board a ship heading for Africa; what we don't know for certain is what country the ship is heading toward. There are 12 possibilities. I assume your crew know about this matter now?"

By 'crew' he meant the Israeli intelligence.

"You assume correctly," Gideon said.

"Our crew have an interest in our product coming back in one piece. With whom should we liaise?" Hunter said.

"The usual inter-crew liaison would be best. I've got to go. I have someone to follow." Gideon ended the call, then with mounting unease, punched in Dani's number.

"C'mon, c'mon, pick up!" he said under his breath.

His quarry was at a crossroad about 200 yards distant. Two women in black burkas exited the apartments next door and walked down the quiet street toward him, chatting loudly. The man looked left, then right, then back the way he'd come. He peered at the women. There was indecision in his stance. Gideon saw the man take out a cell phone and make a call. He spoke to someone for several seconds and then started to run in the direction of Avenue De la Liberti.

Suddenly Gideon's call went through. "Yes," said Dani.

"Dani, I have no time to explain. Call Uncle Ahmet now and tell him we have been compromised! Tell him to get out of the house, now! I'm making my way there!"

"What, Gideon? Slow down!"

"We have no time! Get a cleaning team to the safe house now if you can!"

Gideon pulled off the shemog and threw it down and started sprinting, his day pack banging against the small of his back as he ran. He did not want to ditch the bag; it had the tools he may need. He closed the distance to the corner quickly and turned left, then sprinted another hundred yards. He turned right onto the Avenue and slowed to a fast walk. Ben's Café was about 150 yards away, his quarry nowhere in sight. The Avenue was a bustling place here too, full of heavy motorized traffic, voices, the occasional angry horn blast. Gideon scanned the street for watchers as he walked. Nothing. Bens' Cafe was full of a hubbub of men speaking to one another over coffee in a hazy smoke-filled atmosphere— no one inside that he recognized.

The feeling of unease grew in his mind. Logic told him that Ahmet had somehow been followed and their adversary knew where they were. He made his way through the vestibule of the apartment block above Ben's Cafe and rapidly climbed the first flight of stairs. The block was five levels of apartments, framing a square courtyard set in the middle. Watery light filtered into the square from the sky above the courtyard. Echoing sound reverberated into the stairwell from below. Through the iron railings Gideon saw a single, forlorn tree reaching up its struggling branches toward the light. Underneath the tree stood a slim young woman in a pair of very tight jeans, a white T-shirt and a hijab. She was gently giving instruction to two small noisy children, who kicked a red plastic ball inexpertly to one another.

Gideon slowed, making his way carefully up the stairwell to the second level, his every sense acutely tuned into the environment – the echoes of the children and their mother, the reverberating tinny whine of Middle Eastern pop music spilling from a cheap radio in one of the apartments above and the muted hubbub of conversation coming from Ben's Café, as well as the steady hiss of traffic noise. The rest of the block was eerily still—the tenants probably at work.

Gideon cautiously took the bag from his back and drew the pistol Ahmet had supplied from its innards. A 365 XL Sig Saur 9mm. It would do nicely. He checked the magazine and then slowly, and as quietly as he could, cocked the weapon. From the stairwell, he carefully peered around the corner and out onto the second floor, his eyes adjusting to the gloom. The door marked 215 was the fifth door along, but he would have known anyway; just outside the door, Beard Guy and another closely shaven man with glossy black hair stood, signaling in silence to one another. They were so intently focused on the door that they had not noticed Gideon's glance. Gideon risked another look. Now both held suppressed pistols in their hands; their clear intent was to harm Ahmet. Beard Guy gently pushed down on the handle of the door—locked.

Gideon drew away from the corner, his mind buzzing. He could shoot them easily enough, but that would attract unwanted attention; the percussion of his fired weapon would be deafening in this enclosed space. He reached into his bag and withdrew the suppressor and wound it onto his gun, then carefully zipped the bag closed and replaced it on his back. Every one of Gideon's senses was now attuned to the slightest sound. He heard the two men whispering to each other, the scrape of their feet, then a loud bang and the sound of splintering wood.

Gideon glanced around the corner again. Beard Guy had kicked in the door, the other man darted forward, gun first.

The young woman in the courtyard below looked up in alarm at the sudden crack of splintering wood. The children too took fright; one began to cry. Gideon gave a quick glance around the apartments to his left and right and then up and down a level and sprinted toward the open door. He heard the thud, thud of a suppressed weapon and then another splintering crash of smashed furniture; another suppressed shot. As he ran, he caught sight of the woman crouched protectively over her children.

Beard Guy staggered from the door as Gideon reached it, bleeding from a chest wound; he still held his weapon. Gideon punched him hard in the face. No resistance, the assassin reeled backward into the room, his gun clattered from his hand as his body hit the floor with a wet thump. He stared up at Gideon with shock-filled dying eyes. Gideon ducked low, entering a short, darkened passageway. A kitchen doorway stood open to his immediate left. His eyes swept the kitchen interior, no hostiles. He moved on, hugging the wall to his left, arm extended, holding the 9 mm, his eyes adjusting to the gloom as he moved. Gideon heard furtive movement coming from the living room ahead of him, and a rasping breath. Behind him the door swung loosely on it hinges in a sudden breeze.

"Gide...?" a gasping, half whisper came from the living room. He could not see the speaker, his view blocked by the passage wall to his left.

70

Another rasping inarticulate whisper. A careful step on shattered glass—then quiet.

Gideon threw himself low and prone around the corner, twisting to his left as he did so. The second gunman stood flattened against the wall that joined the passageway, his weapon ready to fire at anyone coming around the corner. His face registered surprise at Gideon's speed and low trajectory, his weapon tracking toward Gideon as he skidded across the parquetry floor. Gideon fired twice.

The thud of the shots filled the small apartment. He felt more than heard the buzz of the gunman's answering shot as it passed close to his ear. The first of his own shots nicking plaster off the wall near the gunman's head, the second caught him just under the collar bone and exited through his upper spinal column. The gunman was rocked back by the shot that caught him, his head hit the wall with a cracking thud and then he slowly toppled over. He was dead before he hit the floor, leaving a dark red streak of gristle on the wall behind him.

"Here," said a weak voice from the gloom.

Gideon rolled, glancing to his right now and saw Ahmet propped up against an overstuffed chair. His pistol lay at his feet, blood oozed from a neat bullet hole through his upper right chest muscle, just under the shoulder joint. The blood had completely saturated Ahmet's shirt from the chest down.

Gideon rose and strode to Ahmet through a debris field of splintered chair and coffee table. Ahmet's steady dark eyes looked directly into Gideon's.

"Get my laptop and the thumb drives, there on the table," he said weakly and nodded toward a small table in the corner of the room.

"Okay, but first let me stop the bleeding. A cleaning crew is on the way."

A cleaning crew was IDF code for an exfiltration team. "Where is the first aid box?" Gideon said.

"Bathroom." Ahmet gasped.

Gideon rose quickly, found the first aid kit and brought it back.

Ahmet's head had sagged, his breath coming in shallow gasps.

"Hey! Stay with me!" Gideon slapped Ahmet hard across the cheek. The adrenalin spike this induced revived Ahmet a little.

Gideon tore open a sachet of blood congealing agent and then ripped open Ahmet's shirt, exposing the wound. He poured out the powdery congealing agent liberally into the wound, pushing some of it into the bullet hole with his index finger. Ahmet flinched with pain, but did not cry out. Gideon gently levered

Ahmet forward. There was a nasty exit wound in his back; he did the same for that wound. Working quickly, he ripped open a thickly padded trauma bandage with a moisture seal and expertly applied one to each side of the wound.

Ahmet became floppy in his arms again.

"Hey! Stay with me! You're not going to die."

Ahmet managed to lift his head again.

"Did you get the call from Dani?" Gideon said in Hebrew.

"Yes. I had about 30 seconds warning," Ahmet answered in the same language.

"Computer…" Ahmet said.

Gideon got up from his squatting position, took a swinging stride across the room and quickly pushed Ahmet's laptop, thumb drives and his own weapon into the backpack.

Gideon noticed how a thick, dark trickle of blood from the corpses had joined together to form a lazily meandering stream into the dark recesses of the apartment, following the path of the less than even flooring—no time to clean up.

"We've got to get out of here, now! There was a woman in the courtyard with children who heard everything,"

"Go, leave," Ahmet said.

Gideon ignored him.

"I told Dani to send a cleaning crew. Let me help you up."

Gideon placed the backpack on his back and bodily lifted the smaller man into a standing position. He draped Ahmet's good arm around his shoulder and placed his around Ahmet's waist and all but frog marched him toward the exit. He seemed light to Gideon in his supercharged adrenalin state.

In the distance Gideon heard the unmistakable wailing of police sirens.

"Shit!" Gideon said with force.

As they passed Beard Guy in the passageway, Gideon fumbled to get his phone from his jacket pocket and took a picture of the dead man's face.

"I want to put this guy through the database," he said.

The wailing of the sirens grew louder.

They moved as quickly as they could toward the door.

"When we split up, I was followed by a woman, so there is at least one more out there."

"Turn right," Ahmet muttered, "fire stair."

As they shuffled down the corridor, a door on the floor above them slammed shut with a loud crack. He ignored it. They did a half circuit of the square and got to a narrow set of stairs. Ahmet moaned in pain as they descended the twisting stairwell. The police sirens were loud now. They made it to the bottom of the stairs and spilled out into a shadowed alleyway, which they shuffled down at considerable speed, Gideon all but dragging a semi-conscious Ahmet along. He heard several cars screech to a halt on the other side of the building. The police sirens stopped abruptly. Gideon and Ahmet exited the alleyway and turned left onto the residential street that he had run up only minutes before.

To his rear, he heard a hubbub of raised voices. Everything inside of him wanted to run and hide, but the still small voice of training held the primitive part of his brain in check. He consciously slowed their pace so as not to attract attention. On the other side of the street an old woman made her way up the hill. She did not look in their direction.

He could feel Ahmet sagging in his arms, almost a dead weight now. They made their way steadily down the hill toward the ocean. A minute later his worried mind found the sanctuary it had been searching for. A nondescript white Opal sedan that reminded Gideon of a dirty fridge, pulled up next to them. The driver eased the automatic window on the passenger side down.

"Get in!" he said in Hebrew.

Gideon opened the back door of the sedan and deposited Ahmet as gently as he could into the vehicle.

"Hurry!" the driver shouted.

Gideon slammed the back door, spun around and opened the front passenger door and jumped in. The driver pulled away from the curb before he had time to close his door. He glanced at the driver, a man slightly older than him, dark hair, shaved very short. A stubbly beard flecked with gray and dark eyes intent on the road ahead. Gideon glanced over his shoulder. Several more police cars roared past the intersection and disappeared up the avenue. It would be only a matter of minutes before they realized the men they were looking for had escaped.

"You okay?" the driver asked in Hebrew. He glanced over at Gideon, quickly.

Gideon nodded. "Yes, but Ahmet very definitely isn't. We need a doctor."

He glanced over his shoulder at Ahmet on the back seat. He was still breathing, but there was an awful gurgling sound that accompanied each breath.

"We have medical supplies at the safe house we're going to. I'm a paramedic; field trained. We'll do our best," the driver said shortly.

A few moments of silence passed as the driver took a corner at speed.

"If you're in Tunis ever again, don't even go near that safe house. It'll be watched for a while. Facilities will get rid of it," the driver said.

Gideon looked over at him. "Yes, I realize we've been compromised. I'm just wondering how and by whom? The only people who know about me are the FBI and CIA agents I spoke to," he said.

The driver did not answer.

"I took a photo of one of the dead guys before we left," began Gideon.

"Not to worry. We can put the photo of our visitor through the database tonight, see if we get a match. Then we'll know who our friends were and what we're dealing with."

Euphemisms. Always euphemism around brass and spooks. Gideon wondered why—the habit of obfuscation? Guilt?

They drove in silence via a roundabout route through the poor southern suburbs of Tunis, checking for a tail—the non-scenic route, Gideon thought to himself.

"We're going in circles. We need to see to Ahmet now! There's no tail," Gideon said with some urgency.

The driver glanced at him again.

"Nearly there. I had to be sure."

Moments later they stopped outside a nondescript house. They pulled into an open garage with an internal doorway to the house. Between Gideon and the driver, they got Ahmet inside. The driver spread a plastic table cloth on a bed and they lay Ahmet down on it in the recovery position. He was very pale and his breathing shallow.

"Take off his shirt and the dressing! I need to see what I'm dealing with, then pour the anti-bacterial around the wound."

The driver handed him a bottle of antiseptic liquid.

"There is an exit wound and I managed to put on some coagulant before we left," Gideon said.

"Good. The blood loss doesn't seem too extreme," said the driver as he examined Ahmet.

Ahmet moaned fitfully. While Gideon administered the antiseptic and cleaned around the wounds with a cloth, the driver set up a drip and stuck a needle into the vein in Ahmet's good arm. "Blood plasma," the driver said by way of explanation. "We need to clear his chest cavity and lungs."

Changing focus, he gave Ahmet a shot of morphine using a syringe and then he checked the wound for bullet fragments with a thin probe. Satisfied the wound was clean, he inserted a flexible plastic tube into the cavity, probing slightly. The tube was attached to an oversized syringe. He pulled upward on the syringe plunger – blood flooded into the syringe from Ahmet's chest cavity. Gideon watched as he did this twice more, until the blood being extracted became frothy.

"Give me the coagulant," he said.

Gideon handed it to him. He mixed the coagulant correctly and syringed this deeper into the wound and then replaced the dressings on both sides, with a small opening in front to let out any trapped air in Ahmet's chest.

Ahmet stopped moaning. His breathing was still shallow, but thankfully steady. The gurgling sound had subsided. Blood ran in a slight trickle from his mouth.

The driver wheeled over a small suction device, much like they used at a dentist. He opened Ahmet's mouth and sucked the excess blood that had trickled into the wounded man's lungs. He then wheeled over a pulse machine, turned it on and stuck a small white cup over Ahmet's finger. Gideon was relieved to hear the steady ping tracking Ahmet's pulse.

The driver looked up at Gideon. "He'll be okay."

Gideon smiled thinly and extended his hand. They shook.

"Thanks for your help today. We would have lost Ahmet otherwise," Gideon said.

# Chapter 6

Gideon picked at his dinner. The action earlier in the day had left him feeling angry. At 7 pm Ahmet had regained consciousness and Gideon had spooned a little chicken broth into his mouth. The driver, "Mahmoud" was his operational name, had given Ahmet some more painkillers with his broth and Ahmet had gone back to sleep.

The call came about a half an hour later. Dani spoke first with Mahmoud, privately, and then to Gideon.

"The PM said he wants you to stay on and finish the operation despite what happened today. We put the photos you collected of the dead guys through the database - both Quds operatives. He's curious about the Quds connection. In fact, the Prime Minister was very pleased with your quick actions and he wished there were more boys like you who took the initiative. But he would say that, he is an old Duvdevan unit member himself. You got a bit lucky today. As you know, it's unusual for Unit 217 members to operate outside Israel, a real privilege. So don't fuck up, okay?"

"Thanks Dani," said Gideon feeling relieved.

"You okay for this? You're the only one who can recognize those men. We have plenty of men who can pull a trigger, but we need someone with your knowledge—and who can think on their feet," Dani said.

"Yes, good to go."

"I won't bore you with the operational details. Mahmoud has them. He'll fill you in on your trip east. Good luck."

Dani ended the call.

Gideon returned to the table.

"Eat, Gideon. You never know when you might eat again in this line of work," Mahmoud said.

"I feel like I messed up. I nearly got Ahmet killed," Gideon said.

There was a thoughtful pause then Mahmoud responded. "That's not true, they followed Ahmet to the safe house, not you. He should have been more careful. The way I see it; you saved his life."

"Yes, but they would not have followed either of us if I had come in on a different passport. I rushed."

Mahmoud shook his head and pulled a face.

"Maybe, maybe not. Does that mean you give up? You traveled on your own passport. It was a risk, but it was necessary. Time is not on our side. My commander has given me orders, I obey them and so must you. I have to get you to Tripoli. Once there, you'll meet up with the Neviot crew who will help you with your surveillance needs."

The Neviot were a surveillance team that collected intelligence for Mossad by break-ins, street surveillance, installing listening devices and other covert methods. Gideon knew of them by reputation only. They were good but not fool proof. He remembered hearing stories about several surveillance missions that had ended badly for Mossad in the late 1990s.

Gideon nodded.

Mahmoud took a mouthful of his food and chewed slowly, then continued, "What the PM wants you to do is find out where that payment is going and to whom it is being made. Once we have the intel, we'll assess the situation. Hopefully by that time Ahmet will have recovered enough to give you your orders from there. Dani made it clear, we are following the money or oil trail if there is one, nothing else."

"And the girl?" said Gideon.

"She's an American. They'll take care of that," Mahmoud said.

"You know how these kidnappings usually end, don't you?" Gideon said, frowning.

"Yes, yes, I do! Not our problem, okay! To get to her and extract her you'd need a team. We don't have a team for that purpose in Libya at the moment. There are many other things going on with higher priority for Israel and closer to home. Besides, Libya, and Tripoli for that matter, is crawling with armed terrorists and insurgents. We can't risk a team for a non-Israeli. The end."

Gideon felt deflated. If he was honest, that was the reason he was here. After five years of soldiering in the West Bank and Gaza, violence no longer bothered him, but the thick streak of congealed blood had brought flashbacks of Ariel, his best friend, dying in his arms. Yes, loss still bothered him and this looked like another loss in the making.

"Look, if it means anything, Hunter, the FBI guy, gave you a bit of praise too. He sent our guys the video. They liked what they saw, and besides, you're the only one who can identify those men. So, look on the bright side. You're the blue-eyed boy for the moment in this operation. Do your job. You're a soldier. You have the backing of the highest in the land." Gideon held the other man's dark eyes for a few moments.

"I take it Mahmoud is not your real name and you have been a soldier too?"

"My real name is none of your business. You know the rules. Just stick to your new cover story."

Mahmoud took another mouthful of chicken and chewed. Pointing his fork toward Gideon, he swallowed and said, "And yes, I was once a soldier like you. In Israel we all have to be soldiers, or we wouldn't exist, so no complaints."

"Who's complaining?" Gideon said.

"You might when you know what you've got ahead of you. It's not easy running people into Libya. Six different factions have control of different parts of the country. They usually shoot first and ask questions later. But Israel needs to know what is going on and we don't have that many good assets on the ground in Libya now—trustworthy ones, I mean. We've got lots of spies, rats, informants—that sort of thing, but the information we get from them is not always accurate."

"How am I getting in?"

"Your cover will be as an English-born war correspondent for the South African Broadcasting Corporation, or SABC. The South Africans currently have good relations with most of the Libyan factions. Nelson Mandela and Muammar Gaddafi were good friends. We'll smuggle you into the area controlled by the government of National Accord. They're the UN-recognized government and they hold Tripoli. There are at least two other groups who claim to be the legitimate government; at last count, anyway. Both El Qaeda and ISIS are active in Libya, but mostly in the eastern parts, near Benghazi, which is controlled by General Haftar's Libyan National Army. To make matters more complicated, these smaller groups often change sides in the conflict and sometimes go it alone."

"Why English-born, why not American? I don't have an English accent."

"Because Americans are likely to be killed right away by most of the factions. They're generally seen as the number one enemy. Don't forget who started that war."

"What's near Benghazi, that there is so much interest there?"

"In one word: oil. A large amount of it. There is a lot of smuggling going on that's fueling the fighting if you will excuse the bad pun," Mahmoud said.

"Who's buying that oil?"

"You name it! Turkey, Egypt, Sudan, Qatar. Even the UAE," Mahmoud said, his mouth twisting into a scowl of contempt.

"But that's old news," he added. "We're interested in the Iranian connection on this one. That's far more ominous. The oil bought by the others is supplying weapons to the Libyan war. Iran, or Hezbollah running oil? If that is what is happening, well that's a different story altogether. Mossad and the CIA have had some success in shutting down Hezbollah's money supply in recent years, but this looks like a new front. That's the only reason why you've got this mission. The only reason, got it?"

\*\*\*

Mahram had the run of the ship so long as she was chaperoned. Her chaperone was either Pinkie Ring, whose name was Jabir, or the man who had punched her in the face, whose name, she knew already—Arash and his gorilla brother, Baraz. She was made to wear a pashmina—something she'd never worn before. It was a large scarf that hung over the shoulder and arms and knotted just above the breasts, with an overhanging piece of material that fell beneath the waist. She was also given some long, loose-fitting pants and a blouse. A hijab was left on her bed, but she refused to wear it, except for when she went for her daily walk Then she was forced into it by Arash and when Baraz was on duty, him too, though he was less forceful. The ship was a cargo ship carrying metal containers full of a mysterious cargo no one seemed to want to talk about. There were long sections of beige painted metal deck on each side of the ship near the hull, down which she walked each day, so that she was able to do a full circuit of the ship, about 70 yards each way. It was certainly the biggest ship she'd been on, but not the biggest she'd seen. As a little girl she'd sometimes accompanied her father to the ports around Tripoli to see the oil being funneled into the waiting oil tankers.

The days were long. She was woken up at 5 am for prayers. The women would perform their prayers separately from the men in a mean little room near the kitchen. All the women on board except Fairuza and herself, were cooks. As far as she could make out, no one else on board were passengers. There were only five women; the rest were men, mostly from Algeria. She was accompanied at prayers and mealtimes by Fairuza, but she was made to eat alone.

Fairuza would sit apart with Delir Hashemi, the injured man. Mahram observed them furtively. Clearly, they were emotionally close. She observed how their legs would touch from time to time, under the table. Nothing obvious, but in a strict Muslim culture even the slightest gesture of intimacy between a man and a woman was haram. Breakfast took place right after prayers and consisted of omelets, with fruit and naan bread and not much variation. The naan was nothing like Indian naan. This bread was baked to rise, about an inch thick and formed into long strips that were cut into squares and was very filling. She learned to eat quickly because she was chaperoned from the dining room as soon as the men entered, then she was locked in her room until lunchtime. Later in the day she would be taken for a walk around the periphery of the ship with one of her three chaperones after which she would be locked in her room until an early dinner.

Her room was a five-by-four-yard cell with a small solid portal, looking out onto the ocean. It was hot and stuffy in the room. The unblinking eye of a CCTV camera stared at her all day. The bunk had no sheet, or blanket—not that there was anything to hang yourself from anyway, she thought darkly.

But she was not suicidal anyhow; what she harbored in her soul was seething, impotent rage born of fear. The only privacy she had was the toilet facility in her cabin, which had a commode and a tiny hand basin behind a flimsy door. Aside from the head coverings, she was given a change of underwear every morning by Fairuza, but no new clothing. Mahram had the distinct impression she was starting to smell, and each morning washed herself vigorously with wet toilet paper in the tiny toilet facility.

Someone had left a few American woman's gossip magazines in the room. She read through them all in about thirty minutes on the first day; they were the usual trash about celebrities breaking up or having affairs. Next to these, placed on the floor, was a one-liter flask of water and a Quran. She did not open the Quran. There was a reason for that too, but she could tell no one. In the evening, she would pretend to spend some time in the toilet facility washing herself again but what she actually did was get on her knees and pray earnestly, reading from the slim New Testament scripture Bible that she had in her jacket pocket. The pocket had a hole worn into it by her car keys and things would annoyingly slip through into the lining of her parka. Then she'd have to painstakingly fish them out—coins and cell phone and the like. This had happened to her small New Testament Bible when they'd jumped her and, somehow, in the rush to escape the USA that ensued, they'd never thought to search her thoroughly. Sure, they had made her turn out her pockets, but as nothing had fallen out, and they'd already confiscated her cell phone and keys, they thought they'd taken everything.

She opened the Bible and tears of grace pricked at the corner of her eyes as she prayed for her safety and the safety of her estranged father. She felt sure she was being used to manipulate him, a man she hardly knew now. She hadn't seen him for many years following the divorce, and then once, when she was 16, he'd come over to the USA to visit them after her brother died in the war. She remembered the furious argument between him and her mother about the way she dressed. She never spoke to him again after that. Her mother encouraged her to write letters to him and she did—a few dutiful letters, but there was never a response. Then after her mother died, she received a terse note from him expressing his condolences, a credit card and a bank account, which he said she could use to buy an apartment and car. But she'd inherited her mother's property in New York and had a job, so she never used the money, though she had once used the credit card to buy herself a diamond necklace from Tiffany's when she turned 21. She smiled at the memory. She did that mostly to see if she could provoke a response from her father, but it hadn't. He didn't even remember her 21st.

Lunch was shared in the galley with her captors. They never joined her at her table, but sat close. It usually consisted of a rice dish, or a stew containing eggplant, tomatoes, onion, and lamb or chicken. The food was fresh and tasted fine considering it was produced in a tiny kitchen for around a hundred people. Today it was served with iced tea. She deliberately ate slowly at lunch, savoring every bite. The afternoon chaperone was usually Jabir. He was gentle and deferential toward her, unlike the other two, with whom she did not feel safe. At first, she had been curt to Jabir and although she was still wary of him, his gentle nature did not change and she wondered if she might be able to get some information from him.

"Why are you doing this, Jabir?" she asked as they walked slowly along the deck on the fourth day.

"I'm a Palestinian," he said simply.

"So that excuses everything for you?"

"Not everything, but it excuses a lot." There was a moment's silence. "I'm not supposed to be talking to you."

She ignored his warning.

"I don't think it excuses anything. Your cause is only as good as your methods."

"We'll never win if that is the case," Jabir said.

"Are you winning now?"

Jabir didn't answer. She could see he was closing down.

"They brainwash you even as children to hate Jews. I know, I have seen Palestinian TV."

"It's easy for you to say. You've not lost family in bombings and as collateral damage."

"Many Israelis would say the same thing."

"They're the aggressors. They're the people who occupy our land."

"The Israelis don't think they occupy your land. They think it is their land by God-given right. They don't even acknowledge the Palestinians as a people group. They would point out that you were part of the Ottoman Empire, that you were never your own people."

"They would be wrong," he said in surly manner. They walked in silence for a few paces.

"The point I'm making is that violence begets violence. It doesn't ever, ever solve anything. And I do know what I'm talking about. My brother died in the Libyan civil war. Who suffers? Only the families who lose sons. In the end, the solutions are always political anyway. There are no military victories in civil war."

"Enough!" Jabir said sharply. He took her back to her room without another word.

So that was interesting, she thought to herself once the door was closed and she lay on her bed. What do I have to do with Palestine? I've never even been there. This definitely has something to do with my father.

Two more days went by. Jabir refused to talk to her. They gave her a novel to read during the day when she was alone. *Identity Man*. It belonged to one of the sailors. It was good. It suited her mood. It was a story filled with violence, but with a strange sense of hope—the ability to change.

On the seventh and final day Jabir spoke to her again. When they were out of sight near the bow of the ship.

"I thought about what you said." Jabir said quietly.

"Really? My captors have a conscience?" Mahram replied softly.

Jabir managed a slanted grin.

"The Palestinian identity doesn't depend on others' perceptions, but our own. You will no doubt say that the Jews think the same. Well and good. Then it is a fight to the death."

"I hope not, Jabir," Mahram said.

He flicked her a quick smile. "You're brave, Mahram. You're a brave woman." She smiled at him.

"Why do you live in the West?" he asked after a pause.

"It's a long story. My mother is a Benghazi Italian. You know—a left over from the Italian colonial days. There're still some Italians in Libya. Anyway, most of my Italian family left in the 70s after the coup. Some went to America; some went back to Italy. My grandfather was in oil, so they stayed. My mother and father met at work. But their marriage was strained. He worked long hours, there were other women I suppose. My mother left him and took me with her when the war broke out. There was nothing to hold her there. She died 6 years ago, a few years after my brother died."

They walked for a time in silence.

"That's a sad story, Mahram."

Mahram could see that Jabir was struggling with something.

"What does my captivity have to do with Palestine?"

"This situation…it's not all that it appears. It's complicated," he said quietly. Mahram looked at him sharply. "What do you mean?"

"I…I'll only say this. Your father…he has concerns about you. That you have gone over to the Infidel."

"My father has had little to do with me in ten years. Why does he care at all?"

Mahram looked into his haunted eyes.

"There is a double purpose. Money, yes, but also your safety. You must allow him to get you to a safe place…there will be war soon. That's all I can say. That's all I can tell you."

As they rounded the curve of the bow, they saw Arash coming toward them.

"Your walk has taken too long! We will be making landfall tonight. Take her below, now!" Arash commanded in an aggressive tone.

The men stared at each other.

"There will be a satellite overhead soon! Did you forget?" Arash said with a sneer. Jabir nodded.

"Come," he said to Mahram.

As they tried to pass Arash put his arm out and grabbed Jabir's shoulder. Jabir looked at the hand and then into Arash's eyes; they were filled with contempt.

"You were talking to her. It is forbidden! It is haram!"

"She's finished her book. She wanted to know if there was another. I said I would look," Jabir lied fluently.

Jabir removed Arash's hand from his shoulder and brushed past him. Arash stared after the two of them until they descended the stairs.

"She can read the Quran! That's all she needs!" Arash's voice followed them down the stairs. "No more books! We make landfall soon!"

# Chapter 7

Gideon and Mahmoud left mid-morning the next day in a dusty dual cab 4x4 utility truck after saying goodbye to Ahmet, who was thankfully conscious and in fairly good spirits. Gideon had heard Ahmet and Mahmoud arguing for a few minutes as to whether Gideon should go alone or with company.

Mahmoud checked Ahmet's wounds and vitals, harrumphing a bit as he did so, but eventually agreed the wounds looked fine and that he would accompany Gideon. Ahmet looked pale and was still a little weak, but the bullet had been a clean shot through muscle and hadn't affected any vital organs. With his right arm in a sling, he was able to move around the house by himself.

"Just make a pot of soup and leave some bread, a few antibiotics and pain killers and I'll be fine. If I start to feel ill, I'll get a team to take me out."

Ahmet gave Mahmoud directions and two GPS coordinates. The first GPS coordinate was where he had to turn into the Libyan desert, the second where to meet his contact. He and Gideon packed the truck under Ahmet's watchful eye and got set to leave. Much to Gideon's relief Ahmet even saw them out onto the street and raised his good arm in farewell. Gideon did the same.

The trip was a long one. Eight-and-a-half hours from the city of Tunis to the little border town of Dehiba. The plan was to refresh at Dehiba, wait until dark, then travel up the lonely dirt C203 road, which ran along the border between the two countries, and cross over at the first GPS point into Libya. There was no border fence or border post along that road and no landmarks to speak of, merely a vast inhospitable desert on either side of the road. At the point they were to cross, they would head due east over hard-packed sand and scattered low scrub bushes for about two miles, after which they would come across another dirt C road, this time on the Libyan side of the border. This was where Gideon had been instructed that he would meet Ezat, his guide.

"No one in their right mind goes out there. So, you should be fine," Ahmet had said. Ahmet also gave him a description of the man called Ezat.

In the back of the truck was a backpack with a good digital camera and some clothing, a laptop with some fake story files, a note pad and pencils. All the gear a typical journalist might carry. A large 20-gallon tank of water and a 10-gallon tank of diesel were strapped to the back of the cab, as well as a mysterious wooden crate about two-yards cubed. Ahmet did not volunteer information about the crate, so Gideon didn't ask.

Gideon had the required visa and papers. His new passport was British and he went by the name David Dunedin. An easy enough name to remember if he was questioned.

There was a fresh authentic-looking Libyan passport stamp in it, dated last week. He had a new cell phone with a tracking device built in, so that friends could keep tabs on his whereabouts in case of mishaps.

"The Back Office is good at this. Tell the boys I said thanks," said Gideon.

"The best," replied Ahmet. He smiled, then added, "and most of them are women, actually." Gideon chuckled.

Mahmoud played the radio and drove in silence. The road was blacktop, single lane, almost arrow straight, and traversed a sparsely featured landscape, broken only by clumps of low growing gorse bush and, occasionally, a small hillock that rose inexplicably from the otherwise flat surroundings. It started getting uncomfortably hot by 11 am and they became thirsty. The air conditioning was only barely keeping the temperature under control.

Mahmoud pulled over onto the side of the road without looking into his rear-view mirror. There was no need; they'd passed possibly three cars on this road once outside of greater Tunis, and the last one about an hour ago going in the opposite direction. Mahmoud got out of the truck and opened a cooler box that rested on the back seat. In it was a six-pack of ice-cold Lion Lager. Gideon got out of the vehicle and Mahmoud tossed him a can of beer. Gideon cracked it open and drank thirstily. It really hit the spot. He pressed the cold can onto his cheeks and the back of his sweaty neck.

"Man, that tastes good," he said with a smile.

Mahmoud smiled back.

"Once we make Dehiba we'll keep a low profile until about 8 o'clock. We'll ride out on the C road and into the Libyan Desert where you'll meet Ezat Naseef.

He'll take you to Tripoli. He's a Coptic Christian and can be trusted. The Copts have real reasons to hate the ISIS and Al Qaeda crowd."

"You don't have to tell me. I've seen their work first-hand in Syria," Gideon said.

They arrived on the outskirts of Dehiba at about 4 pm and checked into a cheap motel, paying cash up front. They spent the late afternoon drinking beer and eating spicy food in their room. The beer was the lager they'd brought with them, the food came from the local market. Mahmoud went out to get it while Gideon lay on his bed, staring at the fly-spotted ceiling—somehow restless, but feeling exhausted all at once. El Jazeera news spilled its peculiar brand of subtle hostility toward the West and Israel into the room.

There was a lot of news about an uptick of drone attacks on Israel coming from Syria. He wondered what his old unit would be up to. Probably tracking down the control vehicles responsible for those drone attacks, he thought.

At about 6 pm they took a walk out into the desert where Mahmoud gave Gideon more detail about the mission.

"You'll make contact with a sayan, Sara is her name. She lives with her grandmother. She'll provide lodging and direction around Tripoli."

A sayan, or helper, is a person of Jewish background who provides logistical support to an operative. Gideon had heard about the sayanim and their valuable work, but had never used or known one, to his knowledge.

"Sara will introduce you to your Neviot team."

Mahmoud made Gideon repeat the names and addresses several times.

The sun sank slowly, but still cast a stunning yellow glow of light at 8 pm. A few minutes later they nosed their battered truck into the town of Dehiba. Mahmoud ran some counter-surveillance before they turned onto the C203. It was no more than a dirt road and in fairly bad repair at that. As they entered it, an army truck full of bored-looking young soldiers roared past them leaving a nimbus of gold colored dust in the fading light behind them. Gideon looked nervously across at Mahmoud.

"I wasn't expecting that," he said.

"They never stop. They're in too much of a hurry to get into town for some fun. As much as you can have out here, anyway. In the meantime get our GPS coordinates on Google Maps."

Gideon got out his phone and hit the Google Maps icon. Mahmoud pointed out roughly where they'd be turning off the road and Gideon eventually matched the coordinates Mahmoud gave him with the GPS numbers shown on the map.

"Got it," he said.

Soon it was dark and they were alone on the road. The moon hung huge and bright in the sky and, without light pollution, the stars were a magnificent spectacle. There was enough light from them to travel with their headlights turned off. Mahmoud noticed Gideon looking at the speedometer—he traveled at a cautious speed.

"No rush, Gideon. The last thing we want now is a punctured tire, or an accident with wild animals, or feral goats. I certainly wouldn't want to have to explain to a friendly army sergeant what we're doing out on the desert road late at night with our cargo."

"Fair enough. What sorts of wild animals are out here?" Gideon asked.

"Gazelle, feral camels, foxes, baboons, you name it. Even some leopards, I'm told."

They traveled in companionable silence for another twenty minutes, just the rumble of rubber tires on the grit and sand of the corrugated surface. The road took a sudden jag to the right.

"We're almost on the coordinates," Gideon said.

Mahmoud slowed even further.

"Here." Gideon said shortly.

Mahmoud stopped. He engaged the four-wheel drive and then put the truck into a low gear and turned perpendicularly off the road and into the desert scrub, tuning on the headlights as he did so. Now Gideon understood why the truck looked so battered. Gideon rocked violently in his seat as they traversed the scrub. He reached over and put on his seatbelt. Mahmoud glanced at him and grinned.

"This is about as bad as the bumps get. The real problem is the sand drifts."

After about ten minutes of constant rocking Gideon saw a quick flash of light, nothing more than a quarter of a second, but startling in the dark.

"There," he said involuntarily.

"I see it," Mahmoud said.

The truck engine grumbled as it churned through sand and skidded over loose grit. At one point Mahmoud sent the truck clean through a screen of low growing gorse bush that sounded like it was violently ripping holes into the undercarriage.

They came to a sudden halt. Just ahead of them, obscured by the coarse gorse was another truck of indeterminate color; probably beige at a guess in the dim light. An old-fashioned-looking Land Rover, but bigger and even more battered than Mahmoud's truck; with large patches of rust on the bodywork.

"Don't let looks deceive you. Ezat Naseef is a smuggler. His vehicle only looks like it's going to fall apart," Mahmoud said, when he saw the dubious look on Gideon's face.

Gideon smiled cynically.

"Ezat's a good man. We've had some adventures over the years, him and I."

Mahmoud stopped his vehicle and got out. The headlamps picking out a squat, powerfully built man before dimming and going out.

Ezat greeted Mahmoud warmly with the standard three kisses on the cheek and hard slaps on the back. He was relieved to see the natural affection between the men. Gideon trusted Mahmoud and this signaled a close bond between them—but caution was still warranted, he reminded himself.

He got out of the truck and saw his breath billowing white into the cold desert air. A faint sweet scent from the gorse bush drifted on the thin desert air. The two men in front of him spoke quietly to each other. Gideon checked his shoulder holster; the Sig Saur 9mm was secure in there under his black jacket. He took his backpack off the truck and hung the camera around his neck.

Mahmoud beckoned him over and introduced him to Ezat. They greeted each other with a hard handshake. Ezat's hand felt like a sandpaper covered vice. His features belied his strength. He was shortish, about five foot seven with broad shoulders and a barrel chest, though he carried a few extra pounds around his middle. His body was fitted into a loose pair of jeans, desert boots and a red shirt. He had an almost comically round head, topped with a mass of thick dark hair, slightly graying on the sides, and big expressive dark eyes in a tanned face. He was one of those men who didn't seem to feel the cold.

"Ahlaan bik—welcome David Dunedin," Ezat said in Arabic. "Anaa laa afham," Gideon answered formally in return.

"Come David, my friend. Mahmoud tells me you're a journalist working for the SABC. We have lots of news to share here in Libya. Come," Ezat said, beckoning Gideon toward his truck.

He pronounced Gideon's cover name "Dawit".

Ezat took Gideon's bag and unlocked the back of the truck. As he opened it the strong odor of livestock washed into the cool air, followed somewhat startlingly by the bleat of a sheep. Gideon looked into the back of the truck and saw a tethered sheep chewing methodically on some hay.

"My cover story," Ezat said, and winked. Gideon handed Ezat his camera.

"I'm a smuggler, you see, Dawit, not a journalist and I need a cover story. My cover is that I'm a farmer who has picked up a journalist, if we are asked."

"I see," said Gideon, a half-smile hovering on his lips.

He flicked a quick glance at Mahmoud who was grinning like a Cheshire cat in the dark.

"Could you help me with the crate? We need to transfer this to the truck. It's the payment for your safe passage to Tripoli."

Mahmoud lowered the tail gate and he and Gideon carried the crate over to Ezat's truck and slipped it into the back with some effort. Gideon estimated it must weigh about 100 to 120 pounds.

Gideon shook Mahmoud's hand.

"Thanks for your help," he said in his best English accent.

"Stick to the mission and all should go well," Mahmoud said in the same language.

Without even a backward glance, Mahmoud got into his truck, started the engine, and left in a swirl of dust. Gideon listened to the whine of the engine as it receded into the distance.

"He's a good man," Ezat said in Arabic.

"He said the same of you," Gideon said. That seemed to please Ezat.

"Come, come we must go before it gets light. These roads are patrolled, and we must be in Al Jawsh before sunrise. That's my home-town."

Gideon clambered into the high suspension truck and put on his seatbelt. Ezat laughed.

"That's good, Dawit, you are a cautious man, but I am a man of faith. I pray to God first."

Ezat made a very elaborate sign of the cross over his chest and then mumbled a few words under his breath.

"I see you're carrying a gun, Dawit, that's good, my friend. Do you know how to use it?"

"I do," Gideon said.

"The reason I'm praying is because we don't want to come across ISIS. If we do, then I'll ask you to hand me my gun that's in the glove box, then we will shoot at them until only one bullet remains and then we will kill each other with our last bullet. You don't want to fall into the hands of those monsters. God will forgive us, I'm sure." Ezat said earnestly.

Gideon smiled mirthlessly at Ezat's macabre pronouncement.

Ezat started the truck and then turned to Gideon and said, "Do you believe in God?"

"It's a good question. I think I do, but I don't think God is much interested in us," Gideon said.

Ezat chuckled to himself. "No, my friend. God is very interested in us. So interested that he allows us to suffer. What shows the reality of the heart better than suffering?"

Gideon tried for a witty retort, but found nothing. "You have a point," he said.

"In the end the heart is what counts, my friend," Ezat said.

Gideon nodded and grinned. He had not expected a philosophical conversation with a smuggler.

"ISIS say they love God and yet look at what is in their heart. Does this disprove God, or does it show something else?"

Ezat backed the truck out rapidly onto a dirt track, then turned onto the road and floored the accelerator. Gideon was glad the truck had good suspension. He did not want to think about the poor sheep in the back. Ezat glanced at him and smiled.

"Are you thinking of the sheep?"

Gideon laughed shortly. "Well, yes."

"He will be our supper. He is lying down there on the straw; he will be okay."

"Excellent," Gideon said somewhat sarcastically.

Ezat laughed.

"So does God mind you being a smuggler?" Gideon said.

Ezat looked at him sideways, then back at the road.

"Where are you from, my friend? You speak Arabic well for an Englishman. Maybe too well."

Gideon didn't answer.

"You look like a soldier to me. So maybe then you know what it's like to fight for your life. God does not mind if we fight for our lives and defend our families."

Close to the bone. Gideon remained silent.

"Do you know what I'm smuggling tonight, Dawit?"

"No. I honestly don't," Gideon said.

"Not what you think. I'm smuggling medicine. Medicine to keep my people alive. No, I don't think God has a problem with me being a smuggler."

Gideon nodded, then said "Yes Ezat, I think you are right, my friend."

They hurtled along the dirt track bouncing ferociously about the cab.

"Ezat, can I ask you a favor, my friend?"

"Yes, of course," Ezat said.

"Could you please slow down, my ass is getting bruised and I want to be able to walk when I get out of this truck."

Ezat laughed uproariously, but did slow down a little.

"Welcome to Libya. Tomorrow you will see what it is like to live on the edge of hell," he said.

*** 

They heard the crackle of automatic gunfire on the night breeze long before they could see the small city of El Jawsh. Gideon retrieved Ezat's firearm from the glove box, a Star BM 45 mm, fed by an 8-round magazine. A heavy, but reliable weapon. There were two boxes of ammunition next to the gun. He checked that the magazine was full and made sure the safety catch was turned to 'on.' Ezat slowed the vehicle and then stopped altogether. He wound down the driver side window and listened carefully. A glimmer of light on the far horizon preceded every crackle of small arms fire.

"They're about 15 kilometers away to the north of the city. We'll come in carefully from the south," Ezat said firmly.

He started the truck and eased off the dirt road. Headlights off. The desert they were in was essentially a flat, stony plain and so the going was slow and bumpy, but fairly straightforward. They both rode with their windows down, listening and looking intently into the gloom. After about 20 minutes, Gideon could see the outline of the city against the emerging dawn light. Ezat stopped the truck again and listened. The gunfire seemed to have eased, now only sporadic and far away. Ezat retrieved his cell phone from the dashboard in front of him and dialed a number. He spoke quickly in Arabic.

"Brother, I'm coming in with my guest, make sure you do not shoot us by mistake. We're coming in from the south."

The person on the other side of the line spoke, then Ezat agreed and rang off.

92

"We must wait until my friend has spoken to the commander in El Jawsh. Otherwise, we'll be shot on approach," Ezat said matter-of-factly.

"Do they know who attacked them?"

"Yes, ISIS. They have captured the black flag. We managed to kill five of them and they're on the run. Two of our men are slightly wounded. It is a good thing I'm bringing medicine. We need it."

Gideon closed his eyes, thinking about all the conflict he'd seen and been a part of in his life. He suddenly felt very weary.

"I'm going to try to sleep while we wait, okay Ezat?"

"Yes, sure, sure. I'll watch and wait for the call."

Gideon wound up his window and placed his jacket under his head, wedging it in the V between the window and the seat, then closed his eyes. He dozed lightly, waking once to hear Ezat get out of the vehicle to take a piss. About five minutes later, the phone rang.

"Good, okay. We'll come in by the road. Tell the commander I have medicine. He will be pleased," he heard Ezat say from outside the vehicle.

The journey took another twenty-five minutes. There was a roadblock a good mile out from the town of El Jawsh. Two stacks of sandbags were separated by twenty yards and on opposite sides of the road from each other, so that a vehicle would be forced to zig zag through the barricade to get through. The road rose here, with steep embankments on either side. Gideon suspected that there must be a riverbed nearby for the road to have been raised this high, presumably to avoid occasional flooding. A machine gun nest squatted ominously behind the second barricade, pointed in their direction.

Ezat slowed the vehicle. "Stay quiet, my friend, and place your hands on the dashboard where they can see them," he instructed.

Ezat brought the vehicle to a stop and got out with his hands forward at shoulder level, shouting his name.

A floodlight sprang to life; the road a searing white line of light. Gideon blinked several times. Out of the corner of his eye he saw a man approach Ezat, holding an AK 47 assault rifle. When he saw who it was, he gave Ezat the three-cheek kiss.

They spoke for a moment and then Gideon could hear the guard yell back at his compatriots.

"It's Ezat. He's brought the medical supplies and a journalist who will tell our side of the story! Let them through!"

The floodlight swung a degree from Ezat and was turned fully onto Gideon. He shut his eyes tightly in order to not be blinded by the light. He did not remove his hands from the dashboard until Ezat came back to the vehicle.

"We're safe. You can put your hands down now," Ezat said, then opened the truck door and got in.

The rest of the trip into Al Jawsh was uneventful. Evidently this small city was a Coptic Christian stronghold. Gideon saw no less than three churches on the way to Ezat's house in the wan light of dawn. This was remarkable, given that Al Jawsh was really a rather small city Gideon estimated, of no more than 50 000 souls. The main road was blacktop and ran almost dead straight through the center of the settlement; the adjoining roads into the suburbs were hard packed dirt. Several larger roads, also tarred, penetrated the city from the four corners of the compass at different points along this strip of road. In the low light Gideon could make out flat-roofed square or rectangle-shaped houses, single or double story. They were really more like compounds. Each home was surrounded by a wall at least seven feet high. A smattering of trees occasionally adorned the front verge of several of the compounds, but there was no greenery at all on the main road through the city. There were no street-lights either. The overall impression was one of bleak, practical necessity underscored by the slight but pervasive smell of diesel.

Ezat put a short call through on his cell to his father. They turned left about five minutes later, down a dirt road that looked exactly like all the others they'd passed in the last few minutes, and finally pulled up in front of an eight-foot-high black metal gate that dominated a breeze block wall painted white. The gate was suddenly pulled open from the inside. An older squat man, clearly Ezat's father, stepped through the opening, looked at Gideon stonily and then peered down the street. Ezat pulled the truck into a concrete-covered courtyard in front of a squat flat-roofed two-story structure, punctured by four small square windows set about three yards apart from each other. The whole structure was painted a slightly off-white color.

They alighted from the truck. Ezat spoke in low tones to his father as Gideon retrieved his bags. He turned to Gideon and gestured for him to join them.

"This is my father," Ezat said in Arabic. Gideon shook the leathery hand extended to him and said "Marhaba," the formal Arabic greeting.

"Ahlan wa sahlan," said the older man; a welcome. Gideon sighed in relief. This greeting was important because it formally put Gideon under the protection of the patriarch.

"I must go and take the medicine to the hospital, Dawit. My father will look after you," Ezat said.

"Yes of course," Gideon said.

"Come!" the older man said and gestured Gideon into the house.

The house interior was modest by western standards. The floors were covered in speckled faux stone tiles, the foyer walls were white plaster. One of the walls on the far left of the room was covered in wallpaper—an odd burgundy sea horse motif on a tan background dominated the swirls. Small mattress-like cushions were arranged around the edge of the room, with occasional throw cushions in burgundy swirls lying on top of the larger cushions. In the far corner was an old-style pre-digital TV.

Three doors led off the foyer, a passage to the left and right and a large wooden and glass door directly in front of Gideon, which led into a sumptuously decorated lounge room. On the floor of this room was a burgundy and tan Persian rug and a dark brown ornate divan. The furnishings were clearly the touch of a feminine hand. The contrast of this room to the two men Gideon had met was almost comical.

"A beautiful room," Gideon said.

A broad smile broke onto the face of the older man. One of his front teeth was missing.

"My wife will be pleased. Come, I will show you your room. You may wash in the basin, then my wife will bring you a meal, then you can rest."

"Thank you, Abba," Gideon said.

They turned into the passage on the left. The first room was clearly the guest bedroom. It was painted light mauve. In it was a double bed with a white and pink duvet and white cupboard. A glass and jug of water were neatly placed on a brass tray on a small round-topped table next to the bed. In the corner of the room there was a utilitarian porcelain wash basin with taps.

"The toilet, if necessary, is down the hall to the right," the older man said, then promptly left the room and closed the door behind him.

Gideon placed his bag on the floor carefully and sat down on the bed. He could feel the fingers of exhaustion making their way up his legs and into his lower back. He rubbed his face. He retrieved his cell phone from a pocket, scrolled down to find his commander's name and sent a quick text to Dani.

"Arrived at friend's home. All well, Abba."

Gideon got up wearily. He thought about shaving then decided against it. A beard would help him to blend in. He strode over to the washbasin and took off his shirt, then washed his face, neck, armpits and chest and dried with a towel he found neatly folded at the end of his bed. He was pleased to note that his wounds were healing well.

He pulled the only other shirt he had out of his bag and put it on, then he sat on the edge of the bed and pulled off his boots, mulling over the mission so far.

There was a polite soft knock on his door.

"Come in," he said in Arabic.

The door opened to reveal an older lady and a young woman. The young woman carried a small low table and a cushion, she placed these on the floor and left. The older woman set down a plate of flat bazin, a sort of slightly wet dough-like substance, drizzled with date syrup, a large glass of goat's milk, and a small side plate of palm dates.

"Shukran," Gideon said, thanking the woman.

"Afwan—you're welcome," said the older lady softly and then left the room and closed the door behind her.

Gideon sat down and tucked into the meal. He had not realized how hungry he was. The meal, though simple, was absolutely delicious and surprisingly filling.

Afterward Gideon lay back on the bed, meaning only to doze for a few minutes. He was startled by the large hand of Ezat, shaking him gently awake by the shoulder.

"It is time to go, Dawit."

The sun had already gone down. Gideon and Ezat had a quick meal of bread dipped in oil and some frothy tea.

The older couple was nowhere in sight. Clearly this family was not buying his journalist cover story. They were making themselves scarce and keeping his visit as quiet as possible.

They left Al Jawsh through another sandbag barricade. The commander of the militia wanted to see his passport. He eyed Gideon dubiously in the dying light.

"You are English?" he said in heavily accented English. "Yes, sir," Gideon said in his best Oxbridge accent.

"Why you tell news stories? Who is interested?"

"The world in general is interested. Remember, this is a war that was started by America, but now where are they?" Gideon said.

"No, not America. Hillary Clinton! Yes? You tell the world that and how El Qaeda and ISIS are now a problem for us, okay!"

"Okay," Gideon said.

"We only defend. We do not make war. We only defend our families! You understand?" said the Commander.

"I do. May I take a photo of you and your troops?" Gideon held up the camera.

The commander smiled. "Yes, yes of course!"

They got out of the truck and all the men gathered around, smiling shyly as they held up their AK 47s in a sort of victory salute. Gideon asked groups of them to sit and stand on the sandbags and then took a dramatic shot of the commander manning the machine gun nest, surrounded by his troops. Gideon noticed that Ezat had a very broad grin on his face the whole time.

"Come Dawit, we must go my friend," he said in English.

"One more thing. Are you all Copts, or are some of you Muslim?" Gideon asked the commander.

"We are both Coptic and Muslim. We are brothers. You see?" He indicated his men. "We have a common enemy."

"I see."

Gideon offered his hand. The gray-haired commander shook it and looked directly into his eyes.

"You are a soldier, Dawit?"

"No, a journalist now," Gideon said, then smiled. "I have seen war zones many times. It does not scare me."

The commander smiled back, but the smile did not reach his eyes. "You have seen what ISIS does, yes?"

"I have," Gideon said, truthfully.

The commander gave him a friendly thump on his shoulder. "Then you are on our side, yes?"

"Yes, definitely!"

Ezat and Gideon got back into the truck and, once on the other side of the sandbagged barricade, Ezat floored the accelerator. Gideon was impressed at how fast the truck could go.

Ezat grinned at him.

"We can go 150 kilometers an hour on a straight road."

"How is it that this truck can go so fast? Forgive me, but it looks old from the outside." Gideon said.

Ezat chuckled.

"I found a Toyota Land Cruiser riddled with bullets and full of dead soldiers, but the engine was still good. I took the engine from it and placed it in my truck. It's a good engine," Ezat said with a grin.

The road trip to Tripoli was mercifully uneventful. There was another police road block adjacent to Tripoli International Airport, about 30 minutes from the center of town. It was early and so there were only a few trucks and cars ahead of them. The stop and search added a good 20 minutes to the journey, but this time the paramilitary police were not interested in papers, they were more interested in what was inside the vehicle. A policeman searched the undercarriage for bombs and limpet mines, and a dog jumped into the back of the vehicle and took a sniff around. Only when the camera was found did the police want to know what brought them to Tripoli.

"I'm a journalist," Gideon said and proffered his credentials to the policeman.

He took a cursory look at the papers and then looked sharply into Gideon's eyes for about three seconds. Gideon held his gaze. The policeman hesitated for a second, thought better of it, and waved them through. Gideon kept a watch on him in the wing mirror as they moved off. He saw the officer take out a small pocket pad and pencil and write something down as they moved off.

"I don't like that. I think he's just noted your registration," Gideon said.

Ezat chuckled. "Not to worry, my friend, he will only find the vehicle belongs to a trading company...registered in Tripoli. I come through this checkpoint regularly."

# Chapter 8

Morning broke with a haze of yellow smoke hanging over the city of Tripoli. Not too long ago this had been, if not a beautiful city, at least a well-ordered low rise, handsome one—with wide boulevards, occasional green spaces, and a central business district with a few western-looking glass and stone high-rises along the waterfront. Now, most of the buildings stood pockmarked with machine gun ball and licked, in what seemed a random way, by the sooty tongue of fire. The shattered buildings looked like the jagged remains of rotting teeth in a gaping mouth.

Ezat cast a sideways glance at Gideon.

"It was a beautiful place once," he said.

"I believe you," Gideon replied softly, his eyes wandering across the shattered buildings again.

A hundred yards from them, Gideon saw a crane rebuilding. The business district looked a little more intact.

"Qaddafi was not a good man, but he did try to look after the people…in a general kind of way," Ezat said.

"If you were in good with him then you were in very good. If not, then things weren't so good. Like that?"

Ezat laughed. "Yes, exactly! You know how we think," he said. "I must deliver you to the address Mahmoud gave me. Once you're there and safely inside and you have made contact with your helper, you must call Ahmet on your cell. There is a number he says is in your cell memory. I don't have to remind you that all calls are monitored."

Ezat turned a corner onto a main thoroughfare and wove expertly between the potholes. Heavily armed government soldiers sat or stood around a flat-bed truck, talking to each other, boredom in their eyes. On the bed of the truck sat a heavy caliber machine gun nest, squat and menacing behind sandbags. The odd mortar shell or artillery projectile was still lobbed into Tripoli by the various militia groups roaming the countryside, though less frequently now. Return fire was expected.

Ezat slowed the vehicle.

"No sudden hand movements or gestures. They need less than the slightest excuse to open fire," he said to Gideon.

Ezat wove the truck around a large section of masonry on the street, smashed from the side of a building by a shell, keeping it between them and the truckful of soldiers. The soldiers cast a look in their direction as they passed by, eyeing them suspiciously. Gideon felt his blood pressure rise, but kept his hands down and eyes averted. Suicide car bombings were not uncommon here. Ezat ignored the soldiers and drove by, slowly. The machine gun twitched in their direction and followed them down the road in a gentle arc. Ezat kept on glancing in his side-view mirror at the soldiers and squinting at the cross-street signs as they traveled along.

"Here it is," he said.

Gideon could hear the relief in his voice. It reminded him a great deal of the Gaza Strip. The same hyper alertness, the same sense of menace, no doubt the same sudden violence.

Ezat turned suddenly and made his way up Al Amrus Rd, a major thoroughfare that had seen some heavy fighting. It led up toward Mitiga International Airport, east of the city, the second of Tripoli's airports.

"The Americans still patrol here. They're based in the UN compound near the airport. They're more likely to stop and search you than the local soldiers."

Along this section of road, the damage to buildings was so immense it was hard to comprehend at first; Gideon's mind just did not want to accept it. He had been in war zones aplenty, but this seemed on a whole other scale. From the reports he'd heard, Gideon knew how fierce the fighting had been, but it was always horrifying to actually see the battle site—the rage of this battle was self-evident. The loss of innocent lives must have been catastrophic. Most of the buildings were soot-stained from top to bottom and pockmarked by heavy caliber bullets, concentrated mostly around window openings, and what looked, to his trained eye, like high explosive blasts from rocket fire, leaving only jagged remains. Some buildings were completely caved in, presumably bombs had been dropped on them from the air.

Ezat sighed as they drove slowly down the blasted road. A makeshift pathway had been bulldozed through the debris-strewn street.

"The government troops had tanks stationed on this road and fired at the militia as they came through the city. The rebels were trying to capture the airport. The fighting was house to house here," he said, barely above a whisper.

"It sure does look a mess, brother," Gideon said, slightly awed. "Let me take a few photos for my cover just in case I'm stopped and searched later."

Ezat stopped the truck and lit a cigarette while Gideon took a few quick photos of the more spectacularly damaged buildings. They traveled on in silence for a minute, Ezat skillfully evading fallen bricks and stones in the street and trying not to make eye contact with heavily armed soldiers on street corners. Gideon noticed the faces of children now, at second and third story windows, looking out at the truck as they passed by. Some waved. He waved back. On several of the balconies he saw washing hanging on lines of rope. Shopkeepers were opening the shops in the buildings that still stood.

Gideon smiled wanly. "But, somehow, life goes on," he murmured.

Ezat gave a quick tight smile in response, but Gideon could see the pain in his eyes as he glanced at his face. Ezat made a right turn and stopped the truck. The narrow street was dark in the early morning shadow, caught as it was, like some furtive slithering creature, between the hulking masses of smashed buildings on both sides.

"You see the pink building up there between the gray one and the one with no roof?"

"Yes," Gideon said.

"I will drop you here. Make your way there indirectly, in case we have followers. Level two, apartment 204. Your contact is 'Sara'. Tell her that Ahmet has sent you. She's probably expecting you."

Ezat extended his hand and smiled. Gideon shook it.

"What did you say you did for a living again, Ezat?" Gideon said with a grin. "Chicken farmer," said Ezat with a straight face. "And importer," he added. Gideon chuckled.

"Don't forget your equipment in the back, mister journalist," Ezat said.

Gideon grinned. "Well, if I never see you again, Ezat, let me say, it's been a pleasure, and please thank your father and mother for me."

Ezat smiled and nodded. Gideon took his backpack out of the truck and shut the door firmly. Ezat pulled away. Gideon watched him go as he considered the Ezats of the world.

They were survivors, no doubt, tough as nails. He felt sure he could trust Ezat, but it always paid to be cautious.

He glanced around, up and then down the street; no movement he could detect. He listened carefully, then hoisted his pack, took two steps forward, and ducked into a shadow covered doorway. Fingers of weak light lanced through the gloom, picking out shards of glass and the occasional miraculously intact window. Somewhere above him he heard the faint sound of a woman's voice and then a child's answering. He stepped further into the gloom, his eyes adjusting to the darkened interior. Bricks, stones, and reinforced chunks of concrete lay scattered like giant clods of earth on a tiled floor. The musty smell of damp cement dust lay over everything. Wires hung in great vine-like loops from the ceiling, and battered metal shelving stood in disjointed heaps; their goods long since looted. This had been a grocery store once. Gideon tried his best to move silently through the wreckage, but his feet made slight crunching noises as he walked over the debris. He looked at his watch then sat on his haunches, waiting silently. The neighborhood was waking up. He heard the splash of water, more murmured adult voices and the louder voices of children, doors closing; the muted signs of human life all mingling and echoing together in the street outside. He flinched slightly at the quick, high sound of a motor scooter buzzing down an adjoining street. Only then did he realize how tense he was. He took a few deep breaths, trying to reach emotional equilibrium, four seconds breathing in, hold for four seconds, four seconds breathing out. This square breathing technique was taught to special-forces soldiers to control their respiration and heart rate. He practiced the technique for about a minute before he heard what he had been waiting for—the call to prayer.

The high, nasal voice of a man sounded the first bars of the call. It echoed loudly down the street and hung like a hovering bird of prey in the blighted atmosphere, seeking out whom it may devour—the weak and the not yet sufficiently deranged. Excellent cover; most devout Muslims would be at prayer. He moved quickly through the building into a passageway. It took him through to the next shop along. Gideon looked carefully through the doorway, nothing moved. This shop was slightly less damaged but still empty, the next the same. He stepped from the building into the next one, not through a doorway, but a jagged hole rent into the wall by what had probably been a rocket grenade. The floor levels between the two buildings were inexact and so Gideon had to step carefully over rubble and down into the next building. This was the target building.

He made his way carefully through the gloom into the lobby area. The shattered remains of a naked concierge desk stood like a grotesque reminder of past attempts at civilization. An effort had been made to clean up the lobby, with rubble pushed back into the building's recesses or unceremoniously dumped on the sidewalk. He clambered over a pile of loose scree, thankful that the chanting of the call to prayer covered his noisy passage.

The chanting ended as abruptly as it had started.

The stairwell stood to the right of the concierge desk and the stairs were remarkably intact and clean in comparison to the rest of the building. It looked like they had been newly tiled, and Gideon thought he could even detect the oily odor of new paint. He'd approached the concierge desk and stairwell diagonally and from the rear, but now, standing in the lobby, he glanced out of the wide front door into the street. The buildings were in a less ruinous state here, still pockmarked with machine gun fire, but not bombed. There was even some glass intact in the windows of the building opposite. This then was where the government forces had managed to turn back the tide of rebels, no doubt.

Gideon listened carefully again; the only sounds came from gurgling plumbing somewhere in the innards of the building and the distant hum of motorized traffic associated with a city waking up. Nearby he heard the oddly cheerful but muted chirping of a flock of sparrows. A sad smile flicked over his face. Those same species had made a nest in a tree next to the barracks he lived in when in Israel. They reminded him of Ariel. As he climbed the stairwell quietly it suddenly dawned on him that he had not had a dream or flashback about Ariel's death for quite some time. He walked with athletic speed up the last flight of stairs, two levels up. His senses had not deceived him. The stairwell had been recently painted in a lovely pastel honey color and the cheerful color continued into the second story corridor. The corridor was tiled in ceramic and very quiet. Clearly, people of middling means picking up the broken pieces of their lives after the war.

Gideon stood outside apartment 204 and flicked open his black tactical folding knife, a wicked-looking weapon. He balled the knife in his fist and placed it into his jacket pocket, taking care not to stab the blade through the material. He hoisted his backpack more securely onto his shoulder and knocked softly on the door with his free hand. It had a spy hole and he looked directly into it, moving to a three-quarter position so that the backpack was between himself and the door. He waited for about 30 seconds and then knocked again, this time a little louder, resuming his defensive stance. He sensed rather than saw a shadow fall across the spyhole. The door opened suddenly. It was on a chain.

"Yes?" said a young feminine voice.

"Uncle Ahmet sent me," Gideon said in Arabic.

The door closed and Gideon heard the chain being removed. When the door opened again, a slim young woman, about his age was standing in front of him. She wore black slacks and a black long-sleeved top. Even although she was well covered, Gideon could detect a beautiful, full figure. He smiled slightly. She had large dark eyes, full lips and an oval face, her hair long, straight and dark, her expression calm and possibly somewhat bemused. She raised an eyebrow.

"Uncle Ahmet, you say?"

"Ah…yes," Gideon replied.

She had the most beautiful voice, high yet somehow smoky at the same time.

Gideon smiled boyishly again; he could not help himself. She moved back to let him into a darkened room. Cracks of light spilled through inexpertly drawn curtains.

"Close the door," she said quietly over her shoulder. She walked toward the curtains and threw them open, allowing daylight to flood into the room.

Gideon did as he was told, making sure the door was secure.

"Are you Sara, or is your mother…?"

"I live with my grandmother," she said. "And yes, I'm Sara."

He smiled again, this time less boyishly, he hoped. In the light he could see that her eyes were a deep navy blue. Arrestingly, shockingly beautiful.

She smiled without opening her mouth. "And you are…Dawit?"

Gideon cleared his throat. "Uh yes, that will do for now," he said. "My cover is Dawit, the journalist."

"Dawit, the journalist who is also my cousin, if anyone asks?" She laughed, not unkindly, and smiled.

"Yes," Gideon said, not quite sure how to take this line of questioning. He put his bag carefully down against the wall and looked around the room.

"Coffee?" Sara asked.

"Sure, that would be good," Gideon said, regaining some of his composure. She walked toward the kitchen.

"Why are you staring at me, Dawit? Are you afraid of me?" she said.

Gideon smiled. "No, I'm just…a little surprised, that's all. I was not expecting someone so…"

"Go on," she said, as she flicked on the electric kettle's switch.

"Your grandmother?"

"Still asleep; it is very early, Dawit."

"Your neighbors?"

"All very old and deaf," she said.

"Thank you," Gideon replied.

"We are safe here," Sara said, changing from Arabic to Hebrew.

Gideon searched her eyes for a second.

"Good," he answered in Hebrew.

"They would not have sent you here if they did not trust me," Sara said.

Gideon sighed. "I know."

"How do you take it?"

"What? Oh, black and sweet please," he said.

Sara gave a short laugh again. Gideon laughed too and grinned. The kettle boiled and she began to pour water into a coffee pot.

"So, are you trained?" Gideon said.

"I'm a sayan; a little trained," she said. "They don't give us helpers much training. A little counter-surveillance training. A little training on some communications devices. Dead drops—that sort of thing."

Sara handed Gideon a cup of coffee.

"Are you hungry?"

"Ravenous," Gideon replied, accompanied by a quick smile.

"I'll make you some toast, but help yourself from now on, okay? I'm busy. I look after my grandmother and have a job."

"Sure, Sara and thanks again. I'll make contact with Ahmet soon."

She smiled, this time the smile made it to her eyes.

"So…where do you work, Sara?"

"I'm a nurse in the local hospital. The truth is I act more like a doctor than a nurse. We're very short-staffed."

"I see," Gideon said.

Sara handed him two slices of toast on a small plastic plate. His stomach rumbled. She giggled. It was a delightful sound.

"I'm glad I amuse you," Gideon said, with a grin of his own.

She said nothing in return, just looked at him steadily with a slight smile hovering on her lips.

"So, do you have a husband, Sara?" Gideon asked.

Her smiled deepened. "No. Why do you ask? Do you think a woman should be married?"

"Well, I just wanted to get the lay of the land, so to speak."

"No, never married. Just too busy to do all that. Things have not been easy here."

"A man could help," Gideon said before he could stop himself. "I mean…"

Sara snorted softly. "Where are you from? Do you know Arab culture?"

Gideon smiled and looked down. "Sorry, I should not have presumed," he said.

"American?"

"Is it that obvious?" Gideon said. "I'm supposed to be an English journalist."

"Your accent is good, but your English idiom is not; it is more American."

"Well, before you do any more guessing, I'd better phone Ahmet."

"Yes," she said quietly. "You'd better. I'm about to wake my grandmother. She's very old and slightly deaf and she'll want to know who you are. You're a doctor from the hospital, who needs a place to sleep for a few nights, okay?"

"She doesn't know you're a sayan?"

"Heavens, no!" Sara replied.

"Don't you get a few people through? Doesn't she wonder about that?"

"All she knows is that I get paid a stipend 'from the hospital…'," she made quotation marks with her fingers, "…to put occasional guests up for the night in our spare room. She is grateful for the extra money, so doesn't ask questions."

"Okay, good. But I don't have a white coat or stethoscope…" Gideon began.

Sara laughed this time. "None of the doctors do. Stethoscopes are too valuable to be removed from the hospital and white coats are non-existent."

Gideon finished his coffee and toast quickly while Sara prepared her grandmother a meal and then she showed him to his room. It was a small room, about 9 by 11 feet and sparsely furnished with a single-sized metal bed that had a blue and white striped duvet on it. At the head of the bed stood a small wrought-iron nightstand and lamp. Set high in the wall above the bed, was a long narrow window, covered by about ten inches of dark blue curtain drawn back allowing weak light to filter in. On the opposite side of the room was a built-in wardrobe made of dark wood veneered particleboard. The floor was covered in an off-white and brown speckled carpet.

"I need to leave in about 20 minutes," Sara said.

"Thanks, Sara, I shouldn't be long."

Sara closed the door quietly behind her as she left the room.

Gideon sighed and sat on the bed. He closed his eyes for a moment as a smile played around his lips.

"God help me," he said under his breath.

She was stunningly beautiful, but that was really not something he should be thinking about now. He shivered slightly and then got up and took his phone from his jacket pocket. He speed-dialed Ahmet's number. The phone rang twice before Ahmet answered.

"All safe, Uncle. I'm with cousin Sara," Gideon said.

"Good to hear. Send my regards to Sara. By the way, this is a secure line so we can talk openly."

"Good to know and will do," Gideon replied. "How are you holding up after your, er, little accident?"

"I'm okay, thanks. A little weak, but okay. No infections, which is the main thing. Keeping my fluids up," said Ahmet.

"Mahmoud?"

"Got back in one piece. All is well." Ahmet said, then added, "Sara will take you to meet the Neviot team today at a location she will arrange. I say team, but really there are only two of them. It's quite difficult to get people in and out of Tripoli these days. You know the mission. I'd say try to get ears into The Northern Oil Company, and the home of Basar Amman, he's Mahram Amman's father of course. If you see the bad guys in town, ears on them too, if possible. My gut feel is start with the father, Basar, and go from there. Do a recon and tell us what you need. Also, Facilities have found you an apartment not far from Basar Ammar's home, a rental only. Don't keep any information there. It's not safe. The team will take you there after they've met you. They're very busy people. This is not our only mission in Tripoli. We're also spying on the UN base at the moment. If things go south, contact the team and they'll try their best to move you to another safe house. If you get caught doing anything, stick to your cover. Just say you're a nosey journalist who got information about a kidnapping and you were looking into it."

"Understood," Gideon said.

"And no heroics, okay? Get in, get out, let's listen and understand first."

"Understood," Gideon said again.

"Oh, and one more thing. Your friend from the FBI, Jack Hunter, is in town. He's just flown into the UN base. We have eyes on him in the base, but we'll struggle to keep up with him outside. It might be worth watching him too."

"I'm one person, Ahmet."

"All roads lead to Basar Ammar. Start there." Ahmet ended the call.

In case of prying eyes Gideon took the opportunity to change his outfit. He extracted a few items from his backpack. It was never advisable to stay in the same clothes too long while undercover.

*** 

Later that morning Gideon and Sara took a brisk walk into the Al Daha district in the north of Tripoli. Sara was dressed in the same black slacks, but she now wore a black miniskirt over her slacks, partially hiding her curves. She'd also donned a slightly more loose-fitting black top and shawl, and black boots. She wore a matching hijab. Gideon wore a pair of dark brown chinos with a white long-sleeved shirt, his desert boots and a black jacket. They looked just like a young Libyan couple. With his dark hair, stubbly beard and a tan coming on, Gideon could pass for a light-skinned Arab. They chatted as they walked. Gideon asked Sara about her family.

"My mother and father were killed in the war. My grandmother is all I have left," she said with tenderness entering her voice.

"I'm genuinely sorry for your loss. The world seems to have gone crazy."

She nodded once.

"What about you? A wife, children?" she asked, looking up at him.

"Who me? Nooo. I've been a soldier since I left senior high. I haven't had time to get married and have children."

Sara smiled.

"Is that something you want?" she said.

Now Gideon smiled.

"Sure. Right place, right time, right woman."

"How about you?" he said.

"Right place, right time, right man," she responded with a half-smile. Gideon chuckled.

The Al Daha neighborhood was the well-to-do end of town and out of range of the self-styled Libyan National Army's artillery. The city remained largely intact in this suburb. The buildings were generally 8 to 15 stories high with a mix of residential apartments, businesses, and some very large two-or three-story balconied residences that looked more like compounds or forts than houses. Most of the buildings were either light beige or gray stone or brick, while some were rendered with light colored painted plaster ranging from white to a dark ochre.

"Tripoli must've been a beautiful city once," Gideon said.

"Yes, it was," replied Sara quietly.

He was pleased to see a thriving café and small business community in the streets and an abundance of shrubs, trees and date palms. It was rather pretty and pleasant and, for that reason, all the more surreal compared to what they'd just left.

The Refak University, Museum of Libya and the all-important Northern National Oil Company HQ graced this suburb. The contrast to the border of the southern suburbs where Sara lived could not have been greater. Foot and motor traffic was building and becoming quite busy.

"We're here," Sara said, indicating a café up ahead.

Café de Paris struck Gideon as a surprisingly elegant establishment, with an outdoor and indoor seating area. White wooden chairs, and tables with glass tops adorned the indoor space, and wicker chairs and tables with white tablecloths, the outer. The walls were covered in painted wooden panels and there were dark gray mosaic tiles on the floor with a white star-like relief, enhancing the look of class and sophistication. To the left were overstuffed gray- and teal-colored divans in a lounging area with low tables and, to the right, booths with dark leather seating. It was there that Sara introduced Gideon to Eli and Nathan. The two men were slightly younger than Gideon, both dark skinned, dark eyed with dark curly hair. They could have been related to each other. Nathan was the taller and more muscular of the two, but neither of them was large when compared to Gideon. They greeted each other in Arabic and continued in that language. Both had half-eaten croissants and a cup of coffee in front of them.

Gideon checked out the other patrons quickly. Aside from the serving staff, there was a young couple on the other side of the room and an older and younger lady gossiping together, quite loudly, among the tables.

"I've got to run," Sara said. She handed Gideon a key. "Let yourself in if I'm not there."

"Okay, I'll see you tonight," Gideon said and smiled.

Eli and Nathan looked at each other.

"Whoa, let yourself iiiin," Eli said.

Sara grinned. The young men laughed good-naturedly.

"Shut up, you twits, and get serious," she said.

As Sara turned to leave, Gideon thought she might be blushing.

"Thanks," he said after her retreating back. Grinning with them at their teasing.

Eli and Nathan chuckled, not unkindly. Sara just raised her hand and gave it a dismissive flick, but did not look around.

Gideon ordered coffee. While they waited for it to arrive, they briefly exchanged their service histories in the IDF in Arabic, quietly and somewhat cryptically. When you lived in Israel, knowing a person's service history told you quite a bit about them.

Both Eli and Nathan had done their national service with the famed and feared Unit 8200, responsible for collecting signal intelligence for Aman, the army's intelligence arm. The enemy databases Unit 8200 had not penetrated were probably not worth mentioning.

"I assume Ahmet has contacted you?" Gideon asked.

"Yes, he has and, wow, never a dull moment with him, is there?" Eli said, leaning in.

"Basar Ammar is only one of the most revered, well known and well-guarded people in Libya."

"Any ideas how we can do this?" Gideon asked.

"The first we heard of this was two days ago. But we've given it some thought. There are a couple of things we can do if we could find a way in," Nathan said.

Gideon looked from one to another. "Okay, shoot."

"Well, the options, as I see them are: we penetrate HQ and get at their hard drive, but that is going to entail getting inside with a thumb drive, inserting it into the system and then using the malware on the thumb drive to break into their hard drive. Second option, we break into his home and do the same thing, or tap a phone to get useful info, or use a drone to try and spy through curtains and eavesdrop with a directional microphone. Or we could try to bribe or blackmail someone like a guard or maid, but that would be extremely dangerous, given where we are. And, of course, they'll have to be compromised in some way to do that successfully."

"Okay, let's start with a recon of his home. I assume you know where he lives?"

"Yes, we've been watching it. Facilities was lucky to find an apartment relatively quickly and close by, on a street adjacent to his house. Basar Ammar lives in a large three-story compound not far from here."

'Facilities' was the euphemism given to the Israeli intelligence arm that dealt with logistics, identity manufacture, travel, and accommodation for agents and assets. They were legends in the business. Operating behind fronts and shell companies all around the world, their turn-around times were reliably some of the best in the business. Gideon knew they were run off a black budget that only the Prime Minister and the head of Mossad had access to. Rumor had it that this caused great anxiety, even among their close government colleagues. Gideon knew he was getting 'star treatment' and was grateful. Facilities usually worked exclusively for Mossad and Aman. The 'cleaners' who had helped him and Ahmet in Tunisia had been part of Facilities' crew. Perhaps this mission was not so low on the priority list after all.

Nathan slid a key toward Gideon. Gideon nodded his thanks.

"Okay, let's go," he said.

The apartment Facilities had rented was located several blocks up from Café De Paris, just off Via Cesare. Gideon would only use it for operational purposes. It was good doctrine to keep the operations as far away from the safe house as possible. Sara's place would be his safe house. Eli punched in the security code to access the block of apartments. Gideon memorized the number as he did so, and they walked up four flights of stairs quickly. No other residents were observed as the three of them, moving rapidly but quietly, approached the apartment's door. Gideon was pleased to see that both men were breathing easily after their climb. He hitched his backpack up a little and then slid the Sig Saur 9 mm from his waistband holster. Both Nathan and Eli looked at him with curious expressions.

"You can't be too careful. The last time I was in a safehouse we were sprung, so forgive my paranoia," Gideon said softly, opening the door and glancing into the room before he entered.

The apartment was a bedsit, sparsely furnished with a single bed, four-seat round dining table, kitchenette and separate restroom. White net curtains covered a window and glass sliding door, which led onto a small balcony overlooking the street. Several pieces of equipment sat on the table. Gideon immediately recognized the curved propellers of a small drone, camera equipment, and of course the universal laptop. He closed the door behind them, locked it, then walked around the table observing the equipment. The young men looked at him expectantly.

"Nice. The same as the drones we use in the Duvdevan."

"Slightly better and a newer model. Quieter. Battery lasts a bit longer," Eli said with a half-smile.

"How far away are we from the compound?"

"Not far. If you go to the balcony and look diagonally right; the second house, well, mansion really, down Via Cesar is our target. We can easily recon with the drone from here, but I suggest we do it after dark. There are armed guards in the compound," Nathan said.

Gideon went to the balcony and eyeballed the target compound through a slight parting in the curtains. The mansion was a good 300 yards away at a three-quarter view. It was a large, walled, flat roofed, two-story home. Most homes had a basement in Tripoli; he guessed this one would not be an exception. Ochre in color, with white trim. Large windows in the front, heavily curtained, but windows that could be opened, he noted. There was a rather ostentatious white painted wrought iron gate in the baroque style housed in a sturdy frame. The frame's posts were set in concrete and Gideon could make out a manned guard pill box on the inside of the gate next to the wall. No one was going to ram their way through that gate.

On the outside of the wall was a security camera and intercom. A brick driveway swept up from the gate to the main colonnaded entrance in an arc and then continued around to a set of large flat-roofed garages. The front of the property held a large round water feature fountain in the Italianate style, slightly raised by a five-inch stone step and set on a well-manicured grass lawn. Tall date palms edged the driveway and swayed in the gentle morning breeze and a very large beech tree near the garage gave shade. Gideon noticed a gardener trimming a set of leafy bushes along the back wall of the compound.

"Have you taken note of who's coming and going on a regular basis?" he asked.

"Three guards on rotation every six hours, one in the guard pill box outside near the gate and two inside. A cleaning crew of three ladies, arrives at 7 am and leaves at 10 am every second day, the gardener also works every second day and he arrives early, about 6 am and stays most of the day. There's a live-in lady cook and her daughter plus Basar Ammar and his driver–and the occasional lady friend. The driver lives on site too and probably acts as another level of security," Eli said.

"Good work," Gideon said, impressed at their thoroughness. "Are the guards the same people every time?"

Eli thought for a moment and said, "Yes."

He handed Gideon a set of small binoculars.

"If you look closely at the far wall, you'll notice a security camera mounted inside the compound near the corner and security spotlights on the front of the house, the same security lights are at the back."

Gideon adjusted the lenses of the binoculars. "Yes, I see them," he said.

"We've flown the drone over a few times and there is a camera in each corner. One of the guards must be monitoring the wall and garden on screens all day and night inside the house.

There's a changeover window at approximately 6 pm, but if they're careful the security recordings are probably played back to check the handover period. The cameras can swivel, but because they are mounted in the corners there'll be blind spots near the center of each wall if they're looking straight on. They may be hooked up to motion detectors and there are at least three laser alarms stretching across the gardens which are visible at night with infrared," Eli added.

Gideon nodded. "Impressive level of security. Okay, this is giving me some ideas. I'm going to take a walk past the house now and check out Northern Oil HQ afterward. Are you guys available tonight, say 8 pm?"

Eli and Nathan glanced at each other.

"Yes, sure," Eli said.

Gideon grinned.

"Don't get excited. I'm not suggesting we get inside tonight, just take a snoop around with the drone. See what we can see. Is the camera any good – infrared?"

"Sure is and we can hear too; it has a directional microphone," Nathan said in the sort of offhand way techies do when they're proud of their skills, but don't want to appear immodest. Gideon smiled.

# Chapter 9

Mahram's thoughts were in a whirl as the ship nosed its way slowly past the long breakwater and into the port of Tripoli. She watched from the porthole as they finally nudged up against the dock.

What had Jabir said? "Your father has concerns for you and something about the infidel?"

What did he mean? He surely could not be so obtuse as to say such an obvious thing, knowing she was the victim of kidnapping—of course a father would have concerns about that. Could he know that she'd become a Christian and if so, how? That would suggest he'd been spying on her. She could not make sense of it. Her train of thought was interrupted by a loud knock on her door and then the grating of the key in the lock. Arash put his head through the door, leering at her as she sat on the edge of the bed.

"Put your hijab on. We are no longer in the West," he said.

Mahram stared at him for a second then reluctantly got up and deftly placed her hijab over her hair.

"Get your things and let's go."

"I don't have anything, remember. You stole all my possessions," she said defiantly.

"Get your coat and pick up your Quran, you stupid spoiled child, or so help me I will give you the beating your father should have given you!" Arash said, harshly.

"If you knew who my father was you'd be more careful with your insults! I will tell him what you said!" Mahram spat back.

Arash smiled, then barked a laugh. He strode into the room, picked up her coat and Quran, and tossed them at her. Mahram caught them deftly.

"You're in for a big surprise, Cat-Meat," he said through a sneer.

Mahram ignored him. She spun on her heel and stalked through the doorway, turned right into the corridor and bounded up the companion way, not waiting for Arash to give her orders.

"Stop!" he shouted, following closely behind.

Out on the deck, Mahram saw the others congregating at the gangway to the dock. She joined them and put on her parka, placing the Quran in her pocket. Fairuza was in a completely black burka. She turned around with a bemused look in her eyes. Mahram took secret delight in seeing Arash arrive behind her looking flustered. Fairuza looked at her and her lip curled into a sneer.

"You have much to unlearn if you want to survive here. You would do well to remember your old lessons," she said quietly, before moving off.

Mahram felt a chill go up her spine and followed Fairuza down the gangway to the dock below. Now there was no chance of escape. She was in the enemies' territory and she harbored a growing apprehension that somehow her father was intimately involved in the organization of this kidnapping. Mahram knew full well that honor kidnapping and even honor killings of women who had become 'infidel' were not uncommon.

The port was busy, with many men and some women, in full burkas, walking the docks. Clearly the Saudi-backed Salafists were in control of the city. For all his brutality, at least Gadhafi had allowed some freedoms to the average people and to women in particular. She'd never seen her mother in a hijab. It was probably why Gadhafi had ended up being killed like a dog, she thought.

Small fishing boats ploughed bravely between large cargo ships, followed by flocks of screeching sea gulls. Given the alleged sanctions in place on Libyan oil, Mahram was surprised to see several massive oil tankers lined up to drink thirstily of the black gold from the circular shaped oil storage tanks. Dozens of gantries were busily loading and unloading cargo. She wondered if her father was nearby. She remembered as a little girl how he would often go down to the oil facilities on the docks.

The group walked slowly along the quay, approaching the majestic Red Castle Fort which lined the far side of the harbor crescent nearest the old city center. She noticed that the facing wall, with the Roman arches and pillars built into the façade, was pockmarked with bullet holes. This was ground zero of the Tripoli uprising in 2011, not far from where her brother was killed. Somehow this depressing site seemed to mirror her mood. She was just a girl when she and her mother left for America. How she missed her mother—a pang of longing and memory coursed through her, bringing a pinprick of tears to her eyes. As they made their way from the quay into the fringe of the old city, she was appalled to see the devastation that the war had wrought on the surrounding buildings. The once lush Green Park was awash with the smashed detritus of war as well as the lean-to housing of refugees from surrounding towns escaping the extremists. The pervasive smell of fresh human excrement hung in the air. A pall of sadness sank into Mahram's heart. The Tripoli she remembered was no more.

She was ushered toward three new black S Class Mercedes Benz sedans that had clearly been waiting for them on the curb of Omar Almukhtar Road, which skirted the park. Several young children and adult refugees from the slums stared at them in open amazement and envy. A little girl with a soot-stained face and grubby dress waved at them with a smile. It almost broke Mahram's heart. She waved back sadly. Fairuza indicated Mahram should get into the middle car and sit; Fairuza on her left and Jabir on her right. Arash took the front right seat next to the driver; a man she did not recognize. Baraz, the twin, was in the car behind them together with the man who was in charge, Hashemi. She did not see the occupants of the first car. She'd not seen much of Hashemi on board the ship. Only at meal times and then he kept to himself. His arm was still in a sling. Arash and his twin were both armed with automatic weapons. Mahram did not know what kind they were, but they looked both wicked and deadly.

They drove fast and, to Mahram's mind, recklessly through the morning traffic. The thumping of her heart wasn't only about the way they were being driven, she realized. They turned off the main road into the more salubrious northern suburbs; her old stomping ground. They had to slow in the heavy traffic. The city surroundings were familiar to her; the constant honking horns and milling crowds, a few donkeys pulling carts and making their way up the road in the traffic. She recognized City Hall and then the Museum of Libya, a place she'd often visited as a school-aged child. Mahram became intrigued as they made their way into the quiet streets of Garden City; the part of the city that held most of the embassies, but also, most importantly, the suburb next to which she had lived as a girl with her mother and father. She wondered where her kidnappers would hold her. Intrigue turned to amazement and then foreboding as they turned into Via Cesare and drew to a halt in the driveway of her old home.

Fairuza glanced at her with a wicked look of cruelty in her eyes and wheezed a short laugh.

"Welcome home," she said, with biting sarcasm, now looking straight ahead.

Mahram's mind was in complete turmoil.

"What is this?" Mahram exclaimed, turning to look at Fairuza.

Fairuza's lips arranged themselves into her familiar smirk, but she kept her gaze forward. Mahram glanced at Jabir. He flicked his eyes toward her and then looked at his lap, pokerfaced.

Arash got out of the car to speak with the guard at the front gate. A guard had never been necessary before the war…and then her mind went numb.

This could not be! As she looked out the driver's window, she saw the young man who had tried to rescue her, sauntering down the street. He'd just turned into Via Cesare from an adjoining street about 50 yards away. No doubt – it was him! When he spotted Arash getting from the car his face registered surprise and then Mahram saw him turn slightly sideways, stop and stoop down as if to do up a loose shoe lace. Mahram looked out of the corner of her eyes, first at Fairuza and then Jabir, to see if they had noticed the young man. Fairuza was focused on Arash, who headed back to the car with a self-important look on his face and Jabir still stared downward, looking at nothing.

Mahram thought quickly, this man appearing must be something meaningful, something good and he clearly was as shocked as she was. For the first time in almost a week, she felt hope blossom.

*Make a fuss, draw their attention away from the kneeling young man! She told herself.*

"Arash, you and I are going to have words together with my father when I meet him! You and that pig of a brother of yours are going to be very sorry!" shouted Mahram shrilly, in Arabic. Fairuza turned sharply toward her and hissed—shock registering on her face.

Arash's face went ashen, and he stood glaring at her for several heartbeats, unable to process the audacity that Mahram had just displayed; then he snorted in derision.

"You're lucky you do not belong to me, stupid Cat Meat! If your father cannot live with the shame of what you've become, I will personally volunteer to end your filthy infidel life!" he yelled at her.

Mahram's eyes flicked back toward the young man; he had turned around and was making his way back in the direction from which he'd come.

"Go!" Arash commanded the driver and slammed the car door.

Fairuza let out a soft malevolent laugh as they pulled away.

"Very unwise. He is a brutal man. You have made an enemy now. He does not care for his own life. He is committed to Shahid. If he thinks of you as the infidel, you will die."

"I count none of you as friends, you stupid bitch!" Mahram shouted back at her. Fairuza turned and struck Mahram a ringing blow across her face.

Mahram held her cheek, but her eyes were busy. The young man had turned the corner and disappeared from sight. Two things became clear to Mahram as they rolled up the driveway and came to a halt in front of her father's mansion. Her kidnapping was bigger than just merely an attempt at extorting money and it was clear that they were not afraid of her father's wrath. One did not treat an Arabic man's daughter like this, unless you wished to insult him. Clearly, they no longer cared about his honor…or much more seriously, hers. To insult him right on the doorstep of his house seemed irredeemably stupid. She concluded it must mean that they thought little of her prospects of survival. Arash had called her an infidel. Surely, surely, they could not know she'd converted to Christianity? Her heart quailed within her. If her father knew, he'd be obliged to kill her. His honor would suffer too much otherwise.

\*\*\*

Gideon's heart beat like a trip hammer. He walked swiftly onto Al Jamahiriya Street, the main thoroughfare in this neighborhood, and turned in the opposite direction to the operations apartment, then ducked into a shop doorway. His intention had been to survey the house and surreptitiously record it using his cell phone. He took out his phone now, pretending to look at its screen, but listening for the footfalls of potential pursuers.

Nothing—only the rush of traffic and the acrid smell of diesel and dust.

His mind raced, trying to make sense of what he'd just witnessed. He moved out of the doorway, changed direction and walked swiftly back toward the apartment, past it, then around the block and waited on Al Jamahiriya Street again, pretending to have a conversation on his phone. He tried to piece it together slowly in his mind. Leaning against a wall in the lee of a building's shadows, he watched the grainy clip on his phone.

Arash exited one of three black sedans pulled up to the gate of Basar Ammar's house. That could only mean one thing, Basar Ammar was in on this whole thing. No kidnapper in their right mind would front their target's residence like that. Then the high voice of a woman in distress, yelling. The picture was wobbly here, but the mic on the phone distinctly picked up two words through the open car door, 'father' and 'pig'—a young woman's voice. Could it be Mahram? Then Arash lost his temper and started to yell back, but at this stage Gideon had been doing his shoelace and the camera was focused on the ground in front of him; the mic though was still picking up sound. He heard the threat, heard the door of the car slam. After that he was facing the wrong way so neither the camera or mic were of any use. Then he'd turned the corner and could not hear or see anything.

He thought fast. Maybe events had progressed more quickly than he thought possible. He needed to know what Hunter knew. If their facts didn't match, then he'd know for sure something more than mere extortion was happening here. Could he trust Hunter, though? They had different agendas, that much was clear. He had to risk it. Gideon took out Hunter's card again as he walked slowly toward the Northern Oil HQ and memorized the number. He crumpled up the card and threw it down a drain and then punched the number into his phone. It went to voicemail. Gideon decided it would be best not to leave a message.

A ten-minute walk took him past Café de Paris and on to the Northern Oil HQ. The building was rectangular in shape, about 200 yards long, with abutting wings set at 45-degree angles protruding from the rear. Six stories in height, navy blue glass, trimmed in white sandstone, with arrow slit windows engineered into the white trim of the sandstone face at roof level. Handsome, but somewhat stark and utilitarian rather than beautiful. The front faced a main road and the side adjoined a large sward of grass graced with several palm trees and a large parking lot with curved brick pathways. There was a lot of motor vehicle traffic around the building, but not much foot traffic at midday. Gideon spotted at least three security cameras as he walked past the front—too risky to try anything at a time like this.

He took out his phone and looked at Google Maps for a well-protected rendezvous point to meet with Hunter. He didn't want to use Café de Paris again; bad trade craft to use a rendezvous twice. There was a likely spot on the edge of the old city with its narrow maze of streets, about a ten-minute walk from his current location. He set out at a fast pace.

Gideon's phone buzzed in his hand.

"Hunter here. Did I miss a call from you?" Hunter had enough trade craft and the good sense not to use Gideon's real name.

"It's David," Gideon said. "We spoke about a week ago in New York."

"Ah, yes, David, what can I do for you?"

"I'm doing a story in Tripoli. Do you know the old part of the city? Cafe de Roma off the Al-Shat Road? Maybe we could meet? It's important."

"Yes…how important? I'm extremely busy and very close to securing an important mission objective here," Hunter said.

"On that score, very specific. Very clarifying, hard evidence," Gideon said.

"Okay, give me ten minutes. Are you close enough for that?"

"Yes, almost there already. See you then," Gideon said and hung up.

Gideon's phone was encrypted, but he did not know if Hunter's was. He had to assume someone had been listening. A person as important as Hunter coming into an Islamic country would almost certainly be under surveillance by government intelligence. Café de Roma was close by, only blocks away, so Gideon made his way via a circuitous route through the old city, its narrow laneways covered by arched pillars and crowded with a hubbub of bazaars, hawkers and people. He saw Hunter walk up the street toward the café and take a seat outside underneath its awning. The streets and café were starting to empty this close to the midday call to prayer. Perfect timing for counter-surveillance. It'd be easier to spot a tail. The muezzins began to broadcast their nasal sounding call to prayer from the three local mosques. The cacophony was mesmerizing. Hunter saw him coming and got up and walked toward Gideon.

"Keep walking. I had a tail, but I think I shook it off. They won't be able to hear us for a few minutes with this racket," he said.

"Who's the tail?"

"Probably the local 'Gestapo'. They're fairly untrained, so weren't hard to spot." Hunter said wryly.

Gideon chuckled. He and Hunter turned a corner onto a quiet street. Gideon handed Hunter his phone.

"I took this video about twenty minutes ago outside the home of Basar Ammar," Gideon said.

Hunter watched the video and then lifted it to his ear and listened, having difficulty hearing it over the call to prayer. They kept on walking.

"So, what am I seeing and hearing here?"

"I went for a recon this morning past Basar Ammar's home and who should I see arriving at the front gate? That's our friend, Arash."

Hunter looked at him sharply.

"Are you suggesting what I think you're suggesting?"

"I'm just giving you what I've got. What've you got?"

"We're hours away from doing an exchange of $30 million USD to reunite Mahram with her with her father. The kidnappers made contact with him several hours ago. As you can imagine, not knowing where his daughter has been, or whether she's alive or dead has left him fragile," Hunter said.

"They're playing you," Gideon replied, his expression serious.

Hunter regarded him for a second, then said, "Either Israel is playing me, or they're playing me."

Gideon shook his head. "Why would we? Israel just wants to know what the money will be used for."

Hunter remained silent, but if his expression was anything to go by, he looked like he was about to explode.

"I took this footage this morning. Do what you need to do. Ask the CIA to run a check for you on the vehicle license plates. See who the cars belong to if you don't believe me. I'll take a bet they belong to the North Oil Company. Any self-respecting kidnapper knows not to take their victim to the home of her father "before" he's paid up and especially if that father is just about to pay up. Why would you risk it?"

"How do you know Mahram's in the car?"

"Do you understand Arabic? Listen. A young woman calling Arash a pig and him saying he hoped her father would allow him to punish her…and this outside Basar's home. It's got to be her. I mean, who else, right?"

"Whatever the case, this is not our shit-show. We're getting our girl and going home with her," Hunter said.

"I'll bet you my shitty condo in Jerusalem, which is all I have in this world right now, that she won't go home with you. They'll make her say she wants to stay. You can't force her out of her father's house. You have no legal sway here. That thirty mill is you being used to launder money for terrorists. They're laughing at you." Gideon said.

Hunter stared at him.

"It's audacious and because it is so brazen, it's calculated so that you would not want to believe a father would do that to his own child…the psychology is perfect," Gideon said.

"I hope for all our sakes, you're wrong Gideon," Hunter said. He handed back the phone, his eyes hard as stone. A look of suppressed fury in his face.

"Right now, I have to prepare for the handover. Let's talk again after that."

The call to prayer ended as abruptly as it had started.

Just then an SUV with heavily tinted windows sped around the corner and slowed, but kept on driving. Hunter's eyes flicked over the car as it nosed its way down the quiet street.

Gideon fumbled in his pocket. He could see Hunter was in two minds now.

"Hunter, I'm one of the good guys. If this turns to shit and you get a chance, give her this thumb drive and tell her to get it into her father's computer, if she can do it safely," Gideon said, then glanced back over his shoulder. The SUV had disappeared around a bend.

Hunter gazed at him stonily for a heartbeat, then took the thumb drive.

"Spyware? I like your chutzpa."

Gideon smiled wryly. "Yes. This is looking mighty suspicious, Hunter," Hunter scowled, nodded once, turned and walked away.

He did not look back at Gideon as he turned the corner.

# Chapter 10

Fairuza, Arash and Jabir escorted Mahram into her father's house and into his study. Arash all but forced her to sit on one of the white leather wingback chairs. The room seemed smaller than she remembered, but she supposed that was always the case with memories of places and spaces from one's childhood. This room had been a sanctuary for her before she and her mother left for America. A place where she had read books, drawn pictures quietly and built Lego houses with her brother while her father worked.

It was a beautiful room. White-painted gilt-edged wooden panels covered the walls. Heavy velvet curtains with a four-sided pattern in dark green, gold, and wine red covered the windows. Fairuza and Jabir sat in the other two wingback chairs around a gilt-edged coffee table in dark wood. In front of them stood her father's heavy fruit tree desk with a white leather business chair neatly tucked into its foot well. The floor was parquetry, covered in a very large and lush Afghan carpet. A wall-length bookcase was stacked with every conceivable shape, size and color of book. To the right of the desk hung three large paintings, depicting scenes from the book *1001 Arabian Nights*, strictly speaking haram to any religious Muslim, she mused ironically. In the center of the ceiling hung a Fontana crystal pendant light fitting.

"Don't you love the paintings?" she said to Fairuza, her tone dripping with sarcasm. Fairuza ignored her, staring straight ahead.

"What do you think, Jabir? Do you like them?"

Jabir smiled. For some reason he'd donned his dark glasses.

"Yes, they're nice. I remember my mother reading to me from the 1001 Arabian Nights when I was young," he said.

"Images are haram. They are forbidden in Islam," Fairuza said stonily.

"And yet, I'll bet you read women's magazines when you can, meat puppet," Mahram said, then chuckled.

Fairuza sighed, closed her eyes and said nothing.

"For whom are we waiting, Jabir?" she said in English.

Jabir took off his dark glasses and glanced at Fairuza. She kept her eyes closed as if in meditation.

"We are making arrangements for your safety," he said to Mahram in Arabic. Mahram snorted in derision.

She heard footsteps in the marbled hallway on the other side of the closed study door and the muffled voices of men in earnest conversation. Then the double doors were opened wide. Arash stepped through the doorway first, the sub-machine gun still slung around his shoulder, followed by Delir Hashemi, and then her father. He looked older, his hair streaked with gray, and he had a full beard. Mahram had always remembered him clean-shaven.

Mahram's heart beat faster. She had not seen her father in ten years. She rose.

"Papa," she said, with a frown creasing her brow.

"Mahram, how good to see you," he replied in Arabic.

She looked over her father's shoulder at a smirking Arash, and an expressionless Hashemi.

"Please, give me a moment with my daughter," he said to the gathered people in the room. Hashemi ushered them out and then closed the doors behind them.

Mahram was alone with her father.

"Papa, what is going on? These people, they've hurt me."

"They have not hurt you. They have helped me. Yes, there has been a level of discomfort, but it has been necessary."

"But Papa, why? You could have just asked me to come. Why this?"

Basar Ammar smiled at her. "You remind me so much of her…your mother. My condolences on her passing. I was not able to make the funeral. The war and its aftermath – you understand? It still continues, despite our best efforts."

Mahram did not answer. An awkward silence grew.

"There is politics at play," he said, walking toward the wingback chairs. He indicated she should join him. She did so obediently and sat.

"I was afraid for your safety, so I acted."

"My safety? I don't understand? What do I have to do with this?"

"In time I will explain all."

Another silence fell between them.

"Time goes so fast. You are a grown woman now and nearly ready for marriage. You are so beautiful, just like your mother. There is a young man I'd like to introduce you to. He comes from a good Saudi family…"

"What?" Mahram exclaimed.

"This young man, he is wonderful…"

"I'm not going to be traded like some cloth. Some cattle!"

"Come now, Mahram, stop this. I'm not trading you. I'm concerned for your future. It is a father's duty to look after his children."

"Stop right there!" Mahram said in English. Her father's eyes hardened.

"I have been kidnapped and abused. I have been held against my will! I have been slapped and tied up! I will not be treated like this any longer! Tell those people to leave immediately, or better still, have them arrested for their crimes!"

Her father sighed and looked at her sternly.

"We do not have time for this now, Mahram. I will explain in more detail later, but suffice to say you were never in any danger from them."

Mahram got up, fury etched into her eyes. "Why did you do this?

"Sit down," Basar said sternly.

Mahram remained standing.

Basar rose too. "You have been in the West too long!"

Mahram glared at him. "What do you care. One visit in ten years!"

His expression took on one of patience.

"I'm not prepared for you to wander from your faith and your culture. I'm not prepared to look the other way. If you bring dishonor to me you will pay with your life," he said softly.

She felt real fear rising in her heart now – did he know about her conversion?

The words came as a blow to Mahram and the lack of emotion in them all the more menacing. Mahram struggled to stop herself from physically attacking her father.

"Honor, you speak of honor?" she shouted. He simply stared at her for several seconds.

"You have been away for too long and have been poisoned by Western thinking," he said.

Mahram laughed derisively.

Now anger flared in Basar's eyes and he made as if to slap her. She flinched, expecting the blow to land on her face.

"Don't you dare laugh at me! If you bring dishonor on this family, you will leave me with no choice! This is not a perverted country like the USA where a woman can do whatever she feels. Here we have standards!"

Mahram stared at her father defiantly, her chest rising and falling with bottled rage.

He turned away and took a few steps toward his desk, speaking over his shoulder, "In less than an hour you will meet a man called Jack Hunter from the FBI. In that meeting you will tell this man that you were kidnapped and abused. You will say that you want to come home and be with your family, with your father. If he offers to take you back to the USA, you will refuse."

"And what if I don't?" Mahram said.

Her father turned, glaring at her. "Then many people will die, including him, and probably you. I will have no power to protect you then."

"Why? Why me? I've nothing to do with these people?"

Basar's expression was incredulous. "I'm not used to explaining my decisions, but since you ask, they get what they want from me and I get what I want from them," he said.

She searched his eyes and shook her head.

"Tell me honestly, Mahram. If I had told you to come home to get married; would you have listened to me?"

"I'm an adult who can make her own decisions."

"You are a young woman who will be looked after by her father."

"Looked after? I have no interest in becoming someone's trophy wife! You have never shown an interest in me. Why now?"

Basar sighed.

"You clearly do not understand Islam or Libyan culture anymore. Neither do you understand what is happening here. In time you will thank me."

"No! I will not!"

Mahram made as if to leave. Basar sighed again. "Mahram, sit!"

She continued to stand.

"Please," he said softly.

Mahram's eye's narrowed, but she sat down again.

Basar sighed again, a look of exasperation on his face.

"I received a visit from an influential member of the house of Saud. He offered me a deal I could not refuse. In other words, pressure was brought to bear on me. Your safety was part of the bargain. Do you understand what I'm saying to you?"

"No, I don't. Speak plainly," Mahram said evenly. Basar scowled at her tone.

"You should know enough about Arabic culture that threats are made obliquely. In not so many words they questioned my loyalty as a Muslim. They said I could help to fight the Zionist entity. They were aware of you. They said they could bring you home safely from the Infidel and give you a sparkling future if I would agree to allow them to use the opportunity…to move funds."

Mahram could see he was struggling with his emotions. His face a stony mask.

"This…idea is a way to move money for the struggle in Palestine without the Americans or Israel suspecting it. I have no idea of the details, but they made it clear that if I did not agree, it would show I wasn't loyal and then they would not be able to guarantee your safety from the reactionary elements within their ranks. The alternative would be to ensure you lead a life of privilege and protection. Is that plain enough for you?"

"And you agreed to this? Why did you not go to the authorities and tell them?"

Basar shook his head and chuckled ironically.

"Mahram, Mahram. Truly? You don't understand. Tripoli and Libya are not the same as you remember. The government is under Salafist control. These people…are the authorities. The Saudis and Turkey are in complete control here. The government is a puppet government for Western eyes. I'm a good Muslim and I do support the Palestinian cause. Believe it or not, I also wish the best for your future."

Mahram could feel the pin prick of tears behind her eyes.

"Please, just do as I say and when this all blows over and they have their money, then things may be different. Can you do that for me, please?" he said and reached out to touch her hand. "Please my little Mahram. Trust me one last time."

Mahram bit down hard on a rising tide of anger. She sighed heavily and drew her hand across her eyes. She did not trust her father at all. A great sadness fell on her heart. She knew, or at least suspected, that she was being used, but really what choice did she have? What psychopath would kidnap his own daughter? He was either desperate, or he was mad.

"Okay," she said, "I'll agree to go along with this charade with this Jack Hunter. But I will not be traded like some cattle by you. I'd rather die."

Mahram could see her father was struggling to suppress his own anger.

"One step at a time, Mahram. Let us save our lives first."

Her father reached out and clasped her hands. He looked at her with a micro-engineered smile on his face. She could see the stone in his eyes. This obsession with Islam had caused the divorce between him and her mother. He was not about to change; she knew that.

"One last thing. I will not travel with either Fairuza or Arash. They have physically hurt me and threatened me."

Basar signed again. "Okay, no Arash in the car, but Fairuza must be there because you are woman. Arash will have to be there when the exchange happens with Jack Hunter. We need a credible baddie."

"I cannot believe I'm doing this!" Mahram said.

"Inshallah all will be well when the dust settles. Come, let us go," her father said, followed by a quick smile.

He led the way to the door and grasped the handles. "I'm sorry our first meeting had to be like this after so many years," he said before he flung the doors wide.

Mahram swept through, ignoring Arash, who had remained in the passage with his submachine gun.

***

Gideon knew he was in trouble the moment he saw the SUV making its way back up the quiet street. The last thing he could afford now was to be picked up and jailed for some made up infringement.

What was he to say about his meeting with Hunter if he was picked up and taken into custody? He crossed the street into one of the many narrow laneways that wound their way through the old town.

The SUV could not follow him. This would force them to come after him on foot. He had known that phoning Hunter and giving him the thumb drive would be dangerous, but nothing ventured nothing gained. Just before Gideon entered the first twist in the laneway that took him out of their direct line of sight, he risked a glance back over his shoulder. The SUV was stationary and three men were piling from the car, one pointing in his direction.

"Stop!" one of them shouted in Arabic.

"Not on your life, buddy," Gideon said under his breath.

He sprinted down the cobbled lane, hearing the pounding of feet behind him. Up ahead was an intersecting laneway; he ran to the right.

"Shit!" Gideon said, as he entered a quiet courtyard surrounded by three story apartments on all sides. Three closed doors faced him; one to the left, one in the center and one to the right.

The echoes of pounding feet behind him grew louder. He tried the door in the center. Locked. The one to the left. Locked. Then the one on the right. It opened. He stepped inside the quiet home and closed the door, then made his way silently up a mosaic tiled stairway. He could hear a woman singing to herself in a room to his left. He walked past the doorway.

"Faizal, is that you?" Gideon heard her say.

Gideon ran up the next flight of steps.

"Faizal?" the woman's voice held a question mark.

Rooms on three sides. He could hear footsteps in the courtyard below.

"See anything?" Came a man's voice.

"Just three closed doors," a younger, more uncertain man's voice answered.

"Well, try them you cretin!" ordered another more imposing voice.

Gideon did not wait. He moved into the room at the top of the stairs. It was a bedroom and held a balcony covered with gauzy white curtains that looked out onto a terracotta tiled roof. He stepped through the doorway and noticed a small boy of about five, sitting on his bed with a small plastic soldier in his hands, gazing at him with big frightened eyes.

Gideon smiled at him.

"Faizal answer me when your mother calls you!" said the woman from downstairs. Gideon knew he only had moments.

He lifted his finger in the universal gesture for silence and placed it on his lips. He walked over to the curtains, shoved them aside and was greeted with a locked pair of French doors. He heard a loud knock on the front door below him. Fortunately, there was a key in the lock. He turned it and stepped out onto the balcony.

"Mother! Mother! There's a man in my room!" the boy screamed.

Gideon heard quick footsteps ascending the stairs as he swung himself over the balcony and dropped about three feet to the terracotta roof below. His right foot went straight through the tiles, but the left held. Above him a woman screamed.

"Thief!"

Gideon extracted his right foot and ran as quickly as he could down the spine of the roof. Behind him another voice, this time a man's, "He's on the roof!"

"Follow him!" bellowed a deeper voice.

Gideon dodged to his left onto another roof running perpendicular to the one he had been on, and was greeted by a gap created by the laneway below. He had no time to think. He vaulted the gap and landed squarely on the roof on the other side with a loud thud. Tiles cracked underfoot, but fortunately the roof held.

"Over there!" shouted a man's voice from below and to his left. "I saw him up ahead and on the roof."

Gideon raced across the terracotta tiles in front of him, vaulted over a low retaining wall and found himself on a flat section of concrete with lines of washing waving in the breeze. He stopped to catch his breath and listened. Below him he could hear pounding footsteps and men calling each other, searching for him. They would be up on the roofs soon and then he'd be done for. He had to get down. Behind he heard a loud thump as a man jumped the laneway, just has he had moments ago, and landed on the roof tiles. Gideon searched his immediate surroundings. His eyes fell on a heavy old galvanized bucket. He snatched it up and waited on the far side of an outhouse. Below and all around him searching calls echoed. The circle was closing.

He heard his pursuer vault the small wall and land with a thud in the courtyard. The pursuer's view was obscured by the waving lines of linen. He blundered through, breathing heavily. As he emerged, Gideon darted forward from his hiding place, swung the bucket in a full arc and hit him as hard as he could on the back of his neck and head. The man reeled forward and landed face first on the cement with a grunt.

Gideon breathed hard, placed the bucket down quietly and kneeled over the man, hoping he'd not killed him.

He felt for and found a fluttering pulse on the man's neck. Good. He turned and quickly made his way back to the outhouse, it contained stairs leading down to the lane below, which he took two at a time. Now he could hear voices calling each other from above. He took a quick glance up and down the laneway and searched the rim of the roofs above him, found no observers, then darted from the shadowy doorway into an adjoining laneway covered with Roman archways. Walking fast, he entered a major arterial laneway, filled with store fronts, hawkers and shoppers.

He continued on up to the busy main road and then filtered his way southeast through back streets carefully, finally stopping at a bustling café. He took a seat at the back of the cool, dark room and ordered some coffee and a falafel. The footpaths were thick with lunchtime patrons after the call to prayer.

He called Sara.

"David here. I'm gonna need a burka that can fit me."

Sara laughed. "Are you being serious?" she said.

He gave her the abbreviated version of what had just happened.

"Never a dull moment around you. I'll see what I can do," she said and rang off.

Gideon sent the video he had of the cars arriving outside Basar's home to Hunter, with a message:

*Check their plates to see who they belong to, or I'm going to send it to my crew to do for you.*

# Chapter 11

Hunter was driven the six city blocks to the Northern Oil Company HQ by a military officer from the United Nations Building. Once there, he was made to wait in the lobby for five minutes until Basar Ammar came downstairs to personally greet him.

"Thank you so much for your presence, Agent Hunter. It's so very reassuring," Basar said smoothly in accented English.

Basar's smile was tight. Nerves? The men shook hands.

"Come, the call will be to my cell phone. Let us go to my office," he said, then turned and led the way, not waiting for Hunter to respond.

Hunter followed.

Once in the elevator, Basar Ammar turned to Hunter.

"I'm surprised you're alone, Agent Hunter. I thought you policemen hunted in packs?"

Hunter smiled sardonically. "I have no legal authority here, except that granted to me by international law. I'm simply here to take an American Citizen, who happens to be your daughter, into my custody," he said.

"I see," Basar said.

"You sound surprised," Hunter said, more of a statement than question.

Basar did not answer. The elevator stopped on the sixth floor and they walked to his suite of offices and entered it through a thick wooden door.

"Mr Ammar, in answer to your earlier question if I may—sadly it has been my duty to negotiate kidnapping releases more than once. Since you have already conveyed to the kidnappers that you are willing to pay the ransom and you do not want your own police force involved, the show or use of military or police force now will only serve to put your daughter's life in jeopardy."

Basar Ammar remained silent, regarding Hunter through hooded eyes.

Hunter continued, "They've given proof of life, now all we do is the exchange. Of course, we must not be naïve. We are not dealing with good or

132

honorable people. I'd suggest you let me handle the exchange because you yourself may become an extortion target if you put yourself in harm's way."

Basar's eyes narrowed. "That seems logical," he said.

"The exchange site we chose is a good one—out in the desert in flat country—it means nothing can hide, less chance for a mistake…on both sides. They come from one direction, we from the other. If they agree to it then we're ready to make the exchange."

"So, do I take some of my men with me, Agent Hunter?" Basar said with a purr to his voice that indicated to Hunter some sort of cultural sneer that he did not quite fathom.

"Yes, and preferably armed, but they stay with you a good distance away. Do you have the cash ready?"

Basar pointed to three very large black reinforced trunks on sturdy-looking wheels with an extender handle.

"It's all there," he said.

"May I take a look, sir?" Hunter said.

Basar frowned. "Yes, if you must. I would not put my only child's life in jeopardy for a few dollars." He walked to his desk and sat down, looking affronted.

Hunter ignored his affront. He lowered the trunks with some difficulty on their sides, opened them and then systematically flicked through the contents. He dug down into the wads of notes and unstacked them randomly from the left, the right, and the center. He flicked through each unstacked bundle noting that the wads of cash were made up of $100 bills equaling $20,000. He did a rough calculation and was satisfied.

"Did you pack these trunks yourself?"

Basar steepled his hands and looked down his hooked nose. "No, of course not. I had a staff member do it. Several of my staff in fact…and I had my personal secretary check the amount through a counting machine. Why?"

"It is important that you're absolutely confident that we're giving them what they've asked for and that no overzealous staff member has, of his own volition, slipped in, say, a dye bomb, or a tracking device, or paper."

Basar nodded, then said in a matter-of-fact voice, "I see your point. I thank you for your thoroughness, but in Libya that just would not happen. You see, if a staff member did that and my daughter died as a consequence, so would they."

Hunter regarded him for a moment with a faint smile, but steely eyes. "I see."

The call came on Basar's mobile, and was spoken in Arabic. It lasted for little longer than a minute. Hunter could not understand the exchange but it was frank and to the point, if not exactly polite. The tone could be understood in any language.

The call ended abruptly and Basar said "They have agreed to your location for the exchange."

\*\*\*

They traveled in convoy in three black Mercedes sedans. There was a guard with a submachine gun in his lap who sat next to the driver. Hunter and Basar sat in the back. The other two cars contained an armed driver and two further armed men. The drive through the center of the city out into the industrial zone surrounding Tripoli took roughly half an hour. They headed for a region called Tajoura, a flat, low desert scrubland on the outskirts of the industrial zone about a hundred hectors square, crisscrossed by dozens of hard-packed dirt roads and tracks. It could be approached from three different directions. The kidnappers would approach from the East, Hunter's entourage from the West. This arrangement was put in place so that the kidnappers could drive directly into the industrial zone after the exchange. The men traveled in silence; a palpable sense of tension building. Hunter looked back several times to ensure they weren't being followed.

"What are you checking for?" Basar said.

"Unwanted attention. The police. I have been followed on several occasions since my arrival. I assume by the local undercover police."

They arrived at their destination at dusk. The low scrub bush was no impediment to their vision and the setting sun made everything stand out in stark relief. As Hunter got out of the car with the other men, he felt for Gideon's thumb drive strapped to his forearm with medical adhesive tape. Still in place, he thought, looking around him. The other men were concentrating on a convoy of identical SUVs making their way through the Tajoura flats, the dust boiling out behind as they drove at speed toward them; a beautiful burnt gold in the gloaming light.

Hunter noted that Basar's armed guard had sensibly arrayed themselves behind their vehicles. The heavy trunks were decanted from the cars by the drivers and wheeled over to Hunter. Hunter indicated that two drivers should take a trunk each and follow him. Without a word, Hunter set off down the dirt road pulling a heavy trunk by the extended handle. Basar did not intervene.

He walked about 30 yards from the cars and looked back to see the men all staring at him. The two drivers deposited their trunks next to Hunter's and then walked back to the line of cars. Hunter brought his trunk around in an arc and as he did so let go of its handle suddenly, as if the wheels had been caught in a rut. Bending down to retrieve it, his body carefully placed between the men at his back and the trunk, he slipped his hand up his arm and pulled off the thumb drive. Then, within the same fluid motion, he lifted the heavy trunk back into an upright position, using both hands. He stood unflinching as the convoy neared him, but was relieved when they stopped about 20 yards away.

Two bull-necked men, another lighter built man, and a woman got out of the second vehicle. Hunter immediately recognized one of the men as Arash. The other man was so similar looking he had to be the twin. The brothers were armed with MP5 submachine guns and the woman, about 25, slim in build and very pretty, was dressed in a burka with a hijab that left her face uncovered. He recognized her as Mahram immediately. The lighter-built man with a wispy beard and sunglasses was not someone Hunter had seen before, but clearly of middle eastern appearance. Hunter noted the shadowy outline of another woman in the SUV that Mahram had just exited.

"Mahram?" Hunter called. "Yes," she said.

"I'm Agent Hunter of the FBI. I'm here to take you into safe custody in exchange for a ransom that your father will gladly pay. Please do everything you are instructed to do by your captors and do not make any sudden moves."

The men grinned and pushed her forward in front of them.

"You have the money?" Arash said in English.

Hunter gave him a sardonic look, "Yes, it's in the trunks."

"Good. Open them."

Hunter pushed the thumb drive between his index finger and thumb while he pushed the trunks over with his knee and then undid the clasps.

A faint evening breeze brought the smell of mesquite and dust. Arash pushed Mahram toward Hunter.

"Stand aside with the agent while we transfer the money," Arash said in English.

He gestured at Hunter and Mahram to stand in the brush, far enough for them not to be a threat, while Wispy Beard inspected the trunks full of money thoroughly. This took about three minutes.

"It's good," said the younger man, looking up at Arash.

"We good? You're satisfied we have met our end of the deal?" Hunter said.

Arash's lips curled into a sneer and he gestured with his weapon.

"Take the Cat Meat and go," he said.

Mahram's eyes burned with pure fury at Arash. He laughed at her.

"Go! Or have you become so fond of me you want to stay now?"

Hunter took her hand and slowly backed off into the road.

"Come Mahram. I'll take you to your father."

They turned together, Hunter still holding her hand.

"I can walk myself, thank you. I'm not a child," she said evenly.

"Just go with it, Mahram. There is method in what I'm doing," he said, his voice low.

Mahram glanced up at him, a confused look on her face. She felt the thumb drive in his hand.

"Take it," he said urgently. She took it.

Hunter glanced back over his shoulder. The men were backing away, all except Arash who lingered, keeping a close eye on them. Wispy Beard had taken the lead and was already back at the SUVs dragging two of the trunks behind him. Hunter's back itched. If bullets were going to fly, it would be now.

"Now buckle at the knees as if you're overwhelmed and allow me to prop you up," he whispered.

She did. Her acting was superb, not overdone. She even managed a few tears. Hunter suspected some of them might be real. Her father broke from his men and strode toward her.

"Wipe your face and slip the drive into your hijab," Hunter said quietly.

"What…?" she began.

"Not all is as it seems," he said.

She stopped, wiped her eyes and slipped the drive under her hijab. She pretended that the wiping of her face had slightly dislodged her hijab off center and adjusted it with her hands—she was doing the overwhelmed demure little woman quite well, thought Hunter suppressing a smile.

Basar arrived.

"Mahram, Mahram!"

Mahram turned and gave a little run into her father's arms. "Papa!" she said.

Now the waterworks started in earnest and Hunter could see real tears of frustration, rage, and fear wracking her slight frame as she sobbed. Her father hugged her, but he noted she did not hug him back. A look of profound sorrow flicked through Basar's eyes.

Hunter squeezed his shoulder in a friendly manner as he passed by.

Basar glanced up. "Thank you, Agent Hunter. My daughter is safe, that is the only thing that matters," he said.

Basar's guards got into the other car, while Mahram sat next to her father in the back seat and Hunter took the passenger seat next to the driver in the second car. The trip home was uneventful.

\*\*\*

55,000 feet above their heads, the unblinking eye of the CIA Predator drone took every detail into its electronic hard drive, then banked steeply to follow the SUVs as they made their way into the darkening city fringe. The motorcade split up as they entered the city. Alda Dibra sat in the CIA situation room in Langley Virginia, her green intelligent eyes taking it all in.

"Follow the SUV that has the money in it," she said to the drone pilot.

"Yes Ma'am," he said and banked the predator to follow the SUV holding the cash.

\*\*\*

Arriving home Mahram said, "I'm very tired. I wish to lie down now for a while and be alone."

"Of course, my child. I will send one of the ladies up to help you," Basar said.

Basar was very solicitous and almost courtly in the way he looked after his daughter's welfare, clicking his fingers at a servant to bring Mahram a sedative and some bed clothes and ordering a light supper for her from the bustling cook.

Hunter only accompanied the family as far as Basar's study, where he was made to cool his heels, but was given a refreshing lemon and rosewater drink while he waited. He was an old hand at the rituals and game playing in eastern cultures and so he spent his time admiring the paintings, pretending to look out of the window and surreptitiously scanning the desk for any useful information. One of the guards joined him in the room and sat on one of the beautiful calfskin settees; his presence like a dark thundercloud, lightning flickering in his eyes, as Hunter passed by the desk on the way to the paintings again.

"You have read 1001 Nights?" Basar said, as he glided into the room.

Hunter turned and observed the man. "Yes, I have actually. As a teen I read the book. It's considered a classic in the West."

"Good, yes, I know. One of my favorites. So much color and life," Basar said.

"But haram to the more conservative mullahs," Hunter replied, somewhat provocatively. Where did this man stand?

"Interpretations differ," Basar said evenly.

"Mahram, I'm sure, will be fine in time. She does not seem physically hurt, though I'm sure she has been emotionally traumatized," Hunter said.

"Yes, no doubt you're right. She will be safe here. She needs time alone with the women. That is how we do things in Libya," Basar said.

"When she is well, we would like to take a statement from her concerning the crime which was committed on US soil."

Hunter could see a vein rise in Basar's left temple.

"Is that entirely necessary, Agent? After all, you have it captured on CCTV camera? And all's well that ends well, no?"

"There are sure to be other pieces of information she has gathered and, with a skilled investigator, we may be able to piece things together. This is a crime that was committed on our soil and though Mahram is your daughter, she is also a US citizen. Naturally we have an interest in prosecuting it."

"You mean interrogating her. I don't think so."

"No, I mean asking her gentle questions that may help us capture these people. I'm sure you want justice to be served?"

Basar gave Hunter a long look. "I will ask Mahram tomorrow if she is willing to speak with you," he said.

Hunter smiled thinly and then put his glass down on the coffee table. "But of course. You have my number, please give me a call when it suits you."

Basar gestured with his hand to the guard. The guard rose.

"My man will accompany you to a car. Where is it you would like to be driven this evening?"

"The UN base will be fine. I have a room there."

Basar shook hands with Hunter.

"Thank you once again for your expertise," he said through his micro-engineered smile. "It would be customary in my culture for a man to reward someone who has done such a brave deed for his child, but I know you in the West do not accept such rewards. You pride yourselves on your professionalism."

Hunter smiled gently, this time, knowing these slight goads were meant to probe for weakness and deceit.

"Your thanks are enough, Mr Ammar. 'Till tomorrow, then," he said.

Hunter was escorted from the house to a waiting car and was back at the UN headquarters in under 15 minutes. Something surely was not right in this situation, he thought to himself as he handed over his passport and FBI badge to the guard at the gate…something is rotten in the state of, well, Libya in this case. Pretty sure Shakespeare's Hamlet had thought something similar. He snorted out loud, wondering if he would ever read another Shakespearean play again, or if it was his lot to die from a bleeding wound in some God forsaken hellhole like this one.

"Excuse me?" said the guard defensively.

"Oh, sorry buddy—just thinking about an issue I'm dealing with and a piece of Shakespeare made it into my mind. I was just snorting in derision at myself."

The guard eyed him menacingly with tired glassy blue eyes. "You sure you're feelin' okay?"

Hunter stared at the marine for a second and could not help the New York cop in himself from saying, "What? Now I'm mentally unstable because I quote Shakespeare to myself?"

The marine shook his head, stamped the passport, and handed it and his badge back.

"Lemme guess, New Yawk?" he said, with a faux Italian accent.

"Got it in one, Pal," Hunter said with a grin.

Hunter walked to his room and locked the door, then phoned Alda Dibra. Alda picked up after the third ring.

"Hunter here. Are we secure?"

"Yes," Alda replied.

"I know it's only been about an hour or so, but do you have any of the intel from the drone and Gideon's video?"

"Not yet from the drone; that's still being analyzed, but we do have something interesting from Gideon's recording. We managed to make out one of the vehicles' registration plates and the vehicle is registered to a shell company in the Maldives. We did a bit more digging and that company appears to be run and owned by the Russian GazNet oil company, and hey, waddya know, GazNet resumed oil exploration in the Zueitina region of Libya last year. So, clearly stealth and prudence in all of these measures and Iran and the Russians cooperating on anything is a heads up for us. The fact that it involves the Libyan Oil Minister and a kidnapping is more than just interesting garnish, I'm sure about that. It looks like our Israeli friends are onto something."

Hunter registered surprise. "That's sus for sure. The Russians? That's…seriously unexpected. So, what do you think? Gideon Dunbar's information has been helpful. I suggest we cooperate more fully with the Israelis."

"Mmm, yes," mused Alda. "Lemme think about it a bit while I tell you what else I found in Shittsville."

"Shoot," Hunter said, smiling sardonically at her black humor.

"Well, secondly the 30 mill that was ostensibly being used to pay for Mahram's release was sourced from a Panamanian shell company and moved via The Foreign and Commercial Arab Bank into Basar Ammar's account. Now you might say, so what, Basar would not be the first oil sheik to have an offshore account, right? Well, you'd be wrong. Clearly, we're supposed to think that Basar Ammarused his own money to pay for his daughter's release. However the shell company is an Islamic charity called "The Palestinian and Levant Orphan and Widows Fund." So Basar is a recipient of the fund that builds orphanages in Syria, to pay for a kidnapping? Give me a break."

"That sounds dubious," Hunter said.

"It gets worse. Our Israeli friends have made quite some headway in tracking dirty money used by the Iranian regime. We regularly update each other on our intel. That particular charity has come in for some scrutiny over the years. They do some good work, but we can't be sure all the money is being used for legitimate purposes. The Saudi Ambassador of Libya is the patron of the fund— Ambassador Al-Ali. He's a long standing Wahabi conservative and makes no secret of funding madrassa schools that churn out radicalized youth in the West. His son, Tariq Al-Ali is on a watch list in the UK for just such activities, funneling suspect funds to radicals. Both have lived in London since the start of the Libyan war. To make matters more complicated, the charity has its HQ in Istanbul, Turkey. The only thing the conservative Wahabis, Turks, Russians and Iranians have in common is their hatred of and opposition to Israel. I mean, for example, the Turks and the Russians back opposite sides in the civil war in Libya. The Turks might not have a direct involvement, but they'd surely know what's happening on their soil."

Hunter scratched his chin. "Okay so let me read that back to you and you tell me what the hell is going on. We have a Saudi sending money via a charity registered in Panama, whose HQ is in Turkey, to Basar Ammar's account to pay to his daughter's kidnappers who we know are an Iranian cell. At the same time, we have the Russian GazNet company in the Libyan Desert acting as facilitator to the kidnapping of the Oil Minister's daughter. Have I got that straight?"

Hunter heard Alda's humorless chuckle through the airwaves.

"I think our young friend Gideon, has just turned over a hornet's nest," she said.

"Whatever the hell it is, it doesn't sound good and we've effectively been made fools of. They are literally using me as a facilitator to potentially fund terror," Hunter said.

"You bet. It's a very sophisticated and clever way to launder money," she said. There was a silence on the line for about ten seconds. Hunter knew Alda's nimble mind was racing through the possibilities, trying to piece it all together, so he did not interrupt her thought process.

"Okay, here're my thoughts," she said finally. "Libya is a complete and utter fuck-up for us since the Clinton debacle in Benghazi, so this has to be a False Flag op. As soon as we tell Gideon anything, he'll tell his bosses. He'll be pressing for intel from you soon, based on what he's given you, or he'll start to think we're holding out on him. My gut feel is we play it straight with the Israelis. We tell them what we've got, but we insist on working through Gideon on this one. That way we retain some control, because he's also an American, but he works with us as an Israeli asset. Mossad are likely to agree, because they'll also want deniability, or to pretend ignorance if he's captured or killed. So, a False Flag operation for both sides if the worst should happen. We help him with information only. Either he succeeds and finds something out that's interesting, or he fails and we're in the clear and the Israelis can deal with the denial mess. The truth is, we've achieved our objective. We've got Mahram back. This looks to all intents like Israel's problem, with all its avowed enemies circling around the same thing. I'll bet my government pension that the money will be for some sort of weapon."

Hunter did not like what he was hearing. "It sounds like Gideon will more or less be on his own if things go bad. Both sides denying any involvement,"

"It can't be helped. It's not our mess. Once we get Mahram back to the States, our involvement becomes information only and keeping tabs on our enemies…and friends, to see what they're up to. We don't want to be dragged into another quagmire in the Middle East if we can help it."

"Timing?" Hunter said.

"As soon as possible with Gideon. I'll handle the liaison with the Israelis," Alda said, then rang off.

Hunter rasped his hand against the side of his face and sighed deeply. He somehow always felt dirty after dealing with spooks—even the good ones.

# Chapter 12

Sara giggled like a schoolgirl when Gideon slipped the Burka robe over his head. They were standing in the spare room in Sara's apartment.

Sara's grandmother was dozing in front of the TV in the living room, they could hear her gentle snores through the open doorway.

The burka caught on his belt and she gently lowered the hem. Gideon adjusted the mirror in front of him, turning this way and that, pretending to admire himself.

"Do I look fat in this?" he said, grinning. Sara giggled again. "Stunning," she said.

"Pass me my make-up bag, would you?"

Sara snorted with laughter.

"Stop, you're going to wake up Granny and if she comes in and sees me like this, she'll probably call the police," Gideon said mock seriously.

Sara made to pass the make-up bag to Gideon.

"Just kidding. But this burka will do nicely, no?"

Sara shook her head. "You're a little too comfortable in that burka, David. You have me worried."

"I do it for a living," he said, and chuckled.

"Now you have me really worried. Is there something you want to tell me?"

He looked at her quizzically, a smile still playing around his lips. "I'm a soldier in the Duvdevan. We, on occasion, use disguise as a method of infiltration."

She nodded. "Okay, now I've heard it all. You mean soldiers getting dressed up as women?"

"Yes. Think how counter-cultural that is in a Muslim setting. Your mind wants to reject the idea of a man in woman's clothing simply because it is not something you would expect. You'd be surprised how effective preconceptions are in under-cover work."

Sara smiled, with a look of skepticism on her face.

"Here, let me prove it to you. Pass me the headpiece of the burka; the veil part that covers the face."

"You mean the niqab?" Sara asked, picking it up from the bed.

"Yes, this is something I will need help with. I'm not very good at putting this on straight and pinning it down."

"Sit," she said, indicating the bed. Gideon did so obediently and she deftly put on Gideon's niqab. Sara's clever slim hands wound the cloth around Gideon's head and clipped the folds into place, sending secret little shockwaves of pleasure through him every time her hand accidently brushed his skin. Only his eyes were revealed now.

"There," she said, and smoothed the folds out around his cheeks. She giggled again. Gideon rose and looked in the mirror. He burst into laughter and so did Sara.

"Well, clearly she needs a bit of hormone therapy," Sara said.

Gideon smiled. "Yes, I'm a bit large for a woman, but still, if I was moving and there wasn't anyone to compare me to for perspective with this full veil..."

Sara's face grew serious. "Yes, it probably would work. Sadly, you do see many more women on the streets of Tripoli these days with a niqab. They've become much more common since the Arab Spring. I need to wear it myself from time to time when the holy men come to the hospital."

Sara's grandmother called from the lounge. She wanted to go to bed.

"I'll put her to bed now," Sara said, and left the room.

Gideon slowly removed the niqab and burka.

Just then his cell phone buzzed. He picked it up from the bed and immediately recognized Hunter's number.

"Hunter, speak to me," he said.

Sara entered the room again and saw Gideon on the phone. She gestured as if to leave and he shook his head, pulling her gently by the hand and indicating she should sit on the bed next to him. She did not resist, and his hand lingered for just a little longer than necessary before he let go.

His expression was serious and she saw his face get progressively paler as he listened and occasionally asked a quick penetrating question. The call lasted for about three minutes, all the while a warm glow spread from her stomach up to her neck. Sara desperately hoped she was not blushing. She got up abruptly and left the room, heading to the kitchen to make coffee. When she put the kettle on, she noticed her hands shaking.

"What is this?" she thought to herself. "Don't be a fool."

Gideon came into the small kitchen a few minutes later. He looked tired. Sara handed him a cup of coffee.

"Thanks," he said, smiling at her. She rested against the kitchen bench, sipping her coffee.

"That was Hunter, the FBI agent I told you about. He was handling the ransom payment. He got some intel for me. Long story short, there now seems to be some Russian involvement, which is making everyone super suspicious. I'm going to have to follow up on that lead. Hunter made contact with Mahram, and managed to slip her one of the thumb-drives the boys gave me, but of course she still doesn't know what to do with it. He also knows which room in the house she's located in, a great advantage to us."

"I see. Why are you telling me this? I'm just a sayan," she said.

Gideon glanced down, smiling, then took a step closer to her.

"Well, three reasons. Firstly Sara, I trust you. Second, I want you to give the boys a message from me to see if we can make contact with Mahram using the drone."

She smiled back at him. He noticed her pupils were very dilated and her eyes dark, even though the florescent kitchen light shone brightly down upon them.

"And the third reason, David?" she asked, looking up at him.

He took a step closer still and reached for her hand. She did not pull away.

"I have come to really like and admire you, Sara. I don't want to bring trouble on you, and I want to make sure you and your Bubbeh remain safe," he said in Hebrew.

She smiled again, holding his gaze.

"If I'm not back in three days, then you must take Bubbeh and leave. Get out of the city and if you or the boys cannot make contact with me, then you must all leave Libya. That can mean only two things, I'm either dead or incapacitated, or captured. If they capture me then it's only a matter of time before they extract information."

"That's three things," she said, lifting herself from the counter gently and bringing herself closer to him still.

Gideon laughed quietly, then he put his arms around her and drew her to him and kissed her deeply. She put her arms around his neck and kissed him back.

"I'm going to call Dani Gilad now. He's my commanding officer. This is not going to be a friendly call, because I've agreed to do something for the Americans without his permission. I should probably do it in private," Gideon said.

"What have you agreed to do?" Sara said, concern creasing her brow.

"I'm going to check out the Russian connection in this whole thing. A Russian company called GazNet owns a property out near Es Sidr. I'm going to snoop around there a bit and see if I can find anything."

They parted and Gideon gave Sara's hands a last squeeze.

"It's time to prepare for tomorrow. I'll see to that now while you talk with Dani," Sara said and smiled up at him. He smiled back.

Gideon's heart skipped a beat. She was so beautiful. He sighed deeply and then left the kitchen to make his call.

# Chapter 13

After the usual thorough search of his person, Dani Gilad walked up the driveway of the Prime Minister's official residence in Jerusalem. If he was honest with himself, he was feeling pretty nervous. Meeting with the PM, the head of Mossad, or his own General was nerve-wracking stuff, but all three at the same time was rather overwhelming. After his brief but sharp talk with Gideon last night, he was even more edgy. He had no doubt that he'd been called to this meeting because of that conversation.

Dani was ushered through the Italian archways of the residence into its cool interior, past the central staircase and out onto the central patio. There was a standing gas heater to warm them on a sunny but cold winter's day and, Dani realized, they were outside because the General and the head of the Mossad were smoking. The PM's wife was notoriously anti-smoking. They were drinking coffee and a small smorgasbord of sandwiches and sweets had been placed on the central table. Several used cups of coffee were on the table and, Dani noticed, there were at least five cigarette butts in the ashtray at the General's side. The men stood when Dani arrived and shook his hand. Dani felt like he'd just entered a room in which he'd interrupted an argument. The PM smiled his crooked smile that never seemed to quite make it to his watchful eyes and indicated that Dani should sit.

"You know the General. This is Yossi, the director of Mossad. Yossi, Dani Gilad serves as Captain in Unit 217, my old unit," the PM said proudly.

Dani nodded at the men. The PM indicated to the butler that he should pour more coffee. The butler did so and then left, closing the patio door behind him. Yossi's eyes communicated all the warmth of a cobras' gaze, thought Dani.

"So, we're here about the news coming out of Libya," said the PM. "The General, Yossi and I have been discussing developments."

A moment of silence fell on the group as all eyes turned to Dani. He nodded and took a sip of his coffee to cover his nerves.

"What are your thoughts, Dani?" the PM said.

Dani placed his small coffee cup down gently and cleared his throat.

"The involvement of so many different nations in a single event would seem to suggest something big. Having Russian and Quds collaboration with possible tacit knowledge by Ankara of whatever this is, on Libyan soil, and Saudi money sponsoring, would suggest something malignant at best," Dani said.

The PM nodded. "Yes, agreed. Any idea, even remotely, what this thing might be?"

"Gideon Dunbar told me that the CIA supplied him with a Geiger counter and some locator beacons without our knowledge. That would seem to suggest at least what our American friends think."

Yossi cleared his throat. "This Gideon Dunbar, he is Aish Machal, a foreign volunteer in the IDF?"

"Yes," Dani said shortly.

"I would still like to know why I did not sign off on this mission in Libya? Dani's report was the first I heard about it?"

The PM put up his hand and smiled. "Shalom, gentlemen, please. I told you already, Yossi, I knew about it. Things unfolded quickly and you were very much caught up on the important matters to our north. I didn't want this to act as a distraction for you. You've seen the video; Gideon took the initiative and I let him run with it. It seemed like a small thing at the time. You had enough on your plate already."

Dani took another sip of coffee and glanced at the General. He stared back and took a draw on his cigarette. The PM turned his gaze back on to Dani.

"I understand, Dani, that when you told Gideon to hold his horses, he said we did not have time and disobeyed a direct command?" the PM said.

"That's correct," Dani said evenly and sighed.

"You trust this little shit?" Yossi interrupted.

"Yes, I do. He's been on many missions and displayed exemplary conduct and courage under fire."

Dani knew that in Israel that still stood for something. They faced death on a daily basis.

"So, this mission, if you can call it that, has become a high priority for Mossad. You tell that little shit that the command of the mission has been transferred to Mossad and he's now officially working for us. If he disobeys my commands that will be regarded as an act of insubordination, and if he shares

148

intelligence in an unauthorized manner with the Americans again—an act of treason. His new contact is called 'Rachel'," Yossi said, his eyes carrying the unblinking message of complete authority.

Dani looked at the General. The General nodded slightly. Then he looked at the PM. The PM smiled.

"This is to be a joint mission between Mossad and Aman, with Mossad leading. Dani, you are to liaise with the Mossad liaison, code name 'Rachel'," the Prime Minister said. "I want a full daily briefing on what is going on here. I want that from you, Dani. Yossi, do you understand? Both of you?"

Yossi nodded. Dani could see he was fuming.

"I'll get his contact details to you. How do I contact Rachel?" Dani said to Yossi.

"We have your and Gideon's contact details already. But please give him a call and let him know the new reality," Yossi said more evenly.

There was another silence.

"In his defense, it was Gideon's intel and the work he did through the FBI Agent Hunter that uncovered the Russian connection. Plus, his original initiative uncovered this mess in the first place. So far, he hasn't put a foot wrong…well almost. The Libyan intelligence know that Hunter made contact with someone. They're not sure who that someone is though."

"Yes, I know. I read the report, thanks, and I got a surprise call from the CIA last night," Yossi said, his eyes starting to take on a snake-like quality.

"Yossi, Shalom. I authorized the use of Mossad back office for this mission. Cool it. Now!" The PM said sharply.

Yossi swallowed hard. He was clearly not happy.

"We're all on the same side here," the PM said more gently. "The young man has done well…so far. The problem is the Americans are clearly using him for their own intel too. Very convenient if he gets caught; a neat False Flag operation."

No one said anything.

"I'm a little worried he's in over his head. So, any intelligence he obtains now goes through Yossi's Department for analysis, Dani," the PM continued. "He is forbidden to give anything to the Americans directly himself, or through a third party without permission. We decide if the Americans get it or not. Also, I think two can play the false flag game—he is an American citizen, yes?"

Dani nodded, his heart sinking.

"Sorry to say, but if he gets captured or killed, he's not one of ours. The fact that he's an American gets leaked. We have a Sayaret Matkal team to do a reconnaissance on the facilities and a Kidon team to be ready to clean up loose ends if he's captured. We'll need to…clean up a few loose ends, you understand. Including the sayan, Sara. It cannot lead back to us."

Dani's eyes once again flicked to the general, who nodded his head.

The PM stood; all the other men stood too. He extended his hand to Dani and smiled his crooked smile again.

"When you speak to Gideon, please extend him my best wishes and tell him that I'm praying for his safety. He has an auspicious name. Let's hope he can emulate the feats of his namesake."

Dani smiled and thanked the PM, "I'll call him as soon as I get back to my office."

"Let my people know when you've contacted him," Yossi said, his eyes gave no warmth, nor did he extend his hand to Dani. Dani nodded and said nothing, then extended his hand to the General, who shook it once.

As Dani walked back down the long curving drive to his car, he wondered how much of Yossi's anger was embarrassment at having missed this intelligence coup and how much of it was the PM enjoying putting Yossi in his place. Chess, with live pieces, he thought. He felt the chill wind on his neck and shivered involuntarily.

* * *

"You left me no choice, Gideon!" Dani said.

Gideon was incandescent with rage. He looked to his left. Ezat was singing along to a Coptic pop song softly as they drove. The call to Dani the day before had not gone well and, the truth be told, he was dreading this follow up call. Dani had basically told him to hold it and he had told Dani to get lost.

"Ezat, stop the truck please."

Ezat obliged and pulled off the Ghashir road to As Sidr port. It was flat desert country and there was not another vehicle in sight as Gideon got out; they were heading into rebel country. Es Sidr was a small unremarkable port city about 100 miles east of Tripoli and 50 miles from their target, the Zueitina region, where GazNet had their drilling facility. Its only importance was that it was the port where most of Libya's oil was stored, and from which most of it was shipped out to the rest of the world.

Gideon got out of the truck and stomped out into the desert. Once out of earshot he let rip.

"Gideon, don't piss me off, kiddo!" Dani interrupted him mid-stream. "Your insubordination is what has got us into trouble!"

"What part of we don't have time to fuck around, don't you people understand?" Gideon spat back. "I had to make a decision. I had to take intel from the Americans. I had no choice. Something big is going down and if we miss the boat, that's it!"

"Gideon," Dani purred. "Raise your voice to me again and I'm going to court martial you when you get back for insubordination and disobeying a direct command, do you understand?"

Gideon swallowed hard. Soldiering was his life. There was silence between the two men for a few heartbeats.

"Look, I did my best to give you cover. Right now, you've still got a green light, but if the people now in charge give you an order, you better obey it! They're people who don't take bullshit…from anyone, okay? I like you enough to warn you. Do not fuck with these people, Gideon!"

Gideon drew a breath.

"Let me finish!" Dani said. "Your new contact is 'Rachel'. When you speak to her, tell her everything. And I mean everything, okay?"

Gideon sighed. "Okay, thank you, Dani. By the way, I'm paying Ezat to take me to Es Sidr and then on to Zueitina to check out GazNet. Does this mean that the Organization is paying now?"

Gideon meant Mossad.

"Mention it to the Organization when you get the call. And the Boss says Godspeed and wishes you well by the way."

"Well, that's something at least. What about our Guy? Does he approve?"

Dani knew he meant their general. "Honest truth, I don't know. He didn't say anything, just smoked and nodded. If my signals weren't messed up, I'd say he got beaten up by the other guy quite badly."

"Okay thanks. Good to know how the land lies," Gideon answered.

"One more thing—a cleaning crew is coming in to tie up any loose ends if that becomes necessary. So, be very careful, okay? And don't you become a loose end, if you get my drift." Dani hung up.

Dani's last words sent a chill through Gideon's heart. If he was honest, he'd expected a little more understanding.

Ezat saw Gideon's face as he walked back toward the car and decided not to ask what was going on. Sometimes it was better not to know.

"So, we still going to Es Sidr?" Ezat said, instead.

Gideon smiled at Ezat's round face, trying his best not to show his concern.

"Yes, my friend, for the moment. I think it is only fair to let you know that this journey has just become a lot more dangerous than I first thought. You still up for it?"

Ezat smiled. "Depends on the pay," he said.

"I'll double it."

Ezat pulled a face. "Triple it and I'm all in."

Gideon raised his eyebrows and then chuckled. "Okay sure," he extended his hand to Ezat and they shook.

"Let's go. Do you have your weapon with you?"

"Always. In the glove box, as before," Ezat said, and grinned.

Gideon open the glove box and took out the .45 Star. "It's not much, but it'll do for now."

"Can you keep a secret, Dawit?" Ezat said.

"Sure, and call me Gideon. I think you know I'm not a journalist."

Ezat grinned again from ear to ear. "Come, let me show you something that will put a smile back on your face. You know I'm a smuggler, but I'm God's smuggler. I only smuggle things that are good to protect my people, you understand?"

Gideon could not help smiling. "I feel sure you're going to show me something I would be safer not knowing about."

Ezat got out of the truck and went around to the back and got in under the canopy, kicking the dirty straw and dung to one side. Then he withdrew a screwdriver from his pocket and pushed it between a section of the cab wall and the utility section floor and lifted. Part of the corrugated floor came away to reveal a wooden box.

"This box looks like it is a petrol tank from the underside of the truck," Ezat explained proudly.

He opened the lid to reveal three greasy AK 47s, several hundred rounds of .762 ammunition, and a few grenades. Gideon whistled. He had a smile on his face.

"See, I told you," Ezat said exuberantly.

"This is for the Copts near the border of Egypt. ISIS is very busy there. I take these weapons to them from time to time so they can protect their families. These ones were taken from one of the factions after they came too close to our territory."

"Are these loaded?" Gideon asked.

"Locked and loaded, as you Americans like to say," Ezat said in a bad rendition of an American accent.

Gideon laughed. "So, you know I'm American? Is my British accent that bad?"

Ezat chuckled. "Yes, it's quite bad, I think, but that's because I have spoken to many Americans in the past. You see, when you speak English, your English accent is quite good, but when you speak Arabic, you can hear that you are American. You speak Arabic like an American. It's strange that way."

Gideon grinned. "That actually makes more sense than you realize. May I?" he said, indicating the weapon stash.

"Sure, sure of course," Ezat said.

Gideon picked up one of the weapons, checked the safety and then checked the magazine. It was indeed loaded and almost brand new by the look of it. A good AK, made in the Czech Republic. Not all AKs were of the same quality.

Gideon checked the other weapons and then examined the hand grenades. They were Russian grenades—very effective ordinance.

"For now, if we get into trouble, we stick with my cover. I'm Dawit from the SABC, covering stories from Benghazi; you are my guide. If the shit hits the fan, we break out these weapons and fight for our lives. Okay?"

"Good my friend. I feel good about it," Ezat said, cheerfully.

"Yeah, me too. All of a sudden, I feel much better," Gideon said.

Ezat squinted at the noonday sun. "It's hot. I have some beer. You want one?" Ezat said.

"Sure. Why not," Gideon said and grinned. "But just one. I've got to be able to shoot straight if that's needed."

They arrived at 2 pm and found a fly-blown motel on the outskirts of the city. This would be their base for a few days. Gideon paid cash. He did some nosing around and found the GazNet logistics warehouse not too far from where they were. He did a quick reconnoiter of the facility on foot, while Ezat bought some supplies, including work overalls and hard hats, so they could blend in with the working men on the dock, or drilling site if necessary. As he walked, he received a call from 'Rachel.' To his surprise they only spoke for a few minutes. She wanted to know what he was planning to do next. He told her.

All she said was, "Good, if you find any useful intel send it through to this number, or give me a call." It was interesting that the conversation was held in English. 'Rachel' had a slight American accent.

The GazNet warehouse was more of a complex of buildings, consisting of two parallel warehouses and an adjacently positioned office block. All were surrounded by a new chain-link fence, topped by barbed wire. It stood on the extreme outskirts of the city, with open lots of desert behind it, neatly flattened to receive a building, but not yet built upon. The ubiquitous gorse bush grew along the sides of the roads and peppered the surrounding desert. Several trees had been planted between the two warehouses and in adjoining lots for some shade. It was the end of the working day and there was a steady stream of vehicles and foot traffic along the dusty roads. Gideon noted that there were armed guards near the entrance of the GazNet property and men were presenting their Identity Cards on lanyards around their necks to be scanned as they left the facility. Gideon skirted the facility, walking down its side and then on toward the back where it grew markedly quieter. There was a security camera fixed to the side of the warehouse nearest him and one on the back of the building. Pretty tight security for a warehouse facility that ostensibly only moved food and heavy drilling gear.

He moved out into the adjacent empty lot and, for the sake of the camera, loosened his trousers and peed on the nearest gorse bush. Then, looking around, he kicked a hole under the gorse bush and pulled down his trousers completely for the sake of the watching camera and squatted, shuffling behind the bush, as if taking a dump. In this position he removed a rectangular black homing beacon from his pants pocket, about the size of a man's hand, with a small antenna attached. He pulled up the antenna, pushed the 'on' button and covered the beacon with sand in the heart of the bush. From the other pocket he took out a similar looking bright yellow object, but this one had a digital screen and dial. He turned it on and the dial flicked to life, reading the radiation level around him. It was in the normal range.

He made a show of pulling up his under clothes and pants and redoing his belt. Once done, he moved along to the next warehouse, one lot down. It looked identical to the target warehouse complex, but this one was all but deserted, with

154

only a few straggling workers focused on finishing up for the night and leaving. This warehouse stored concrete-based prefabricated products such as paving blocks and the like. Not much in the way of security at all. You can't run very fast with concrete blocks, Gideon thought to himself. With its similarity to the target warehouse, Gideon walked all the way through to the other side and out the front door, memorizing the details of its floorplan; doors, windows, pulley systems, and office space. No one challenged his presence, although he did get one or two curious looks from workers leaving the building. Excellent – he smiled to himself.

***

That night Ezat insisted on coming along with Gideon, so they donned their overalls to look like nightshift workers. Gideon ripped out a small black detachable nylon bag velcroed into his backpack before they left and placed it in his pocket; this was a standard issue operational pack Ahmet had given him and contained the tools of his trade. He also placed the burka inside the backpack. Ezat grinned at that.

"Just in case. You never know," Gideon said.

They took a circuitous route back to the warehouse, approaching the target from the opposite direction Gideon had taken earlier. Parking the truck on a quiet street near the warehouses, they walked silently through the eerie silvery light cast by a high moon, riding like a sailing ship in the star-studded sky. The warehouse containing the concrete blocks was shrouded in darkness. By contrast the target warehouse was well lit, front and back. Gideon and Ezat stood momentarily outside the unlit warehouse. Gideon retrieved the small pouch from his pocket and removed a lock pick. He scanned one more time for a security camera, security lights, or alarm and then got to work. The lock was a standard cylinder one and Gideon had it open within ten seconds. He looked up in to Ezat's gleaming eyes.

"You must show me how to do that," he whispered to Gideon.

They stood on the verge of the darkened interior of the concrete goods warehouse, adjusting their eyes to the gloom and sounds. Nothing moved. The silvery light penetrated weakly through the dusty windows several yards above their heads; it was just enough light for them to move quickly across the warehouse floor directly to the opposite wall where another side door was located. This one required no pick because it opened from the inside. That was the easy bit done. Now they put their plan into motion.

From his backpack Gideon handed Ezat a beer and a small phial of metal shavings. Ezat exited the door, opened the beer and stumbled down the fence line toward the front of the warehouse, singing to himself, as if drunk, taking a swig of beer every now and again. Ezat sprinkled the metal shavings on the fence surreptitiously as he walked—no sparks meant the fence was not electrified.

Soon the security camera on the target warehouse opposite began to swivel as it tracked Ezat's slow progress. Ezat made as if he'd stumbled again and landed heavily against the chain link fence. Then pulled at it heavily to right himself, making an almighty racket. The camera buzzed slightly and Gideon could see the lens focus in on Ezat. Now Gideon worked quickly. He slid through the doorway, leaving it slightly ajar. Keeping half an eye on the camera, he pulled out a set of pliers and cut ten links across, ten down and ten across again lower down, pushed open the hole, climbed through and then neatly replaced the fence so that no one would be the wiser.

Ezat, pretending to have just noticed the camera, pulled down his zip and began peeing on the fence, then pretending lust, thrust his pelvis back and forth through the fence while laughing raucously. Gideon chuckled softly to himself, ran in a crouched position to the side of the target warehouse, and made his way stealthily along the wall until he was positioned just under the security camera. Ezat moved on, singing and stumbling. Gideon's heart skipped a beat as he heard the pivot mechanism of the camera giving short whirrs, moving to track Ezat's unsteady progress. He knew a guard would be out shortly to move Ezat on. Gideon retrieved the lock pick from his pocket and ran to the side door of the target warehouse. It was an exact replica of the warehouse door in the adjacent lot. There must be only one builder of warehouses in this small dusty city. Gideon had the lock picked in several seconds, but the door did not budge. He pushed against it again and then crouched. Looking through the crack of the frame as he pushed, he could just make out that the door was bolted from the inside. To his left Gideon heard but did not see a guard shouting at Ezat to move off. Ezat, having reached the end of the warehouse, began swearing at the guard and challenging him to come over the fence and tell him to his face. There was nothing for it; Gideon stepped back and kicked the door squarely over the bolt mechanism, the door burst open with a thump. To Gideon's eternal gratitude, Ezat saw his distress, picked up sizable stones and started throwing them in a haphazard, drunken manner at the warehouse opposite, making a booming noise every time one of them hit the wall. Gideon saw the guard angrily storming toward Ezat as he closed the door. He hoped Ezat would be okay. There was a fence between them, so he should be. Gideon tried to make the damaged bolt look as normal as possible, but it was extremely buckled and hung limply from one screw.

He found himself in a large warehouse behind a long line of shelving upon which stood wooden and metal crates. The warehouse was well-lit and several very large shipping containers, all painted a military green, sat solidly in the center of the floor. To his extreme left, at the end of the warehouse, was an office space behind a large windowpane, with a bank of monitors in it. Gideon could just make out a security guard moving around the office, making himself coffee and speaking to someone on his cell phone; probably the guard outside. Well, he hoped that was the case.

Gideon squatted down for a moment, allowing his eyes to adjust to the new environment. It was dark behind the shelving. He did not know how many guards were on the premises, so he had to be vigilant. He refocused his eyes on the shelves themselves. Curiosity bloomed into alarm when he read the writing on the side of the crates. This was military ordinance. Gideon took his cell phone from his pocket and got a few photos. Not any ordinary ordinance either. The crates were large and if the labeling on the sides was accurate, contained 2k22 Tunguska surface to air missiles. The words were written in Cyrillic script on the side of the cases, but were discernible enough. In a much smaller font on the side of each case were the words "Kraznodar Inc". Gideon took another picture of this. Taking a piece of cloth from his kit, he wiped the surface of one of the crates and placed it in a small phial. The swab would very likely be able to detect what kind of explosive was in the crate.

Gideon eyed the shipping containers and could guess what was in them. The Tunguska missile system was a mobile one and those containers were big enough to contain the trucks from which these missiles could be launched. He made his way silently down the row of shelves, keeping a lookout for guards and any sort of alarm system.

Gideon smelled the smoke of the guard's cigarette before he saw him. He edged toward the end of the shelving and carefully peered around it. A large man in military fatigues sat on a pile of wooden crates, an AK 47 resting next to him, looking at the screen of his smart phone. He was at three quarter view to Gideon, looking inward toward the center of the warehouse floor and facing the office side of the warehouse. Gideon knew he had to have a look inside the shipping containers, so the guard would need to be distracted.

He circled the guard, whose whole attention seemed to be absorbed in a Russian soap opera on his small screen. He was a heavy set, muscular, large Russian and so Gideon did not want to take any chances. His eyes roved the floor searching for a method of distraction. What he found propped up against the far wall near the roller doors was a very large, flat truck's tire still on its rim, some old nut heads, and a wrench.

Gideon smiled and picked up the wrench, turned and walked silently toward the guard. The guard detected Gideon's presence just as he swung the first blow. The wrench head struck the guard between the back of the jaw and the neck and he grunted, trying to roll away from his assailant. The next blow was to the base of his skull and the guard was out cold. Gideon felt for a pulse; his jugular fluttered weakly. He did not like killing people unnecessarily. He took the belt from the guard's waist, propped him into the recovery position, just in case he vomited, and secured his hands behind his back. He slid the man off the pallets and stowed him behind them, listened intently for a moment and then made his way as stealthily as possible to the first shipping container. It was locked with a round Yale lock. He retrieved his lock pick and, within less than thirty seconds, was in.

Gideon's breath caught at the back of his throat. He had been expecting it, but now it was there in front of him, a KAMAZ 8 x 8 truck used to launch missiles. He took a photo. Gideon could guess what was in the other containers and he was right. In the next container were the missile tubes and the two radar stations that attached to the truck to make it a very effective mobile missile launcher. Once again Gideon took a picture and moved to the next two containers. These contained the guns that sat alongside the missile tubes and ammunition. In all, Gideon counted a row of six containers, double stacked. There were likely to be two full Tunguska missile systems here. Why would an oil drilling outfit need two such sophisticated air defense weapons? They were clearly meant to defend something very valuable. Gideon moved quickly and took a snap of each shipping container number. Before he left, he put a tracking device under the front curved fender of the truck and locked all the shipping containers again. Then he rolled the Russian guard over and took a photograph of his face and uniform. That there was a Russian in military uniform guarding this material was interesting in itself, but not unexpected, given GazNet was a Russian business. Still, it was clear now that GazNet was being used as a front for smuggling in Russian made weapons to fuel the civil war. That in itself was useful intel, but Gideon could not piece together in his mind how it necessarily posed a threat to Israel. He replaced the guard's belt. Then he dragged the unconscious man from his position and placed him near the crates. He pushed one of the smaller crates off its shelf and placed it near the guard's head. It would simply look like a crate had somehow fallen onto him as he did his rounds and knocked the guard out. Any crazy story the guard might tell of a man with a wrench would be viewed with skepticism in the face of this overwhelming evidence.

Before Gideon exited the warehouse, he heard a terrible commotion coming from the front of the building. He could hear voices raised in anger. He made his way out of the side door and back through the fence. He could see Ezat in the bright lights. He was in trouble. A guard had him by the scruff of the neck and another covered him with a raised weapon. Gideon turned the backpack around to his front and dropped the straps to their lowest setting, then donned the burka and veil in a rush. He looked like a pregnant woman in the right light.

"Ezat!" he cried in a high-pitched voice. "Please don't hurt my husband. I'm with child! What will I do without a husband!" he shouted in Arabic.

All the men turned in astonishment, including Ezat.

A look of profound humor, covered over quickly by a look of mock outrage, covered Ezat's face.

"Come home, my husband, please!" Gideon implored in his high-pitched voice and fell to his knees dramatically.

Ezat beat his chest and shouted to the guards, "Kill me now! Kill me. Look what God has done to me! You wonder why a good Muslim man gets drunk and rowdy!"

The guards looked at each other with frowns on their faces and then both began to smile.

One of the guards turned to Ezat. "Who is this woman?" he said sternly. "God have mercy. She is my wife," Ezat said with a sob.

The guards looked at each other and then at Gideon through the gauzy veil. Both of them were struggling not to laugh.

"Go back home, you imbecile! I was going to call the police, but I think God has already punished you enough," one of the guards said unkindly to Ezat.

"Come back home to me, please my husband!" Gideon said, imploringly and got up from his knees. Now the guards openly guffawed.

"There, be a good man and go back to you wife," the taller of the two said sardonically and then laughed again, cruelly and gave Ezat a shove in the direction of his 'wife'.

Ezat pretended a shiver ran through his spine and walked dejectedly toward the burka covered Gideon. He walked right past Gideon without a glance or word and disappeared into the night, a forlorn figure. Gideon, in his flowing burka, hurried after him.

Uproarious laughter from the guards followed them into the darkness.

They got back to the truck and got inside and then both of them burst into laughter themselves. Ezat shook his head. "That was A class acting! Not even an Oscar would be good enough for that!"

Gideon took off the veil, still grinning.

"Let's get outta here," he said.

Ezat started the engine. There was a brief silence while the two men collected their wits.

"All good?" Ezat asked.

"Yes, a very useful recon. Your acting was superb too, by the way. I had a hard time not laughing out loud," Gideon said.

Ezat smiled his Cheshire cat grin in the dark "Where to?"

Gideon though for a moment. "Let's pick up our gear and head back to Tripoli. I need to talk to Hunter about this information," he said.

As they drove, Gideon sent the photos he'd collected, twice—once to Rachel and again to Hunter with a short explanation.

He'd technically just committed treason, he knew, but he needed the Americans on his side. Hunter had proven a solid ally and he wanted to keep it that way.

Gideon had an idea. As they drove, he made two phone calls: one to Sara and one to Hunter. The call to Hunter was a bit more difficult, but in the end, Hunter agreed it was worth a shot. In the light of this new information, they desperately needed to get into Basar Ammar's laptop for some sort of clarification on how the Russians were involved, and Mahram was their only asset.

# Chapter 14

The interview with Hunter was scheduled for just before afternoon prayers a few days after Mahram's return. To her great surprise Jabir had joined her father's security detail. This scared her and lent some credence to what her father had said about a deal with the Saudi Ambassador.

"Why is that man part of our security now?" Mahram asked him.

Her father sighed. "Leave the politics to me, Mahram. Get ready for your interview and remember what I told you to say. You're staying in Libya because you feel unsafe in the USA."

"Is that why Jabir is here. To ensure I stay? To ensure you comply?"

Her father gave her his hooded-eye stare for a few moments, then said, "I told you, your safe return to me was part of a deal which I cannot guarantee if there is even a single deviation. The young man called Jabir is here to report that all goes well. Do you understand?"

"No, I don't," Mahram answered tartly. "It looks like I'm still a prisoner in my own home and we are in danger. They have their money."

"Get dressed and wear the burka and stop questioning everything!" her father said with force, looking pained.

"No! I will never wear that idiot outfit!" Mahram said firmly. "I'm not a little girl who gets told what to wear!"

She could see her father's face become ridged with anger.

"You will be with the guards. I don't want them looking at you! Do you have no self-respect?"

Mahram sighed and shook her head. "No. I will wear the hijab, but that's it!"

"Suit yourself. But remember, shame is a commodity I cannot trade in. In Libya the wages of shame is death," Basar said quietly and turned away.

The interview was to take place at the UN Head Quarters in Tripoli. Accompanying Mahram was her fathers' heavily armed driver, his lawyer, Abdullah Ghanem, together with Farah, his cook's daughter. The drive there was uneventful, but the security to get into the building was awkwardly tight. They insisted on doing a body scan, which of course was an X-ray machine that could 'see' under clothing. Abdullah became incensed when they indicated that the male guard would be taking a scan of the women.

"On no account!" Abdullah said, raising his voice.

Hunter arrived just at that moment and told the guard that his female assistant would search the women in an adjoining room. Farah would accompany Mahram of course—it was just procedure and obviously no exceptions could be made. Abdullah reluctantly agreed.

Sara, dressed in marine army fatigues, smiled pleasantly at the two young women and indicated that they should accompany her into a room behind a curtain.

Once inside, Sara smiled pleasantly at them both. "Do either of you speak English?" Sara asked in English.

"Yes, I do," Mahram said smiling back.

"Does your assistant understand English at all, because unfortunately I don't speak Arabic," Sara said.

"Not a word, but I can translate into Arabic," Mahram said.

"Excellent. Please ask her to take off her hijab and jacket and shoes."

Mahram did so. The young woman looked nervously at Sara, but she took off the garments and Sara approached her with the metal detector wand.

"Now explain to her that I just have to run this across the length of her body, but I do not need to touch her."

Mahram complied.

As Sara lifted the wand, she asked Farah to turn around, then she spoke to Mahram as she drew the wand over the nervous younger woman.

"When I do this to you, I'm going to hand you your hijab when I'm finished. In the lining will be a note with instructions. Please follow these when you get home. It is important. Tell her she can get dressed now. I work with Hunter. We believe you are being held against your will. Tell me now if that is not so."

Sara turned and held Mahram's eyes with her own. Mahram's eyes indicated shock, but she managed an unsteady smile and told Farah to get dressed again.

Farah searched Mahram's face. "Are you alright? Am I in trouble? What is the matter?" said the younger woman in Arabic.

"Nothing is the matter. It is just my turn now," Mahram said consolingly to the younger woman.

"What is this about?" Mahram asked in English, taking off her hijab and handing it to Sara.

"It will help us catch those men and stop them from doing something very bad here," Sara said.

"Does this have to do with the—" Mahram started.

"Yes, but don't say the M word," interrupted Sara, as she moved the wand around Mahram's head. "That word will be recognized in any language."

"…ah, I see. The payment, then?" Mahram continued.

Mahram once again smiled for the sake of Farah.

"I will require a fuller explanation at some point. I know something bad is going on, but I don't know what, and, yes, I'm being held against my will," Mahram said softly.

"When you hear knocking on your window tonight at 10pm, you will get the explanation," Sara said, and smiled back in a friendly fashion.

Mahram frowned slightly and nodded her head as Sara handed her, the hijab.

Farah watched the interaction between the two women closely, wondering why so much verbal interaction was required.

In under four minutes, Sara had the women scanned and dressed. She jerked back the curtain. As she did so she caught the angry eyes of Abdullah, who stood impatiently on the other side of the X-ray machine. Abdullah came forward and immediately asked Farah what happened.

The timid girl said, "The nice woman asked us to take off our hijabs, jacket and shoes and used the stick in her hand to see if we were carrying bombs."

Abdullah nodded and turned.

"Come, follow me!" he said authoritatively in Arabic. The two women obliged.

"I apologize to the ladies for any inconvenience. Merely procedure, you understand?" Hunter said solicitously.

"Perfectly," Mahram said in English, smiling. If the truth be told, her heart was beating like a piston, but she tried her best to hide it.

"This way if you please—the interview should not take long," Hunter said, indicating the elevator.

\*\*\*

Later that evening, Sara and Hunter walked to Gideon's apartment, off Via Cesar, near the Ammar compound.

Gideon had phoned Sara earlier and asked her if Mahram had agreed to help them.

"Yes!" said Sara excitedly and told him what had happened.

"I want you there too," he said. "We need a woman's perspective on this. Too much testosterone in the room tends toward recklessness and our subject is a woman after all. We don't want to scare her away."

Sara knocked on the door to the apartment and Nathan let her and Hunter in. Nathan shook hands with the older man, and then he relocked the door.

"Jack Hunter, FBI," Hunter said softly.

From the center of the room Eli said, "Don't worry, Gideon explained who you are. Come in. Do you want a coffee? It might be a long night."

Hunter looked at Sara who smiled back.

"And who are you?" Hunter asked.

"Better you don't know," Eli said in accented English. Hunter nodded, and smiled his lopsided smile.

"You two sure you weren't followed?" Eli said, peering carefully through a crack in the curtains into the street.

"We both did a counter-surveillance routine and we only met up in the lobby moments ago," Hunter said, his impatience showing. Eli chuckled.

"Gideon will be joining us later. He's traveling in from Es Sidr," Sara said.

"What's he doing out there?" Nathan said.

"A very long story I'm sure he can fill you in on when he arrives," Sara said.

"Okay, so what's the plan, Sara?" Nathan asked.

Sara quickly filled them in on what had happened earlier in the day at the UN HQ. The note that Sara had given Mahram in the changing room had told her to expect a drone visit at 10 pm that night and to flick her bedroom light off and on three times when it was safe to receive said drone at her window.

Nathan pursed his lips. "Good work. Nice exchange. And she seemed okay with it all?"

"Yes. If it was going to go pear-shaped with her, it would have already," Sara said.

"So, to sum up, she's expecting a drone visit tonight at 10 pm and we gave her the note explaining we want her to insert the thumb drive into her father's laptop, or a work computer. She also knows we want his password, but what we don't know is if any of this is even possible?" Nathan said.

"That's about the size of it," Hunter said. "Actually, on second thoughts, I might have that coffee."

"The percolator is on and full, help yourself," Eli said.

"Well, there're a few things we need to do then. We need to find out what she can do and then help her if she needs it. But we're not going to get more than a few chances to do this, so the drone should contain a package of goodies and clear instructions for her—to give her options," Nathan said.

"Agreed. I've given it some thought. I've actually been inside the house, so I have an idea of what might work," Hunter said.

He poured some coffee and then sat down and started to talk. Sara took a small notebook from her shoulder bag and a felt-tipped pen and started to jot notes. Nathan and Eli scurried around while Hunter spoke and collected what he thought they might need.

After fifteen minutes of this, what lay on the table before them was the small quad copter drone, a tiny listening device, and a tiny pinhead camera that Nathan had painted white with some nail polish; he had a whole row of polish colors available for just such contingencies. Sara put the finishing touches to the neatly written notes with instructions in Arabic, and included an extra piece of paper and a thin pencil that usually went in the spine of her notebook. She dropped these into her sunglasses' black nylon drawstring bag and gave it to Eli who attached it to the undercarriage of the drone.

Eli and Nathan spent a few minutes adjusting the drone's propeller pitch and rotation speed. Tonight's mission was all about stealth, not speed. They flew the drone around the room a few times. Sara could not help feeling impressed at its dexterity and ability to maneuver, but it made her skin crawl when the boys made it hover almost silently in front of her face—boys with their toys. Hunter smiled. One of the neatest things the boys had done was to rig up a blue tooth camera feed to the drone's nose, so that you could see what it was 'seeing' in real time on a small screen. This was critical for night maneuvers.

\*\*\*

As 10 pm neared Sara kept an eye on Mahram's room from the balcony of the apartment. As hoped, the lights were flicked off and on three times in quick succession at exactly 10 pm.

Sara turned back into the room where the men were putting the finishing touches to their drone and discussing next steps.

"It's game time. She's flicked the lights," Sara said excitedly.

"Excellent," Hunter said, smiling at Sara's excitement.

Eli and Nathan moved to the balcony, checked for observers, and then launched the drone quickly into the sky. The drone seemed to have no trouble at all with its payload. There was no pedestrian traffic at this time and very little vehicular traffic down Via Cesar, though there was more on the main road. Eli dexterously flew the drone above the halo of light cast by the streetlamps. Right now, they were flying by sight but soon they would only be able to fly by camera feed as they lost sight of the drone behind the trees in the front garden and the silky darkness of night.

***

Mahram locked her bedroom door and opened the window slightly, peering through a crack in the curtains into the gloom. The guard at the gate would make a round soon and she did not want him to see her open window. Right now, he was in the guard hut and his vision of her room window was obscured by a tree. She didn't know where Jabir was either and that worried her. She'd seen him only at a distance, speaking with her father, when she came back from the UN HQ. All they'd done was exchange glances. They'd not spoken at all since she'd come home. She'd thought about what the woman at the UN HQ had said to her all day, and had read the note about a dozen times since. She concluded that Hunter was about the only person she trusted and the only one that had her best interests at heart. She resolved to remain open minded until she knew what was going on and what Hunter proposed. He'd seemed quite upset in the interview when she told him that she did not want to go back to the States.

She caught her breath in fright as the small drone swooped into view and slowly approached her window, something dark dangled from its undercarriage. Heart hammering, she glanced around the grounds of the compound again. She could just make out the guard listening to the radio in his hut from her vantage

166

point. He was facing the drive; she risked it and threw her window wide open and opened the curtains.

The drone made its way carefully into the room and dropped onto her bed. Mahram closed the window and curtain so no light would spill onto the grounds to invite attention, then turned, her heart beating like a drum, toward the ominous black contraption on her bed. An involuntary shiver went down her spine. She drew a breath and approached it carefully. Taking the pouch from its undercarriage, she spilled the contents onto her quilt. Two electronic objects that mystified her, a pencil, a blank piece of paper, and a piece of paper with some Arabic writing on it fell to the bed. She picked up the piece of paper, unfolded it, and read:

*Place the drone behind the curtain in case someone enters your room.*

Mahram looked nervously at the contraption as if it could bite and then gently picked it up. The body was slightly bigger than both her hands and with protruding stick-like extensions on which the four propellers were attached. It was surprisingly light in weight. She placed it carefully behind her curtains on the windowsill.

Next instruction:

*Switch off the main light and put on your bedside light.* She did so.

*Place the two electronic items in your pocket.* She did have a sleeping bra on so she tucked the gizmos in there.

Back at the safehouse, Eli and Nathan looked at each other with smiles on their faces. The tiny spy camera was already on. They had forgotten to tell Mahram that.

"Oh, grow up you two," Sara said, feeling a sisterly concern for Mahram as she watched the camera feeds.

*Take the two electronic items to your father's office. Take the adhesive tape off the back of each object. Place the white one as high up and to the left on the wall to the back of your father's desk with a good view of the desk surface.*

*Take the black one and attach it to the underside of your father's desk. These will allow us to hear what is being said as well as see his password. Once we have that password, we will get it back to you. We need you to log into his computer and insert the thumb drive that Hunter gave you.*

167

Mahram swallowed hard. She felt afraid and guilty and very alone. Clearly these people meant to spy on her father. She read on:

*I'm sure you have questions. I will try to answer some of them. If I'm not able to answer all, write them on the blank page with pencil provided and send back to us when you send the drone back. Please accomplish as much of this as you can tonight. We cannot wait.*

*The men who kidnapped you are Iranian Quds Force terrorists. The money your father gave to them is likely to be used to purchase a very powerful and deadly weapon. We represent the United States Govt. Please help us help you. Destroy this note now.*

Mahram shivered slightly. She ripped up the note into tiny pieces and burned them, then placed the ash in her incense burner and lit the incense wick to cover the smell of burned paper. She got up, unlocked the door and padded silently along the passageway, stopping outside her father's study door. No light shone underneath. She leaned in slightly, listening, and then gently tried the handle. The door opened silently on its well-oiled hinges. She stepped in and closed it quietly behind her. All she could feel was the coolness of the parquetry floor beneath her bare feet. The room was pitch black with the heavy drapes drawn for the night. She moved over to the window and pulled down on the drawstring that silently opened the curtains, flooding the room with a silvery moonlight.

The beauty of the silver light as it reflected off the white paneled walls and paintings was lost on her; she was just too nervous. Working quickly, she retrieved the two devices and took the tiny adhesive off the back of each object. She placed the white one as high as she could reach on the painted panels behind the desk. It blended in well on the wall. She refocused on her father's desk and placed the second device under the side paneling and up against the underside of the desk's surface. She had to push quite hard to make this one stick in place and hoped she had not damaged it.

As she turned to exit the study, she heard her father talking to someone on his cell phone, just outside the study door. Her heart leapt in fright. He seemed upset, speaking rapidly in Arabic. Her mind in a panic, her first thought was to hide, but she could see that there was nowhere that would conceal her. Instead, she moved to the curtains, drew them closed quickly, and then bolted to the settee facing the paintings. She slid across its smooth calfskin surface, and turned on the lamp next to the coffee table, so that it cast a beautiful yellow glow up onto the paintings. The door handle turned and the door opened.

"Ya Allah!" Basar exclaimed in surprise as he entered the room and saw Mahram lying on the sofa.

"I'm sorry, Papa. Did I surprise you?" Mahram said in English, as she lay on the settee, looking up at the paintings.

"Ah, yes. I was not expecting anyone to be in here!" Basar said, as he walked toward his desk. "What are you doing in here at this time of night, anyway? I thought you were in bed," he said, trying not to sound annoyed at his own surprise.

"I couldn't sleep. I came in here to look at the paintings. They remind me of when we were all together as a family," Mahram replied.

Basar sighed. "Yes. I've been meaning to talk to you about that." He sat down heavily in his executive chair, opened the top right-hand drawer of his desk and took out his laptop.

He leaned over his desk on his elbows and rubbed his eyes tiredly.

"On Saturday we're going to have some dinner guests over. About forty or so. I'd like you to get involved in arranging that."

"Who are our guests to be?" Mahram said, a sense of unease growing in the pit of her stomach.

"The Saudi Ambassador and his family and entourage, including his son."

Mahram sat up straight. "I told you, Papa, I will not be traded like some cattle."

"I am not trading you, Mahram! I'm simply concerned for your future like any good father should be."

"What does the Saudi Ambassador's son have to do with my future?"

"It's complicated."

"We have time now. You said you'd explain this to me."

"Actually, I don't have time. I have to do some work; but I will give you the short version."

Mahram said nothing, just stared at the stranger who was her father.

"The Saudi Ambassador has a charity through which money is moved to help the Palestinian cause. As you know I'm sympathetic to that cause. You cannot wage a war without money and while the Saudis and Iran hate each other, there are elements within Saudi Arabia who hate Israel even more, so they are willing to work even with the Iranians. Delir Hashemi is a member of the Quds force and the Saudi Ambassador is willing to help him wage the war against the Zionist entity—indeed more than willing. It was the Ambassador's idea to stage a kidnapping to raise money. They approached me as someone who could help them move money through the charity to give to Iran."

Mahram frowned. "But that doesn't make sense. Why do they need to go through you? Why does this Saudi not give money directly to Quds?"

Basar gave a short laugh.

"Dear child, that is not how the world works. The Saudi Ambassador is doing this against his governments' wishes. If he was caught giving money to the Iranians, he would be shot for treason, or worse. The Israelis are also very good at tracking money and if they knew who was giving money to Quds, the Zionist entity would eliminate them. The Zionists have made it difficult for Iran to spend large amounts with all their sanctions."

There was a moment of silence between them while Mahram processed this new and disturbing information. She could not help but flick her eyes up to the camera behind her father.

"So, you agreed to use me as a cut out to move money to finance terror?" Mahram said, anger raising in her voice.

Basar stood; his body language agitated.

"It is for a good cause and fighting the Zionists is not terror. Anyway, I told you already, I had no choice! This was a test of my loyalty to the cause. To the liberation of Palestine and I got you back to Libya safely, did I not?"

He stared at her for several seconds.

"I can see you don't understand…" Basar began.

"Oh no. I understand," Mahram said sharply. "Some friends you have! They threaten to murder you, or me unless we cooperate? Is that what you're telling me?"

Basar glared at Mahram, but did not answer.

She nodded her head in outrage at what she'd just learned; a look of profound anger blazing in her eyes.

"…and on top of that you want me to be some show pony for the Ambassador's son!" Mahram's voice choked with emotion.

Basar shook his head. "It's not like that. I negotiated the best deal I could!"

"Deal?" Mahram shouted.

"Don't raise your voice to me! I was saving our lives!" Basar yelled.

"Saving your life, you mean! I would not need protection if I was back in New York and no one had dragged me to this place against my will!" Mahram continued, ignoring her father's warning.

Basar stalked over to Mahram and slapped her hard across the face. Rocking her head backward. Mahram raised her arms against further blows.

"Don't you dare show me that kind of disrespect!" he screamed "Do you know what they would do to you if I disagreed? Do you!"

Mahram did not answer.

"Let me tell you want they have done to people in the past who have been accused of collaborating!"

He turned and walked a few short steps only to turn back again.

"They chop their children up into small pieces and leave their remains in a plastic rubbish bag on the front doorstep of their father's house to be found in the morning!" he screamed. "They sell the daughters into prostitution and take videos of them being abused by men and send these videos to the father!"

Mahram did not answer.

"Do you think I would let this happen to you? I-did-not-have-a-choice! I did the best I could!"

Mahram stared up at him, still shaking her head.

"No, I don't suppose you had a choice…but at least you have your precious money for the Palestinian cause," she said sarcastically.

A snarl of hate crossed her father's face and she thought he was going to punch her, but instead he turned away.

"Is everything justified in your obsessive hatred of the Jews? You should have gone to the American authorities and told them…"

"We have been over that already, Mahram. I cannot protect you from this war simply by letting you go back to New York! The people who…removed you from New York made that clear to me."

"You can provide protection to me here, then. That is why I'm here, is it not? Why do we need the Ambassador?"

Basar sighed heavily. "I'm getting old. Soon I will be a nobody…a has been. Then I will not be able to provide any protection and you will be vulnerable."

"Vulnerable to what? To whom?" Mahram said angrily.

Basar simply looked at her. "Have you not listened to anything I've said? Are you under some illusion that Libyans control Libya? As your father I insist on your trust. As much as you do not want to hear it, I'm looking after you in an imperfect world in an imperfect situation. This world is not a safe place for me and, because of that, it isn't for you either."

Mahram swallowed the angry sarcastic response that rose in her mind. She had to get control of this situation and anger would not help.

"What about the Americans? Can't they help us?" Mahram said evenly. Basar laughed derisively.

"They started this mess. Who could trust the Americans? They don't care. They certainly don't care about you. No, the only way is for you to go to Saudi Arabia. There you will be safe and you will have a comfortable life. A good life."

"I will decide my own fate," Mahram said softly, rising as she did so, but still holding her inflamed cheek.

"No, you will not! I have spoken! You will listen to your father! And what are you doing walking around the house in a nightdress! Don't you know there are men in this house and cameras? Guards patrol! At least put on a dressing gown!"

"I know there are cameras, but presumably not in your office. That is why I came in here. I don't even feel my own house is private! How can you live like this?"

They glared at each other. Complete strangers.

Mahram thought quickly. Perhaps her father could now see his mistake. What monsters these people were. How compromised he'd become. She softened her tone.

"You can join me in the States. There you will be safe and so will I," Mahram said imploringly.

Basar shook his head. "Mahram, don't be a fool. You don't know what I'm up against, or how powerful and ruthless these people are. A member of the Saudi family has condescended to take an interest in us...in our welfare. That is not nothing. I'm not in a position to refuse. This is not America. The States is not some sort of safe space to hide away. Especially not for someone like me. My political profile, my beliefs, will make me a target and an enemy of everyone and a friend of no-one. I would not last a week and I frankly do not want to spend the rest of my days holed up in some God forsaken cabin in the middle of the woods. These are important people. This may very well be my last chance to secure your future and mine. A refusal would be a mortal insult...fatal to us. Swallow your pride and accept that your father has some wisdom and has worked this out."

Mahram put her hands on her hips, "I will help you with your dinner, but I will by no means be helping you with anything else," she said and then stalked out of the room, slamming the door behind her.

Basar, sat down at his desk, then thumped his closed fist making his laptop jump. He shook his head and keyed in his password. He had work to do and the last thing he needed was a sassy daughter to deal with. How he regretted allowing his late wife to take her to the USA. Inside the safe house, Eli and Nathan whooped with delight and high fived each other. Hunter smiled. They had the password. They saw Mahram pick up the drone, write a quick note and then fling the drone out the window. Nathan dove for the controls and was only just able to rescue the drone from hitting the ground.

"She's very upset," Sara said, looking on. "I don't blame her either." They'd heard everything.

Nathan managed to steer the drone back to the balcony and Eli caught it with a large fishing net on the end of a pole. No time for finesse. He brought the drone inside, opened the pouch, took out the note, and handed it to Sara who read it out loud.

*If you want my help you must promise to get me back to the USA. I'm an American citizen.*

The three young people turned to Hunter and Hunter regarded them steadily.

"Well, that changes things a bit," Hunter said. "When her lawyer was present, she said she wished to remain in Libya with her father."

"She had no choice," Sara said.

Hunter sighed deeply. "What a mess…it would have been so much easier if she'd allowed us to take her into custody on the UN base."

"Well, from the exchange with her father, we can clearly see there was a level of coercion in her decision-making. She did tell me that she was being held against her will," Sara said.

Hunter frowned. "Yes, no doubt you're right. Write back to her with her father's password and instructions to put the thumb drive I gave her into the computer to download the virus and also say, *'You are a US citizen, you have rights. We will try our best to extract you. In the meantime we need that information to keep people safe'*."

Sara wrote the note and Nathan sent the drone back toward a darkened window. They had to gently knock the drone on Mahram's window three times before she opened it and received the drone.

They saw her quickly write a note and hold it up in front of the drone's camera.

*Got it. Buzz three times if you can see this note. Will try thumb drive on Saturday, during dinner party.*

Nathan gave three short bursts of the propellers. Mahram nodded, folded the note and put it in the pouch and chucked the drone unceremoniously out her window, then turned off her light.

"And that, my friends, is that," Hunter said. "Sara, let me know when Gideon gets back, please. I need a word with him."

"Will do," Sara said.

"I'll be in touch," he said to the young men, and walked out of the room.

Once the door was closed the three of them looked at each other.

"He's got chutzpah," Eli said. "I like his style."

"We need to keep an eye on Mahram, look for an opening to get her out and make sure she doesn't get cold feet. Sara, can you help us? Especially if she goes shopping and into women's stores and things like that? She said she'd help prepare for the dinner party. I presume that means she'll be out and about. We must make sure she doesn't talk to anyone she shouldn't," Nathan said.

"I don't get the impression Mahram shows signs of getting cold feet. I see someone incandescent with anger. And rightly so," Sara said.

\*\*\*

Ezat dropped Gideon off at Sara's apartment late that night.

"Are you sure you don't want to sleep for a while, Ezat? I'm exhausted. I can't imagine you feel any better?"

"No, my friend, I'm fine. I'll sleep when I'm dead," Ezat said with a smile.

Gideon chuckled.

"Okay, go well."

Gideon handed Ezat a wad of $100 dollar bills. They shook hands, then for the second time in under a week Ezat was off with a wave and a smile on his face. Gideon marveled at his irrepressible spirit of optimism under such trying conditions.

Gideon trudged up the stairs and used the key to let himself in as quietly as he could. He went to his room and was just taking off his shoes when a he heard a soft knock on his door.

"Come in," he said. Sara stepped through the door and closed it without making a sound then turned. She smiled shyly down at him.

"You look beautiful in your nightie, Sara," Gideon said, smiling back at her.

He lay down on the bed and patted the pillow next to him. She lay down beside him. He ran his hands down her body and settled them on her slim waist.

"You have the silliest smile on your face, Gideon," she said.

He laughed softly. "You're making it very difficult for me to be good," he said.

She smiled at that. "Would you like me to go?"

He chuckled again. "No, definitely not."

He kissed her softly, and then more deeply. She kissed back, but gently stopped his hands from exploring her body.

"Just a kiss," she said.

He sighed, then kissed her again.

"I have to get some sleep. I have work tomorrow," she said.

"I have to sleep too. But I'm not sure how I'm going to accomplish that now," he said.

She giggled, gave him one final kiss and sat up. "You'll manage, I'm sure. Have a cold shower."

Gideon snorted and threw a pillow as she got up. Sara laughed.

"We got some good information from Mahram tonight. The whole thing went very well. But I'm concerned for her safety," Sara said. "If we don't help her, she's likely to do something stupid to save herself."

She caught Gideon up on the developments of that evening.

Gideon looked thoughtful, but then rubbed his eyes tiredly. "That was excellently done and really confirms everything we suspected all along," he said. "I still don't see how the Russians fit into this though. I can't think clearly now. I need sleep. I'll talk to Hunter and Rachel in the morning and we can figure out where to go from there."

# Chapter 15
# Sevastopol, Crimea, Belbek Military Airport

The Gulf Stream G650 banked steeply over the picturesque city of Sevastopol in the Crimea and lined up for a landing at the Belbek Military airport on the city fringe. On board, Delir Hashemi and Fairuza sat together. Fairuza admired the view from the window seat as Delir punched in a number on his cell phone from memory. His dislocated shoulder had healed well and he'd removed it from its sling. Behind him, Arash and his twin Baraz spoke together quietly, their dark glasses reflecting the exquisite tan leather interior of the airplane and the nervous faces of the four Iranian nuclear scientists and engineers they'd picked up on the way to the Crimea. Fairuza noted that all of the men of science looked tired—probably hadn't slept a wink; she smiled mirthlessly. They were not soldiers, but they were useful anyhow—full of vengeance for their colleagues who had been assassinated by the Mossad.

"Konstantin! Delir here. We're just about to land at Belbek. I assume all is in order?" Delir laughed at something Konstantin said.

"Good, good. Yes, of course we have the money. Every last dollar. It was almost too easy. The Americans seemed to take the bait. But we may have a problem. There is a young Jewish American who has interfered with our plan. We picked up a trail of this man in Tunisia and we suspect he has been nosing around Basar in Tripoli. Our intel is that he might be an Israeli soldier. Do you think you can take care of that for me?"

Delir listened for a moment.

"His name? Gideon Dunbar. Yes, not a very Jewish sounding name, but there you go. You can never tell with Jews. They breed like flies and with anyone. But one thing. We need his body. Dead or alive, it doesn't matter. This is crucial to our plan."

Another round of forced laughter.

"Excellent, well that seems to have gone very smoothly. We'll see you tonight, then." The line went dead.

"Is all well?" Fairuza said.

Hashemi glanced at Fairuza. "Yes, barring any last-minute problems, better than expected," he said.

"It'll be best when Gideon Dunbar is gone. Konstantin will send someone to take care of it," he added after a pause.

***

Gideon and Hunter agreed that both sides needed to meet and thrash things out. This jealousy over intel was going to end badly and so both men put pressure on their sides. Finally, it was Alda Dibra from the CIA who called the meeting.

Gideon met Hunter at the UN Headquarters in uptown Tripoli. The security procedures were rigorous, and Gideon was pleased that his journalist cover story scanned well with the UN HQ security staff. Hunter and Gideon ascended swiftly to the fifth floor of the building and entered a large brightly-lit meeting room, filled with a boardroom table and at least 20 chairs in UN light blue as well as a semi-circular bank of LED screens on the front wall, allowing for a multi-party video conference. Hunter phoned them into the CIA's network as Gideon closed the door.

One by one the invited guests joined the session. Alda, because she had called the session, was on when they joined, then Dani came on, followed by Rachel and Yossi. Gideon noted that 'Rachel,' his contact, was sitting on the opposite side of the table to Yossi in shadow and her exact features could not be discerned. Finally, Carl Sullivan, the FBI Director, joined the call.

"Okay, all here," Alda said. She did a quick round of introductions. Clearly there was a bit of tension in the room.

"Let's recap," Alda said, and gave a quick précis of events to date. "Which brings us to events two days ago, when Gideon took the initiative under the Prime Minister's directive, I understand, and did some reconnaissance. Could you give us an update please Gideon?"

"Yes certainly." Gideon gave an outline of the intelligence he'd collected.

"So, missile trucks and missiles and the Russian soldier that Gideon photographed. Kraznodar Inc is a Russian mercenary outfit. Do the Israelis have any idea who the Russian soldier is?" Alda asked.

177

"Yes, we do," Yossi said.

They all waited for several seconds while Yossi stared at his screen. Finally, he spoke.

"His name is Nikolai Petrov, aged 25. We have information that he is working as a mercenary for Kraznodar Inc. Kraznodar is, as you say, a Russian mercenary outfit. Petrov's latest deployments were in Syria and now Libya."

"Thank you, Yossi," Alda said. "That's very interesting and I'll tell you why in a bit. First, thanks to the great work done by Gideon in getting the serial numbers of the shipping containers, we were able to track the delivery of the missiles to the Al Khadim Airfield using old satellite data."

Alda flicked a satellite picture up on the screen of an airfield about 100 miles from the Es Sidr port.

"And the delivery of the actual trucks, which are much bigger, via sea to the Es Sider port last week. Clearly separation of the trucks and the missiles is meant to obscure their arrival at the same destination. Most interestingly of all, the trucks were delivered on board an oil tanker named the "*Andromeda*" registered in Liberia. We were able to follow the *Andromeda* back to Sevastopol using older satellite and shipping data. The shipping container numbers have also been obscured. The intelligence gathered by Gideon shows numbers that do not correspond to containers that went through Sevastopol, so once again a clear attempt at obscuring origins, not to mention that oil tankers usually don't carry…well, shipping containers. We've also noted with interest that *Andromeda* did fill up with oil at Es Sidr and is on her way back to Sevastopol now. We presume she went through the Bosporus Strait this morning, heading into the Black Sea."

"What about the money? Were you able to track that?" Yossi asked.

"Yes, we had an eye in the sky the night it was exchanged. We can't be 100% sure, but we believe that money made its way via Al Khadim airfield in Libya, on board a Gulf Stream G 650."

The slide flicked over to a grainy shot of an aircraft, then several shots showing four people disembarking from a dark SUV and moving the trunks of money into the cargo hold of the waiting airplane on a desert runway.

Alda continued, her intelligent green eyes seeming to bore into the eyes of the watchers.

"The airplane landed at Doshan Tapeh Air Base in Iran. What is interesting is that we've been keeping watch with satellite over that base, and four nuclear scientists, two with engineering qualifications, boarded the plane this morning. We're tracking the flight now, but to all intents and purposes it looks like it's on its way to Sevastopol."

"Very curious," Carl Sullivan said.

Yossi cleared his throat. "As you can imagine, we keep an eye on Iranian nuclear scientists for good reason. We can confirm that four of them were in the region of the Doshan Tapeh Air Base yesterday, but we cannot confirm that they left Iran," Yossi said, in a more conciliatory tone.

"We have intelligence that they boarded the G 650 this morning. The same plane that flew in last night," Alda said.

"Your intel is very concerning to Israel," Yossi said. Clearly, his interest had been piqued.

"What's in Sevastopol?" Hunter said.

"Glad you asked. Very simply, the HQ of Kraznodar Inc," Alda said.

"The same outfit the young mercenary works for and whose markings were on the rocket casings," Carl Sullivan muttered, more statement than question.

"Yes," said Alda, "but we did some more digging on Kraznodar. The owner of the mercenary outfit is one Konstantin Bogatov. He also happens to sit on the board of GazNet."

A silence fell over the room as the members of the group digested the intelligence. Alda flicked up another picture.

"This is Konstantin Bogatov—he got his start in the first Chechen war and soon after formed his private security firm, peopled mostly by ex-Russian, Chechen, and Ukrainian soldiers. Kraznodar Inc. started off doing grunt work but has slowly risen in the ranks of prestige and now has a full-time staff of lobbyists and sales people all around the world. It's become almost indispensable in Russian foreign policy, and its global economic ambitions, when deniability is needed. The group deploys up to 5,000 mercenary soldiers around the world to bolster Russian economic and political interests. Their work ranges from diplomatic protection to training, arms smuggling, and protection of mineral and oil fields. They've been involved in every major conflict Russia has had an interest in since the Chechen wars. They're occasionally deployed via Russian military aircraft, are treated in Russian military hospitals when injured, and are considered for military medals for their actions in combat. According to Ukrainian sources, Kraznodar troops are known to travel on passports validated by Russia's military intelligence, which as you know, also issues the travel documents of Russian agents."

Each of the members of the meeting remained silent as they digested the new information.

"Gideon, you've been involved from the beginning; your thoughts?" Alda said.

Gideon noted Yossi's eyes narrow. Yossi did not like him. Well, the feeling was mutual. Gideon chose to ignore him.

"My thoughts are that Iran needed money to buy what looks like some kind of weapon, possibly from this Konstantin character; possibly nuclear, based on the fact that Iranian nuclear scientists are being flown to the Crimea. The Iranians have tried hard to hide the money trail via an elaborate kidnapping scheme using a Saudi charity and the Libyan oil minister's daughter. We also now know, from his own mouth, that Basar Ammar is up to his neck in this plot. My guess is that the intention is for this weapon to be transported and stored in Libya. Hypothetically, if those scientists are able to transfer, say a nuclear warhead into a 2k22 Tunguska surface to air missile, then that missile could possibly be launched via one of those missile-launch trucks we found in Es Sidr. They have enough of a range to hit Tel Aviv on the coast of Israel. Hidden in plain sight in a war zone; deniable if you will, and given cover by a legitimate-looking Russian oil drilling operation. Whatever the case, three things have to happen in my view—we need to find out what has interested Iranian nuclear scientists in Sevastopol, we need to make sure that whatever it is, does not get transported to Libya or Iran and we need to knock out the launch vehicles at Es Sidr. I'm sure that the target must be Israel; I cannot see any other logical reason why Iran would be interested in transporting a nuclear weapon to Libya."

Silence once again descended on the meeting.

"Seems like a fair assessment to me," Carl Sullivan said.

"One thing is clear," Yossi said. "The Russians and Iranians are keeping a plausibly deniable distance between themselves and whatever is in Crimea. No money trail, the use of a mercenary outfit. No military Quds force members. If we are to knock out this operation, Israel needs deniability, especially if it's to happen in Russian controlled territory."

"What do you propose? It cannot be led by the US either for the same reason," Alda said quickly in return.

"First, we need to know what is going on, but we also need to be able to react very quickly if we find that this is a real threat to Israel. Gideon, so far, has done a fine job. I say we keep the legend of David the journalist going; an English correspondent for a South African TV network. Rachel will remain his contact. If we need a team over there to do wet work, we will send someone from Europe," Yossi said.

The energy in the conversation had changed. There seemed to be a new spirit of cooperation and if Gideon was not mistaken, even a note of respect in Yossi's voice.

"Do you think it is wise to try to assassinate Iranians on Russian soil?" Alda said.

"Alda, I have known you for a long time. You know that Israel has never and will never allow Iran to get hold of a nuclear weapon. Period. And anyway, technically the Crimea is Ukrainian soil," Yossi said firmly.

There was silence in the room again for a few heartbeats.

"We don't know anything for sure yet," Alda said. "After all, the Iranians have total plausible deniability. They could just as easily say they are moving their top Iranian scientists to a safe country like Crimea to keep them from assassination in their own country. We're making assumptions about their motives."

"That's why we take a look first, but Israel reserves the right to act if we feel it to be necessary. Anyway, you all know that terror cells are never obvious if they are effective and know what they're doing," Yossi said.

Alda sighed. "The CIA should have a call on this. After all, it was our citizen…"

"Gideon's report states that she is being held against her will, even although the ransom was paid, and I do not need to remind you that the ransom was paid despite Israeli wishes. This payment may well have endangered Israel," Yossi cut in.

"Taking out Iranian scientists on soil controlled by Russia will endanger Mahram Ammar. She is being held against her will and she is about to help us get into her father's computer. We need to ensure her safety," Hunter said.

"The main game has moved on to Sevastopol," Yossi said, "Gideon will take a look, we will run him. He's still the only person who can identify the whole crew. I suggest you keep an eye on the personal bank accounts of Konstantin Bogatov and Kraznodar Inc. and any of their shell companies. We will do the same. We share all intel. If we see 30 mil move through their accounts, or even an appreciable fraction of that, we will know the Iranians are paying for a nuclear service. Then Israel has no choice, we have to act."

After another pause Alda said, "Agreed, but with one caveat; if you intend to take someone out, we need to know first. We also have assets to look after."

The meeting ended in a business-like fashion soon after and Hunter and Gideon walked from the building. Hunter shook hands with Gideon and headed to the UN living quarters.

Gideon took a call from Rachel as he walked through the city and then made a call to Sara. He could not help feeling that what lay ahead was a suicide mission. Yossi had made very clear that there was to be complete deniability for Israel and that essentially meant only tacit support from Mossad.

"I want to see you before I go," he said. "I'll try make it there by nightfall. There have been developments."

It was a short two-mile walk from the United Nations Building to Martyrs Square, where Gideon drew a large sum of cash from an ATM and stashed it in his backpack. He picked up a tail not too far from the square – possibly two. One of them on a white scooter, the other on a red one. He walked slowly and stopped for a coffee so they would have to circle the block and do a stop and start to follow him. At the same time, he kept an eye out for pedestrian surveillance. He noted at least two on foot. He was in a classic box surveillance trap – two on foot behind and two in front, possibly more. He walked back toward Martyr's Square, stopped, made a quick phone call and then jogged across the square, changed direction by 90 degrees halfway through the massive square and sprinted for 100 yards toward the adjoining street. He saw a white Toyota Corolla making its way at speed toward him. He snuck a look over his shoulder as he got into the Toyota, Hunter at the wheel. The change in direction and speed had messed up the surveillance box they'd fitted him in, with two of the would-be watchers at his rear, meeting the two boxing him in from the front; one of the scooter riders rode up to the two footmen, eyeballing Gideon meanly. Hunter pressed down on the accelerator and sped off into the thickening evening traffic.

"There's another one on a red motor scooter. Keep an eye out," Gideon said.

"Will do," Hunter said, grinning. "It's probably the local boys keeping an eye on anyone resembling you, since you beat up one of their men. We should get you outta here as soon as possible."

They zigged and zagged to throw off any would-be surveillance. Hunter dropped Gideon off a block from Sara's apartment in the shattered part of town, and then made his way back to the main road and the UN building.

Gideon carefully stepped through the back passages in the rubble the way he had on his first visit and let himself into the apartment.

Sara had just finished making dinner for her grandmother, who was eating it comfortably in front of television once again. The grandmother lifted her hand and smiled in greeting at Gideon.

"Hello Mia," Gideon said. They were on a first name basis now, which pleased Gideon.

Several minutes later dinner was served and Sara and Gideon sat at the dining table talking quietly.

"They put a tail on me today, after my meeting at the UN building."

"Who is *they*?" Sara said, a slight note of anxiety in her voice.

"Probably Libyan intelligence. Don't worry, we lost them before we got here."

Gideon explained to her what had just happened and the outcome of the meeting.

"So, it's goodbye, then?" Sara said, trying to hide the disappointment in her voice.

Gideon smiled gently.

"I don't want to bring grief to you, Sara."

"We'll be fine," Sara said and sighed.

"I have something for you. It's in my bedroom," Gideon said.

"Oh, very smooth," Sara said with a laugh.

Gideon could not help but smile. "Come," he said.

When he had her alone in his bedroom he turned and held out his hands. She put her hands in his and he gently drew her to him and kissed her deeply. Gideon could feel her smiling through the kiss.

He drew away. "You're not laughing at me, are you?" he said, playfully.

"No. You're so melodramatic," she said.

"Excuse me for trying," he said.

"I didn't say I didn't like it," she said.

They stood in each other's arms. "It's getting very dangerous here, Sara, and I couldn't live with myself if harm came to you or Mia because of me."

"We'll be okay, Gideon, I'm sure."

"I'm not sure and I want to be sure. Please just to do this for me."

"And what is it you want me to do?" she said.

Gideon pushed himself away and opened the backpack that was on the bed. He took out a large sum of American dollars and a hand-drawn map.

"This is for you and Mia. My family owns a small cottage in the hills in Lougosanto in Sardinia. It's in the northwest of the island. A granite stone cottage with two rooms on two acres; nothing special, but very peaceful and safe. I used to go there as a child for winter when we lived in New York. My mother hated the cold. Ironically, now she lives in England with her sister."

"They sometimes go back there for the summer, but it's winter now, so no one will be there. Please take Mia and go there until I come back. If I don't make it through then you can come back here and the danger will have passed for you."

Sara searched his eyes.

"These are very bad people, Sara. If I get captured, they'll be out for blood. There are ways of extracting information from a man that are too horrible to describe. As much as I may resist, they will get all the information in the end and that will endanger you."

Sara shuddered slightly.

"I can't imagine being happy ever again knowing there is a woman like you in the world and I did nothing. We don't have time now, but give me your promise that you will be safe and that will be the incentive for me to get back in one piece," he said.

She smiled up at him. "Okay, I have some leave I can take, about a month, but when it runs out, I'm coming back here," she said. "This place is all I've ever known."

He kissed her again and felt her trembling slightly.

"Text me when you're safe, okay?"

She nodded. "Okay."

He picked up his backpack and kissed her one more time.

"I miss you already," he said and then walked through the apartment, feeling like a man condemned, and let himself out.

# Chapter 16

Delir Hashemi observed the scientists with a barely controlled look of scorn on his face as they carefully examined the two W35 nuclear torpedoes, salvaged from the wreck of the USS Scorpion. The torpedoes lay neatly on long wooded trestle tables with sturdy A-framed legs. They were a nondescript green color and about four yards in length, top to tail, with a rounded nose cone on the front and a propeller about the diameter of a man's chest at the rear. In his heart he despised these shuffling academic cowards. They always looked so inept and unprepared in their ill-fitting suits—every one of them with a look of fear on their faces, speaking quietly together. He wondered if any of them were truly prepared to die for the Islamic Revolution.

"I'm sure they're fissile," said Konstantin in English, his baritone voice carrying around the warehouse. "They're in good condition. If your scientists cannot determine these things, I'm sure I can get Russian scientists who can," he added.

"Patience Konstantin. These things take time," Delir said in the same language.

Delir and Konstantin walked toward the group of scientists and engineers who were carefully removing the nuclear warhead from the booster of the first torpedo. It looked tiny compared to the rest of the device, roughly about the size of an over-inflated soccer-ball, but slightly elongated at both ends.

"What can you tell us, Dr Hosseini?" Delir said.

Dr Hosseini raised his bespectacled, balding gray head. "Not much at this stage," he said, his eyes communicating the irritation he was too afraid to voice.

"You've had three hours. Tell me what you have so far!" Delir snapped. His patience was always tried by these technocrats.

Dr Hosseini swallowed hard and cleared his throat. "We're dealing with the W35 class of tactical nuclear warhead used in torpedoes, as you no doubt can see. These were manufactured in the late 1950s by the USA. That is a long time for any nuclear warhead to have gone without any maintenance."

"Is it fissile? Can we get it to explode?" Delir said.

Dr Hosseini adjusted his gold-rimmed spectacles. "Well…yes, but it depends on a few things. It's still radioactive if that's what you mean. The W35 uses the melt-cast high explosive Octol, a variant of HMX and TNT as the material for its implosion lenses. And the gas which boosts its explosive yield has of course all leaked out over the years. So right now, it's unlikely to be anything more than a dirty bomb."

"Can you get it back into working order?" Delir demanded, rubbing the back of his neck. He felt like slapping the doctor.

"Well, that depends," the scientist replied in a flaccid tone.

Delir's eyes narrowed. "On what?" he said, barely above a whisper.

The scientist cleared his throat again, nervously, "Well, on the way you deliver it. We could not, for example, use this torpedo. It is too old and it needs an electronic wire system to steer it, which we don't have."

"Let's say we had one warhead strapped into a small dinghy and filled the rest of the dingy with high explosives and set that off in a harbor. Would that work?"

"Yes, if you shaped the explosives correctly and you refilled the warhead with the appropriate gas and it was a surface explosion, then it would yield an appreciable explosion."

"How appreciable are we talking?" Delir said.

"Once again, hard to say after so many years. Brand new, this type of warhead produced an 11-kiloton nuclear explosion—slightly smaller than the Hiroshima blast."

"Remind me of how effective the Hiroshima blast was. I seem to recall it was fairly devastating to that city?" Konstantin said.

Dr Hosseini eyed both men for a few seconds. "A single one of these would incinerate everything within a one-mile radius and likely level, or substantially destroy about 20 city blocks. The two of them together, because of their age, possibly a third more. Whatever the case, if it was used effectively, it would make a very profound statement."

Konstantin guffawed loudly. "Profound statement! I like that. Yes? I think it would be a profound statement! Delir, what do you think?"

Delir regarded the scientist and his team with a slanted smile. "Make sure it's in working order. Get your engineers to work shaping the explosives around one warhead for the dinghy and let Konstantin know what you need—the types of gas, the explosives. Prepare the second warhead, but we will transport this separately. I have a different plan for it. We'll meet again in a few days."

Delir turned to Konstantin and extended his hand. "Well, my old friend, I have relied upon you many times and you seem to have delivered again. We'll shake on it now. Pending any difficulties with the impregnation of the gas into the warhead, you will get the full payment."

Konstantin and Delir shook hands vigorously.

"Good! Gentlemen, a drink. Let us stop to have a drink, yes? I think even you Muslims will drink a toast to the end of Israel as we know it! A fitting revenge for all the nuclear scientists that have been assassinated by Israel, Dr Hosseini, wouldn't you agree?"

***

The flight was uneventful. Gideon and Rachel were seated together as man and wife. The sun was going down as they landed in Sevastopol, a baleful red eye over the darkening sea, casting spears of light on the rippling tide. Rachel was an attractive, slim brunette, her hair in a bob cut. Gideon guessed she was about thirty-five years old, with light blue eyes, hidden behind a large pair of sunglasses, and alabaster white skin. She wore a dark blue pants suit, sensible but elegant calfskin boots, and a modest pair of gold earrings and bracelet, with a black woolen coat for warmth. She'd not spoken much to Gideon at all during the flight, but had been content to read a novel. For his part Gideon had not minded. He caught up on some sleep. Gideon wore chinos and a sports jacket over a white shirt and black leather shoes with rubber soles and an overcoat for the cold. When he got up to disembark, he carried a black backpack while she carried a shoulder slung black leather briefcase. Going through immigration took all of 20 minutes on British passports. Their driver was an older taciturn man who did not ask where they were from or what they planned to do in Sevastopol—his discretion probably a holdover from the Communist era, and just as valuable today after the violent Russian annexation of Crimea.

They drove in heavy rush hour traffic via the pretty city center full of low-rise classical architecture and tree-lined streets, and headed for the south west,

187

still tree-lined, but with a more art nouveaux look to its architecture. Rachel pointed out things that interested her, like a tourist would, keeping in character with her cover. She gave the impression of being a consummate professional in Gideon's mind.

Facilities had booked them into an unpretentious three-star hotel called the "Ukraina Art Otel" which, as its name implied, boasted a great deal of art—mainly, paintings and some sculpture in its lobby. Gideon paid the driver with his credit card and then hauled out their single suitcase and carry bags from the trunk, while Rachel went ahead and organized their key and a rental car at the concierge desk.

Gideon walked up to the desk and spoke to Rachel in his best English accent—he was getting better at it. "I just have to go to the lavatory, Sweetheart. I'll be right back."

He left the bags with Rachel but carried his backpack with him toward the restrooms. As he entered, he scanned the area for security cameras. Generally, cameras in restrooms were unacceptable anywhere in the world, but he took nothing for granted. It was clean and quiet, painted white with a heavy marbled washstand. He moved to the last of three basins on the left of the room. He placed his backpack on the bench next to him and began washing his hands, his eyes flicking over the room reflected in front of him. He started whistling the Verdi aria 'La Donna e Mobile' to himself.

A toilet flushed in a row of four behind him and a young man with a dark beard and greasy hair exited one of the stalls and came and stood next to him. He carried a very similar looking backpack to Gideon's and placed it on the floor between them, then washed his hands and tidied his slightly scruffy hair and left. As he turned, he picked up the backpack that Gideon had placed on the bench moments before. Gideon continued to wash his hands. Just as he was about to reach down and pick up the backpack the young man had left, an overweight middle-aged man and his teenage son entered, speaking loudly in Russian. Gideon tracked their movements in the reflection of the mirror as they walked to the urinal. The teen boy guffawed at a comment made by the older man as they both relieved themselves. All seemed innocent enough.

Gideon picked up the backpack at his feet; it was appreciably heavier than his had been. He slung it over his left shoulder, grabbed a paper towel on his way out, and walked briskly toward the elevators where Rachel waited for him demurely with several other guests. She kissed him softly on the lips as he came up.

"All well?" she asked.

"Ah yes, just the flight food, you know, it doesn't agree with me. I don't know why I eat it. I guess it's just boredom," he said.

A fisheye security camera observed them and the other guests, in slightly uncomfortable silence, as they rode to the third floor and were pinged out. Gideon dragged their bag behind him on the carpet, leaving welted tracks in the thick green and gold pile. They walked in silence, observing that the corridor to their room had a security camera at its far end.

He opened the door and then shut and locked it behind them and threaded the small security hook in place. They found themselves in a moderately large room with a separate restroom. The décor was mainly light green with furniture that was more art nouveau inspired than anything else. The couch had rounded wooden arms, as did the single seat chair, the carpet was plush and the theme of gold leaves edging a geometric design continued in the carpet inside their room. Heavy green curtains covered the netted windows.

Rachel dumped her briefcase on the queen-sized bed and removed a small device the size and appearance of a hand-held transistor radio. She raised the aerial and adjusted the dials on its facing side, then swept the room for listening devices and anything that might be emitting an electronic signal or feedback. She did this through several frequencies. Gideon dumped his backpack on the bed too and did a quick but thorough physical inspection of the light fittings, bed, tables, TV set, bathroom, and cupboards.

"Looks like we're okay," he said.

Rachel nodded.

Gideon unzipped the backpack and flapped it open to reveal two Glock 19 pistols, velcroed in place, together with two suppressors, an extra clip of ammo each and fifty rounds of ammunition stacked neatly in their red and blue cardboard boxes, plus a small drone and a satellite phone. He quickly inspected the weapons. They had a full load of 15 in them, but no round in the chamber—the way Mossad liked to operate. The extra magazine was also fully loaded. Gideon chuckled to himself.

"What?" Rachel asked, as he threaded the suppressors.

"55 rounds each—two full mags, plus an extra 25. We're pretty well armed for a fight, I'd say," Gideon said.

"You wouldn't want to go in unprepared. It's quite probable we're going to have to kill people, Gideon. This situation potentially poses a great threat to Israel," Rachel said.

Gideon smiled wanly at her, then said, "You know I'm a soldier, right?"

"I've read your record. I know you're a good soldier. I wouldn't have agreed to work with you if I didn't think you were up to this. The difference here is that we're more or less alone. We have a few contacts, a safe house if we need it, but we'll be disavowed if we get caught. It might be better to die fighting than get caught. You understand?" Rachel said.

Gideon held her eyes, then smiled thinly. "We'll be okay," he said.

Rachel smiled lopsidedly. "Typical man. I appreciate the reassurance, but this is not my first rodeo,"

Gideon ignored the goad. "You hungry?"

"Sure, they have a restaurant downstairs." Rachel said. There were a few moments of silence and then she added, "or we could order in?"

"Probably best to go downstairs," Gideon said. "Cement the cover story."

"When we get back, I notice there's only one bed. I guess we'll have to share it like a proper married couple," Rachel said, smiling in a worldly fashion.

A real femme fatale Gideon thought, then grinned. He wasn't sure if she was joking. "Mmm, tempting, but I'll sleep on the couch," he said.

"That little Sayan in Tripoli—is that why?"

"Yes, that's why," Gideon said.

"She is rather pretty," Rachel said and smiled knowingly.

***

Delir looked at the same glowering sunset while he and Fairuza sat at dinner with their Russian hosts in an upmarket restaurant in Sevastopol.

"Konstantin said one of his warehouse guards in Es Sidr in Libya was found with a mysterious wound on his head. He swears he was knocked cold by an intruder. A side door looked like it had been damaged and then when we did a sweep of the facility, we found a tracking device under one of the trucks," Delir said quietly to Fairuza in Farsi.

"That sounds ominous. Still, we expected a level of interest from the FBI and CIA. Hopefully their gaze will be fixed on Libya as planned. We've left a trail about a mile wide to hold them there. It sounds like they've been fooled."

"It's not the FBI and CIA I'm worried about. It's this Gideon Dunbar man. We've found out he has Israeli defense connections. Someone fitting his description has been snooping around Tripoli," Delir said quietly.

Fairuza sat thoughtfully for a moment, then said, "We double our objective if they don't act to knock out the missile trucks; we have effectively opened three fronts on them. Even if Israel has a suspicion and they take out the trucks, we still achieve our objective," she said.

Delir smiled at her. "Yes. True. You're a formidable woman, Fairuza. I should have married you."

Fairuza had taken care of her appearance this evening. She wore makeup and her hair was free, long and curled and she was wearing a bright red dress. He'd noticed a few men's heads turn as she walked by with him.

Fairuza smiled. "As a Muslim man you are able to take more than one wife. Why don't you?" Delir did not answer, but stared at her until she lowered her eyes.

"You know why…my father-in-law would object. That would put you in danger."

Fairuza's heart swelled with hatred at the truth, but she smiled at Delir. That damned General Ostovar, she had a mind to take matters into her own hands.

Delir sighed. "I don't know why, but I just feel as if they're here…you know, in Sevastopol. It's like I can feel their malignant Jewish fucking presence."

Fairuza put her hand in his. "I'll come to you tonight. It's been a tense time," she said.

He smiled warmly at her.

"Has Konstantin organized a guard?" she said.

"Yes, he has."

"Do you trust him?" Fairuza said.

Delir sighed again and rubbed his eyes and jaw tiredly with a hand. "Yes. They're professionals and this is their hometown. They know what they're doing."

She did not answer.

Delir looked deeply into her eyes.

"Then you shouldn't worry. There's absolutely no way they can know we've got two atomic weapons in Sevastopol and, even if they did, what could they do? We're surrounded by Russian military," Fairuza said.

He took a mouthful of the succulent lamb dish he'd ordered and she took a sip of his red wine.

"Yes, true and besides, if there is shooting to be done, I'd prefer the losses were Konstantin's not mine," Delir answered.

He looked sideways at Arash and Baraz. Both were grinning wolfishly at the beautiful blonde Russian girls who'd been supplied by Konstantin; both were swigging back vodka shots to the admiration and encouragement of the girls. No doubt the girls would be paid well for their efforts, he thought.

***

Gideon and Rachel were woken by a call on Rachel's cell. Gideon turned on the couch as Rachel took the call. She listened intently, exchanging a few short sentences in English.

"They've found the location of the Kraznodar warehouse. Let's take a look," she said. Both were naturally early risers, so a 3 am start was not difficult for them. Gideon got up and pulled on his chinos and laced his shoes. He caught Rachel looking at him. She smiled.

"They've also been able to track the money. There was a transfer of two separate payments of 15 million US dollars into a numbered Swiss bank account that lists a Kraznodar Inc. shell company as one of its clients—'The Canton Land Bank.' A not too big and not too small bank, popular with Russian Oligarchs and wealthy Europeans looking for legit land tax breaks."

"Who did the sleuthing?" Gideon asked.

"8200, who else. They're good, those guys," Rachel answered.

"Rachel, it's nice to be confident in our guys, but don't forget who we owe here. The only reason we know anything about anything is because Mahram helped us. If they even vaguely suspect her, she'll be killed. I hope to God they didn't leave any tracks."

"Relax, Gideon. They know what they're doing," Rachel said.

Gideon shaved as Rachel got dressed. When he came out of the bathroom, she was ready and waiting in a tight set of stretch jeans, a black T-shirt and chocolate-colored leather jacket, and combat boots, her hair tied in a tight, short ponytail.

Gideon drove them in the Audi sedan Rachel had rented. The address they were given was a ten-minute drive away on the corner of Industrial'na and

Promyslova Street in the Leninsky District, an industrial part of the city. The streets were all but deserted in the suburban fringe as they traveled through wan pools of neon light, but occasional heavy trucks lumbered toward the port, heading in the opposite direction. It was cold and their breath came out in white billows even in the car.

"Put on the heater," Gideon said. "We don't want cold hands."

Rachel did so.

"How did they find it?" Gideon said.

"This warehouse is owned and operated by Kraznodar Inc. It's allegedly where they store a lot of their weaponry before shipping it overseas. It was pretty easy to locate. Why do you ask? Do you doubt the accuracy of the information?" Rachel said, slight annoyance edging her voice.

"I keep on going over and over the information we have. It feels like we've missed something," Gideon said.

"What do you mean? You've woken up in a bit of a skeptical mood, haven't you?" Rachel said.

"You said they had tracked two payments of 15 mill to an account associated with Kraznodar Inc. Why two?"

"We don't know what we don't know, Gideon. That's why we're taking a look," Rachel said.

"A good friend of mine was killed because of bad intelligence. I just want to be sure we're not walking into something we're unprepared for," Gideon said, glancing at her as he drove.

"We don't have time for this now, Gideon. The reason we're here is to see what these payments are for," Rachel said.

Gideon felt his blood-pressure spike. This reminded him so much of the operation when Ariel was killed in an ambush. Incomplete intel, going in half prepared, underestimating the enemy. They had been expecting them then, too. They'd been played…and walked directly into an ambush. His mind analyzed, trying to find the fault in their plan, probing, prodding.

Gideon shut his eyes hard, trying not to visualize Ariel lying dead. His mind starting to race.

"Gideon?" Rachel said sharply.

"Fuck!" Gideon said, "Sorry."

A few minutes later he came to a halt about 200 yards short of their target. Gideon grabbed his backpack from the back seat before they both got out and walked toward the hulking mass of the warehouse, its massive Kraznodar Inc. signage in Cyrillic script impossible to miss. The building consisted of three long interconnected slope-roofed warehouses side by side. The only light came from the glow of a lonely streetlamp, and a pale patch of light barely visible at the back of the massive structure. Otherwise, it lay in darkness and an eerie silence filled the industrial precinct.

Gideon and Rachel glanced at each other warily. Both drew their weapons from inside their jackets before turning into the lot next door and in a low crouch, walked along the fence line under the cover of sycamore maple trees, toward the pool of light at the back of the structure. The faint noise of human voices, machinery and movement within the warehouse filtered into the chill night air, carried on a breeze coming off the harbor. The fence was ramshackle and rotting, about five feet high with many of its planks missing altogether and so would be easy to breach, if necessary, but it provided sufficient cover from prying eyes. They moved silently, crouching even lower now, beneath the fence line, until they came to the halfway point. Gideon removed his backpack and took out a small helicopter-shaped drone, about the size of his palm with a coin-sized camera lens attached to its front. He connected his satellite cell phone to the device via Bluetooth, checked the controls on the cell phone keypad, turned on the power and threw it up into the air. The images appeared on his cell screen almost instantly.

The satellite link took a moment and then started beaming recordings to Mossad headquarters in Tel Aviv in real time. Both placed earpieces in their right ears and Rachel connected them to Tel Aviv.

"We're on," she murmured.

A silence fell over the Operations room at Mossad HQ, as Yossi, Alda, the Director of Operations—Uzi Cohen and several Israeli and US armament experts watched the screen with keen interest as the images started to tumble in.

*\*\**

The Saudi Ambassador, his wife, and their younger daughter arrived in a silver Bentley, while the Libyan guests, consisting of the interior minister, the foreign minister, and several high-ranking employees in the oil company and their families arrived in the almost ubiquitous black Mercedes Benz Maybach.

Not to be outdone, the son of the Saudi Ambassador, Tariq Al-Ali, and his sister arrived in his late model Maserati.

The cars swept into the crescent driveway and the men and women disembarked. All of the Libyan men wore the traditional Farmilia, a richly embroidered stitched jacket, and a Jalabia, over snow white knee-length shirts and loose-fitting trousers with satin pull-on slippers. The younger men's zaboun were more exuberant in colors ranging from deep burgundy to blue, or striped, while the Saudi men wore their traditional long-sleeved robe, and dramatic black shoulder cloaks with gold edging and white head coverings secured by black headbands.

The Libyan women also wore the stitched jacket, but theirs were embroidered with gold and silver threads with elaborate designs and set off with gold and silver buttons over sleeved, full-length brightly colored dresses with matching gauzy head scarves. The Saudi women looked stunning in highly embroidered gold blouses with brightly colored floor-length skirts and matching Shayla style head coverings pinned at the back.

Mahram stood next to her father on the steps of their mansion, welcoming their guests. They too were dressed in the traditional Libyan style. Mahram wore a white and gold highly embroidered jacket over her sky-colored dress, while Basar wore a similarly embroidered black and white zaboun with silver buttons over a snow-white ensemble. Mahram graciously accepted the sweets and gifts that the guests brought and handed them to a servant who placed them on a small wooden table to her side. She spoke kindly to each guest and shook the hands of the older men.

When it came time to greet the Saudi Ambassador, Basar Ammar shook hands with him for at least two minutes and the men spoke warmly to each other.

Mahram took a moment to scan the crowd. She found who she was looking for. Jabir stood near the gate in a dark suit and wore dark glasses. He gazed up at her unabashedly. Mahram gave him a quick smile and he smiled back at her, then turned away.

The ambassador finally introduced his son and wife.

"Please, my son, Tariq Al-Ali, and my wife."

Basar briefly shook hands with Tariq and then turned to Mahram.

"My daughter, Mahram Ammar."

Tariq was a tall handsome young man with a trimmed beard and flashing large brown eyes. He stepped toward Mahram and produced a small richly wrapped gift and gently handed it to her. She accepted it with both hands.

"My mother wishes to present you with this gift," Tariq said correctly and respectfully.

Mahram smiled briefly at Tariq and then bowed her head slightly toward the ambassador's wife who accepted the bow with a condescending smile.

All the guests, about forty in total, were ushered into the large second-story dining room where men and women were seated separately on highly decorated lounge pillows in front of long low tables. The position of honor at the middle of the rows of tables was reserved for the Saudi Ambassador, with Basar seated to his right. Mahram showed the ambassador's wife to her position at the middle of the women's table. A bowl of highly scented water was passed around at each table for ritual cleansing. Once done, Basar pronounced the name of God and then the first communal dish was served with a thick, sweet hot tea. The dish was a variety of different aromatic and spicy finger foods from which the ambassador and, at the women's table, his wife, were served first by Basar and Mahram respectively. The dishes began to flow in from the kitchen and conversation commenced and soon the dinner party was in full swing. Mahram's eyes flicked up to the guards who stood in the room. Jabir sat at the foot of the men's table. Once again, she caught him gazing at her. Jabir quickly looked away.

Mahram made small talk with the ambassador's wife and her daughter, Tahani.

They spoke a lot about their home in England and Mahram asked intelligent questions.

"You must come and visit us in England," said Tahani Al-Ali kindly. The ambassador's wife clucked her approval.

Mahram graciously accepted. "That is most kind. I shall ask my father."

*She had no intention of ever going near them, but they could not know that and must never suspect.*

The ambassador's wife smiled approvingly at her modesty.

"Oh, this is so exciting," Tahani said. "There are so many things to do in London. I can't wait! The shopping is so good. The restaurants are fine and Tariq can take us to the park and the zoo!"

Mahram smiled warmly at the idea, making appropriate enthusiastic remarks.

Once the guests had been asked by their host to have seconds and the traditional resistance to seconds was finally given in to, desserts were served and performers came into the large room to play music and dance. These were traditional Berber musicians and dancers, both men and women. There was much joy and clapping and the younger of the men and women were urged to get up and dance with the troupe. Mahram noted that the Saudis did not get up to dance.

It was at this point that Mahram excused herself from her guests saying she had prepared a special surprise for them. She picked up her small purse and made her way past the men's table; her father, deep in conversation with the ambassador, did not seem to notice her departure.

She walked quickly toward the kitchen, heart hammering in her chest. The special surprise she wanted to check on were small cakes for each male guest in the shape of a Libyan flag and a posy of icing covered edible miniature roses for the women. They were of course all perfectly prepared, or being prepared. She looked on at the busy kitchen staff for a moment and then quietly slipped out and down the corridor toward her father's study. She looked back down the hallway nervously before opening the door to the study, then entered and quickly closed the door behind her. She stood with her back against the door trying to compose herself. Her breath was coming in short sharp bursts and she was in danger of hyperventilating. She inhaled deeply to try to calm her racing heartbeat.

She snapped open her small purse and took out the thumb drive, walked resolutely to the desk, opened the right-hand drawer and removed her father's laptop, switched it on, and waited for it to boot up. It felt like an eternity, but was roughly only 15 seconds or so. Mahram quickly entered the password that had been given to her by Hunter, but made a keying mistake on the first attempt and had to try again.

"Crap," she said under her breath.

Finally, she was in. She inserted the thumb drive. She saw the malware inject itself into the computer hard drive and connect to the internet. She waited nervously for about 30 seconds listening intently for any noises coming from the corridor. Done. She removed the thumb drive, turned off the computer and shut it. As she was about to lift it, to put it back into the desk, she heard the door behind her opening. She spun and took a quick step toward the door and all but walked into Jabir's arms.

"Oh, you startled me, Jabir," she said in Arabic.

Jabir flinched in surprise, but looked down at her for a moment then said, "Your father sent me to find you. He wants you to speak with Tariq…the ambassador's son. They are dancing now."

There was a moments silence between them.

They said each other's name at the same moment, then laughed.

"You first," Jabir said, smiling.

"You know I continue to be a prisoner here in my own home. You seem such a nice man, but here you are following me around keeping tabs on me. Why?" Jabir's expression was controlled, but he looked affronted.

"I know what it looks like, but my mission was chosen for me long ago. I did not expect to meet such a fine woman when I met you, Mahram…I simply follow orders."

Another moments silence fell between them. Mahram took a small step closer to Jabir. He took a small step back.

"You know what my father is planning, don't you? I'm going to be forced into a marriage…"

Jabir looked miserable, but his eyes rose over her shoulder and fell on the computer on the desk.

"What are you doing in this room?" he said evenly, looking down at her again.

"The question is what are you doing in this room, Jabir? What are you looking for? What is this mission you are on?" Mahram said, taking another small step closer.

Jabir stepped backward again, on the doorway threshold now, putting distance between them. Mahram knew he could smell her perfume and she could see its effects on him.

Mahram touched his arm. Jabir withdrew.

"What are you doing? I'm a shahid-a martyr. I must keep myself pure."

Mahram searched his eyes.

"What are you saying? A martyr for what?"

His eyes burned into hers.

"Please don't do it, Jabir. They are brainwashing you. You're a man of peace. I can see it in your eyes," Mahram said softly.

Jabir looked once more at the computer on the desk and then back at Mahram.

"What are you doing here? I searched all over, even in your room…"

"I left my purse in here," Mahram lied fluently, "it has my lipstick." She raised her hand to show him her purse.

"Your lipstick is fine. Come! Your father wants you. You must face your fate like I must. He's protecting you from what he knows is coming."

"What do you mean, 'what is coming'?" Mahram said.

"War, Mahram. War with Israel that will stop them in their tracks…they will never recover."

About five minutes had elapsed since Mahram had left the party. She could hear it was in full swing down the hallway. She knew she had to get back to allay suspicion, but she also knew that Hunter was listening into this conversation. She moved toward the doorway.

"War is nothing new to Israel," Mahram said as she passed through the frame of the doorway.

"Nuclear war is," Jabir said quietly.

Mahram's heart was hammering. She shut the door after Jabir came through. They walked together down the hallway; their hands almost touching.

Mahram turned and looked straight into Jabir's eyes.

"You cannot be serious, Jabir? How can you justify this before God?"

Jabir held her gaze for a moment and then looked away.

"You don't understand. Come, we must hurry. Your father will be wondering where you are." They walked together in silence, now her hand brushed his in the darkness of the corridor.

"All I will say is that as a man, I'm glad you will be safe and out of harm's way in England," he said. Mahram reached out and touched his arm.

"You go ahead…I will follow after. We must not be seen together," Jabir said.

Mahram squeezed Jabir's arm and then moved swiftly back to the party where she finally joined in the revelry with the other young people. All told she had been missing from the party for about six minutes. She felt her father's gaze as she joined the group.

***

Two blocks away Eli and Nathan whooped with joy. "She did it, we're in!"

Hunter smiled thinly at their youthful enthusiasm and watched as their fingers flew nimbly over their keyboards. He let out his breath slowly, realizing he'd been holding it as he listened to the exchange between Mahram and Jabir. He wondered if he was getting too old for this work. Eli had given him a real time translation as they spoke.

"We're looking for any information about the transaction between Basar Ammar and the kidnappers, the contacts, the payments, any email traffic, and any encrypted files," Hunter said.

"Send me a copy of the transcript between Mahram and the guard called Jabir. I recognize him. He was at the handover."

Hunter sent a text to Alda Dibra and Yossi letting them know they were in. He ended with:

*Disturbing conversation between Mahram and a guard called Jabir, I recognize from the money handover. She seems to have struck up a friendship with him while a prisoner. In not so many words he indicated that he would soon be martyred and that there would be a nuclear war with Israel.*

*Transcript to follow.*

# Chapter 17

Gideon hovered the drone carefully over the join between two of the warehouses in a shadowed section of the roof and carefully steered it toward the roof edge. He stopped it once he had a good view on the inside of the truck parked at the rear of the building. He and Rachel watched with fascination as the tiny drone angled in on a rubber dinghy being maneuvered into the truck with a small crane. At first, he could not make sense of what he was seeing—a rubberized dinghy full of what looked like packages?

He zoomed in on the tender. Alarm bells rang in his mind. It was clearly packed with explosives and wired to what disturbingly looked to be a nuclear warhead, about the size and shape of a distended soccer ball.

"Oh, my God," he heard Rachel say softly, next to him.

They heard a faint crackle in their earpieces and then a deep male voice said, "Focus in on the silver football-sized object at the front of the vessel. That may be a warhead."

Gideon did as he was told. A faint serial number could be seen.

"Take a still picture of that serial number and send," he heard Alda say.

"Take a picture of the wiring and the canister connection," the male voice instructed again. Gideon did so.

"Focus in on the packages in the rear of the dinghy."

Once again Gideon followed the instructions smoothly and focused in on dozens of rectangular packages with the word 'Octol' printed on them. "What is Octol?" he heard Alda say.

"It is an older explosive that you Americans made in the 50s and 60s; a variant of HMX and TNT. It was used to implode the lenses in nuclear warheads of that era—American warheads," said the Israeli accented male voice.

"What are you suggesting?" Gideon heard Alda say.

"I'm suggesting that this is a captured American nuclear warhead—they mean to detonate a false flag warhead—a dark star. With the intel we received from Hunter in Tripoli just moments ago; we must act."

A chill ran down Gideon's spine, clearly something had gone down in Tripoli. Perhaps they'd found something on Basar Ammar's laptop, but there was no time to clarify that point.

"Gideon, focus in on the faces of the men involved in this work. I want clear pictures of each of them and I want you to get that drone into the warehouse to see what else is there," he heard Yossi say.

"Copy that," Rachel whispered.

Gideon began to take snaps of the men as they worked; waiting for them to turn their heads or walk back toward the warehouse. There were four of them in total, one working the crane and another three helping to strap down the dinghy inside the flatbed truck. Finally, they let down the tarpaulin on the side of the truck and secured the flaps to the edge.

The microphone on the drone was picking up someone speaking in accented English, giving the men directions from the door of the warehouse—a person Gideon's drone could not see from this angle.

He flew the drone vertically, high into the air above the corona of light shed by the warehouse fluorescents and then turned the drone camera on to the faces of three men standing in the doorway—Gideon instantly recognized Dr Hosseini from the picture the satellite had picked up in Iran. The man to his left was one of his companions, probably an engineer, and the man to his right Gideon did not recognize.

"Those three men must be terminated tonight," Yossi said.

"Confirm instruction. Termination of Dr Hosseini and his scientist companions?" Rachel said in a quiet voice.

"Confirmed," Yossi said.

"Think this through, Yossi. We have no evidence..." Gideon heard Alda begin.

"Alda, forgive me. That man has just constructed a nuclear weapon using American material. He is an avowed enemy of the state of Israel. We have intel confirming a planned attack on my country. A fair question would be how did they get hold of an American nuke..."

"You may not act on our behalf, Gideon. As an American citizen you will be disavowed if you do," Gideon heard Alda say.

Then there was radio silence. Clearly, an argument had broken out between Yossi and Alda Dibra. Not good.

Rachel searched Gideon's eyes for several seconds, her own eyes agate hard.

The driver of the truck got into the cab with another armed man and turned over the engine, then maneuvered the truck slowly toward the driveway.

"Let's get a look inside the warehouse," Gideon said, breaking eye contact with Rachel.

Gideon hovered the drone just above the corona of light, waiting for the moment that all eyes either followed the truck or turned away from the entrance. He did not have to wait long. Dr Hosseini and the engineer hugged each other.

"Allah Akbar!" Dr Hosseini shouted. His companions echoed his call with smiles and pats on the back, turning back into the warehouse.

Gideon skillfully maneuvered the small drone to a hover just below the upper lip of the entrance and took a sweeping shot of the inside. He noted several heavily armed guards in tactical gear. He took several zoomed in still shots of various items, including what looked like two gutted torpedoes and sent them back to headquarters.

"Bring it back now," Rachel said.

Gideon obeyed her order and brought the drone back to them in under 30 seconds.

"Mute your comms."

Gideon did as she requested.

"You've got a choice to make, Gideon. You either help me, or I'm going in alone," Rachel said.

"You saw the guards. We're heavily outgunned," Gideon said as he stowed the drone into his backpack, placed it on his back, and tightened the straps.

"Yes, but we have no choice," she said.

"This is a suicide mission," he said.

"Something in Tripoli confirmed Yossi's fears. We have people to kill. Are you coming or not?" Rachel said with a snarl shaping her lips.

Gideon gave her a hard look for several moments. Her eyes did not waver.

"Fuck!" he said with quiet force.

"I can't let you go in alone, Rachel, so I'm coming with you, but against my better judgement. So, if we do this, then we do it my way."

"I'm in command," she said.

"How many buildings have you cleared of heavily armed enemy combatants in your life?" Gideon said quietly.

She did not answer, then nodded.

"I'm going to give you three minutes to get to the front of the building and let the air out of the front tires of the cars in the lot. On the three-minute mark I will open the assault from the back entrance. When that happens, the scientists will run for the front entrance and try to escape in their cars. When they exit, shoot the armed men first; they are the immediate threat. Stay on air, but radio silent as much as possible," Gideon pointed to his earpiece and unmuted again.

"Commencing assault," Gideon said to the audience in Tel Aviv.

Rachel nodded and left in a crouched run. She made it to the front of the building, still shrouded in darkness, extracted a short-bladed knife from her boot and began to slash the front tires of the motor vehicles in the parking lot. There were six in total, four gray SUVs and two black sedans. She was halfway through the debilitation of the fourth motor vehicle when the shooting started.

\*\*\*

Gideon counted to 180 slowly taking off the backpack again and stowing it behind some rubble and then took off his jacket and placed it over his shooting arm, obscuring his weapon. It would give him several seconds of surprise. He pushed through an opening in the fence and walked briskly to the entrance. Ambient noise greeted him from inside the structure; men shouted instructions and the whine of several forklift engines drowned out most of the other sounds. An armed guard stood at the entrance to the building, smoking a cigarette and staring into the night. He turned to Gideon with a surprised look on his face when he was only a few feet away, his assault rifle lowered, not immediately detecting the threat Gideon posed. Gideon shot him twice in the heart with his suppressed weapon and grabbed the man and his assault weapon before he hit the ground. Blood gushed from the wounds onto Gideon as he did so. Gideon dragged him behind a line of nearby crates and lowered the guard to the ground, relieving him of his weapon, looking once into the man's unseeing eyes. He replaced his jacket, covering the blood on his shirt, thrust his suppressed weapon into his belt, and checked the assault weapon, a Scorpion 9mm carbine—a good weapon for close contact work. The clip was full and the weapon cocked. He eased off the safety and then took a few deep breaths to steady himself and peered around the corner of the crates. Two guards in black tactical gear, wearing body armor and carrying assault weapons, walked easily with their backs to him, chatting to one another. The older of them stopped and looked back, frowning.

"Alexi! Stop jerking around. Finish your smoke. We have to go!" he called in Russian.

His eyes caught a glint of light off Gideon's barrel aimed at him, just before Gideon drilled him between the eyes. He died with a surprised look on his face. His friend's head was instantly covered in a spray of blood, bone and brain matter. The younger man wailed in fright and disgust, trying to swing his carbine around and firing madly into the roof. A gout of blood erupted from his neck and lower face as Gideon double tapped him, taking out his brain stem, his blue eyes devoid of life as he crumpled to the ground like a sock puppet.

The explosion of shots was deafening in the confined area and Gideon knew it would have an instant effect. Those who would live would run, those who would die, would freeze. Two more guards spun around, trying to locate the source of the sound. One at a mezzanine level above the glassed-in office space at the mid-point of the building and another at ground level. He judged the mezzanine guy to be a greater threat. In one fluid motion, Gideon crouched, making himself a smaller target and shot the man on the mezzanine level, hitting him in the chest. The man spun backward, his weapon clattering to the floor below. Gideon suspected he was still alive. He dove to his right just as the guard on the ground picked him up in his sights and levelled a burst of fire in his direction. The aim was panicked and sloppy, kicking up cement dust, lead and wooden splinters from the nearby crates. Gideon rose to one knee and double tapped him in the face. He reeled backward into the glass front of the office and it shattered on impact.

Gideon ran swiftly toward the office. He could hear someone speaking frantically into a radio calling for back up. Gideon leaned over the sill to see a man crouching near a desk with a cell phone and shot him in the chest and face. The man collapsed where he squatted and shat himself as he died. Gideon ducked down behind the sill, ignoring the stench. He discarded the weapon he held and picked up the one the guard on the mezzanine had dropped earlier, cocking it as he did so. This one was an AK 47. A more powerful weapon. He listened carefully. He heard the guard above crawling and moaning softly, clearly wounded. Up ahead he heard the quick furtive scurrying of panicked feet and whispered voices. He knew that Rachel and he only had about two minutes to get this done before they became severely outnumbered and outgunned. He hoped Rachel would be sensible enough to walk away if the numbers became unmanageable.

He worked his way around the office to the right and took a quick look around the corner. Gunfire erupted at the front of the building and Gideon knew that Rachel had been engaged. He darted back to the steps rising to the mezzanine level and made his way carefully to the top. Gideon put two shots into the gasping body of the wounded guard crawling toward its edge. He took the last three steps in one stride, bolted onto the mezzanine and scanned the area. Time was not on their side. Fierce gunfire erupted from the front of the building. He could hear Rachel's answering shots among the rattle of the AKs.

From this vantage point he could see over the crates in the center of the floor, into the vestibule of the building where four more guards fired through the wide-open front door into the night. Two of their colleagues lay dead, a neat hole between each of their eyes. Three scientists cowered on the far side of the doorway, one looked like he'd been hit. Gideon took a deep breath and double tapped the guard closest to the door. Dead. The next, he shot in the shoulder and neck as he turned. He would bleed out and was as good as dead. The other two turned and unleashed on him with their assault rifles. A spray of bullets ripped up the railing and floor where Gideon had been moments ago. He jumped from the mezzanine, bullets zipping past his head missing by millimeters, following his trajectory down. As he landed, he rolled for cover behind some stacked wooden pallets. A storm of bullets hit the pallets, sending lead shrapnel and wood splinters in a furious spray that stung his right shoulder and back. He kept rolling to get behind some nearby crates, away from the angry firepower of the AKs. He prayed that the crates were not full of explosives.

"Go, now!" he heard one of the guards call as they stormed out, en-masse, into the parking lot. Gideon heard the pop of Rachel's pistol and then the booming chatter of the AKs response.

Gideon took a quick peek around the side of the crates and was met with another burst of automatic fire.

Car doors slammed.

"Now! Now!" screamed a Russian voice.

Gideon heard the sound of scurrying feet as the last of the guards exited the building. An engine roared to life and one of the SUVs took off at high speed, crashing over the shrubs that lined the parking lot and onto the road. Gideon raced forward, emptying his magazine into the fleeing SUV as he ran. There was wild answering fire from the vehicle, the bullets ricocheting madly around Gideon, but none finding their mark.

Gideon dropped his empty AK and drew the pistol from his belt. He had not heard Rachel firing at the fleeing car from outside; that was a bad sign.

"Rachel!" he yelled. No answer.

Rachel was either down or had fled. Alarm filled his heart as he raced for the exit. One of the Iranian scientists crawled feebly across the concrete hardtop in the entrance, leaving a thick streak of blood behind him. Gideon dispatched him with a shot to the back of the head. He ran forward and found Rachel lying in a pool of blood behind one of the sedans. The sedan looked like a sieve it was so covered in bullet holes.

"Rachel, Rachel no, no, no," he whispered.

She was still alive, but bleeding profusely from a wound through her lower abdomen. Gideon pushed his hand onto the wound, trying to staunch the flow and felt the strong pumping of blood through his fingers. Rachel moaned feebly.

"Fuck, fuck, fuck!"

He picked her up in his arms and ran as fast as he could back to their car and placed her gently on the back seat.

"I'm gone, Gideon," she whispered.

"No!"

Gideon touched his earpiece "Are you still there, HQ?"

"Yes," came a curt reply.

"Man down, man down!"

"We heard everything," Yossi's voice said. "You know where the safe house is. We have a doctor on the way there."

Gideon got into the driver's seat, fumbled for the keys and dropped them; his hands were so slick with Rachel's blood.

"Get in, you fucking fuck!" he cried out at his clumsiness. He picked up the key and shoved it into the ignition.

The car roared to life, wheels spinning. He shot forward onto the street, tires screeching on the black top as they gained traction. The industrial park was deserted on this early Saturday morning, but as they hit the urban area the traffic picked up; Gideon did not slow down. Cars honked at him as he sped past. The directions started flowing through his earpiece, reminding him where to turn. On the other side of the highway, several black SUVs bristling with men, sped past heading for the industrial park.

"Stay with me, Rachel! Stay with me!" Gideon shouted as he raced to save her life.

*** 

Gideon brought the car to a screeching halt outside the safe house. The medic was expecting them. Together they picked Rachel up bodily. She felt as light as a feather. They rushed her inside and laid her on a bench where the medic immediately sought a vein and plunged an intravenous needle into her exposed arm, pumping in plasma. He worked quickly, cutting away fabric around the wound then trying to staunch the flow of blood, frantically, using coagulant, but his eyes told Gideon everything he needed to know. There was no hope in them. The safehouse manager, an older man, brought in a blood pressure monitor. The reading was very low. Miraculously, though, Rachel was still conscious. In the end the medic stitched the wound and covered it with a pressure bandage, gave her another and heavier dose of morphine for the pain and then let Gideon hold her hand. He left with a shake of his head.

Rachel managed a smile as her life slowly ebbed away.

"I always thought I'd be a mother," she whispered.

"You'd be a perfect mother," Gideon said softly, fighting back tears.

Rachel fell unconscious and died three minutes later.

Gideon gently placed Rachel's hand on her chest when she closed her eyes for the last time, then rose and took a shower, washing off the bloodstains on his hands, neck, and face. He sobbed quietly in the shower, allowing the raw emotion to have its way and escape him as he watched Rachel's blood wash from his body and stream down the drain.

He changed into a fresh pair of black jeans, black rubber soled combat boots, a white T-shirt over which he put on ultra-light-weight low-profile-fit body armor, a durable canvas workman's shirt, and a black leather jacket. He reached for the satellite phone on the bedside table and speed-dialed Dani on speaker phone while he walked into the kitchen, indicating that the house manager should listen in.

Dani answered.

"She's gone," Gideon said simply, in Hebrew.

"HaMakom y'nachem etkhem b'tokh sh'ar a'vaylay Tzion v'Y'rushalayim," he said. "May God comfort you among the other mourners of Zion and Jerusalem."

"Thank you," Gideon said.

"Forgive me for asking, Gideon. I don't mean to be callous, but I need to know—did you manage to stop the scientists?"

"I don't think so. I know for sure we killed one, because I shot him, but the others got away. I don't know in what state. Rachel may have injured them, but they overwhelmed her in the last rush."

"We need eyes out there, Gideon. We have no satellites over Russia. At this stage we don't know where the bomb is."

"Bombs, plural Dani. There were two gutted torpedoes…the CIA?"

"At this stage they've gone silent. Yossi and Alda had an almighty row…"

"Yes, I heard. Tell Yossi for me he's a fucking dick! He killed Rachel."

"You're upset, Gideon."

"Damn straight I'm fucking upset! Fucking clowns! That was a suicide mission!"

"I remind you that there are potentially two loose nukes out there and, as you know, they're likely aimed at Israel. We do what we need to do. Yossi made the right call."

There was silence between the two men for a few seconds while Gideon fought to take control of his emotions.

"Any clues where I should start? I imagine it will be an amphibious assault based on the fact that one of the bombs is strapped to a dinghy?" Gideon said.

"Yes, those are our thoughts too. I think the best bet is to check out the ship 'Andromeda.' That's our only lead. She's still berthed at the wharf in Sevastopol and taking on cargo. We've hacked the server to the Sevastopol Harbor Authority—she hasn't been given permission to sail yet."

The manager of the safe house followed the gist of the conversation and gave Gideon a new phone, weapon, tactical knife, car keys, earpiece, dark glasses, beanie, and gloves. Gideon nodded his thanks as he kitted up, still talking.

"Have you found out where the warheads came from? What are we dealing with?"

"Yes, the video footage you took revealed older style American torpedoes. Probably a lost nuke…and we suspect it's from a sunken nuclear submarine; and yes, they are nuclear torpedoes. When you were inside can you remember seeing only the two torpedoes? The reason I ask is because those nuclear subs usually carry more than two nuclear warheads. That class of submarine was usually armed with four."

"It was not my main focus at the time, so I can't be absolutely sure. But, yes, I saw only two that I can remember," Gideon said.

Gideon nodded his thanks at the safehouse manager and left the building via a door that took him into the adjoining garage. In it was a turbo charged Subaru Liberty; he climbed inside. A fresh black backpack lay on the passenger seat. The house manager opened the garage door while Gideon continued speaking to Dani.

"I want you to stay online and in contact with us at all times. Ask the—"

"I have the new kit already. I'm on my way. Give me Alda's number. I'll phone her directly. I'm going to ring off this phone and ditch it. The Russian military will be trawling the ether for satellite chatter given what's just happened and they'll be trying to triangulate around similar ongoing signals. I'll call on the new burner."

Dani gave Gideon Alda's number and then ended the call.

Anger boiled in Gideon's heart, but he clamped down on it hard. He dialed Alda's number, placed the earpiece in his ear, then gunned the engine and drove as quickly as he could, without attracting undue attention, in the direction of the harbor.

Alda answered with a curt, "Yes."

"It's Gideon."

"I should just hang up on you. You disobeyed a direct command. Our ambassador has already been accused by the Russians of harboring terrorists who assaulted a warehouse in Sevastopol," Alda said.

"Please don't. We need each other. Just as a matter of interest, I agreed with your assessment but I had no choice. We lost an agent this morning in the assault."

"What happened in the warehouse?"

"We killed a lot of mercenaries and one scientist. Rachel was wounded and died of her wounds earlier this morning."

"I see. I'm sorry for your loss. The scientist killed?"

"Not Dr Hosseini."

"So, in other words, a complete, fucking balls-up!" Alda said bitterly. "And now they know that we know."

Gideon changed tack. "There's definitely more than one warhead and we only have the lead on one. My instincts tell me they're sacrificing this one as a potential diversion; not putting all their eggs in one basket? It's a clever tactic, because we're compelled to put all our effort into stopping this one anyway, only to have another one, or three for all we know, explode somewhere else."

"Three? What makes you think there's another three?"

"The torpedo comes from a drowned American sub class that usually carried at least four warhead-tipped torpedoes."

"Pure speculation. We have only evidence of two torpedoes…" Alda began impatiently.

"Alda, could we just leave the politics out of this please. I'm on my way to the *Andromeda*—the ship is in port at Sevastopol. Israel does not have the SIGINT resources that the CIA has at its disposal. I need you to help me. I'm one man. They're expecting me…I need help."

"You certainly do," she said.

He did not answer.

Gideon heard Alda sigh, then say "Shit," very loudly.

"What?" Gideon said as he dodged through the early morning traffic.

"New intel you're probably not aware of yet came in from Hunter and your 8200 crew. It was being analyzed while you were clearing the warehouse and that report has just landed in front of me. We overheard a conversation between Mahram and a person called Jabir; clearly someone she knew from the kidnapping. We thought he was only boasting, trying to impress Mahram, but this Jabir admitted to her that he was committed to jihad. I have the transcript here. He said, and I quote 'I'm a shahid-a martyr. I must keep myself pure', but then he spoke of the jihad he's to take part in involving a nuclear explosion."

"That's very, very, very fucking bad. We need to keep an eye on him. He may very likely lead us to the second warhead," Gideon said.

There was a silence.

"Alda, are you there? Did you hear what I said?"

"Yes, I heard what you said, Gideon," she said softly.

"I need you and Mossad working together. Please believe me, I know how angry you are with Yossi. I'm doubly angry. I just lost a colleague unnecessarily. Alda, this situation is really bad. We need each other."

"Tell them we'll feed them intel. What do you need?"

"I need eyes on the *Andromeda*. I need to know where she is, how many crew there are, whether the truck took the dinghy there…"

Alda cut in. "We believe the dinghy is aboard *Andromeda*. Our satellite followed the truck to a warehouse at the port. We couldn't see what happened inside the warehouse obviously, but we can confirm that a number of shipping containers were moved from that warehouse to the *Andromeda*…that much I can confirm."

"Were you able to see the serial numbers, or any identifying marks on those containers? My plan is to get aboard the *Andromeda* and confirm the bomb is aboard. If we know for sure, then we can take measures to intercept the ship, or sink it. You'll need to work the finer details out with Yossi."

"We don't want fireworks in the Med, Gideon! The United States government will never sanction that. The Turks, the Russians, the EU will all have something to say about having a nuke go off in their backyard, even if it is an underwater explosion."

"Well, then I guess it's a good thing you have plausible deniability about me. After all I'm not a CIA operative."

There was silence on the line again.

"Yossi's right about one thing. We can't allow that ship anywhere near Israel," Gideon said.

"If it heads past the southern tip of Cypress and we know for certain the warhead is on board, then we can take some kind of action. That's what I will be pressing with Yossi," Alda said.

Gideon thanked Alda, ended the call, and then recalled Dani with the news that the Americans would be supplying the SIGINT via Mossad and everything else that had been shared between them.

Dani confirmed the intel that Alda had just shared and then gave him the coordinates of the *Andromeda*.

The day dawned, the sky a wet dishcloth of clouds that soon gave way to a fine misty rain. He had to drive around the harbor from his present location on the South Shore to the North Shore of Sevastopol Bay and into the Gollandiya district, the North Shore's industrial zone. There were several large destroyers and a frigate berthed in the harbor near the *Andromeda*. It was an understatement to call Sevastopol harbor enormous and, for that reason, it was almost impossible to keep secure, so it was easy to find a quiet street nearby on which to park the car behind some warehouses.

Gideon donned the black beanie and tucked the sheathed knife into the back of his pants, while securing the suppressed Glock 19 in his backpack and an extra clip of ammunition in his leather jacket. He took a quick glance at himself in the rear-view mirror before exiting the car—with his five o'clock shadow and beanie he'd pass for a deck hand and was unlikely to be recognized for the man who attacked the Kraznodar warehouse.

Gideon checked the connection of the new satellite phone to his earpiece and then placed the cell into the other inside pocket of his jacket and took a leisurely-paced stroll into the harbor precinct. There were no trees or street furniture here and the strip had a bleak, utilitarian feel about it in the light drizzle.

The *Andromeda* was easy to spot. She was a massive ship, but still only mid-sized for a tanker. A number of shipping containers were securely lashed to her foredeck; about twenty or so. He observed her easily enough from his vantage point on a street running diagonally toward the harbor. Several shops lined the streets that gave onto the massive body of water, all still shut at this hour and mainly industrial services, but there was a café of sorts that served pies and other baked goods and coffee. His last meal had been with Rachel the night before and, although he didn't feel particularly hungry, he knew he should eat. He stepped inside the rotunda-like façade of the all but deserted café, astonishing the proprietor. She was a plump lady with rosy cheeks and bleached blonde hair, wearing a pink knee-length waitress uniform under a white apron.

"Oh," she exclaimed in surprise at Gideon's sudden appearance. "You're very early."

Gideon's Russian was basic and so he only got the gist of what she was saying. Gideon made as if to leave, but she flapped her hands, plumped her hair and fussed him into a booth, handing him a menu with pictures of the food next to the name in Cyrillic script. Gideon didn't want to chance his accent being picked out as foreign and so ordered via grunts—a coffee, several flap jacks, a pork meat pie and something that resembled a Cornish pastie to take with him. He had a hunch it'd be a while before he ate again.

***

Dani arrived at Mossad HQ just outside Tel Aviv about thirty-five minutes after his conversation with Gideon. He had been invited into the Mossad HQ to run the operation after he updated them on Gideon's movements. He was ushered into the equivalent of the USA's situation room. In their inimitably practical fashion, the Israeli impatience with melodrama meant that their "Situation Room" was called by the much more practical moniker of the "Operations Room." It was a surprisingly plain room, soundproofed from the outside with a thick double door, guarded by a single armed soldier in the vestibule area between the doors. It was his job to ensure no electronic equipment went into or out of the Operations Room, except what was already supplied, and that included mobile phones. Dani was made to step through a metal detector and then ushered into the Operations Room. The room itself was large and rectangular, well lit, with a bank of TV monitors rising from the floor to just below ceiling height. At the back of the room was a gently curved semi-circular table facing the wall of monitors on a slightly raised dais and, below the dais, two neat rows of six monitors and their PCs. The semi-circular table was studded with comfortable chairs around its circumference. A sideboard along the far length of the room was stacked with a coffee machine, an urn of tea, a large glass jug of fresh milk, water, and four large silver trays of sandwiches and pastries. A feed of constantly updated data was coming in from an American satellite on one of the large monitors in the center of the video conferencing wall, right now focused on the *Andromeda,* while another monitor was dedicated to Gideon's cell feed and audio. At this time, the visual on Gideon's phone was the ceiling of a café and the audio was of him eating his breakfast.

The Director of Mossad Operations, Uzi Cohen greeted Dani. They had not met, but knew of each other professionally. They shook hands and Dani nodded a greeting to Alda Dibra who was online on one of the screens from Langley Virginia.

"Alda, glad to see you," Dani said, with a genuinely warm smile.

She smiled back thinly. She looked exhausted. Dani sat down at the semi-circular table while the low murmur of voices rose from the officers below them, all working on humming monitors.

"Dani, thanks for joining us. I speak to all in the room and you too, Gideon. Dani Gilad will have the lead on this Operation. He has the best knowledge of the situation and the soldier. Dani, as I'm sure you've inferred, Gideon is online and can hear our conversation. He will not participate immediately for obvious reasons." Uzi said.

"Morning all and to you too, Gideon," Dani said somewhat loudly. The officers in the mosh pit, as it was affectionately known, all turned to greet Dani with smiles and nods.

The Director smiled. "We're mic'ed up at the table, no need to raise your voice."

He continued, "We have some interesting but disturbing news. Jack Hunter, together with our two 8200 operatives in Tripoli, managed to penetrate Basar Ammar's laptop. We concentrated on the payments he made to the kidnappers of his daughter. As you know, the ransom was set at thirty million dollars. That was taken in cash and banked in an offshore account. The money then got transferred to a Tehran account and two separate payments of 15 million apiece were made to Kraznodar inc. one day apart. We now know what the payments were for; clearly the warheads that we have all seen. At the time it was not clear how many of them there were. Now we can infer two weapons at 15 million apiece. Gideon and Rachel only saw one warhead weaponized, and both payments were made after the known warhead was weaponized—in other words, the payments were not half payment for the recovery of a single 'working' warhead. What this indicates is that there may be two weaponized devices out there," Uzi announced.

Dani felt the blood pressure in his body rise appreciably, so much so, that he quickly sat down.

"That is certainly not a welcome development," he said quietly.

"Yes, disturbing. Still a little speculative at this stage but can easily be inferred as accurate. There is some corroborating evidence, though. We may have a lead on the other bomb. Some excellent intelligence work led us to a young Palestinian man known only as Jabir, who claims to be a shahid intent on jihad involving a nuclear device. We're keeping an eye on his movements in Tripoli," Alda said.

"This is a very clever ploy if accurate. I guess it was Gideon's gut feel on the matter once again that made us look more carefully at this. We are in a heads they win, tails we lose situation." Uzi said.

"So, what are the options?" Dani said.

"Well, as Alda suggested, we have to try to track the movement of the other members of the kidnap team identified by Gideon. It's too dangerous to send a large team into Russian territory, so the capture of Hashemi or any of his crew while they are still on Russian soil is not an option. Gideon will have to follow the lead and eliminate one of the threats for us. He will stay with the *Andromeda* connection. We have other assets following the lead on Jabir."

"Okay, that's reasonable. Have we worked out how to get Gideon on board the *Andromeda*?" Dani said.

"Not yet. I suspect it might be one of those situations where an opening will present itself. If not, we'll get him to the Yavuz Sultan Selim Bridge that crosses the Bosporus in Turkey. He'll have to belay onto the ship as it passes underneath the bridge superstructure, but that's plan B and super risky. We must stay vigilant for that opening today, or manufacture one if that is not forthcoming before the *Andromeda* leaves port."

Gideon paid with cash and left, shouldering his backpack filled with a few more snacks and opened a packet of cigarettes, bought at the café, and lit up. He'd noticed a few sailors goofing off on a smoke break on his way in, so smoking was a good cover for simply standing around and not garnering too much attention. He wasn't a smoker, so had to try hard not to cough when he inhaled. He ambled down to the waterfront and observed the *Andromeda* and the quay generally, understanding the layout and then turned back to the ship. She was lying side on with her guy ropes attached to the pier. Several other ships lay at anchor close by, with their sterns to the peer. Gideon walked diagonally toward the hulking decks of the *Andromeda* and suddenly registered a familiar face walking with purpose toward the gangway onto the ship's deck.

"Check, 11 o'clock, one of the twins. It's the one called Arash," Gideon mumbled past his cigarette.

Dani took a good look and turned toward the pictures they had laid out on the table of the kidnap team.

"Confirmed."

Gideon slowed his pace to a standstill and took a drag of his cigarette while leaning against a large wooden crate on the docks, about one-hundred yards from the ship itself. He observed how Arash produced a pass tag on a lanyard at the gangway entrance guarded by a fairly bored-looking young man in marine army fatigues with an automatic weapon slung over his right shoulder. The check was thorough and done by eyesight, as well as using an electronic pass wand, no doubt reading a microchip in the pass. The soldier turned back and spotted Gideon. His eyes flicked over him appraisingly. Gideon took his measure behind the smoke screen. An idea formed in his mind. He finished his cigarette and then made his way to a public restroom he'd passed earlier. It was, for some reason, an absolutely huge room with something like twenty toilet stalls and as many basins. He entered the fifth stall along, listening for other patrons, heard none and climbed onto the commode and pushed the hung ceiling up to stow his backpack. As he was climbing down, he heard an upbeat tune being whistled by someone who'd just entered the facility. Gideon's blood pressure spiked. The man walked past his toilet stall, continuing to whistle. Gideon wiped his footprints off the commode with some toilet paper, flushed and opened the stall door to see a man with mop and bucket, wearing a cleaner's uniform, starting to clean the floor on the side furthest from the entrance. Gideon lit another cigarette as cover, ignoring the cleaner, and walked from the toilet, noticing a van full of cleaning implements with the name of the company neatly stenciled on its side. He withdrew his mobile took a picture and sent it to Dani.

'What does this mean in English," he wrote.

"*Sparkling Cleaning Services," came the reply*.

"What do you have in mind?" said Dani in his earpiece.

"Not sure yet. Just collecting ideas," Gideon murmured.

He sauntered past the soldier guarding the *Andromeda*, ignoring him too, and on, toward the vessel docked close by. He noticed his hand holding the cigarette shaking slightly. *Get a grip, he thought.* This whole shaking thing at the slightest bit of danger was a new thing for him.

Gideon could feel the eyes of the soldier on him as he ambled toward the gangway of that vessel. Men were busily unloading a provedore's truck filled with a range of foodstuffs and drink. Gideon watched them closely as he headed their way, looking for their rhythm. As one of the men picked up a plastic crate filled with water bottles, he threw down his cigarette and stomped on it and then pocketed the pack of cigarettes and picked up the next crate, following the man in front of him toward the gangway. The driver of the truck gave him a long look in his side mirror, but said nothing, as he walked in the direction of the gangway; looking for all the world like a lazy deckhand arriving late and having a cigarette before work. None of his fellow deckhands even gave him a second glance, just glad his help meant less work for them.

Dani smiled as he saw the charade play out over the satellite feed.

"What's the plan?" he said.

Gideon walked with energetic purpose toward the galley entrance following the man in front of him. When he had a clear patch he said, "Let me know when the soldier at the gangway to the *Andromeda* goes for a toilet break, or knocks off shift. I won't have much time, but can't be seen on the quay; they're watching for me and I got the beady eye from that soldier twice already."

Gideon did two more trips down to the truck and back to the galley before he got the call.

"Seems to be a changing of the guards about to take place," Dani said.

Gideon quickly put down a crate of eggs on one of the galley counters and made to turn.

"Hey, you! Not there!"

Gideon turned to see a cook gesticulating at him to move the eggs to the cold store. He picked them up dutifully and moved them to the cold room.

"Now you can help me move the meat!" the cook said loudly in Russian. Gideon did not understand him completely.

"He wants you to help him move the meat," Dani said in Gideon's ear.

"Get a move on, the soldier is about to leave. I see another making his way from the barracks toward the *Andromeda* gangway," Gideon heard in his ear.

The cook led Gideon into the further recesses of the kitchen toward a hunk of beef sitting on a counter, a hook already speared through the ankle bone.

Gideon looked around the kitchen surreptitiously; they were alone. Above his head hung a rack of cast iron pans and skillets.

"Why you deckhands think we cooks can move these things by ourselves is a mystery! You always do half a jo…"

In one fluid motion Gideon unhooked a small but heavy cast-iron skillet and gave the cook a good hard smack on the back of his fat neck with the flat of the skillet. The cook lost consciousness as if someone had flicked a switch. Gideon only just managed to catch him by his collar before he fell onto his face.

"Sorry shithead," he said to the unconscious cook.

"What did you do?" Dani asked.

"One cook out cold," Gideon replied in a whisper.

He lowered the cook to the ground, dragged him behind a counter and then laid him gently in the recovery position. He took a quick look around, no one in sight. He unzipped his jacket and placed the heavy cast iron skillet against his chest and then rezipped, just as several men entered carrying a haunch of beef. They were shouting to each other good naturedly and laughing, no doubt cracking jokes, as young men do all over the world as they work. Gideon shifted past them and made his way toward the gangway. Out of the corner of his eye he could see the soldier handing over the electronic device to another soldier in uniform on the quay. They exchanged a few final words and then the first soldier turned smartly and made his way down the quay. Gideon walked quickly and with purpose as if on an errand, closing the distance between himself and the young soldier. No one took any notice of him at all.

"Talk to me. What's ahead?" he said to Dani.

The soldier turned the corner of the warehouse and Gideon lost sight of him for a moment.

"He seems to be making his way to a warehouse near the military barracks that is listed as having a gym and sauna inside it."

Gideon glanced at his wristwatch: 11 am. The gym would not be too busy this late in the morning, particularly with a heavily male workforce on the docks. He followed the soldier at a discrete distance and observed him from outside the warehouse. The soldier was at the reception desk talking to a pretty blonde attendant. She laughed at some comment he made and scanned his gym ID, then took his automatic weapon and placed it in a pigeonhole and gave him a tag. The marine pushed through a turnstile into the gym. Gideon knew he wouldn't get through without a pass, or a fuss, and he was less than happy at the thought of knocking out a female attendant…unless…Gideon retraced his steps in a jog to the public toilet.

"Dani, I'm going to try and get my hands on that soldier's pass and uniform. Get your boys to check if the gym has a contract with *Sparkling Cleaning Services* cleaning company."

"Just a minute," came Dani's voice. "What do you have in mind?" Dani said a minute later.

"There was a cleaner in the toilets. If the same company does the cleaning for the gym, then I might be able to get past the reception desk."

Gideon entered the toilets again. The cleaner was still there and had left the mop and bucket at the door. Now he was busy with soap and brush, cleaning each of the toilets. Still whistling tunelessly. Gideon noted he was wearing an iPod now; he could hear the tinny music spilling from the earbuds.

Gideon looked around and then went to the urinal. A toilet flushed and a deckhand in denims left the restroom. Gideon was pretty sure there was no-one else there except the cleaner. He felt a little bad about what he had to do next, but there was no other way. He removed the skillet from his jacket and dinged the attendant on the back of his head as he lent over the toilet, cleaning. The young man went down without a fight; Gideon caught him as he fell. He lowered the cleaner to the ground and felt for a pulse. Still strong, just out cold. Working quickly, he removed the cleaner's shirt, pants and lanyard, then his own and put his shirt over the unconscious man and then his own jacket. *At least he scored a good leather jacket out of the bargain and with any luck won't say anything so he can keep it, thought Gideon.* He didn't bother putting his pants on the other man, just leaving them for him when he regained consciousness. It would buy him a bit of time, anyway. He placed the unconscious attendant in the recovery position and tied his hands behind his back with the iPod cord. On his way out he retrieved the mop and bucket and then hurried toward the gym.

"Gideon?" Dani said.

"Speak to me."

"It's not the same cleaning company."

"Shit. We'll just have to improvise," said Gideon.

"Tell me how to say 'new cleaner' in Russian, then I'll hand my phone to the attendant and you can spin her some bullshit about a new contract having been signed."

As he entered the warehouse containing the gym, with his mop and bucket, the attendant looked up and gave him barely a glance. She was a military lady, he thought.

"New cleaning service," Gideon said in his best Russian, displaying his lanyard and then quickly handed the attendant his phone.

She frowned at him "Da ee deityyou—are kidding?" the woman exclaimed with a look of mistrust on her face, but accepted his phone.

"Hello?" she said.

Dani spoke fluent Russian. His family had come to Israel from Russia a generation earlier.

He watched her as she listened. Her face seemed to register confusion, then acceptance, then finally humor.

Gideon pointed at his watch.

The woman gave him his phone, then gave him a once over from top to bottom and made as if to buzz him in, still chuckling to herself. Gideon took a step away with his bucket and mop.

"Where is your pass?" she said.

Gideon held it out to her, but held his ground, not coming any nearer.

The woman's eyes narrowed.

"Your boss said to me you were a Persian idiot, but he could not find a Russian to clean the toilet," Dani did a real time interpretation for Gideon. Then he told Gideon what to say in response.

"I'm a fucking cleaner," Dani relayed to him. Gideon repeated, then tapped his watch again, looking chagrined.

She giggled, but then buzzed him through with a condescending look on her face.

"Hurry up," she said and gave him no more attention, getting back to her beauty magazine.

Gideon snorted under his breath and walked toward the sauna, mop and bucket in hand, scanning the gym. It was relatively empty of patrons, as predicted. The soldier he was after was not on the floor. *Must be in the changing room.* He opened the door to the men's changing rooms and walked along the front vestibule filled with benches and hooks, on which a number of clothing items hung. No soldier here. He continued along the shower stalls toward the back, where the sauna steamed behind a closed door. Two soldier's uniforms hung on the hook, together with the soldiers' ID cards and their boots neatly tucked in below the bench. Steam came from below the sauna door and Gideon detected slight movements in the sauna stall, then a splash and hiss as one of the soldiers threw more water on the steamer.

A grin appeared on Gideon's face.

"My lucky day," he said under his breath.

He heard the soldier sigh, then swear. Gideon put down his mop and bucket and quickly stripped off his clothes.

"I need to take a piss," one of them said.

"Not in here!" the other answered.

He put one of the soldier's pants on and was just going to put on his shirt when the sauna door opened and one of the soldiers stepped out.

Both Gideon and the soldier exclaimed in surprise at the same time in different languages.

"What are you doing? Thie…" the soldier began.

Gideon did not let him finish. With tremendous speed, Gideon pivoted and delivered a roundhouse kick to the soldier's face that sent him reeling backward into his friend. The second soldier ricocheted off the first into the steamer. He put both his hands out to push himself off the piping hot steamer, screaming in pain. Gideon descended on the mop and spun it around delivering a sternum blow to the second soldier with its point, winding him and then finished with a frontal dragon kick to the head.

Both soldiers were out cold.

Gideon caught his breath, thinking quickly. He dragged both men off the bench and into the recovery position, feeling for pulses and hoping he had not killed either of them. After all, they were innocent of any wrongdoing.

Both men lay prone. Gideon listened carefully for any sign of movement in the changing rooms; none he could detect. He might just get away with this.

"Talk to me, Gideon," came Dani's voice in his ear.

"The soldier you saw earlier, and another, both out cold," he said breathing hard.

"I'll stow them in the sauna. No one will be the wiser and I'll walk out of here in one of their uniforms."

Gideon turned the sauna off and closed the door behind him.

"How are you going to get past the receptionist?"

"Not sure yet," Gideon mumbled, as he worked quickly to put on the Marine's uniform. His judgement had been correct; it was almost a perfect fit; the boots were a little large though. He pulled the soldier's cap low over his head and, noticing the other soldier had a pair of eyeglasses, he put them on too. Except for the stubble, he had a passing resemblance to the first marine, who was also dark haired.

Gideon looked around him. High up on the wall above the bench were three louvered glass windows that let in filtered weak sunlight. He wondered if he could repeat the feat of escaping through a gym window like he'd done in New York, but these were just not big enough for him to squeeze through at the shoulders.

"Crap," he said under his breath.

The door of the changing room opened and swung shut; someone had entered.

"One more thing I have to do before I go," he said in a whisper.

"What's that?" asked Dani.

"Shave. No self-respecting soldier would be unshaven on duty," he said.

He shoved his discarded clothes under the bench. He placed the marine's lanyard over his head so that it swung neatly from his neck around the middle of his chest, making sure the photo ID was turned the wrong way around. He pocketed his wallet and had a quick look through the wallet of one of the soldiers, removing only the gym ID. A shower in the next vestibule area sputtered to life. Gideon made his way past the shower stalls. Another man, young, with his back turned to him soaped himself in the shower. In the changing rooms he spotted what he was looking for, a shaving kit left on the bench by one of the patrons. He unzipped it and liberated the razor and a small can of shaving foam, which he put in his jacket pocket.

He left the changing room and walked slowly toward the back of the gym. Several men were in the throes of their various workouts and did not give him a single glance. The wall at the back of the gym was solid, no door. One of the side walls had a fire exit, but it looked like it had a contact alarm attached. There was nothing for it; he'd have to risk leaving via the front door. Relief flooded him as three men wearing marine uniforms walked in, joking and making a ruckus and flirting with the attendant. She was all bouncing breasts and laughter, as they had their IDs checked by her and left their carbines on the front desk for her to stow safely. Gideon took the opportunity to exit the turnstile just as the attendant checked the first Marine's gym ID. He kept his cell phone to his ear and said "Da" a few times as he moved through the reception area. Gideon kept an eye on the attendant's reflection in the front window. She glanced after him with a slight frown on her face and then a shrug as she helped the other marines. Gideon jogged to the public restroom. The cleaner was nowhere in sight. He retrieved his backpack, took a quick shave, and left the restroom in under three minutes.

"Nice moves," Gideon heard in his ear, followed by a dry chuckle. "What's the plan now?" Dani said.

"Not sure," said Gideon.

"We've been working on a few scenarios. Best to use the 'General would like to have a word with you, scenario.' You know the one; it'll be effective since we're on a military base. We'll need a ship's manifest though." Dani explained what he had in mind.

"Sounds like it has legs, I'll try that, but I've got to hurry. They're going to discover the soldiers in the sauna soon and the kid cleaner I knocked out earlier is nowhere in sight, but the good news is he didn't see who knocked him out. The soldiers did though," he said to Dani.

"Who does your ID say you are?" Dani said.

Gideon glanced at his ID. "Private Medvedev."

Gideon walked up the dock and into a busy warehouse. It was a large import/export business. He received a few cautious glances from several workers as he strode toward the office space at the back of the warehouse, no doubt because of the uniform.

He entered the office and shut the door behind him.

"Can I help you?" said the middle-aged lady behind the counter. Her hair was dyed jet black, her lipstick a blood red stain on a powdered white face.

"Da," Gideon mimicked the lines being fed to him through his earpiece.

Gideon saluted the lady and then handed her his phone. "The General," he said.

Dani took over.

The woman took the cell phone from him with a scared look on her face.

"Hello?" she said timorously.

"This is General Balakin. I need to see the manifest for the ship, the *Black Sea Star*," Dani said in flawless Russian. *The Black Sea Star* was a ship that was currently being loaded.

"What do you need it for?" said the woman.

"It is a delicate matter of some importance," Dani said.

The woman stared at Gideon who held her eye, unsmilingly, his hands behind his back. A look of uncertainty crept into her eyes.

"All I need is a copy, not the original. There is a piece of equipment on board that we understand has been stolen from the military and disguised as something else. Please give Private Medvedev a copy of the manifest and keep this matter strictly confidential. This is a national security matter."

Gideon continued to stare at the woman. He could see her becoming nervous. Her eyes went from registering uncertainty to fear. She cleared her throat.

"Okay, but can I get some ID please? This is highly irregular. I will have to tell my boss." Gideon sighed and extended the ID on his lanyard for her to see, a very quick glance. "Private Medvedev?" The woman made a show of taking a note of his name.

"That is correct Madam, now if you don't mind…and while I appreciate this is irregular, please get your boss to call me when this is done." Dani continued.

Dani gave her a military number, garnered by his 8200 analysts, to jot down.

She was clearly a little overawed being involved in a military matter. She handed Gideon his phone.

Gideon accepted the phone and continued to stare at her unblinkingly. The woman typed a few keystrokes and a second later Gideon heard the whine of a printer. It chattered for a full minute while the woman stared back at him, uncomfortably. She got up, with a sulky look on her face and snapped a staple through the top of the left corner of the manifest and handed the document to Gideon. He glanced at it and then thanked the woman in Russian, stowed it in his backpack, turned and had to clamp down hard on an urge to run from the building.

He made his way over to the *Andromeda* gangway and stood near the guard. His cell phone rang.

"Da, Private Medvedev here," he said loudly enough for the guard to hear. The guard turned his attention to Gideon.

"Yes, I have the documents," he said copying the words Dani fed him, and put his backpack down at the feet of the guard then removed the documents from his bag.

"Yes, Captain Andreyev…?" Gideon said, as if taking instructions.

The guard's attention sharpened. Captain Andreyev was the Captain of the *Andromeda.*

"Da, General Balakin…" Gideon continued as if in conversation. Gideon walked up to the guard and looked at his name tag.

"Private Egerov, General Balakin," Gideon said, eyeing the blond, prematurely balding young man menacingly.

"General Balakin wants to talk," Gideon said to the young soldier, keeping it simple and handing private Egerov the cell phone.

The young private visibly blanched and accepted the handset, the reddish pimples on his skin now standing out fiercely.

"Private Egerov, this is General Balakin. Is Captain Andreyev aboard the *Andromeda* yet?" Dani said authoritatively, once again in perfect Russian.

"Yes, I believe he is," said the private scanning his clip board.

"I have a confidential message to deliver to the captain. And I need the captain's signature on the documents Private Medvedev has with him. Private Medvedev has an important task to perform. I want you to sign him in as usual, but tell no one else that he has seen Captain Andreyev, under any circumstances, is that understood?"

"Completely General."

"Good man. I shall remember your name. I reward loyalty."

"Thank you, General."

"Pass me back to Private Medvedev."

Gideon held up the ID attached to the lanyard with his finger slightly obscuring the face.

Private Egerov solemnly scanned the ID. It beeped as it should have and so there were no further questions asked.

Gideon replaced the documents in his bag and then dramatically zipped it up, keeping eye contact with Private Egerov. He nodded his head in a slow downward motion; a conspiratorial gesture.

Private Egerov nodded back and then opened the gate to the gangway. Gideon sauntered up and headed toward the bridge. Crew for the *Andromeda* were starting to arrive in large numbers now.

"Our boys are in the ship's system now. We'll wipe the name of Private Medvedev boarding from the log," Dani said.

"All good. Do you have a layout of the ship you can send me?"

"One step ahead of you," Dani said.

Gideon felt a gentle buzz in his pocket as an email landed in his inbox with the ship layout.

"Borrow some clothes from one of your shipmates and ditch the uniform when you can. Right now go to the engine room. There are quite a few nooks and crannies down there, you can hide out until nightfall," Dani said.

The crew on board were getting ready to cast off and did not pay much heed to a Russian marine on board with official looking documentation in his hands. Gideon was able to make his way carefully down into the engine room. There was no shortage of places to stow away. Three stories of massive engine, piping, wiring, and ducts gave him ample opportunity to find a spot in a quiet dark corner behind some air conditioning ducting. He squatted down, checked his weapon, and then took out one of the pasties and a bottle of water. Gideon decided to wait for roll call before finding suitable clothing.

# Chapter 18

Mahram woke with a sense of foreboding she could not shake. She did not like the way the ambassador had looked at her as the guests departed. She slipped on some jeans, a white T-shirt, and a sensible pair of shoes and went down to the kitchen for breakfast.

"Morning Mahram! What a wonderful party," the cook said as Mahram entered the kitchen.

Farah was there too and smiled shyly at her.

"All thanks to you Fatima, and you too, Farah. The food was delightful!" Mahram said with a smile.

"Thank you for letting Farah watch the dancing. That was kind of you, Mahram."

"Farah is my friend. She was most welcome."

Farah smiled again and bobbed her head.

"Your father wants you to join him for breakfast in his study. I have taken the things through already."

Mahram frowned slightly. "Okay, thank you Fatima. I will go."

Fatima sighed heavily. Mahram knew the sign.

"What is it, Fatima?"

"Mahram, I have known you since you were a little girl."

Mahram smiled at Farah. "This sounds serious." Farah giggled.

"You are of an age when a woman must marry. A father is right to care for his children," Fatima said solemnly.

"What are you trying to say, Fatima?"

Fatima teared up. "I only want you to be happy, Mahram my darling. Libya is not like America. They are godless people in America…"

Mahram walked over to Fatima and gave the plump older lady a warm hug.

"Please don't worry about me."

Fatima burst into tears.

"Honor is still important to a man here in Libya. Please don't dishonor your father. I could not bear the consequences."

Now Farah started to cry too.

"Fatima, please. Calm down. What has made you so sad? Tell me. You're scaring me."

"I know how headstrong you are, Mahram. You have always been like that; even as a little girl. I remember, just like your mother. I fear for your safety."

"Why?"

"I overheard the Master talking on the phone to the Sheik about you. They have agreed to marry you to the Sheik's son. He is a fine, good-looking young man. He is wealthy. You will be happy."

Mahram felt shock rising from her stomach into her mind.

"What are you saying?" Mahram said.

"I have said too much. Please don't let your father know I've said anything. He will not forgive me."

Now anger started to mount in Mahram's heart.

"He cares for you, Mahram. It is a father's duty. Please, I'm like a mother to you now. You were such a sweet little girl. Now you're all grown up. My only concern is your safety."

Tears threatened to overwhelm Mahram, but she fought them down.

"Don't worry, Fatima. I will be sensible," Mahram said. She gave Fatima a final hug and squeezed the hand of Farah and then left the kitchen, closing the door gently behind her.

Once out in the passageway to her father's study, Mahram leaned on the wall. She squeezed her eyes shut, willing the tears away. Clamping down on her fear, she said a fervent silent prayer for protection. She detoured into the bathroom, washed her face, and then rubbed her cheeks vigorously with a towel to get some color back into them and looked into her own eyes in the mirror. She was not going down without a fight. Her lower lip quivered. She grabbed it and squeezed it between her fingers until the pain made her eyes tear up. She washed her face again and dried it on a towel then turned, resolute.

Mahram knocked on the door of her father's study.

"Come in," her father said.

"Hello, my dear daughter. Come in and have some breakfast with your father."

"Thank you, Papa. I'm not disturbing your work? I'm sure you are busy," Mahram said. Her father got up as she sat down and poured her a cup of coffee.

Mahram sat and buttered some toasted naan bread and spread some strawberry jam on it.

"No, no. I always have time for my daughter. Last night's party was fun, no? You looked like you were having a good time."

"Yes, Papa, it was fun. I think our guests left happy."

"Yes, the ambassador and his family are good Sunni Muslims. Though they are good people, they are not too strict. I think the trick is balance in this life. Do you agree?"

Mahram did not answer.

"The ambassador understands things are changing. His son is close to the Prince, you know – almost the same age. They went to the same school together in London. Did you know that?"

"How interesting. No, he didn't mention that when I spoke to him," Mahram said.

"What did the two of you speak about?"

"Well, he did most of the talking. He seemed to be very taken with the nightlife in London and spoke about his house in Knightsbridge quite a bit. He also appeared to have some interest in horses and fencing, you know, with a sword…and he mentioned he is patron of a few madrassas in England."

Basar looked at her then chuckled. "It is very difficult to impress young ladies these days, it seems. I feel sorry for the young men."

"I was not aware he was trying to impress me."

"I saw you leave halfway through the meal?"

Mahram hesitated just a fraction before she answered. "A good hostess must check on the serving staff to make sure all is well."

"My security guards said you came in here, into my study, and were in here for a several minutes."

"Did they now."

"Why were you in here when you had guests to look after?"

Mahram laughed lightly. "I had forgotten my purse in here earlier." His eyes narrowed. She could see he was trying to search his memory. "In my study?" he said.

"It's my favorite room in the house. Before the guests arrived, I came in here to relax. I was a little nervous…I came in here for solace," she said.

"Solace. What do you mean?" he said.

Mahram knew she had to nip this in the bud and quickly. Attack was the only way forward.

"I came in here for solace because I know you are trying to pawn me off to the Sheik's son."

She could see her barbed words had struck home. Now he was on the defensive.

"I'm not trying to pawn you off! That is a rude and disrespectful thing to say! A father has a right to seek the best for his children's future. We have been over this already! I'm not going to let you marry some American, if that's what you think!"

Mahram remained silent, her thoughts racing. She could become defiant, but that way was blocked to her. At best she would be a prisoner in her own home, at worst she could be killed for dishonoring her father. She had no doubt he was capable of that and Fatima's tears hinted at that possibility.

"You're in Libya now and this is the way we do things in Libya!" he said in a sullen tone.

Mahram could feel her face twitch slightly. How she wanted to claw this man's eyes out. She clamped down hard on her hate. She would live to fight another day.

"Yes, Papa. I see. I'm sorry I showed you disrespect."

Basar's eyes narrowed as he observed his daughter. He took a slow sip of his coffee.

"Tariq Al-Ali has asked me for permission to pay you visits. I have agreed to this arrangement."

Mahram took another bite of her toast and chewed slowly, lest her bitter anger make her say something she would regret.

"One more thing before I go to work. You must start to dress like a woman and not a little girl. I do not want you wearing tight clothing out in public, especially if you are seen with Tariq."

Mahram's heart leapt in hope. Here was a possible break. She could get out of the house. She knew Agent Hunter and that other young man were out there somewhere, watching, waiting.

"Yes Papa. I will need to buy some clothes if I'm to go out with this man. I assume you will want me to have a friend along? Farah can come with me when I'm with Tariq and when I shop. She is a good girl."

Basar sighed heavily.

"Of course! I will also send one of my guards. Don't worry, he will stay at a discrete distance from you."

There was a moment of silence when neither of them would look at the other.

"You are not the only one who misses your mother, you know. She would have been much better at this than me," he said.

Mahram smiled at that admission and bit down on a sarcastic retort. Her mother would definitely have been better at this. She would not have approved of an arranged marriage for a start, but she said nothing.

He took his wallet from his suit jacket pocket and handed her a credit card.

"I've been meaning to give this to you, but was looking for a measure of responsibility from you before I did. Now that I've seen it, I'm happy to give you this. I know you will be sensible."

"I will, Papa. Thank you. I will go after lunch today to look for appropriate clothes. Something more conservative," she said.

Basar searched her eyes again.

"I know things have been very tough for you lately. But please believe me when I say, if you knew what I knew, you would also be concerned."

"You keep on saying that—hinting at trouble, Papa. What is it? You can trust me."

Basar gave his daughter another searching look and sighed, then shook his head.

"Please believe me when I say, my daughter, it is better you don't know. Knowledge is sometimes very dangerous. When one has it, one is forced to make decisions and that is what you are seeing me do. Hard decisions, bitter decisions—let me make them. It's my duty to do so."

Mahram nodded but said nothing. It felt like a sputtering candle had just been snuffed out in her heart. He would not trust her; she knew without a shadow of a doubt now she could not trust him. One thing was undeniable; something was deeply amiss in all of this. If Jabir's hint to her had been true, then her father was complicit in a great act of planned evil. Something that involved her and the exchange of a large sum of money. What had Jabir said to her, a nuclear war? Powerful forces were at work all around her.

At that moment she made up her mind. She was determined she was not going to be used anymore.

"I must go now. I have work to do," her father said. He got up and smiled condescendingly down at her. She put up a front, smiling back.

As her father left the room, she could not help but look up at the wall where she knew the hidden camera stared at everything, unblinking and all knowing. She gave it a long hard look and nodded slightly.

Hunter did not miss that look. Soon he had a transcript of the conversation and was on the phone to Alda and Dani. They had to act soon.

*** 

The call came through just after Sara had convinced her boss to give her two months leave.

"Hi Sara, Hunter here."

"Hunter? Wait a second."

Sara moved into the ladies' bathroom at the hospital and made sure she was alone in the facility. She moved the aluminum rubbish bin toward the door so that anyone coming in would strike the edge of it just slightly and she would be alerted to their presence. She entered a toilet stall but did not close the door entirely.

"What is it?" she said, softly.

"Long story. Suffice it to say it's important and urgent. Can we meet?"

Hunter gave a short description of what had transpired between Mahram and her father. They agreed to meet at the apartment.

"Hunter, I have an idea. This might just be the best timing ever. Gideon wants my grandmother and I to go to Sardinia while he's away. He believes it's unsafe for us here. Well…what if Mahram comes with us? I can give you all the details now."

"Ok," Hunter said thoughtfully. "It sounds intriguing. Let's talk more when we meet."

Sara left work after finishing her night shift. She called in to the Café de Paris for a coffee on the way to the safe house and deliberately left her phone on the seat she sat on, knowing full well that if it was found, it would be handed in to the staff. Her phone was a potential electronic marker she could not afford to have on her now. After making a detoured trip and checking for tails, she made it to the safe house and knocked on the door.

232

Eli let her in and, after a quick greeting, she made her way directly to the table where Hunter and Nathan sat talking quietly to one another.

Hunter smiled up at her. "Sit down and check this out, then we can talk."

The first bit of footage was of Basar speaking to the ambassador and then Tariq about dating Mahram. The second bit was the conversation between Mahram and her father, and then Mahram's long look directly at the camera.

"I've spoken to Alda Dibra, the Deputy Director of Operations in the CIA. She says that we shouldn't take Mahram out of the mix, but should continue to use her in place as she could be a great asset for us if she ever gets close to the ambassador's son."

Sara frowned. "That's completely unethical. Mahram is a US citizen and she's quite clearly being held against her will. She didn't place herself in this situation."

Hunter nodded. He seemed a little shamefaced.

"And yet I cannot disobey an order and there is some logic to Alda's argument," Hunter said.

Sara searched his eyes then looked at Nathan who remained impassive, then at Eli, who smiled at her.

"What? Am I missing something?" she said.

"Well, while I have to follow orders, you don't. What if a boat was made available for you, Mahram and your grandmother and what if that boat sailed to Sardinia and you holed up at Gideon's house until this whole thing blew over?"

Sara smiled, then said, "That sounds great, but there is only one problem. I don't own a boat and, secondly, I don't know how to pilot one."

"We know just the man. We use him all the time. In fact, you may know him as Ezat," Eli said.

"The smuggler? Yes, he brings guests to my house."

"We've had a preliminary discussion with him. If you know Ezat, you know he is a man that can do just about anything with an engine. He says he can organize a fishing trawler. It won't be the Ritz but..."

"Okay. So, we potentially have a boat and a Captain in Ezat. How do we get my grandmother and Mahram on board?"

"There is a little harbor and fishing village near Al Hamidiyah. You know the suburb; to the north east of Tripoli? Ezat will wait for you there. You can take your grandmother to him before returning to meet Mahram."

Sara looked skeptical.

"We can't do this without your help. It has to be quick and Mahram has to be in agreement. We just don't have the numbers to do this by force—it has to be by way of deception."

"Where will I make contact?"

"We have a camera on the front of the house that we placed by drone. Basically, we wait for her to leave and follow her."

Sara looked at the men looking back at her.

"Where will you be in all of this, Hunter?"

"A long way away. I should be on an airplane back to the States when all this goes down, so my fingerprints cannot be traced back to this."

"Who's paying for this? I don't have much money to spend on boats and motels and paying captains."

Eli and Nathan looked at each other, then looked at her and laughed mischievously.

"Why do I get the impression you two have just done something bad?" she said with a half-smile.

"Basically, we have what Eli and I like to call our emergency 'get out of Dodge' fund. Don't misunderstand us; it's just insurance money. We have an offshore account that we can use in emergencies. We've developed a program that allows us to…well, borrow money from bad people," Nathan began.

"Yes, don't look so skeptical, Sara. Basar Ammar is going to be paying for this little holiday of his daughter's as he should have all along. Instead, he agreed to funnel money for a terrorist organization. We're simply going to use some of his money for the safety of his daughter…while she is in our care."

Sara grinned.

"So, you're stealing some of his money to pay for this."

"Stealing? Meh. Such an unfortunate word. We have access to his computer. We infected it with a Trojan. We can follow keystrokes. So now we have his bank details, passwords and bank account numbers. He has several offshore accounts. He's a naughty boy and a very wealthy man. We're going to help him be honest for a change and ensure his daughter's safety. If he was a righteous man, he would be grateful to us. Or so we believe." Eli said, then cackled with laughter.

Hunter chuckled. "Just so that you know, I'm going to check my bank account after I leave today. I'm glad we're on the same side."

They all laughed nervously.

"Okay, enough fun. Here's the plan," Hunter said. He took out a street map of Tripoli and outlined his plan.

"So, unless we somehow get more information before she leaves, Sara, you will need to follow her into a shop. Your play will be an old high school friend. Eli, Nathan, you need to dig around in your computers to find out where Mahram went to school and what year she graduated. Sara, you need to get her alone. Perhaps in a change room or something and tell her to take her entourage for lunch at the Shwaya Steak House. It's really important that it is this restaurant and no other, because there is a back entrance off the toilet facility that leads onto a quiet street. Eli and Nathan will be waiting on that street for Mahram with a van. Understood?"

Hunter paused, looking at each of the young people.

"I know its fly but the seat of your pants stuff, but it's all we have. We have to use every opportunity we get."

Everyone nodded their heads.

# Chapter 19

The siren sounded for roll call. All crew moved to the deck as the ship cast off. There was a rush of footsteps and good-natured banter and laughter as the men trooped up to the main deck. Gideon waited for a minute for any stragglers and then moved quickly to the crew quarters, using the map of the ship Unit 8200 had sent him earlier.

The ship was large and Gideon had to walk up several gangways to get to the crew quarters. He entered a dorm door left open in the rush to roll call. Each room slept four. Several half-stowed bags lay on bunks. Some had hung up their clothes in their lockers, others had left their clothing on their bunks as they sorted through the items. Gideon worked quickly and cleanly, knowing he only had moments. The first to go was his shirt replaced with a black T-shirt featuring Led Zeppelin, next a green bomber jacket from another locker and then a pair of dark denim jeans measured against his legs and a black beanie from yet another locker. The jeans and fatigues he'd taken off were stuffed under his arms. Placing the beanie on his head, he walked quickly back toward the engine room as he heard the men breaking up after roll call and making their noisy way back.

There was no turning back, the ship was underway now. Gideon cautiously returned to his hideout and changed slowly. He screwed the suppressor into his weapon and placed it on the ground within easy reach of his hand. He tightened the laces on his combat boots and placed the knife in its sheath under his belt. He ate the rest of the food in his backpack and drank a full bottle of water. Sitting cross-legged, his back wedged into the corner of a wall with his Glock resting on his lap, he did some square breathing until his mind calmed completely. He went into a deep meditative state between sleep and wakefulness, his ears and other senses acutely attuned to his environment. This was a state of consciousness that had been taught to the soldiers in his unit by their special forces instructor. There were often times they'd have to wait quietly in a confined space for hours for their quarry to show up and so it was necessary training to stop the fidgets while they waited. After about an hour of meditation, he slowly brought himself to full consciousness again.

It was late afternoon and the sun at these latitudes would be sinking quickly in the west. He felt refreshed, in tune with his body and mind, and ready for action. Digging into his backpack, he withdrew his satellite cell phone. The reception was weak down here, but still probably strong enough to send a text. He wrote a quick one to Dani and sent it, but it stuck in the outgoing box.

"Shit," Gideon said under his breath.

He got up quietly and retrieved the paperwork he'd come on board with as cover and made his way silently up the nearest companionway. He saw several engineers below him working at gauges. None looked up; they were all engaged with the management of the ship.

He made his way up a second companionway and with a quick glance down a corridor, sauntered toward a doorway that led onto the starboard deck. As he opened the door, he felt the phone vibrate in his hand. He looked down. His SMS had gone through. He stood under some piping. A deck above him, he could hear men talking indistinctly to one another. On the bow, about 200 yards distant, he could make out men moving around the shipping containers. He noticed a guard in tactical gear patrolling the bow section, carbine in hand.

The phone vibrated again. A reply to his SMS.

*"Locate package. Beacon, Geiger counter and spike drone bomblet in backpack. 55$^{th}$ Airborne unit are preparing and will deploy to engage once we are sure the package is aboard and Andromeda in international waters. Confirm message."*

Gideon wrote quickly.

*"Good, copy. At the present rate of knots when will we reach international waters?"* he sent.

A minute later another vibration.

*"12 hours for Andromeda at present speed to enter Aegean Sea. 55th Airborne is gathering now. Confirm."*

Gideon confirmed and turned back to see a young sailor making his way toward him on the starboard deck.

"Hey," the man called out to him and waved.

Gideon waved back and moved toward the door, adrenalin seething through his system, readying him for action.

"Hold up!" the young sailor walked toward him with a smile on his face and took out a packet of cigarettes.

"You have a light?" making the action of a lighter.

Gideon smiled back "Nuit," he said, then pointed to the manifest. He opened the door and closed it quickly behind him.

He could see the young sailor frowning at him through the portal. Gideon pointed to the manifest and made a running motion.

The sailor grinned.

Gideon sighed his relief as he turned and quickly made is way down to the belly of the ship. He passed by another sailor on a companion way, going in the opposite direction, who grunted at his friendly nod. He saw no-one else.

Once Gideon was safely behind his air-conditioning unit again, he decided to do an inventory and took out all of the contents of the backpack, making sure everything was in working order. He eyed the 'spike,' essentially a flying drone grenade. That could do some serious damage in a confined space, he thought.

***

A file was opened and a military investigating officer was assigned to the case of an assault on Private Medvedev and Private Pushkin. Both were found in a military gym sauna at about the same time the *Andromeda* cast off.

They'd been taken to hospital. Private Pushkin regained consciousness in hospital, but Private Medvedev did not. A scan was performed and he was rushed into surgery with bleeding on the brain. The surgery had been successful and he would survive, but he was in an induced coma for the moment. The blow more damaging than at first anticipated.

Officer Votyakov was assigned the case at 5 pm. He sighed heavily as he read the case details. Probably some sort of dispute between soldiers; about a girl no doubt. It usually was. He'd investigate tomorrow, he thought.

Just as he was about to close the email, he noticed that the weapon used for the assault was a mop—the same had been reported stolen by a young cleaner, he was sure of that. And then there was the assault on a cook earlier on a nearby ship. Three vicious assaults in one day and a stolen mop was highly unusual on base; coincidence? If experience had taught Investigator Votyakov anything it was that there was no such thing as coincidence. On second thoughts, Private Medvedev was lucky he'd not been killed; this was a serious matter and Private Pushkin has steadfastly refused to acknowledge that he'd had anything to do with the assault on Private Medvedev; rather he had a forcefully repeated a fanciful tale about a karate expert having knocked them both out with a mop. There was a fleeting description of the alleged assailant.

His interest now piqued, Votyakov flicked through the cases of the day until he found the one containing the assault on the cook. He read the cook's description of the assailant. Dark haired, about 6.1, wearing a beanie. Now he flicked back to the case involving the soldiers. In a description, all but ignored by the interviewing officer, the receptionist at the gym said that a suspicious cleaner had entered the gym earlier in the day saying that he was a new cleaner and he had gone to the men's changing room directly—description of suspect, tall, dark and a beanie, with an unshaven face. The assaults could have taken place only minutes apart.

Investigator Votyakov felt a surge of excitement. Almost certainly the same man, he thought. He stared, unseeingly at the glowing computer screen in front of him, his ice blue eyes computing images and information running through his mind. He was so deep in thought, not even the bustle of his colleagues leaving for the evening intruded. There was something else trying to make its way into his memory, something he'd heard in passing that just would not quite surface, lurking below his line of consciousness.

Think. What did Private Medvedev and Pushkin and the cook on a cargo ship have in common? Where had Private Medvedev and Pushkin been just before the scene of the assault? Votyakov brought up Private Medvedev's log. He'd been guarding the tanker *Andromeda's* gangway; Pushkin had been in his office. Medvedev had handed over to a young Private Egerov. There was a handover at roughly the same time as the cook had been assaulted on the cargo ship *Pegasus*. Excitement surged through him again as he realized that the *Pegasus* had been berthed right next to the *Andromeda*. That too was surely not a coincidence! He sat for another full hour trying to puzzle out what the connections were, but finally gave up, as his stomach grumbled and then his wife phoned wondering what was keeping him.

Votyakov sighed and switched off his computer for the night. He drove home, still puzzling through the connections.

"Is there something wrong with the fish, my dear. You seem so quiet tonight," his wife said.

"No, no, not at all. In fact, the fish is wonderful. It's just this case I'm working on—it's got me worried. I'm missing something—I know it is important, but I just can't figure out what it is," Votyakov said.

His wife smiled; he was such a serious man. But that's why she loved him—intelligent and serious—she hated triviality. Her father had been such a trivial man. A drunk. A man who laughed at everything, including his own health as he died of liver disease.

"I'm sure if you relax it will come to you," she said with a smile.

"I'm sure you are right, my love," he said.

"Perhaps after the little ones are asleep, we can make love? That should fix you up," she said, still smiling.

He chuckled. "That always fixes me up. Let's get these babies to bed," he said with gusto.

Just after midnight Votyakov woke from a dream. He sat bolt upright in bed. A thin film of sweat soaked his chest, despite the cold night.

The sudden movement disturbed his wife.

"What is it, Alexander?" she said irritably, still half asleep.

"I have it! I know who he is!"

"Who what is?" she said, now coming fully awake.

Votyakov got out of bed and started to dress in his uniform.

"What are you doing, my love! It is only midnight!" she said in a shrill voice.

"I know, I know. I have to check on a few facts before I report what I've found. I must get to the office. This is important! This is the terrorist that shot up the factory and killed some security guards in Leninsky two days ago. I'm absolutely certain it's the same person!"

Mrs Votyakov looked at her husband with admiration and got out of bed in her nightdress.

"I'll make you some coffee and a sandwich my dear. I will do this while you dress."

"That would be excellent, my love! I'll need all my wits about me today and my strength," he said, "but I must be in the car in less than five minutes. If I'm right I shall be speaking to none other than the General!"

# Chapter 20

Mahram got on her knees beside her bed and prayed silently but fervently that God would help her to get out of the awful situation she found herself in. She now knew that she'd been foolish to go along with her father's wishes to stay silent. She should have said something to Hunter, but she had genuinely feared for Hunter's life and her own. Her father had said that he would likely be killed if he helped her. Still, he was a policeman. She should have told him.

Tears sprang to her eyes as she beseeched God to not be forced into a marriage of convenience. She prayed for the safety of those people who would rescue her and the safety of her father too. She prayed for the safety of Farah and for her own courage not to falter.

She got slowly from her knees and picked up the envelope that contained a letter to her father and placed it in her bag, together with a change of underwear. She applied some makeup to her face using her vanity and then checked the door behind her to make sure it was locked, and stepped back toward her bed and felt under the pillow for the handle of the steak knife she'd surreptitiously liberated from the kitchen in the early morning, while pretending to have a drink of orange juice from the fridge.

She stared at the knife in her hand and then placed it in her bag.

"Never again," she thought. "I will never go down without a fight, ever again."

She donned her hijab and then placed her bag over her head and shoulder. Ready.

She walked to her father's study and knocked on the door. He was working from home this morning since it was Saturday.

"Come in," she heard him say.

Mahram opened the door and stepped inside the study. A pang of sorrow lanced through her heart. It was such a beautiful room and reminded her so much of a happier time in their family life—a time before the war. She walked over to the desk where her father sat.

He smiled at her.

"I'm going into town now with Farah. Which one of the guards should come along?"

"Jabir will drive you."

"I will go to the Mungo clothing stores first and then the shoe store. All of them are on Al Jarabah Street. You know the ones?"

"Yes. Yes. Enjoy yourself and be sure to buy Farah something."

"I will," she said.

"Jabir will meet you out front," he said.

"Okay, thank you Papa…"

A fleeting look of misgiving crossed Basar's face. "Stay safe, now," he said, then smiled again.

As soon as she shut the door, Basar called the guard house.

"Faisal, tell Jabir I want him to drive my daughter this afternoon to do some shopping. There is something not quite right here. Make sure a second car follows and ensure the man in that car is armed. Do you understand?"

Basar put down the phone and looked at the painting to his right. Something about the way Mahram was acting made him suspicious. The way she'd looked at him and the painting when she left. The sadness in her voice—almost like she was saying goodbye. He sighed heavily. Maybe it was just her becoming a woman, leaving her childhood fantasies behind and taking on her responsibilities. In truth, he'd never really understood his late wife and daughter. They were too Western.

\*\*\*

Sara's grandmother was very excited at the prospect of an overseas holiday, but when she found out they would be traveling to their destination by fishing trawler she became less enthusiastic. But she regained her composure and then her enthusiasm after she met the captain of the vessel. He simply introduced himself as Ezat and was very charming. Not being a Muslim, he'd kissed her hand as she stepped aboard. That had not happened to her since the sixties, she thought with a smile.

He was very solicitous and showed her to a comfortable berth, which she would share with Sara and helped her lift her very heavy and large suitcase onto the bed. Then he left her and Sara to unpack their things, but later came back with some hot sweet tea and biscuits.

"I will show your grandmother around the boat while you finalize your arrangements," Ezat said to Sara.

"Thank you. We shouldn't be too long, but will probably want to leave as soon as we arrive back."

"Who is this 'we' you keep on talking about? Is it that nice young man who was staying with us? Is he going to come along too?" Mia said with a sly smile. Ezat could not help laughing.

Sara laughed too. "No, he isn't. I'm just going to pick up my girlfriend. You know, the one I said would be joining us. I told you about her at the apartment. She needs a break. She will be staying with us in Sardinia for a little while. I'm just going to help her pack now."

"Oh yes," Mia said. "I forgot about that. I do hope she is well behaved?"

Sara laughed; she knew her grandmother was doing this for effect to impress Ezat.

"This is a big boat to run all by yourself?" Mia said to Ezat.

"Yes, but I'll have some help. There're two young men who will help me. All will be well, you will see, dear lady. I will show you around the vessel and then I will get you comfortably set up in the saloon. There is a TV there and we have a satellite dish."

"Thank you, Ezat," Sara said.

"You have things to do, Sara. Your grandmother will be safe with me. I will look after her well," he said, waving his hand in mock dismissal.

Mia laughed and Sara smiled and walked down onto the gangway to the dock. She got in behind the wheel of a white minivan with a sliding door as she saw Ezat leading her grandmother gently into the bridge to show her the instruments. Sara started the engine and nosed out of the harbor, then dialed Eli hands-free.

"Okay, all set here. Where should I meet you?"

Eli gave her the address then said, "Just be aware that she's going to have company. Farah, the housekeeper's daughter, will be her chaperone and a driver called Jabir, with another car following." He ended the call.

She drove the van cautiously, not wanting to attract attention from the authorities unnecessarily and felt her adrenalin elevate as she entered the central city precinct. Everything depended on the next few minutes. As she drove, she said a silent prayer and donned her dark glasses. How she wished Gideon was here. His presence always made her feel calm. She sighed and hoped he was okay.

Sara parked the white van under a tree on a quiet street running parallel to Al Jarabah street, which was a busy main thoroughfare and one block down from her planned rendezvous point with Mahram. Mahram, of course, was 'flying blind.' She only knew that at some point someone was going to make contact with her. So, Sara had to be careful. Mahram was going to be accompanied and probably quite jumpy. Sara placed her earpiece into her ear, donned her light hijab, and kept her large dark glasses on. She grabbed her bag and cell phone, then carefully locked the vehicle and walked the route she hoped Mahram would take to get away, checking for obstacles. Nathan had reconnoitered the route already, but Eli had told Sara to familiarize herself with it, just in case she had to improvise. She was fairly familiar with this part of the city, but checked her Google maps app just to be sure.

She made her way up Al Jarabah street and entered Mungo, the first of the shops Mahram said she'd visit. It was a large, upmarket, two-story store, exclusively for women and Sara figured it would be best to go and check clothes out near the changing rooms. She kept an eye on the front door from the back of the store, taking several dresses off the rack and holding them up against her body, then she moved to the scarf rack.

"That one looks so nice on you," Sara heard someone say.

She turned and found a sales assistant beaming at her.

"Oh, thank you. I'm waiting for a friend and just looking right now," Sara said in her most dismissively polite voice.

"Do let me know if you need any help. I saw you looking at those dresses. Do you have a formal occasion?"

Sara spotted Mahram and Farah walk into the store.

"I'll be fine, thanks," Sara said more forcefully. The assistant nodded with a hard smile on her face.

"You know where to find…" the assistant began.

"Yes, thanks," Sara said with hard little smile of her own and walked slowly toward the hijabs.

Sara could see that Mahram and Farah were not alone. A man in a suit stood at the door of the store giving it a once over. He made to come in.

"No, Jabir. This store is for women only," Mahram said quite sharply.

"Oh, forgive me. I had no idea. I'll wait out front then," Jabir said, looking suitably chastised.

"Yes, that is fine," Mahram said dismissively.

Sara's lips twitched a smile. Mahram could pull the real prima donna when she wanted to. The sharp-eyed sales assistant had not missed the exchange and decided she would wait a while before pouncing on her next sales victim.

"Ok, making contact now?" Sara whispered into her earpiece.

"Remember, she went to Tripoli Girls' High school," came Nathan's steady voice.

"Yes, yes I remember," Sara said.

A moment passed.

"Aya Ibrahim, classmate," Nathan said.

"Yes, I remember. I can't think when you're talking into my ear." Sara said, checked around the shop. It was not terribly busy, just another five customers, two of them a mother and her daughter.

Sara swallowed hard, then made her approach.

***

"Mahram? Mahram Ammar?" Sara said, walking toward Mahram with a big smile on her face. Mahram looked up sharply.

"It's me, Aya Ibrahim. Do you remember me? We went to the same school. Tripoli Girls' High School?"

It took a second for Mahram to register that this may be her contact.

"Ayaaa, of course I remember you!"

Farah smiled delightedly, then frowned; there was something familiar about this woman, she thought.

Sara opened her arms and she and Mahram hugged.

"Remember our little joke. The one we did in English class together?" Sara said in Arabic. "Remind me, I don't remember," Mahram said, frowning slightly. In the back of her mind, she realized she was speaking to the same woman who had searched her at the UN headquarters. Her disguise was good beneath the hijab, large dark glasses and make-up; she looked like a completely different woman.

In accented English Sara said, "Laugh when I finish the sentence. I will tell you next that I'm looking for a gown and would like an honest opinion from an old friend and will get one size too small. Send your friend to get a size up for me."

Mahram laughed and put her hand to her mouth. "You were always the class joker," she said in Arabic. "Farah, this is an old friend of mine, Aya Ibrahim. We met at school."

Farah bobbed her head in greeting. Sara beamed at her.

"Pleased to meet you, Farah. You know, are you ladies in a hurry? I need a gown for a formal function I'm attending shortly and I'd really value an honest opinion. I'm not sure I'm getting it with the attendant," Sara said the last part in a whisper.

Farah smiled conspiratorially.

"Of course, we'll help. We're in no hurry," Mahram said.

Sara cast a quick glance at Mahram's security detail. Jabir stood in the doorway, frowning at Sara.

"Your man outside doesn't seem all that happy," Sara said, mostly for Farah's benefit.

"Security, they are never happy. I guess they're not paid enough to be happy," Mahram said.

Sara led the way to the gowns and picked out two that she knew would be too small. She left a burgundy colored one on the rack that she actually liked that was the correct size.

"Let's see how these fit," Mahram said and led the way into the fitting room. The attendant eyed Sara balefully, following them into the fitting room.

"Would you like some he…"

"No thanks, my friends will help me choose, thank you," Sara said.

"Very well," the attendant said and turned on her heel.

"Optimistic," the attendant mumbled just loud enough to be heard, as she left the changing room area.

"That's very rude. Did you hear what she said?" Farah said.

"Not to worry, Farah. She's probably right, but the point is you don't know what will be best until you try a few different colors and sizes. Half the fun of shopping is finding the right thing. Haven't you found that something you don't think would ever suit you actually does suit after trying it on?"

"So true," Mahram said.

Sara undid her pantsuit and tried to wriggle into one of the gowns. Farah blushed slightly.

"Would you like me to leave?"

"No, my dear. We are all women here," Sara said, smiling.

"Oh dear. I'm afraid the attendant was right. These are too small for me."

Farah looked forlorn.

"Farah, would you be a dear and take this one back to the rack. I don't want the attendant to get that small victory over me. There is a burgundy dress that I also like which is one size up. Would you mind?"

"I'd love to help," Farah said smiling.

"Thank you," Mahram said to Farah.

Farah left the changing room with the dress and noticed the attendant smirking near the register. Farah ignored her.

Sara turned to Mahram, smiled and said in English, "Forgive my undress, but we have no time. Hunter and I are working to get you out. We have heard everything."

Mahram's heart beat like a trip hammer. "Ohh, thank God!" she said.

"There is a steakhouse down the road called Shwaya Steak House. After lunchtime prayers go there and order a big meal for you and your security detail. Get them to sit separately from you. Halfway through the meal, tell Farah you have to go to the bathroom. There is a back security door, go through it. We'll take it from there. There is only one way in and out of that street. Also, be aware that there are at least two men on security detail today—your driver and another in a second car."

"Okay, will do. I didn't know about the second man," Mahram said, alarm in her voice.

"Not to worry. We'll take care of it.," Sara said.

Just at that moment Farah arrived with the burgundy dress.

"Thank you, Farah. As you were bringing it here it occurred to me that I should have taken that dress in the first place. What a beautiful color!"

"Yes, it is so beautiful! To me it is the most beautiful," Farah said. Sara slipped on the dress and it did look stunning on her.

Mahram fussed at the back of the dress, getting Sara's hijab to fall correctly.

"Perfect!" Farah said, beaming once again.

"I think you're right, Farah, it looks great," Mahram said.

"Ladies, I do believe I've found what I'm looking for. I have to run, but it has been such a pleasure meeting you again, Mahram, and making your acquaintance, Farah. Thank you so much for your help. We should meet again. Mahram, may I have your cell number?"

"Yes, of course, Aya, and I yours."

The women exchanged numbers and said their goodbyes.

Sara slipped out of the dress and back into her pantsuit. She quickly paid for the dress with cash, ignoring the attendant's pout, and waved goodbye to Mahram and Farah as they continued to shop. As she left the building, she noted Mahram's security guard giving her a suspicious look and when she had her back turned, she caught him whispering into his cuff in the reflection of a shopfront window across the street. Within less than a minute she had a tail. Sara walked another block toward the steakhouse she'd told Mahram about and entered a women's clothing store called Mira. It was closing in on lunchtime prayers and so she knew the shop would stop for prayer soon. She saw the man who had followed her, waiting across the street. Sara took some jeans off the rack and entered the changing room. There was no one there so close to prayer time.

In Arabic she whispered, "Eli, Nathan? There is a man at 6 o'clock waiting for me outside the Mira store. Can you deal with him? The ladies will be going to lunch soon."

"Describe," Eli said in her ear.

"Tall, dark hair, pockmarked face, light blue shirt, dark pants."

"Copy." There was a momentary hiss on the line. Then: "Target acquired. We'll deal with him once prayer is over."

The call to prayer sounded and everyone on the street faced east while they recited the prayer. The tail kept vigil on the door, despite his need to face east.

After prayer, Sara left the shop. She walked past the steakhouse restaurant and turned left toward where she had left the van. As she turned, she glanced up the street and was gratified to see Mahram and Farah making their way toward the restaurant, chatting and smiling and carrying their new purchases.

Eli and Nathan raced past Sara on a scooter.

"You still have a tail. Bring him one block up. The ladies have just entered the steakhouse," Eli said in Sara's ear.

Sara walked another block and turned left into a quiet, leafy residential street and resisted the urge to look behind her. Up ahead Eli and Nathan stood in front of their scooter with their helmets on chatting to each other and ignored Sara as she walked past them. At the juncture of the next block, Sara hesitated and then crossed the street to a bus stop and sat down. Her tail hesitated too, whispered into his cuff and then continued to walk up the street toward Eli and Nathan, who were still chatting. The tail kept Sara in his peripheral vision across the street. As the tail passed Eli, Sara saw Nathan casually draw a taser from his jacket pocket and shoot the man in the back. The man shook wildly for a second and then went down like a dropped plate of jelly. Eli caught him and dragged him to the nearest tree trunk, his hand over the man's mouth. Eli propped him against the tree and then stepped back while Nathan tasered the man again at close range for good measure. He was out cold, his system overwhelmed with the amperage. Sara hoped the boys had not killed him.

Eli signaled for Sara to move. She got up and walked back toward the van. The last she saw was Eli taking the man's earpiece out of his ear. Although there were children and a few women walking up the street, their backs were turned to the incident and because everything had happened so quickly and quietly, none of them noticed. Several cars slid by in the opposite direction but did not stop. A minute later Eli and Nathan buzzed passed her on their scooter.

"Slight change of plans," she heard Eli say in her ear.

"The tail is not dead. When he comes to, there will be hell to pay. Get Mahram out now!" Sara took her cell phone from her jacket pocket and dialed Mahram's number.

On the third ring Mahram answered.

"Hello?" she said, a worried note in her voice. Clearly, she had not expected a call so early.

"Go to the toilet now. Walk past the ladies' toilet and toward the back of the restaurant. There is a metal door that leads to the courtyard. It's open. Go through. There will be two men waiting for you outside the back of the restaurant. Follow the men from there. They will bring you to a white van that I'm driving. I had a tail. We have dealt with him. Do you understand?"

"Yes of course," Mahram said in a falsely upbeat manner so that Farah would not become suspicious or alarmed.

Mahram took an envelope from her bag containing the letter she'd written to her father and slipped it onto her lap. Just then, their drink order came through. Farah had ordered a coke and Mahram some tea.

"What a lovely day we are having," Farah said contentedly.

"Yes," Mahram said with a tight smile. She swallowed hard, a lump forming in her throat.

"Is all okay, Mahram? You look a little pale," Farah said.

Mahram reached across the table and squeezed Farah's hand.

"You've been such a dear friend. There are big changes ahead for me. I don't want you to worry at all. Here is a letter I've written. Give it to your mother when you can. It's a letter of thanks for all she and others have done for me through the years."

Farah took the letter, a look of sweet confusion on her face. "I'm sure you will really enjoy being married, Mahram. The Sheik is a great man."

Mahram smiled.

"Are you happy with your gifts?" she said to the younger woman.

Mahram kept an eye on the waiter while she listened to Farah gush.

The moment the waiter engaged Jabir for his order, she said, "I'm just going to go to the ladies. I need to change. I'm not feeling well because of my cycle."

Farah looked concerned.

"Order me some lamb and couscous when the waiter comes," Mahram said.

She squeezed Farah's hand again, got up with her bag, and walked into a narrow passageway that led toward the ladies' restroom. She looked around fleetingly and saw Jabir speaking into his cell phone earpiece with a frown on his face. She opened the ladies' restroom door and went inside, but did not let the door close all the way, keeping a small gap between the frame and the door. She leaned her head on the door frame for a just a moment and felt her hands trembling as she did so.

From her vantage point, behind the door she could just see Farah. She waited until Farah turned to the window to her left, her attention caught by the movement on the street. As Farah turned, Mahram slipped through the door and down the passageway, walking to the metal trellis door, opened it and stepped beyond. Once outside she spotted a waiter smoking in the courtyard. The waiter glanced at her as she pushed through the door. Waiting just out of sight of the waiter and beyond the corner of an adjacent building was a young man in a leather jacket with curly dark hair. He nodded at her and turned, indicating with is hand that she should follow. She took another nervous look at the smoking waiter. He smiled at her knowingly. She ignored him, then stepped out into the courtyard and made her way toward the young man, her heart in her mouth.

***

Back inside the restaurant, Jabir's phone rang. He picked it up off the table and, as he did so, looked sideways and saw that Mahram was not at her table. He immediately stood in alarm; she had been sitting there chatting with Farah just moments ago.

"Where have you been, Faisal. I've been trying to reach you!" he said.

"Jabir, I've been mugged! Two men shot me with a taser. Check the girl! I think they are trying to take her! Check!"

Jabir did not wait to ask questions. Mahram had been acting strangely all day. He covered the floor between his table and Farah's in two easy strides. "Farah!"

She jumped in her seat, a look of fear on her face as she looked up at Jabir.

"Where is Mahram!"

"She went to the ladies…"

"Where?" he shouted.

Farah pointed in the direction Mahram had gone, near tears already. Jabir stalked into the ladies' bathroom, banging the door open on the way in and almost taking it off its hinges.

"Mahram!" he shouted as he went in. He looked under the toilet stall doors—no feet.

He banged his way back through the toilet door out into the hallway and looked left toward the metal trellis door and courtyard beyond. As he did so, the metal door shut with a sickening little click on its pneumatic spring mechanism. He raced toward it and wrenched it open.

"Mahram!" he bellowed.

Jabir glared at the waiter outside, who looked at him with pale fear.

"The woman, which way!" he shouted.

The waiter nodded his head in the direction of the corner building.

Taking the three steps in a giant leap, Jabir raced toward the exit of the courtyard to the street beyond. He was rewarded with a glimpse of Mahram's face turned toward him, a look of fear but also determination on her pretty features as she entered a white van, assisted by a young man in a leather jacket. Jabir took a step through onto the street and drew a pistol from a shoulder holster under his jacket.

"Stop, Mahram, or I will shoot!"

Jabir heard the distinct click of a cocked hammer behind him and to his left. A pair of cool dark eyes appraised him from behind a pistol.

"What are you doing, Mahram! Don't be a fool. They'll kill you. This will bring dishonor on your father! They will kill him!"

"Kidnapping me has brought dishonor to our house. Using me to pay for terrorism has brought dishonor!"

Jabir raised his weapon.

"Don't. I will kill you. Drop the gun," said the cool voice to his left. Jabir stared at Mahram for a moment, then dropped his weapon. He held her eyes.

"Why Mahram? Why? If you knew what was coming, you would know that your father is only trying to look after you…you don't understand."

"I will never be forced into a marriage, Jabir! Never!" Mahram shouted defiantly.

"Get in!" Sara cried and pulled Mahram into the vehicle. Nathan gunned the engine.

Jabir turned to see the man behind him lower his weapon. What he had not seen was the helmet in his other hand. The man swung his arm and the helmet made heavy contact with the back of Jabir's head. He felt like an explosion had gone off in front of his eyes. The next moment he realized he was lying on the dirt and leaf litter, looking at his attacker's running feet. The man leapt into the back of the van, tires squealed and the van disappeared from view. A black mist rose before his eyes, threatening to engulf him.

***

Inside the restaurant, Farah looked nervously at the letter, heard Jabir's bellow of rage, and then picked up her phone, trembling uncontrollably. She dialed her mother's number.

"Yes Mamma, it's me. I think something has happened to Mahram. I think she's in trouble," she whispered through tears.

# Chapter 21

Gideon peed into the empty water bottles, not wanting to move around the ship unnecessarily. He did some squatting leg exercises and press ups in the cramped area, doing his best to reduce lactic acid buildup in his muscles, as he waited patiently. At around 10 pm the *Andromeda* sailed through the Bosporus and into the Sea of Marmara, another hour at the present rate would take the *Andromeda* into the Aegean Sea and into Greek territorial waters. The activity on board noticeably decreased after they sailed through the Bosporus and several lights were extinguished in the engineering section for the night. Gideon prepared a quick text. It would send automatically as he reached the top of the companionway.

"Moving onto first. Check for guard activity."

He holstered his weapon, pulled the beanie low over his head to just above his eyebrows and retrieved the document from his backpack as well as the Geiger counter and placed the latter in his jacket pocket. The document would provide him some cover if he was stopped by anyone; the Geiger counter was the mission. He shouldered the backpack. He wedged the capped plastic bottles of pee in behind some piping and bulkhead—no point in leaving evidence lying around.

Gideon checked the map of the ship on his phone and then made his way up to the accommodation section ablution block. The steady hum and vibration of the engine grew slowly weaker as he moved away from the belly of the ship. As he reached the top of the companionway on the first deck, he felt his cell buzz in his pocket. Just outside the ablution area a florescent light flickered its dying blue white light as if in warning. Gideon opened the door and stepped into a humid, warm environment. Someone was having a late-night shower, mumbling to himself. Gideon moved quietly into a toilet stall, closed the door, and emptied his bowels with some relief. He felt the buzz he was waiting for and checked the text.

*Rotation of armed guards around the shipping containers located on foredeck. Two guards at any one time. Change every four hours. Six in total. Next change due in ten minutes. Make way to port side of the vessel. There is a darkened passageway leading to the foredeck. Guards armed with carbines and are to be treated like enemy combatants if challenged.*

Gideon could feel his adrenalin levels spiking again. He did some square breathing for two minutes and then checked his watch; 10.55 pm. He left the ablution area undetected and walked with a relaxed authority toward the port side of the vessel, carrying the document in his left hand. He climbed another stairway from the first deck onto the main deck and walked to a metal door in the bulkhead with a small porthole in its surface. He looked through into a dark overcast night. Several dim lights spaced every few meters threw jagged shadows of convoluted piping, duct openings, and other machine parts. Beyond the piping was the distant shoreline of Turkey, filled with winking night lights. Gideon moved through the doorway, closing the door soundlessly behind him. A chill breeze blew with the faint but pervasive odor of diesel and grease wafting in the night air. He listened carefully, but all he could hear was the low hum of the engine and the more proximate sound of waves slapping against the hull of the ship. He looked to his left and right, and, waiting for approximately 40 seconds for his vision to adapt to the new light, set off toward the forecastle deck.

\*\*\*

There was no doubting Investigating Officer Votyakov's competence, thought General Balakin. Once he'd gotten over his initial grumpiness and the shock at the fact that his own good name had potentially been used to perpetrate such a foul deed, he could see the facts. The tearful confession of Private Egerov sealed it. He picked up the phone and was patched through to the captain of the *Andromeda.*

"Captain, we have reason to believe that there is a violent stowaway on your vessel connected to a terrorist act that took place in Leninsky two nights ago. Where is your vessel now?"

The grumpy Captain, having been woken by the first mate, rubbed his unshaven face.

"We've just entered Greek waters. In the Aegean. Why?"

The General grimaced. "We need to search the vessel," he said.

"Not to worry, General. I have several heavily armed security men aboard. We'll make a thorough search and go about it quietly in the first instance; I think that is best. We don't want to alert the stowaway to our knowledge. We will let you know how things stand in about an hour or two."

"Very well. I will wait for your call, but please be advised that I will need to speak with the Kremlin shortly to give them an update. This is most important."

As the general put down the phone the captain smiled to himself and turned to the first mate.

"Wake Arash and his men. Our hoped-for guest has indeed made an appearance, it would seem."

After the first mate closed the cabin door and the captain was sure he could not be overheard, he dialed a number and waited impatiently as it rang five times.

Delir Hashemi's sleepy voice answered. "Hello?"

"Captain Iravani here. We believe he's on board."

"Excellent. When you kill him, strap his body to the dingy. We want the coast guard at Tel Aviv to see him and believe he is in control of the dingy before it blows."

\*\*\*

Gideon heard the crackle in his earpiece just as he spotted the guards. He ducked behind the cover of an air duct and peered around the edge of it carefully. Four of the guards spoke urgently to one another, then another two joined them, one of them he recognized right away—Arash.

"Gideon!" Dani's voice sounded urgent but tired in his ear. Gideon knew he probably hadn't slept either.

"There's been an uptick in the communications to the ship coming from the Crimea. I think they know you're on board."

"They definitely do. I see six guards, not two," Gideon said.

"Hold," came the answer.

Gideon waited impatiently in the cold. He would need to have the situation under control by the time the 55th airborne took control of the vessel. They could not deploy unless they knew for sure there was a bomb on board; he knew that. Acts of piracy would be levelled against Israel and the diplomatic fallout would be vast if they took over a Russian vessel that was essentially not a threat.

"We need to know where that bomb is, urgently." Dani said.

"I know that!" Gideon whispered impatiently. He risked another look around the edge of the air duct and felt the first drop of rain and then the delicate sound of distant thunder.

The group broke up. Three guards remained on the forecastle, two of which patrolled the entrance and one was sent further forward, to a location Gideon could not see from his vantage point. Gideon watched as Arash directed a guard down the port and starboard side of the ship and then walked back into a doorway at the bottom of the bridge.

"Confirm sighting of Arash as commander. He is giving orders in Farsi," Gideon whispered and drew the suppressed Glock with his right hand and the tactical knife with his left.

"Confirmed," Dani said.

"Check the location of the point guard on the forecastle deck. I think that'll give us a good indication of where to start looking for the bomb."

The guard sent down the portside walked carefully along the lengthy corridor, his weapon raised at shoulder height, eyes searching for the slightest flicker of movement. The rain started to fall in earnest now. The guard ducked under the cover of an overhead pipe and squatted, about five feet away from Gideon's position.

A faint electrical crackle and then Gideon heard the guard call his sign.

"Check 5," he whispered in Farsi.

That was what Gideon had been waiting for.

The guard rose to a standing position again and made his way carefully down the open corridor for another ten steps, passing the point at which Gideon hid. If he looked back now, he would see Gideon, a shadow in the rain. Another crackle and then the guard called his sign-in again. "Check 5," he whispered.

It was clear what Arash meant to do. Flush him out by causing a contact between him and one of the guards, and then rush in for the kill with all his men. An open mic meant this would have to be a silent kill. What was in Gideon's favor was that Arash did not know he could understand and speak Farsi fluently. Gideon placed his Glock carefully on the deck, swapped the knife to his dominant right hand, rose, took two swift, silent steps and plunged the five-inch blade through the fourth and fifth vertebrae in the guard's neck, severing his spinal cord and vocal cords, while at the same time jerking the guard's right arm forward and out, away from the carbine's trigger. The guard fell forward and then swung in the air as his body weight pivoted against his right arm, which Gideon held in a vice-like grip. Surprise and terror flickered briefly in the guard's eyes and then he was staring sightlessly as his life blood gushed out onto the deck. Gideon dragged him into the superstructure of convoluted piping and took the guard's earpiece, and plugged it into his left ear, just has he heard the electronic crackle and the word in Farsi.

"Report."

Gideon waited for the other guards to cycle through their call sign. The dead guard's turn.

"Check 5," Gideon said in Farsi in a low whisper.

High above the *Andromeda*, the all-seeing eye of the infrared camera on the satellite peered through the cloud cover.

Dani held his breath while he watched the infrared image of Gideon pick up the dead guard's carbine and retrieve his own Glock. A few seconds later a text pinged into his inbox.

*Radio silence required. I'm on enemy frequency. Text only.*

Dani wrote back, *Confirmed.*

Gideon felt the buzz of Dani's confirmation.

*Strategy to confuse enemy. Will not be able to take out more than one or two guards without them knowing,* Dani read.

A new piece of intel pinged into his microphone and onto the screen in front of Dani.

*Arash has set himself up with a sniper's rifle on the foredeck of the bridge. 20 minutes to zero.*

Gideon looked down at the text and then moved silently back into the ship's interior.

Zero hour was when the 55th Airborne would send in paratroopers to take command of the vessel.

"What are you doing?" Dani said to himself. He didn't want to distract Gideon with too many texts, but moving indoors meant he could not see Gideon.

Dani risked it. *What is your objective moving indoors?*

*Sow confusion, cut off head,* Gideon wrote back.

*Negative. Get back out there and find the bomb! That is an order!* Dani wrote.

*Negative. Out.* Gideon replied.

Dani heard Gideon say "Check 5" again as he disappeared off the screen. The thickness of the bulkhead was too much for the infrared camera to penetrate.

An anxious minute went by. Dani saw several young faces glance upward at him surreptitiously from the floor of the Ops room.

"Does that young idiot listen to anyone?" Yossi said, standing behind Dani. Dani jumped in his seat.

"Ah, sir, you startled me. I didn't know you were in the room."

Yossi smiled wanly, holding a cup of coffee in each hand. "I was just wondering how the mission was going. The 55$^{th}$ is in the air now and the Prime Minister wants an update."

Dani indicated the chair beside him.

Yossi passed Dani a cup of coffee; he accepted it gratefully. He remained standing for a few seconds and then took a seat next to Dani.

"Check 5," both men heard again and then saw Gideon's infrared image emerge on the starboard side of the ship via a doorway.

Dani texted. "Number 4 is about 200 yards to your left."

Gideon looked at his screen and nodded. This side of the ship was better lit and had less superstructure in place, but there was a large air vent on the deck between Gideon and Guard 4. When Guard 4's back was turned, he ran silently to the nearest vent and squatted behind it. He waited for the next call sign-in.

"Report" came the Farsi command. "Check 1"

"Check 2"

"Check 3"

"Check 4"

Gideon looked at his watch. Ten minutes to zero hour. 55$^{th}$ Airborne would be above the ship soon. Rain drifted in gray curtains out to sea. Gideon stood, saw the look of surprise bloom in the eyes of Guard 4. He shot him between the eyes and saw his head kick backward, his brain exploding in a pink mist in the florescent light behind him.

The suppressed weapon made a distinct popping noise as he fired, knowing Arash would hear it and understand what it meant.

"Check 5," Gideon said. Silence.

"5 come in," Arash said.

"Check 5. What was that noise?" Gideon said and slipped through the doorway again, moving quickly through the ship to the port side. It was 12 am, no one in sight.

"Shut up. Silence!" Arash screamed in his ear.

"Check 4 come in," Arash said. Silence.

"Go! Go! Go!" he heard Arash shout. "He's on the starboard side!"

Gideon rushed toward the port side, through the door again, and out into the dark corridor. He could hear the terror in the heavy breaths of the other guards.

"2 and 3 find cover. 5 come in? Where are you?"

"I'm making my way to the stern. We'll get him in a pincer move." Gideon said.

"1 stay where you are. 2 and 3, push down the starboard side. 5 push up the starboard from the stern when you get there.

"Copy 5," Gideon said.

Gideon sprinted in the exact opposite direction that Arash had just ordered, toward the forecastle and the shipping containers. He kept his eyes on the Portuguese bridge that jutted out from the wheelhouse, looking over the bow where he knew Arash had been a moment ago. He felt a buzz in his pocket and ducked down behind some piping.

The text read, *Arash is on the starboard side of the Portuguese bridge. You have a clear run onto the forecastle.*

"Report," he heard in his ear.

Gideon kept to the shadows of the pipework, the rain making it all but impossible for him to see more than 10 feet in front of him. He made it to the foredeck and looked up to the front of the Portuguese bridge. He could see Arash leaning over the starboard side looking through the scope, searching for a shot as the cycle started again.

"Check 1."

Gideon was just about to scuttle from the shadows to the safety of the bulk of the first row of shipping containers when he saw Arash glance back toward the forecastle area where he knew Guard 1 would be. He froze in the shadows, waiting for Arash to turn away.

"Check 2."

Arash turned his head toward Guard 2 and then turned his attention to the starboard side where he knew Guard 3 to be.

Gideon darted across the brightly lit deck and into the shadow of the shipping containers.

"Check 3."

Gideon took several steps in the direction of the forecastle of the ship, his weapon raised and ready. Now Guard 1 was the greatest danger.

There was a pause where Guard 4 should have been.

"Check 5."

Silence, Gideon deliberately did not answer, sowing more confusion.

"Check 5. Come in," he heard Arash say urgently. Silence.

"2 and 3 make your way carefully toward the stern. He's between you and the end of the ship."

"Copy," said a voice in Gideon's ear.

The ruse had worked. They thought Guard 5 had just been taken out at the back of the ship, near the stern.

Guards 2 and 3 moved carefully down the starboard side of the ship toward the stern. Guard 3 stepped over the body of Guard 4 and called it in, "Confirm 4 down," Gideon heard him whisper.

Back in the operation room, Dani glanced from the big screen to Yossi's face.

"Clever move, I'll give him that much—getting them moving in the wrong direction," Yossi said. Dani felt a surge of pride for his soldier.

"Five minutes to zero. Are you in comms with the C 130—Hercules pilot and commander?" Yossi said.

"They're online and standing by."

Yossi nodded, his eyes straying back to the image of Gideon.

Dani texted again.

*Move to earpiece.*

Gideon took the earpiece of the dead guard from his ear and replaced it with his own.

"Guard 1 is two shipping containers up and three along," Dani said.

"Copy, keep commentary going if he moves. Which way is he facing now?" Gideon whispered.

"Toward you."

Gideon glided forward, a shadow among shadows.

"He's turned now. Looking straight toward the Portuguese bridge, now crouching. Trying to see Arash through the rain."

Gideon ran along the outer edge of the shipping containers in shadow until he reached the end of the row which was three deep and three high. He ducked down a passageway to his right between the outer row and the next row of shipping containers in front of it.

"Confirm you are now behind Guard 1," he heard in his ear.

Gideon moved quickly down the breadth of the row and then glanced around the corner of the last container to his right. To his delight, he saw Guard 1 on one knee with his carbine pointing in the wrong direction.

Gideon stepped out of the shadows and took several silent and cautious steps toward the guard, his weapon pointing at the target. He could have taken the shot from where he was, but he was about 50 yards away and a closer shot would be more certain. Two things happened simultaneously as he closed the gap to within striking distance: Gideon heard the guard call in his sign and then the Geiger counter in his pocket let out an almighty shriek – somehow the Geiger counter had turned on in his pocket.

The guard spun as Gideon dove forward. The guard's carbine letting loose an ear shattering spray of deadly lead; bullets thudding into the containers behind Gideon and sending sparks flying. In mid-air, Gideon pulled his trigger, sending a bullet through the guard's neck and the next through his open mouth. Gideon saw a ribbon of blood splatter onto the shipping container to his right.

Gideon rolled to his left as he hit the floor and back into the shadows of the containers and then scuttled backward on his haunches facing the bridge, waiting for Arash to show his face. The Geiger counter screamed again as he moved past the last shipping container in row two. Gideon fumbled in his jacket pocket swearing mightily under his breath and switched the damned thing off.

In his ear Dani said, "Arash is moving back toward the front of the Portuguese bridge and the other two are sprinting forward." Gideon shook his head.

"Two hostiles making their way up the starboard side. Arash is still on the Portuguese Bridge."

Gideon thought for a second, then deliberately put down his pistol and took the spike drone from the backpack. He put the guard's earpiece back into his ear. He unsheathed the drone, flipped the switch on the eight-inch contraption—a tube filled with high explosives and ball bearings and a propeller attached to the top, small wings which flipped out on each side once unsheathed, and a wide-angle camera on the bottom. It was a simple device in design, but highly effective. Silence on both lines in Gideon's ears as he sent the drone shooting high into the air above the silvered halo of light pouring down onto the shipping containers. The rain made perfect cover.

Overhead the C-130 Hercules roared into view, flying low over the ship.

"We need to know if the bomb is on board, Gideon," he heard in his left ear.

"What the hell was that!" he heard in his right ear from one of the guards.

The rain continued to drum down, disguising the low frequency whine of the drone's propeller.

"It doesn't matter, move forward! We have him pinned down!" he heard Arash shout over the comms. If he moves down any of the middle rows, I'll nail him. You take the lateral lines."

Gideon brought the drone to a hover above the bridge and then slowly edged it over the side. 20 feet below it, the camera picked up Arash in a crouch, looking through the scope of his high-powered rifle, searching for a shot. It was probably this that ensured Arash had not seen the drone shoot up into the night sky. In the periphery of the camera vision Gideon caught a glimpse of the two other guards moving in a careful leapfrog formation, as one gave cover to the man moving forward. They had just reached the forecastle deck. They would be upon him in less than a minute. Gideon lowered the drone another ten feet and then another five.

"Look up Arash. I'm behind you," Gideon said softly.

An immense sense of justice flooded his soul as Arash glanced up and a look of sheer terror passed over his features. He tried frantically to bring his rifle to bear on the object hovering just out of reach.

Gideon heard the explosion and knew that Arash was dead. No one could survive a spike explosion from that proximity.

He dropped the console, got up and moved quickly toward the dead guard, picking up his carbine and a spare clip, and loaded the weapon.

Over his earpiece he could hear the other two guards praying.

"Arash is dead," he said to them. "You will follow soon if you do not put your weapons down now."

"Who are you?" one of the guards said.

"You will die if you do not surrender," Gideon said.

Gideon thought for a moment. He put his weapon down and brought out the Geiger counter again and turned it on, then moved toward the bow. As he was about to cross a lateral passageway the Geiger counter began to shriek. Something radioactive was in the container to his immediate right. He left the shrieking Geiger counter there and crossed the passageway and waited in the shadows of the container on the other side of the passageway directly opposite the shrieking counter.

"Allahu Akbar! Allahu Akbar! Allahu Akbar!" Gideon heard over his earpiece. A note of triumph in the voice.

"They're about five shipping containers away from you on your left and coming fast down the passageway," Dani said in his earpiece.

The two guards came charging forward, brandishing their weapons and turned the corner ready to kill, thinking they had Gideon cold, in front of the shipping container housing the bomb. Too late, they saw the Geiger counter lying forlornly in the rain, but no man. Each man turned in the opposite direction, frantically searching for the intruder. Three shipping containers up Gideon stepped from around its corner and shot the guard who faced him between the eyes. The other guard spun trying to save himself, only to have two bullets thud into his torso. The guard fell, his weapon clattering to the floor. Gideon moved carefully toward the last of the downed guards. He was still moving, trying feebly to draw a side arm. Gideon shot him through the head at point blank range.

"Come in, Dani," Gideon said, turning off the Geiger counter.

"Forecastle clear of bogies. Send paratroopers to take control of the vessel," he said.

"Confirmed. We want eye on, I repeat eye on the bomb before we take command of the vessel," Dani said.

Gideon shot the lock off a heavy chain that secured the door to the container in front of him. He opened the door of the shipping container. Inside was the dinghy with the warhead attached.

Gideon turned the Geiger counter on again. The Geiger counter was off the charts.

"Confirm bomb on board," Gideon said breathlessly.

"Go, go, go. Paratroopers are in the wind," Dani said.

A few seconds later, he heard the mighty roar of the C130 Hercules as it flew overhead again.

Gideon watched as the first of the paratroopers glided like a black hawk out of the predawn sky, descending with silent and admirable efficiency into the narrow corridors between the containers.

"We'll take it from here, soldier," he heard the commander say in his earpiece.

Now another five or six paratroopers thudded down around him, their chutes quickly stowed. Several commandos moved passed him, weapons raised, a look of admiration and victory lighting up their young eyes.

# Chapter 22

The voyage across the Mediterranean was pleasant. Ezat was a good sailor and Eli and Nathan seemed to know their way around a boat too. Mia had been filled with joy at all the company and was delighted to discover that Eli and Nathan spoke Hebrew.

The last part of the journey was nerve-wracking. They made landfall at night in the tiny harbor town off Isola Rossa. Ezat helped them on to land with a dinghy. Mia showed great spirit and resilience getting aboard the dinghy despite her advanced age, but allowed herself to be lifted out by the young men and piggy backed ashore though the surf. Sara smiled, wondering if her grandmother was secretly enjoying all the male attention.

"I'll say my goodbyes here," Ezat said. "Eli and Nathan will help you get to the house."

They waved goodbye to Ezat as he nosed the dingy back toward the trawler.

Nathan and Mahram walked into town from the beach and about an hour later came back in a taxi minibus. They loaded all of their goods onto the bus and set off again in great spirits. The taxi driver was a young man who had been drinking with friends when Nathan and Mahram enquired at the local Taverna if there was a taxi available. Mahram could speak Italian and was able to translate for Nathan. He was a little drunk but insisted on driving his own taxi back to where the others were waiting. However after seeing there was an old woman to transport, he agreed that Eli could drive the taxi while he gave directions from the front passenger seat.

A fifty-minute drive along the highway took them to the outskirts of Lougosanto and a further ten minutes to the isolated farmhouse owned by Gideon's family. Sara found the key where Gideon said it would be and opened the house. Once again, Nathan and Mahram took a drive into the local town and after waiting for 45 minutes, chatting with the driver, who was an affable, if not very bright young man, the local shops opened and they bought food and a few other items to keep them comfortable. When they got back, they found that Sara had tidied the house and Eli had got all the electronics working, started the fire stove heater and turned on the TV for Mia.

Rain started to fall just as they arrived. Nathan sent the driver off with a large chunk of cash.

"How about some coffee?" Sara said and there was a chorus of agreement.

A breaking news story interrupted the inane flow of morning TV chatter and brought every one of them to a stop. Sara picked up the remote and turned up the volume.

A helicopter hovered above a ship moving slowly out into the Mediterranean Sea. The ship was surrounded by naval vessels. A breathless commentator spoke.

*In the early hours of this morning, European union authorities were alerted to a vessel allegedly carrying a live atomic warhead. Authorities now have control of the vessel and are sailing it out into international waters. We have been given to understand that a specialist unit has diffused the bomb and it no longer poses a threat.*

*Authorities were alerted to the threat by an as yet unknown source, saying that they had received credible intelligence that an atomic warhead was on board and that the ship's target was Tel Aviv in Israel. Information has come to light which suggests that there was a confrontation between the alleged terrorists and commandos resulting in the death of all the armed terrorists on board.*

*Anonymous material received by Al Jazeera and the BBC in London alleges that the terrorists were of Iranian origin and that the ship had recently taken on cargo in the disputed waters of Crimea.*

Several grotesquely bloodied and pixelated pictures of dead men were flashed up on the screen in various states of damage.

*The EU was quick to condemn the Iranian and Russian authorities, both of which deny any responsibility or knowledge of the alleged terrorist plot. An investigation is ongoing. Meanwhile, the Turkish authorities have closed the Bosporus corridor and vehemently deny any knowledge of the ship's passage, or the incident.*

*The crew of the ship, who also deny any involvement in the incident, have meanwhile been taken into custody and are being processed on the island of Cypress.*

Eli looked at Sara who was as white as a sheet, then he looked at Mahram who also looked pale and shaken.

"I'm sure he's okay," Eli said.

"How can you be sure? There was fighting, there were so many bodies," Sara said, almost in tears.

She left the house and burst into tears. Eli made to follow, but Mahram stopped him.

"I'll go."

Eli phoned Mossad HQ and gave them an update of their situation, then asked if they had news of Gideon. He waited for several long seconds before he was patched through to Dani in the Operations room.

Once he'd identified himself, Dani said, "Yes, the operation went well. Aside from a few bruises and bumps, Gideon is fine. He's asked to be transported to Sardinia. He told me about the move of his friends there for safe keeping."

"You might want to tell him to contact his girlfriend. She saw the news this morning and is very worried." Eli said, grinning.

"Girlfriend? He never mentioned a girlfriend. He mentioned the Sayan and gave elaborate excuses as to why she and her grandmother had to be removed from Libya. I'll let him know after his debrief."

Eli stuck his head out of the door. The rain had stopped and a wan sunlight was breaking through. He waved at the women with a big smile on his face, holding his phone in the air. They looked back with a look of hope blossoming on their faces.

"Good news! Come back! I'll tell you all about it!"

# Epilogue

Delir Hashemi watched Dr Hosseini and his technicians give the warhead one last check over. The bomb rested like an alien jewel on the flatbed of the Toyota utility. It always amazed him that such fury and power could be held in something so small.

A car pulled into the warehouse. In it sat Jabir with two other mujahidin.

Delir watched the young man get out from the car. The flight from Libya was a short one, but the last few hours had been intense and he could see the exhaustion in Jabir's eyes, as the young man approached him.

"We are now committed, Jabir," Delir said, turning to the young Palestinian man.

"Arash and his brothers gave their lives in Shahid, but we knew all along that that would be the most dangerous part of the mission. If it had succeeded, it would have been spectacular."

Delir Hashemi searched the young man's eyes.

"Let me see the wound on your head for myself," Delir said.

Jabir turned slightly and showed him the bruised contusion where he'd been struck by the helmet.

"You obeyed well when I told you to kill Basar, but you looked…regretful to me," Delir said.

Jabir held Delir's gaze steadily. "I showed you the pictures. What more do you want? I shot him in his face after we discovered the camera in his study."

Jabir reached into his shirt pocket and took a small white object from it. The two men behind Jabir looked at Delir questioningly. Was Delir just about to have Jabir killed?

Delir held the younger man's eyes, then put out his hand and Jabir gently placed the object into his palm. Delir looked at it closely, controlled rage crossed his features and animated a burning hate in his eyes. He shook his head and pocketed the device.

An uncomfortable silence grew as the two men stared at each other.

"Now it's your turn, Jabir. To revenge the life of your family against the infidel and the Zionist entity and the brothers you have just lost." Delir said, his eyes hooded.

"Insha'Allah, if God wills, it will happen," Jabir said in his soft voice.

"The Quran says, *Let those fight in the way of Allah who sell the life of this world for the other. Whoso fighteth in the way of Allah, be he slain or be he victorious, on him We shall bestow a vast reward.*"

Delir searched the eyes of the young man again. Jabir's eyes did not flinch.

"Your reward is before you, within your grasp. All that is required now is courage and the will to avenge," he said.

Jabir nodded once. "I wish it to be so. My entire family is dead. The woman I rescued from the infidel has betrayed me and her father. I'm ready."

"You have done your ritual cleansing and video?"

Jabir nodded again. "At the hotel when we landed. The brothers have it." He indicated the two young men behind him.

"Then go in peace, brother. May Allah reward you for what you do next," Delir said, and handed Jabir the keys to the Toyota truck.

Delir indicated that the fiber glass top should be affixed to the back of the utility. Several young men came forward, picked it up and carefully placed it over the bomb, obscuring it from view completely.

"The route is through Syria. First stop is the town of Cariqli. The brothers there will get you across the Euphrates and then into Lebanon where you are to wait for further orders. Once we have a route through the border into Israel, make your way to Tel Aviv, if you cannot make it through, then you are to detonate the bomb and kill as many infidels as you can."

Jabir nodded again. "Insha'Allah."

He took a step toward the truck. Several of the young men came forward and shook his hand and gave him a kiss on both cheeks, then he got into the utility and started the motor, punched his destination into the GPS, and set off. He nosed the utility out of the corrugated iron shed and onto the dusty road, leading to the border town of Cariqli in Syria, moving slowly over the lumpy surface at first, but then picking up speed. Dr Hosseini had reassured him that he could not detonate the bomb with a bump, but all the same.

Jabir looked into the rear-view mirror. A truck with several men followed behind him. They would see him through the Turkish border crossing and into Syria. He let out a long sighing breath. He genuinely though that after the mess-up with Mahram, Delir would kill him. Fortunately, Basar Ammar had worn the blame. The cut and bruising on the back of Jabir's head and the witness of the other guard, Faizal, convinced Delir of the truth of his attempt to stop Mahram's kidnapping.

Basar on the other hand had not been so fortunate. His killing had been brutal. Delir had made him video conference the execution. In the end Basar had shown admirable courage. He had stared up at Jabir while he sat on his executive chair at his desk in his study and in front of his laptop, while Delir looked on through a video hook-up. Jabir had shot Basar between the eyes. Basar had not said a word and had died instantly. Delir had made Jabir lift the laptop up to his smashed face so as to ensure he had done a thorough job.

Jabir examined his conscience. Something niggled at him. In his mind, Basar had been dishonored and deserved to die…but yes, if he was being honest, there was no regret. Basar's voiced intention was to kill Mahram for the dishonor she'd brought to the house of Ammar. For his own part, he had been so sure of what lay before him before the kidnapping, but somehow now he could not shake the beautiful green eyes of Mahram and her sweetness. Her words had penetrated his heart like a knife. What were they?

*The point I'm making is that violence begets violence. It does not ever, ever solve anything. And I do know what I'm talking about. My brother died in the Libyan civil war. Who suffers? Only the families who lose sons. In the end the solutions are always political, anyway. There are no military victories in civil war.*

Those words seemed to be burned into his heart…and her sweet face. He shook his head, trying to clear it. It was God's will in the end, he thought, but he just could not get rid of her haunting green eyes and her sweet smile. The truth, he thought with rising anxiety, is that now, he did not want to die.